"The Yellow Wallpaper"

Women Writers
Texts and Contexts

SERIES EDITORS

THOMAS L. ERSKINE
Salisbury State University

CONNIE L. RICHARDS
Salisbury State University

SERIES BOARD

MARTHA BANTA
University of California at Los Angeles

BARBARA CHRISTIAN
University of California at Berkeley

PAUL LAUTER
Trinity College

VOLUMES IN THE SERIES

CHARLOTTE PERKINS GILMAN, "The Yellow Wallpaper"
    Edited by Thomas L. Erskine and Connie L. Richards, Salisbury State
        University

FLANNERY O'CONNOR, "A Good Man Is Hard to Find"
    Edited by Frederick Asals, University of Toronto

KATHERINE ANNE PORTER, "Flowering Judas"
    Edited by Virginia Spencer Carr, Georgia State University

LESLIE MARMON SILKO, "Yellow Woman"
    Edited by Melody Graulich, University of New Hampshire

ALICE WALKER, "Everyday Use"
    Edited by Barbara Christian, University of California, Berkeley

HISAYE YAMAMOTO, "Seventeen Syllables"
    Edited by King-Kok Cheung, University of California, Los Angeles

"The Yellow Wallpaper"

❏ CHARLOTTE PERKINS GILMAN ■

Edited and with an introduction by
THOMAS L. ERSKINE
and CONNIE L. RICHARDS

Rutgers University Press
New Brunswick, New Jersey

Library of Congress Cataloging-in-Publication Data

Gilman, Charlotte Perkins, 1860–1935.
　　The yellow wallpaper / Charlotte Perkins Gilman ; edited and with an introduction by Thomas L. Erskine and Connie L. Richards.
　　　　p.　　cm. — (Women writers : text and contents)
　　　Includes bibliographical references. (p.　　).
　　　ISBN 0-8135-1993-4 (cloth) — ISBN 0-8135-1994-2 (pbk.)
　　　1. Gilman, Charlotte Perkins, 1860–1935. Yellow wallpaper.
2. Feminism and literature—United States.　3. Women and literature—
United States.　4. Sex role in literature.　I. Erskine, Thomas L.
II. Richards, Connie L., 1939–　　. III. Title.　IV. Series: Women
writers (New Brunswick, N.J.).
PS1744.G57Y4534　　1993
813′.4—dc20　　　　　　　　　　　　　　　　　　　92-42099
　　　　　　　　　　　　　　　　　　　　　　　　　　　CIP

British Cataloging-in-Publication information available.

for our daughters
Jennifer Grantham Erskine
and
Caitlin Elizabeth White

❏ Contents ■

❏ Acknowledgments ■

We are indebted to the many people who have helped us with this book: to our graduate students Lori Beste and Steve Ryan for their research and help with reprint permissions; to our secretaries Sydney Webster and Jane Trimmer for their technical assistance; to Carol Farley Kessler, Penn State, for her suggestions regarding selections; to our colleague, Bill Zak, for his helpful ideas regarding the critical pieces; to Paul Lauter, Trinity College, and Martha Banta, UCLA, for their useful criticism and suggestions; and especially to our editor, Leslie Mitchner, for her foresight, clear-headedness, critical eye, and patience. We thank you all.

❏ Introduction

■ THOMAS L. ERSKINE and
CONNIE L. RICHARDS ■

Introduction

Although most fiction is to some extent autobiographical, there are few short stories so dependent on personal experience as Charlotte Perkins Gilman's "The Yellow Wallpaper," which has during the last twenty years received more critical attention than perhaps any other American short story. Like William Faulkner's "A Rose for Emily," which also concerns a female protagonist's "imposing" descent into madness, it is a story readers seem unable to forget. For Gilman herself, however, the tale was much more than grotesque Gothic fiction. It was a fictional exorcism of a particular, painful portion of her own personal life experience, as well as her first commentary on the conflict between women's familial duties and their public responsibilities. Indeed, the author, who had undergone medical treatment from Dr. S. Weir Mitchell, a prominent nerve specialist, wrote the short story in the hopes of effecting a change in Mitchell's methods of dealing with nervous prostration. She even sent Mitchell, who is identified by name in it, a copy of the work. The best introduction, then, to the story's complex import might well begin with its author's biography.

Born on July 3, 1860, in Hartford, Connecticut, Gilman was related through her father, Frederick Beecher Perkins, to the illustrious Beechers, a family which provided her with a number of models of public women activitists. Although Harriet Beecher Stowe, the author of *Uncle Tom's Cabin* (1852), was the most notable of her female relatives, Catherine Beecher wrote an advice book for young women, and Isabella Beecher Hooker campaigned for women's emancipation. The most significant Beecher influence—if also a negative one, however—was Charlotte's own father. An intellectual who left his family, he made only sporadic financial contributions to support them, and was responsible for Gilman, her mother, and her brother moving nineteen times in eighteen years. Although Gilman described her father as only an "occasional visitor," she made repeated efforts to contact him and apparently went on to express her resentment and frustration with him through the fictional fathers she depicted as "explosive, tyrannical, self-centered, suffocating, and unloving." Gilman, however, was ironically very much like her father in important ways, for she "abandoned" her daughter to her husband and, like him, preferred to deal with her emotions at a distance—in letters, books, or in her fiction.

Gilman was also critical of her mother, who was a stern disciplinarian and proved to be as distant, rejecting, and emotionally stunted as her father. Without any physical or verbal affection from either parent, Gilman found herself emotionally isolated. Her mother refused to allow her to have intimate friends, so she created them in the fairy tales she wrote during her adolescence. The tales predictably feature powerful female friends, good-but-ineffectual older males, and unhappy older females. Chafing under her mother's prohibitions (novels also were outlawed), Gilman finally rebelled at the age of fifteen; this confrontation with her mother opened "an entire new world" of protest.

Although Gilman subsequently developed friendships with young men and women, her most intense was with Martha Luther, a lifelong friend. Their relationship, as expressed in Gilman's letters, was ambiguously affectionate, suggesting the possibility of repressed homosexuality; but close friendships, often expressed in romantic if not erotic language, were not unusual between artistic intellectual women of the day. Throughout her life, Gilman enjoyed close ties with other women, but the nature of those relationships remains unresolved. In her autobiography, *The Living of Charlotte Gilman: An Autobiography,* Gilman herself felt compelled to dismiss the idea that her relationship with Ms. Luther had a "Freudian taint." Not surprising, however, when Martha met Charles Lane, Gilman saw him as an "interloper" and opposed the relationship, which—her objections notwithstanding—resulted in Martha's marriage to Lane in 1881.

Less than a year later Gilman met Charles Walter Stetson, an artist whom she married on May 2, 1884; but their

4

courtship was marked by friction and misunderstanding that continued through their marriage and led to their formal separation in 1888 and eventual divorce. While Walter's bohemian, rebellious lifestyle appealed to Gilman, his thoroughly conventional ideas about women and marriage were at odds with Gilman's own struggles between choosing a "masculine" world of public service and a "feminine" world of domesticity. To preserve her own identity, she resisted his efforts to possess her, and her concern with her own work did not square with Walter's expectations that she devote herself to furthering his work and career. The birth of Katharine Beecher Stetson on March 23, 1885, did not resolve their differences. Because it seemed to fix Gilman in the domestic sphere, it probably only aggravated them. Walter, who had ignored Gilman's ideas and assumed she would "reform" and accept her traditional role, had similarly dismissed the recurrent depressions she experienced during the courtship. After Katharine's birth, the depressions deepened until Gilman could no longer care for her child. As Ann Lane points out in her biography, Gilman's life at this point was marked by a "peculiar bifurcation": she was active and energetic outside the house, but inside she was fatigued and depressed.[1] Actually the bifurcation is not so peculiar because it reflects the continuing internal conflict that she had subconsciously resolved in favor of public life.

Gilman's choice was inadvertently reinforced by her visit in the winter of 1885 to Pasadena, California, where she stayed with Grace Channing's family. She and Grace, who succeeded Martha as friend and confidant, wrote plays together, and their friendship and collaboration produced a complete recovery in Gilman, who understandably feared a return to marital domesticity. Shortly after her return to Walter, she experienced depression and lethargy, and once again her relief came from outside activity, particularly her column for the *People,* a weekly Providence newspaper. But finally, her domestic cares overwhelmed her, and in April 1887, she turned for help to Dr. Mitchell, who had treated many female patients.

The usually expressive Gilman did not record in her diary any of the details of her stay at Mitchell's Philadelphia sanitarium, and even her autobiography is sketchy about her treatment there. However, because he was a prolific writer,

Mitchell's views about the care of his female patients (some of which are included elsewhere in this volume) were well known. He prescribed extended bed rest, isolation from family, overfeeding, and massage—all of which tend to transform an adult woman into a dependent infant. After a month of infantilization, Gilman was "cured" and sent home to a regimen that stressed domestic life, permitted "but two hours' intellectual life a day," and prohibited painting and writing. Adhering to these prohibitions almost drove Gilman insane, and her autobiography contains details about creating a rag baby and retreating both literally and emotionally to closets in order to escape from her distress. By November 1887 she decided to "cast off Dr. Mitchell bodily, and do exactly what I pleased." This decision seemed to coincide with resolving her marital dilemma, for in September 1888, she went to Pasadena with Katharine, leaving her husband behind.

Before she left for California, Gilman had been active in public life as a lecturer, a role she continued to play throughout her life, and as a writer, though she was always recognized more as a journalist/propagandist than as a creative writer. After healing herself from the effects of Mitchell's cure, she did collaborate with Channing on *A Pretty Idiot,* a feminist play about gender roles in courtship and marriage. It was not until she moved to California, however, that she applied her creative abilities to her stay in Mitchell's sanitorium. Perhaps geographical and emotional distance from her experience were necessary; whatever the cause for the delay, she did not complete "The Yellow Wallpaper" until 1890. The story was prompted, she suggested in 1913, by her desire to "save people from being driven crazy." Her comment suggests the aesthetic problem with much of Gilman's literary work; often her sociopolitical agenda overwhelms the characters, who become one-dimensional mouthpieces for different ideas. Propaganda all too often threatens art. With the possible exception of *Herland*, her futuristic feminist novel, "The Yellow Wallpaper" alone unequivocally transcends its didactic origins and agenda.

Gilman sent her story to William Dean Howells, who as novelist, critic, and editor had the power to establish or destroy literary reputations. He had, fortunately, already declared his admiration for two of her poems and was also intrigued by her story, which he recommended to Horace Scudder, editor of the *Atlantic Monthly*. Scudder did not unequivocally share Howells' enthusiasm for "The Yellow Wallpaper"; he refused to publish the piece despite its power, declaring "I could not forgive myself if I made others as miserable as I have made myself!"

Gilman hired Henry Austin, a literary agent, who finally placed the story, with Howells's intervention and support, in *New England Magazine* in 1892. The initial critical responses, some by physicians, tended to stress the clinical rather than literary aspects of the work, which was thought dangerous, presumably because it might "infect" female readers who would also question medical authority and assert their own rights. When in 1920 Howells included her story in his *The Great American Short Stories,* he noted that he "shiver[ed] over it as much as I did when I first read it in manuscript." Howells's "shivering" reflects the contemporary critical response to "The Yellow Wallpaper" as a horror story with Gothic overtones, but by including it he rescued it from probable literary oblivion and stamped Gilman as a peer of Jewett, Wharton, James, and Twain, authors who also appeared in his anthology.

Over the following fifty years, however, Gilman's literary reputation declined, in part because her focus on women's causes was expressed through her journal, her nonfiction, and her lectures, though she did not entirely abandon fiction. It was not until the Feminist Press's 1973 reissue of Gilman's story that she regained her literary reputation, due in large part to Elaine Hedges's lengthy and incisive "Afterword," an essay that reassessed the story in terms of feminist theory. Since 1973 "The Yellow Wallpaper" has become, with Kate Chopin's *The Awakening,* a key feminist text that has attracted varied critical elucidations.

The most famous quoted text is *The Madwoman in the Attic* (1979), by Sandra M. Gilbert and Susan Gubar. They place "The Yellow Wallpaper" in the tradition of other late nineteenth-century fiction patterned in the "enclosure and escape" mode, the narrator's choices being submission to male dicta or insanity. When the realities of such social experience are transformed into fiction, Gilbert and Gubar feel that women authors "are secretly working through and within the conventions of literary texts to define their own lives." Gilbert and Gubar point to the nineteenth-century metaphor of woman as house, to be owned, inhabited and confined. Women's desire to escape their social conditions, like the narrator of Gilman's tale, leads these authors to believe that this is "*the* story that all literary women would tell if they could speak their 'speechless woe.'" For them, the story is triumphant, even if momentarily so, for its recognizes women's need to save and reveal themselves and, by extension, "the progress of nineteenth-century literary women out of the texts defined by patriarchal poetics into the open spaces of their own authority."

By contrast, Conrad Shumaker's "'Too Terribly Good to Be Printed': Charlotte Gilman's 'The Yellow Wallpaper'" (1985) assumes a counter-revolutionary approach to the story. He wants to step back into the innocence of not treating it in feminist terms. While Gilbert and Gubar make the story and its social implications a matter that cannot be ignored, Shumaker wishes to realign it with the "dominant tradition" in the nineteenth century rather than isolating it merely as precursor to feminist ideology: "Woman is often seen as representing an imaginative or 'poetic' view of things that conflicts with (or sometimes complements) the American male's 'common sense' approach to reality. Through the characters of the 'rational' doctor and the 'imaginative' wife, Gilman explores a question that was—and in many ways still is—central both to American literature and to the place of women in American culture." Because the rational fears the imaginative, it seeks to control, especially when the imaginative is a quality of the "weaker sex." Shumaker argues that the narrator's comments suggest that she "understands John's problem yet is unable to call it his problem, and in many ways it is this combination of insight and naiveté, of resistance and resignation, that makes her such a memorable character and gives such power to her narrative." Shumaker goes on to suggest a "powerful dramatic irony" here as "the reader gradually puts together details the meaning of which [the narrator] doesn't quite understand." Following the established tradition of her gender, the narrator objects to the state she finds herself in but cannot openly rebel. In fact, Shumaker argues that she is "not always aware of her own actions or in control of her thoughts and so is not always reliable in reporting them." Unlike Gilbert and Gubar, Shumaker sees the ending as a bitter triumph.

In view of the obvious and extensive relationship between the narrator's descent into madness in "The Yellow Wallpaper" and the author's account and analysis of her own breakdown and struggles as a woman in a world controlled by men, it is hardly surprising that the lion's share of the critical interest in Gilman's tale immediately subsequent to the Feminist Press reissue in 1973 should be focused on the relationship of the author's work to her life and how, by symbolic extension, Gilman herself becomes representative of every woman's plight in a culture largely defined by patriarchal condescension. As Elaine Hedges declares in her "Afterword," "The Yellow Wallpaper" "is one of the rare pieces of literature we have by a nineteenth-century woman which directly confronts the sexual politics of the male-female husband-wife relationship." What is surprising though is how variously the relationship between Gilman's experience as a woman and "The Yellow Wallpaper" has been characterized.

Among the early critics of this text, Beate Schöpp-Schilling, Patricia Meyer Spacks, Mary Hill, and Juliann Fleenor discuss the tale primarily in terms of the relationship between Gilman's life and the experiences of the tormented narrator in "The Yellow Wallpaper." Beate Schöpp-Schilling's article "'The Yellow Wallpaper': A Rediscovered 'Realistic Story'" (1975) uses Adlerian depth psychology to explore "the relationship between Gilman's life and this specific literary work from a psychological point of view," and subsequently to evaluate "the story as a psychologically realistic account of the causes and the progressive stages of mental illness."[2] Patricia Meyer Spacks's *The Female Imagination*, also published in 1975, moves in a slightly different direction, yet still emphasizes the intimate relationship of Gilman to the narrator of the story, noting that Gilman's "situation literally duplicated that of her fictional heroine." Spacks takes special note of Gilman's tortured relationship with her mother and her debilitation in marriage. In "Charlotte Perkins Gilman: A Feminist's Struggle with Womanhood" (1980), Mary Hill shifts the discussion of the Gilman/narrator relationship in the direction of Gilman's early quest for independence, the story allowing Gilman to say in fiction what she cannot say in life.

Juliann E. Fleenor's "The Gothic Prism: Charlotte Perkins Gilman's Gothic Stories and Her Autobiography" (1983) reads the Gilman/narrator relationship in yet another way, arguing "that the Gothic form [in which "The Yellow Wallpaper" is cast] is one framework through which Charlotte Perkins Gilman shaped her autobiography as well as generalized about the female experience. Its use is both limiting and yet revealing—limiting in that it reduces Gilman's life to that of a victim; revealing in that its use suggests that the major conflict in her life was with her female self, with her mother, and with the very act of creation." Fleenor compares Gilman's autobiography to three Gothic stories she wrote in close proximity to one another: "The Yellow Wallpaper," "The Rocking Chair," and "The Giant Wistaria." Fleenor argues that on the surface "these stories, like her autobiography, convey her continued rebellion and anger over the treatment women received in a patriarchal society. On closer examination, however, they also reveal an ambivalent relationship with the mother, one that is duplicated in the autobiography. And, finally, they reveal an ambivalence about the capacity of female imagination and female creativity," the latter including Gilman's own discomfort with her body and reproduction. Fleenor concludes that for Gilman, ever out of step and alone, "The Gothic prism had become the Gothic prison."

As different as these four diagnoses of the author's psychological trauma and crisis are, one thing they hold in common is an unquestioned conflation of the meaning of the narrator's experience in the tale and Gilman's own life experiences, especially those related to her personal breakdown. As we shall soon see, however, this is not an assumption unreservedly shared by all readers of the story. These early feminist commentaries are all likewise agreed in defining the story as a reflection of the nugatory plight of women trapped in a cultural context dominated—both then and now—by patriarchal control and condescension.

Because subsequent readers could take for granted many of the advances in our understanding of the tale made by this first group of readers, a new wave of feminists, beginning with Annette Kolodny in 1980, began to make a secondary move away from the text of the tale in itself, its relation to Gilman's life, and even from the broad issues of cultural politics comprising much of the tale's meaning. For this second wave of feminist critics these frames of critical reference do not exhaust our understanding of Gilman's disturbing tale. Instead of reading the text of "The Yellow Wallpaper" by the light of a feminist critical analytic that merely lays bare the imprisoned plight of women in Gilman's and our cultural moment, they "re-read" the tale with a contemporary spin, seeing in the silenced narrator's quandary a prophetic and cautionary emblem of the difficulties women must face and overcome somehow if they hope to redress the neglected state of women and women's discourse and advance their own cause. In foregrounding the fact that the chief means of patriarchal control exerted over the anonymous narrator in this story is the husband, John's denial of her access to "texts"—both those she might read and those she might write—Annette Kolodny and Judith Fetterley both see in the story an anticipatory reflection of the current power struggle in academic circles over revision and reformation of the "literary canon," that body of "stories" handed down from generation to generation as our common cultural inheritance, context, and image of ourselves. If the stories by and of women are not accorded a "room of their own" in the "ancestral house" of fiction our children inherit and will inhabit, these feminists fear that future generations of women will be treated no less patronizingly than was the unfortunate narrator of Gilman's tale. Like her, they will remain imprisoned in the childish nursery of men's creation, their very subjectivity seriously compromised, their stories unheard and unread, their full human identities neglected—indeed negated.

It is precisely the heroic quest to liberate woman from her own imprisonment that these critics applaud in the narrator of "The Yellow Wallpaper" and that they themselves seek to emulate in an analogous enterprise of their own, the freeing of Gilman's tale and other distinguished female stories from an arbitrary confinement and neglect suffered at the hands of the male literary establishment presuming to determine what women may or should read. For them, Gilman's narrator's efforts to write and then read a discourse separate from the constraints "learned" male authority figures in her life would impose upon her is—however paradoxical and even tragic its results—her only possible escape from the demeaning shackles of patriarchal domination she has long endured in silent frustration and anxiety. It is likewise the cultural model under whose banner they would revise the literary canon.

In "A Map for Rereading: Or, Gender and the Interpretation of Literary Texts" (1980), Annette Kolodny takes as her point of departure Harold Bloom's argument in *A Map of Misreading* (1975) that poets write in response to other poets, with no work having its genesis as a single, separate entity. Bloom's theory has its basis in the Freudian notion that the son needs to "slay the father" symbolically in order to assert his own identity. Likewise, the poet, writing within the tradition of the literary canon, wishes to slay his or her precursors—that is, displace the old poet with their own poems. While this indeed is a simplified version of Bloom's theory, one can see that the theory itself assumes the central importance of a shared sense of literary tradition: "Bloom assumes a community of readers (and, thereby, critics) who know that same 'system of texts' within which the specific poet at hand has enacted his [or her] *misprision* [misreading]" of the literary progenitors who inspired them.

Kolodny argues that the reading audience of 1890 might have seen "The Yellow Wallpaper" as Gilman's misprision of Poe's "The Pit and the Pendulum," for "both stories, after all, involve a sane mind entrapped in an insanity-inducing situation." But Gilman's story never entered the accepted literary canon:

> Insofar as Americans had earlier learned to follow the fictive processes of aberrant perception and mental breakdown in [Poe's] work, they should have provided Gilman, one would imagine, with a ready-made audience for *her* protagonist's progressively debilitating fantasies of entrapment and liberation. As they had entered popular fiction by the end of the nineteenth century, however, the linguistic markers for those processes were at once heavily male-gendered and highly idiosyncratic, having more to do with individual temperament

> than with social or cultural situations per se. As a result, it
> would appear that the reading strategies by which cracks in
> ancestral walls and suggestions of unchecked masculine will-
> fulness were immediately noted as both symbolically and se-
> mantically relevant did not, for some reason, necessarily
> *carry over* to 'the nursery at the top of the house.'

For this reason, Kolodny argues, "Poe continued as a well-
traveled road, while Gilman's story, lacking the possibility of
further influence, became a literary dead end." So, too, the
narrator in the story, unable to "write" her own text, turns to
the wallpaper and begins to "read" her own text, ending only
in isolation and culturally condemned deviance. As Kolodny
notes, "Liberation here is liberation only into madness: for in
decoding her own projection onto the paper, the protagonist
had managed merely to reencode them once more, and now
more firmly than ever, within." What Kolodny argues for is a
literary tradition that includes women's texts, with men learning to read women's texts in the same manner that women
have learned to read men's texts. Asking for this in a public
way, she acknowledges, places women writers and critics "in
a position analogous to that of the narrator of 'The Yellow Wallpaper,' bound, if we are to survive, to challenge the (accepted
and generally male) authority who has traditionally wielded
the power to determine what may be written and how it shall
be read." A public acknowledgment of women's texts, she asserts, would "allow us to appreciate the variety of women's literary expression, enabling us to take it into serious account
for perhaps the first time rather than, as we do now, writing it
off as caprice or exception." Recognizing and learning to read
women's fiction would be salutary: "*Re-visionary rereading*"
of the stories of men and women alike.

In her discussion of "The Yellow Wallpaper" in "Reading about Reading" (1986), Judith Fetterley argues that like
"Mark Twain who must learn to read his river if he wants to
become a master pilot," so too must men learn to read women's
texts if they wish to understand women. Gilman's story then
is a story of rebellion: "Writing from the point of view of a
character trapped in that male text . . . Gilman's narrator shifts
the center of attention away from the male mind that has pro-

duced the text and directs it instead to the consequences for women's lives of men's control of textuality . . . As man, husband, and doctor, John controls the narrator's life. That he chooses to make such an issue out of what and how she reads tells us what we need to know about the politics of reading." Until this changes, women forced to read men's texts "are forced to become characters in those texts. And since the stories men tell assert as fact what women know to be fiction, not only do women lose the power that comes from authoring; more significantly, they are forced to deny their own reality and to commit in effect a kind of psychic suicide."

Whereas the earlier feminist critics discussed would align Gilman herself with the narrator, Fetterley points out that unlike the narrator whose choices are to agree to become a character in John's text (which she sees as madness) or to refuse to become a character in his text and opt to write her own (which he will deem madness), Gilman herself chose yet a third option: "that of writing 'The Yellow Wallpaper'" though it is also true that she "implicitly recognizes that her escape from this dilemma is the exception, not the rule." The narrator remains trapped in the patriarchal text. Fetterley asserts that, "More insidious still, through her madness the narrator does not simply become the character John already imagines her to be as part of his definition of feminine nature; she becomes a version of John himself. Mad, the narrator is manipulative, secretive, dishonest; she learns to lie, obscure, and distort." With the roles reversed at the end of the story, the narrator momentarily masters and the husband faints. When he awakens, "John will tell his story, and there will be no alternative text to expose him." In this article, Fetterley seeks to heighten our awareness that "the struggle recorded in the text has its analogue in the struggle around and about the text, for nothing less than our sanity is at stake in the issue of what we read." Here again, the related issues of social canon and change are very much the focus of critical discussion.

As we have just seen, Kolodny and Fetterley form a second wave of feminist response to Gilman's story and implicitly acknowledge that the tragic ending of the narrator's efforts to create a discourse of her own by means of her private engagement with and imaginative projection upon the wallpaper threatens to undermine and indeed "contradict" the heroic tale her rebellion also tells. In response to the crippling inhibitions that male authority figures impose upon her in an attempt to control her voice (severely restricting what she may read and write), the narrator persists in an undaunted effort to identify and uncover her own true story to herself, writing and reading it through the symbolic mediation of the wallpaper. Hers is clearly a heroic resistance and innocent self-defense, one that these feminists justifiably admire; but it nevertheless results in miserable failure: madness, self-defeat, and further marginalization in a world controlled by male authority figures. Heroic resistance concludes by further isolating the narrator and reconfirming the prevailing suspicion among the "authorities" still presiding over her fate that female experience should be considered deviant. It is somewhat surprising then that Kolodny and Fetterley are not more suspicious than they appear to be that their adoption of the narrator as a culture heroine to emulate in their own battle to legitimize a "separate female discourse" within the literary canon may be fraught with hidden perils to their contemporary feminist agenda as well. That potential irony is not lost, however, on the most recent feminist writers represented in this text— Janice Haney-Peritz, Marianne DeKoven, Susan Lanser, and Elizabeth Ammons. For them, the narrator of Gilman's tale makes a fatal error when she passes beyond sympathy for the imprisoned female figure whose story she reads in the wallpaper to total identification with that figure; in doing so she confuses the imaginary with the real, losing all sense of the potentialities of her own distinctive self in her attempt to assert and liberate that self, only, as Haney-Peritz puts it, to "encrypt herself" as a mad "fantasy figure" by tale's end. Contemporary feminists, they argue, should not repeat the narrator's mistake in their analogous "identifications" with her.

Haney-Peritz's 1986 study of "The Yellow Wallpaper" establishes the narrator's condition from beginning to end of the story as an "unheard of contradiction" and accepts previous feminists' analysis that the way the narrator protects her condition is through her private reading and writing of the paper (or her own textuality).

But Haney-Peritz argues that the majority of feminist

critics writing about the tale may be reenacting the ironic "triumph/failure" of Gilman's narrator on a broader cultural stage. Instead of seeing the story as a reflection of their condition that can be mediated in language, they completely identify with it, thereby becoming marked as deviant and separated from the fullest understanding of their condition. Haney-Peritz feels that the reader's proper stance is *sympathy* for the narrator rather than *identification* with her: "Like the narrator of 'The Yellow Wallpaper,' some contemporary feminist critics see in literature a really distinctive body which they seek to liberate through identification. Although this body goes by many names, including the woman's story, female meaning, *écriture féminine,* and the maternal subtext, it is usually presented as essential to a viable feminist literary criticism and celebrated as something so distinctive that it shakes, if it does not destroy, the very foundations of patriarchal literature's ancestral house." Haney-Peritz suggests that women readers, writers, and critics must wish to do more than simply "shake" the "ancestral house"; they need to look to Gilman herself as their model rather than the story's narrator. Gilman did not go mad but labored to change the social conditions imprisoning females. What Gilman may have learned in the course of writing "The Yellow Wallpaper" is that "until the material conditions of social life were radically changed, there would be no 'real' way out" of mankind's ancestral prison.

Marianne DeKoven also deals with mankind's ancestral prison in "Gendered Doubleness and the 'Origins' of Modernist Form" (1989). Placing modernism historically (1890 to World War II) and noting that modernist fiction hinges on inconsistencies and "continually denies itself," DeKoven argues that Kate Chopin's *The Awakening* and Gilman's "The Yellow Wallpaper" helped "birth" the modernist form as much as James, Yeats, Conrad, Pound, and Joyce—the male writers usually credited for this achievement. While these two works are not usually considered among the "proto-modernism or the high modernist canon," DeKoven defines their modernist form features.

Like Haney-Peritz, DeKoven focuses on the "unheard of contradictions" in "The Yellow Wallpaper," illustrating how the story represents the "doubleness of female modernism" in its use of "dream structure to enact self-contradiction." Given the situation the narrator of this tale finds herself in, the struggle becomes "her own against herself." DeKoven sees this entrapment/freedom ambivalence in the narrator's symbolic projections into the wallpaper, which she rightly notes "have been insufficiently appreciated." Her excellent analysis of the narrator's relationship to the paper offers a fuller appreciation of this aspect of the story while furthering our understanding of the contradictions within the text. Although the narrator's success at tearing away the paper and crawling over her husband rings of triumph, DeKoven, like Haney-Peritz, acknowledges that "she has defeated him and his world of anti-female laws at far too great a cost to herself." In the wallpaper and the narrator's reaction to it, Gilman has created "a self-defeating duality of prison and prisoner" which represents, DeKoven feels, "the story's double figure of ambivalence about female freedom." On the one hand it is desired; on the other, feared. The desire for freedom "invents" the paper. The ambivalence toward freedom "divides it into front and back patterns" and sets them "at war with each other."

Had *The Awakening* and "The Yellow Wallpaper" not been cast in modernist forms, DeKoven argues, their content would have been "too threatening" for the times. The subsequent suppression of both works was, as DeKoven sees it, a "turning away from the rage expressed in both texts at the female condition," allowing readers to temporarily forget that modernism "had mothers as well as fathers."

It is precisely to further explore these contradictions that Susan Lanser argues for deconstructionist readings of the story. In "Feminist Criticism, 'The Yellow Wallpaper,' and the Politics of Color in America" (1989), Lanser recounts the critical reception and suggests that seeing the story through the eyes of a deconstructionist might reveal additional meaning. She points out that no one seems to have noticed that virtually all feminist discourse on "The Yellow Wallpaper" has come from white academics and has failed to question the story's status as a universal woman's text: "A feminist criticism willing to deconstruct its own practices would reexamine our exclusive reading of 'The Yellow Wallpaper,' rethink the implications of its canonization, and acknowledge both the text's position in ideology and our own." Wishing to make more of the color yellow in the tale than other critics have done, Lanser asserts that "in privileging the questions of reading and writing as essential 'woman questions,' feminist criticism has been led to the paper while suppressing the politically charged adjective that colors it."

Using Gilman's later work, particularly *Concerning Children*, the *Forerunner* essays, *Herland*, and *Moving the Mountain*, Lanser reflects on Gilman's own prejudices against non-Aryan people and her conclusion that to accept them into the melting pot would produce an inferior country because they were not ready for democracy: "For Gilman, patriarchy is a racial phenomenon: it is primarily non-Aryan 'yellow' peoples whom Gilman holds responsible for originating and perpetuating patriarchal practices, and it is primarily Nordic Protestants whom she considers capable of change." For this reason, Gilman was critical of immigration practices that would impede her vision for social reform.

The conclusion of Lanser's article points to the same inconsistencies and contradictions noted by Haney-Peritz. Contradicting Gilbert and Gubar, with whom this critical survey began, Lanser asserts that "The Yellow Wallpaper" is "no more '*the* story that all literary women would tell' than the entirely white canon represented in their *The Madwoman in the Attic* is *the* story of all women's writing or the only story those (white) texts can tell" and that it has been able to pass for a universal text "only insofar as white, Western literature and perspectives continue to dominate academic American feminist practices even when the most urgent literary and political events are happening in Africa, Asia, and Latin America, and among the new and old cultures of Color in the United States." The inherent "contradiction of ideology" within Gilman and "The Yellow Wallpaper" force Lanser to note "a political unconscious in which questions of race permeate questions of sex" and allow her to conclude that one of the messages of this story—albeit unwittingly on Gilman's part, of course—"is that textuality, like culture, is more complex, shifting, and polyvalent than any of the ideas we can abstract from it, that the narrator's reductive gesture is precisely to isolate and essentialize one 'idea about sex and gender' from a more complex textual field." Lanser acknowledges the important work of earlier critics of this study, but she is hopeful that a new course of critical readings acknowledging our historically complex and ever-changing social structure will emerge.

Elizabeth Ammons's "Writing Silence: 'The Yellow Wallpaper'" (1991) is a good place to conclude our review of the range of critical perspectives the story has generated, not only because her overview of the story's implications builds upon and neatly consolidates the recent history of critical debate we have ourselves been tracing at greater length, but also because her powerful and detailed account of much of the story's language and symbolic action returns us, as all good criticism should, to renewed attention and focus upon the specific language of the story itself.

Ammons concludes that the story is, on the one hand (as the initial wave of feminist critics argued), a heartening account of a "middle-class white woman's attempt to claim sexual and textual authority" for herself, a conflict in which she successfully transforms herself "from the position of victim to that of agent." But, on the other hand, Ammons is likewise quick to concede (with Haney-Peritz and Lanser), that the story is nonetheless a "very dark and hopeless one" in which even the imprisoned heroine's most likely source of aid—solidarity with other oppressed women—remains but a private fantasy and an increasingly maddening one at that. By the end, as Ammons ironically notes, the "heroine has become the cripple her class has worked hard to create."

Ammons's carefully balanced recognition of the hopelessly ambiguous meaning and import of the narrator's experience should remind us of Haney-Peritz's important claim that Gilman viewed the narrator's case and character in profoundly paradoxical terms from the very beginning to the shocking end of her confinement. The crucial phrase revealing Gilman's complex attitude towards the protagonist of her tale comes early on in the story when the narrator describes the wallpaper as having "lame uncertain curves . . . [that] suddenly commit suicide—plunge off at outrageous angles, destroy themselves in unheard of contradictions." The words the narrator uses to describe her frustration in "reading" and writing what sense the paper might make are also the words communicating, at one remove and metaphorically, the author's frustration in reading and writing the sense her narrator—and more generally—her own "paper" might make, i.e. what sense the short story itself might make. It may well be, then, that ultimately the problem, as Gilman sees it, is that the narrator remains from first to last an "unheard of contradiction" in important ways, a woman unwittingly committing suicide even as she acts to affirm a life lived as an independent human spirit. In other words, the self-contradiction the narrator embodies is virtually "unheard of" in the usual idiomatic sense of that phrase because her protests against the conditions she endures remain "unheard of" in a more literal sense. Though she consistently feels inclined to challenge the wisdom of her well-meaning "guardians," she never does find the will to speak out in any public way against the treatment she feels oppressing her, her only protest being her hesitant and finally aborted effort to detail her frustrations in the personal journal entries she acknowledges from the outset will never see the light of day nor be read by any other living soul. Even sane, she is as "imprisoned" by her own shortsightedness as she is literally walled off from self-determination by the blindness of an oppressive social order. By the end, although she can madly assert "'I've got out at last, in spite of you and Jane,'" this ambiguous "spite," a foolishly triumphant boast and embittered curse, is about the only satisfaction she could gain from such a protest because from now on Jenny and John will alone be publishing her "story," not her. Nor, tragically, will she protest that fact, either; the narrative informs us that the mad narrator no longer even seeks her own freedom when the opportunity presents itself. In freedom, she fears she might "lose her way." Better to crawl in a vicious circle about the margins of her cage.

It is our view that Haney-Peritz also speaks for Gilman herself, too, then, when she declares that the narrator is virtually an "unheard of contradiction" in terms: a woman who remains simultaneously well and ill, a woman who is at once rightly asserting herself and wrongly suppressing herself. At the end, when the narrator appears to assert herself most triumphantly and unambiguously by shouting her rage at John and then subsequently crawling over the prone body of her jailor, she remains a self-destroying, thoroughly ambiguous being—neither human nor beast. A simple beast would seize the opportunity to flee its captivity; sane human beings do not forfeit the opportunity for self-reflective thought and moral self-determination. But the mad narrator has abandoned all reflective self-regard and fear for her own personal well-being. Even as the story nears its conclusion, she is still sane enough to acknowledge a human scruple when she reflects that it "must be very humiliating to be caught creeping by daylight"; but by the end she has lost all signs of the shame that traditionally distinguishes human beings from the other animals. For Gilman, this is no genuine liberation to celebrate. As she communicates it to us through her tale, bringing the narrator's abandoned journal entries to a meaningful conclusion, the human choice we must make is terrifyingly simple: in oppressive circumstances we must stand up for ourselves and make ourselves heard—or go mad. Gilman herself apparently learned this lesson the hard way, nearly losing her own sanity before venturing on her lonely way to her own literary voice.

Having gone full circle, the criticism of "The Yellow Wallpaper" returns to the question of power. Feminists should not, like the narrator, confuse the imaginary and the real by fantasizing that a separate female discourse they have uncovered can by itself become a voice and story so distinctive that it will have the power "to shake, if it does not destroy, the very foundation of patriarchal literature's ancestral house." Even if such a reversal could be realized, it would, as Haney-Peritz implies, mean little more than the masters and slaves would have exchanged uniforms, since its motive is implicated in the pattern of erotic domination and aggression feminists have long deplored.

Although Gilman continued to write poems and fiction about the need to break free of restrictive traditions and to find creative solutions to problems posed by the domestic/public conflict in women's lives, her creative work was plagued by the didacticism that she kept in check in her masterpiece. "Dr. Claire's Case," a positive reworking of the "The Yellow Wallpaper" situation, reads less like fiction than an anecdotal account of how distraught women can be cured. Even "Making a Change," which is included in this volume, seems more

21

concerned with message than character; Gilman demonstrates how a creative woman, in this case a musician, can
escape her maternal role, practice her craft, and alleviate the
family's economic problems. The Utopian fiction, particularly
Herland, is more engaging, lively, and clever in its promotion
of Gilman's ideas about gender roles but fails to emotionally
engage its readers the way "The Yellow Wallpaper" does. In
"The Yellow Wallpaper" she demonstrated her considerable
creative talents and her triumph over patriarchal control by
chronicling her narrator/writer's own emotional and creative
failures. It is therefore interesting and ironic that Gilman herself turned away, for the most part, from the expressionistic,
"literary" style admired by her feminist critics to adapt a jour-
nalistic, prose style which could be described as stereotypical
"masculine" public discourse.

In fact, though she is known by most readers as the
author of "The Yellow Wallpaper" and the novel *Herland* (published in 1915 and reissued to receptive audiences in 1979),
Gilman was regarded until 1973 as primarily an internationally recognized social theorist, journalist, and lecturer. Her
Women and Economics (1898) was particularly well received,
and her feminist concerns are reflected in non-fiction like *His
Religion and Hers: A Study of the Faith of Our Fathers and
the Work of Our Mothers* (1923) and *The Man-Made World;
or, Our Androcentric Culture* (1911). Her later life was devoted to lecturing and to her autobiography, *The Living of
Charlotte Perkins Gilman,* published in 1935, the year she
died of an overdose of chloroform. Just as her work was "of a
piece" with consistent ideas that were reworked through lectures, her journal, and her books (both prose and fiction), her
life was the living out of those ideas. She remains an indomi-
table figure and her haunting tale—demanding that attention
be paid to gender issues and social practices—continues to
reveal its shocking truth a century later.

In addition to "The Yellow Wallpaper," three other selections by Gilman are included in this volume: two short
stories, "Through This" and "Making a Change," which
nicely complement "The Yellow Wallpaper," and "The 'Nervous Breakdown' of Women," which was published in *The
Forerunner* (1916). "The Hysterical Woman: Sex Roles and

Role Conflict in Nineteenth–Century America," by Carroll Smith-Rosenberg, provides a historical background for the narrator's illness in the story, and the selections from Dr. S. Weir Mitchell, who treated Gilman, suggest the medical treatment women received. The nine critical pieces, already discussed here, attest to the wonderful power and richness of "The Yellow Wallpaper," which continues to fascinate readers.

⬜ *Notes* ∎

1. *To Herland and Beyond: The Life and Works of Charlotte Perkins Gilman* (New York: Pantheon Books, 1990), p. 105. Much of the biographical material in this introduction is drawn from Lane's biography.

2. Works cited in the introduction but not reprinted here are listed in the bibliography.

❏ Chronology ■

1860	Born Charlotte Anna Perkins in Hartford, Connecticut.
1884	Marries Charles Walter Stetson, a painter.
1885	Gives birth to her only child, Katharine Beecher.
1887	Enters Dr. S. Weir Mitchell's sanitarium just outside Philadelphia and is subsequently pronounced "cured."
1888	Moves to Pasadena, California, and renews friendship with Grace Ellery Channing.
1892	Publishes "The Yellow Wallpaper" in *New England Magazine*.
1893	Publishes *In This Our World*, her first book of poetry.
1894	Sends daughter Katharine to live with Grace and Walter Stetson, who had just married.
1895	Lectures throughout the United States.
1898	Publishes *Women and Economics*.
1900	Marries George Houghton Gilman, her cousin; publishes *Concerning Children*.
1903	Publishes *The Home: Its Work and Influence*.
1904	Publishes *Human Work*.
1909–1916	Edits and writes *The Forerunner*, a monthly magazine in which she serializes three of her novels (*What Diantha Did*, *The Crux*, and *Moving the Mountain*), which are later published separately. *Herland* is serialized in 1915, but not published separately until 1979.
1923	Publishes *His Religion and Hers: A Study of the Faith of Our Fathers and the Work of Our Mothers*.

1932   Diagnosed as having breast cancer.

1934   Husband dies.

1935   Dies of a self-administered overdose of chloro-
            form; *The Living of Charlotte Perkins Gil-
            man,* her autobiography, published post-
            humously.

1973   "The Yellow Wallpaper" is reissued, marking
            the beginning of current scholarly interest in
            Gilman.

❏ The Yellow Wallpaper

☐ The Yellow Wallpaper

It is very seldom that mere ordinary people like John and myself secure ancestral halls for the summer.

A colonial mansion, a hereditary estate, I would say a haunted house, and reach the height of romantic felicity—but that would be asking too much of fate!

Still I will proudly declare that there is something queer about it.

Else, why should it be let so cheaply? And why have stood so long untenanted?

John laughs at me, of course, but one expects that in marriage.

John is practical in the extreme. He has no patience with faith, an intense horror of superstition, and he scoffs openly at any talk of things not to be felt and seen and put down in figures.

John is a physician, and *perhaps*—(I would not say it to a living soul, of course, but this is dead paper and a great relief to my mind)—*perhaps* that is one reason I do not get well faster.

You see, he does not believe I am sick!

And what can one do?

If a physician of high standing, and one's own husband, assures friends and relatives that there is really nothing the matter with one but temporary nervous

From *New England Magazine*, January 1892.

depression—a slight hysterical tendency—what is one
to do?

My brother is also a physician, and also of high
standing, and he says the same thing.

So I take phosphates or phosphites—whichever it
is—and tonics, and journeys, and air, and exercise, and
am absolutely forbidden to "work" until I am well again.

Personally, I disagree with their ideas.

Personally, I believe that congenial work, with excitement and change, would do me good.

But what is one to do?

I did write for a while in spite of them; but it *does*
exhaust me a good deal—having to be so sly about it, or
else meet with heavy opposition.

I sometimes fancy that in my condition if I had
less opposition and more society and stimulus—but
John says the very worst thing I can do is to think
about my condition, and I confess it always makes me
feel bad.

So I will let it alone and talk about the house.

The most beautiful place! It is quite alone, standing well back from the road, quite three miles from the
village. It makes me think of English places that you
read about, for there are hedges and walls and gates
that lock, and lots of separate little houses for the gar-
deners and people.

There is a *delicious* garden! I never saw such a
garden—large and shady, full of box-bordered paths,
and lined with long grape-covered arbors with seats under them.

There were greenhouses, too, but they are all broken now.

There was some legal trouble, I believe, some-

30

thing about the heirs and coheirs; anyhow, the place has been empty for years.

That spoils my ghostliness, I am afraid, but I don't care—there is something strange about the house—I can feel it.

I even said so to John one moonlight evening, but he said what I felt was a *draught,* and shut the window.

I get unreasonably angry with John sometimes. I'm sure I never used to be so sensitive. I think it is due to this nervous condition.

But John says if I feel so, I shall neglect proper self-control; so I take pains to control myself—before him, at least, and that makes me very tired.

I don't like our room a bit. I wanted one down-stairs that opened on the piazza and had roses all over the window, and such pretty old-fashioned chintz hang-ings! But John would not hear of it.

He said there was only one window and not room for two beds, and no near room for him if he took another.

He is very careful and loving, and hardly lets me stir without special direction.

I have a schedule prescription for each hour in the day; he takes all care from me, and so I feel basely ungrateful not to value it more.

He said we came here solely on my account, that I was to have perfect rest and all the air I could get. "Your exercise depends on your strength, my dear," said he, "and your food somewhat on your appetite; but air you can absorb all the time." So we took the nursery at the top of the house.

It is a big, airy room, the whole floor nearly, with windows that look all ways, and air and sunshine ga-lore. It was nursery first and then playroom and gymnasium, I should judge; for the windows are barred for little children, and there are rings and things in the walls.

The paint and paper look as if a boys' school had used it. It is stripped off—the paper—in great patches all around the head of my bed, about as far as I can reach, and in a great place on the other side of the room low down. I never saw a worse paper in my life.

One of those sprawling, flamboyant patterns committing every artistic sin.

It is dull enough to confuse the eye in following, pronounced enough to constantly irritate and provoke study, and when you follow the lame uncertain curves for a little distance they suddenly commit suicide—plunge off at outrageous angles, destroy themselves in unheard–of contradictions.

The color is repellent, almost revolting: a smouldering unclean yellow, strangely faded by the slow-turning sunlight.

It is a dull yet lurid orange in some places, a sickly sulphur tint in others.

No wonder the children hated it! I should hate it myself if I had to live in this room long.

There comes John, and I must put this away—he hates to have me write a word.

We have been here two weeks, and I haven't felt like writing before, since that first day.

I am sitting by the window now, up in this atrocious nursery, and there is nothing to hinder my writing as much as I please, save lack of strength.

John is away all day, and even some nights when his cases are serious.

I am glad my case is not serious!

But these nervous troubles are dreadfully depressing.

John does not know how much I really suffer. He knows there is no *reason* to suffer, and that satisfies him.

Of course it is only nervousness. It does weigh on me so not to do my duty in any way!

I meant to be such a help to John, such a real rest and comfort, and here I am a comparative burden already!

Nobody would believe what an effort it is to do what little I am able—to dress and entertain, and order things.

It is fortunate Mary is so good with the baby. Such a dear baby!

And yet I *cannot* be with him, it makes me so nervous.

I suppose John never was nervous in his life. He laughs at me so about this wallpaper!

At first he meant to repaper the room, but afterwards he said that I was letting it get the better of me, and that nothing was worse for a nervous patient than to give way to such fancies.

He said that after the wallpaper was changed it would be the heavy bedstead, and then the barred windows, and then that gate at the head of the stairs, and so on.

"You know the place is doing you good," he said, "and really, dear, I don't care to renovate the house just for a three months' rental."

"Then do let us go downstairs," I said. "There are such pretty rooms there."

Then he took me in his arms and called me a

blessed little goose, and said he would go down to the cellar, if I wished, and have it whitewashed into the bargain.

But he is right enough about the beds and windows and things.

It is as airy and comfortable a room as anyone need wish, and, of course, I would not be so silly as to make him uncomfortable just for a whim.

I'm really getting quite fond of the big room, all but that horrid paper.

Out of one window I can see the garden, those mysterious deep-shaded arbors, the riotous old-fashioned flowers, and bushes and gnarly trees.

Out of another I get a lovely view of the bay and a little private wharf belonging to the estate. There is a beautiful shaded lane that runs down there from the house. I always fancy I see people walking in these numerous paths and arbors, but John has cautioned me not to give way to fancy in the least. He says that with my imaginative power and habit of story-making, a nervous weakness like mine is sure to lead to all manner of excited fancies, and that I ought to use my will and good sense to check the tendency. So I try.

I think sometimes that if I were only well enough to write a little it would relieve the press of ideas and rest me.

But I find I get pretty tired when I try.

It is so discouraging not to have any advice and companionship about my work. When I get really well, John says we will ask Cousin Henry and Julia down for a long visit; but he says he would as soon put fireworks in my pillow-case as to let me have those stimulating people about now.

I wish I could get well faster.

But I must not think about that. This paper looks to me as if it *knew* what a vicious influence it had!

There is a recurrent spot where the pattern lolls like a broken neck and two bulbous eyes stare at you upside down.

I get positively angry with the impertinence of it and the everlastingness. Up and down and sideways they crawl, and those absurd, unblinking eyes are everywhere. There is one place where two breadths didn't match, and the eyes go all up and down the line, one a little higher than the other.

I never saw so much expression in an inanimate thing before, and we all know how much expression they have! I used to lie awake as a child and get more entertainment and terror out of blank walls and plain furniture than most children could find in a toy-store.

I remember what a kindly wink the knobs of our big, old bureau used to have, and there was one chair that always seemed like a strong friend.

I used to feel that if any of the other things looked too fierce I could always hop into that chair and be safe.

The furniture in this room is no worse than inharmonious, however, for we had to bring it all from downstairs. I suppose when this was used as a playroom they had to take the nursery things out, and no wonder! I never saw such ravages as the children have made here.

The wallpaper, as I said before, is torn off in spots, and it sticketh closer than a brother—they must have had perseverance as well as hatred.

Then the floor is scratched and gouged and splintered, the plaster itself is dug out here and there, and this great heavy bed, which is all we found in the room, looks as if it had been through the wars.

35

But I don't mind it a bit—only the paper.

There comes John's sister. Such a dear girl as she is, and so careful of me! I must not let her find me writing.

She is a perfect and enthusiastic housekeeper, and hopes for no better profession. I verily believe she thinks it is the writing which made me sick!

But I can write when she is out, and see her a long way off from these windows.

There is one that commands the road, a lovely shaded winding road, and one that just looks off over the country. A lovely country, too, full of great elms and velvet meadows.

This wallpaper has a kind of sub-pattern in a different shade, a particularly irritating one, for you can only see it in certain lights, and not clearly then.

But in the places where it isn't faded and where the sun is just so—I can see a strange, provoking, formless, sort of figure that seems to skulk about behind that silly and conspicuous front design.

There's sister on the stairs!

Well, the Fourth of July is over! The people are all gone, and I am tired out. John thought it might do me good to see a little company, so we just had Mother and Nellie and the children down for a week.

Of course I didn't do a thing. Jennie sees to everything now.

But it tired me all the same.

John says if I don't pick up faster he shall send me to Weir Mitchell in the fall.

But I don't want to go there at all. I had a friend who was in his hands once, and she says he is just like John and my brother, only more so!

36

Besides, it is such an undertaking to go so far.

I don't feel as if it was worthwhile to turn my hand over for anything, and I'm getting dreadfully fretful and querulous.

I cry at nothing, and cry most of the time.

Of course I don't when John is here, or anybody else, but when I am alone.

And I am alone a good deal just now. John is kept in town very often by serious cases, and Jennie is good and lets me alone when I want her to.

So I walk a little in the garden or down that lovely lane, sit on the porch under the roses, and lie down up here a good deal.

I'm getting really fond of the room in spite of the wallpaper. Perhaps *because* of the wallpaper.

It dwells in my mind so!

I lie here on this great immovable bed—it is nailed down, I believe—and follow that pattern about by the hour. It is as good as gymnastics, I assure you. I start, we'll say, at the bottom, down in the corner over there where it has not been touched, and I determine for the thousandth time that I *will* follow that pointless pattern to some sort of a conclusion.

I know a little of the principle of design, and I know this thing was not arranged on any laws of radiation, or alternation, or repetition, or symmetry, or anything else that I have ever heard of.

It is repeated, of course, by the breadths, but not otherwise.

Looked at in one way each breadth stands alone, the bloated curves and flourishes—a kind of "debased Romanesque" with *delirium tremens*—go waddling up and down in isolated columns of fatuity.

But, on the other hand, they connect diagonally,

and the sprawling outlines run off in great slanting waves of optic horror, like a lot of wallowing seaweeds in full chase.

The whole thing goes horizontally, too, at least it seems so, and I exhaust myself trying to distinguish the order of its going in that direction.

They have a horizontal breadth for a frieze, and that adds wonderfully to the confusion.

There is one end of the room where it is almost intact, and there, when the crosslights fade and the low sun shines directly upon it, I can almost fancy radiation after all—the interminable grotesques seem to form around a common center and rush off in headlong plunges of equal distraction.

It makes me tired to follow it. I will take a nap I guess.

I don't know why I should write this.

I don't want to.

I don't feel able.

And I know John would think it absurd. But I *must* say what I feel and think in some way—it is such a relief!

But the effort is getting to be greater than the relief.

Half the time now I am awfully lazy, and lie down ever so much.

John says I mustn't lose my strength, and has me take cod liver oil and lots of tonics and things, to say nothing of ale and wine and rare meat.

Dear John! He loves me very dearly, and hates to have me sick. I tried to have a real earnest reasonable talk with him the other day, and tell him how I wish he would let me go and make a visit to Cousin Henry and Julia.

But he said I wasn't able to go, nor able to stand it after I got there; and I did not make out a very good case for myself, for I was crying before I had finished.

It is getting to be a great effort for me to think straight. Just this nervous weakness I suppose.

And dear John gathered me up in his arms, and just carried me upstairs and laid me on the bed, and sat by me and read to me till it tired my head.

He treats her like a Baby.

He said I was his darling and his comfort and all he had, and that I must take care of myself for his sake, and keep well.

He says no one but myself can help me out of it, that I must use my will and self-control and not let any silly fancies run away with me.

There's one comfort, the baby is well and happy, and does not have to occupy this nursery with the horrid wallpaper.

If we had not used it, that blessed child would have! What a fortunate escape! Why, I wouldn't have a child of mine, an impressionable little thing, live in such a room for worlds.

I never thought of it before, but it is lucky that John kept me here after all, I can stand it so much easier than a baby, you see.

Of course I never mention it to them any more— I am too wise—but I keep watch of it all the same.

There are things in that wallpaper that nobody knows but me, or ever will.

Behind that outside pattern the dim shapes get clearer every day.

It is always the same shape, only very numerous.

And it is like a woman stooping down and creeping about behind that pattern. I don't like it a bit. I

"A woman stooping down and creeping about like a pattern"

wonder—I begin to think—I wish John would take me away from here!

It is so hard to talk with John about my case, because he is so wise, and because he loves me so.

But I tried it last night.

It was moonlight. The moon shines in all around just as the sun does.

I hate to see it sometimes, it creeps so slowly, and always comes in by one window or another.

John was asleep and I hated to waken him, so I kept still and watched the moonlight on that undulating wallpaper till I felt creepy.

The faint figure behind seemed to shake the pattern, just as if she wanted to get out.

I got up softly and went to feel and see if the paper *did* move, and when I came back John was awake.

"What is it, little girl?" he said. "Don't go walking about like that—you'll get cold."

I thought it was a good time to talk, so I told him that I really was not gaining here, and that I wished he would take me away.

"Why, darling!" said he, "our lease will be up in three weeks, and I can't see how to leave before.

"The repairs are not done at home, and I cannot possibly leave town just now. Of course if you were in any danger, I could and would, but you really are better, dear, whether you can see it or not. I am a doctor, dear, and I know. You are gaining flesh and color, your appetite is better, I feel really much easier about you."

"I don't weigh a bit more," said I, "nor as much; and my appetite may be better in the evening when you are here, but it is worse in the morning when you are away!"

"Bless her little heart!" said he with a big hug,

"she shall be as sick as she pleases! But now let's improve the shining hours by going to sleep, and talk about it in the morning!"

"And you won't go away?" I asked gloomily.

"Why, how can I, dear? It is only three weeks more and then we will take a nice little trip of a few days while Jennie is getting the house ready. Really, dear, you are better!"

"Better in body perhaps—" I began, and stopped short, for he sat up straight and looked at me with such a stern, reproachful look that I could not say another word.

"My darling," said he, "I beg of you, for my sake and for our child's sake, as well as for your own, that you will never for one instant let that idea enter your mind! There is nothing so dangerous, so fascinating, to a temperament like yours. It is a false and foolish fancy. Can you not trust me as a physician when I tell you so?"

So of course I said no more on that score, and we went to sleep before long. He thought I was asleep first, but I wasn't, and lay there for hours trying to decide whether that front pattern and the back pattern really did move together or separately.

On a pattern like this, by daylight, there is a lack of sequence, a defiance of law, that is a constant irritant to a normal mind.

The color is hideous enough, and unreliable enough, but the pattern is torturing.

You think you have mastered it, but just as you get well underway in following, it turns a back-somersault and there you are. It slaps you in the face, knocks you down, and tramples upon you. It is like a bad dream.

The outside pattern is a florid arabesque, reminding one of a fungus. If you can imagine a toadstool in joints, an interminable string of toadstools, budding and sprouting in endless convolutions—why, that is something like it.

That is, sometimes!

There is one marked peculiarity about this paper, a thing nobody seems to notice but myself, and that is that it changes as the light changes.

When the sun shoots in through the east window—I always watch for that first long, straight ray—it changes so quickly that I never can quite believe it.

That is why I watch it always.

By moonlight—the moon shines in all night when there is a moon—I wouldn't know it was the same paper.

At night in any kind of light, in twilight, candle light, lamplight, and worst of all by moonlight, it becomes bars! The outside pattern, I mean, and the woman behind it is as plain as can be.

I didn't realize for a long time what the thing was that showed behind, that dim sub-pattern, but now I am quite sure it is a woman.

By daylight she is subdued, quiet. I fancy it is the pattern that keeps her so still. It is so puzzling. It keeps me quiet by the hour.

I lie down ever so much now. John says it is good for me, and to sleep all I can.

Indeed he started the habit of making me lie down for an hour after each meal.

It is a very bad habit, I am convinced, for you see I don't sleep.

And that cultivates deceit, for I don't tell them I'm awake—oh, no!

The fact is I am getting a little afraid of John.

He seems very queer sometimes, and even Jennie has an inexplicable look.

42

It strikes me occasionally, just as a scientific hypothesis—that perhaps it is the paper.

I have watched John when he did not know I was looking, and come into the room suddenly on the most innocent excuses, and I've caught him several times *looking at the paper!* And Jennie too. I caught Jennie with her hand on it once.

She didn't know I was in the room and when I asked her in a quiet, a very quiet voice, with the most restrained manner possible, what she was doing with the paper—she turned around as if she had been caught stealing, and looked quite angry—asked me why I should frighten her so!

Then she said that the paper stained everything it touched, that she had found yellow smooches on all my clothes and John's, and she wished we would be more careful!

Did not that sound innocent? But I know she was studying that pattern, and I am determined that nobody shall find it out but myself.

Life is very much more exciting now than it used to be. You see I have something more to expect, to look forward to, to watch. I really do eat better, and am more quiet than I was.

John is so pleased to see me improve! He laughed a little the other day, and said I seemed to be flourishing in spite of my wallpaper.

I turned it off with a laugh. I had no intention of telling him it was *because* of the wallpaper—he would make fun of me. He might even want to take me away.

I don't want to leave now until I have found it out. There is a week more, and I think that will be enough.

[handwritten marginalia: she thinks everyone is looking at the pattern]

[handwritten marginalia: → she has something to look forward to]

43

I'm feeling ever so much better! I don't sleep much at night, for it is so interesting to watch developments; but I sleep a good deal in the daytime.

In the daytime it is tiresome and perplexing.

There are always new shoots on the fungus, and new shades of yellow all over it. I cannot keep count of them, though I have tried conscientiously.

It is the strangest yellow, that wallpaper! It makes me think of all the yellow things I ever saw—not beautiful ones like buttercups, but old, foul, bad yellow things.

But there is something else about that paper— the smell! I noticed it the moment we came into the room, but with so much air and sun it was not bad. Now we have had a week of fog and rain, and whether the windows are open or not, the smell is here.

It creeps all over the house.

I find it hovering in the dining-room, skulking in the parlor, hiding in the hall, lying in wait for me on the stairs.

It gets into my hair.

Even when I go to ride, if I turn my head suddenly and surprise it—there is that smell!

Such a peculiar odor, too! I have spent hours in trying to analyze it, to find what it smelled like.

It is not bad—at first—and very gentle, but quite the subtlest, most enduring odor I ever met.

In this damp weather it is awful, I wake up in the night and find it hanging over me.

It used to disturb me at first. I thought seriously of burning the house—to reach the smell.

But now I am used to it. The only thing I can think of that it is like is the *color* of the paper! A yellow smell.

There is a very funny mark on this wall, low down,

A yellow smell

near the mopboard. A streak that runs round the room. It goes behind every piece of furniture, except the bed, a long, straight, even *smooch,* as if it had been rubbed over and over.

I wonder how it was done and who did it, and what they did it for. Round and round and round— round and round and round—it makes me dizzy!

I really have discovered something at last.

Through watching so much at night, when it changes so, I have finally found out.

The front pattern *does* move—and no wonder! The woman behind shakes it!

The woman behind shakes it

Sometimes I think there are a great many women behind, and sometimes only one, and she crawls around fast, and her crawling shakes it all over.

Then in the very bright spots she keeps still, and in the very shady spots she just takes hold of the bars and shakes them hard.

And she is all the time trying to climb through. But nobody could climb through that pattern—it strangles so; I think that is why it has so many heads.

They get through, and then the pattern strangles them off and turns them upside down, and makes their eyes white!

If those heads were covered or taken off it would not be half so bad.

I think that woman gets out in the daytime!

She thinks the woman gets out

And I'll tell you why—privately—I've seen her!

I can see her out of every one of my windows!

It is the same woman, I know, for she is always creeping, and most women do not creep by daylight.

She sees her creeping

I see her in that long shaded lane, creeping up and down. I see her in those dark grape arbors, creeping all around the garden.

45

I see her on that long road under the trees, creeping along, and when a carriage comes she hides under the blackberry vines.

I don't blame her a bit. It must be very humiliating to be caught creeping by daylight!

I always lock the door when I creep by daylight. I can't do it at night, for I know John would suspect something at once.

And John is so queer now, that I don't want to irritate him. I wish he would take another room! Besides, I don't want anybody to let that woman out at night but myself.

I often wonder if I could see her out of all the windows at once.

But, turn as fast as I can, I can only see out of one at one time.

And though I always see her, she *may* be able to creep faster than I can turn!

I have watched her sometimes away off in the open country, creeping as fast as a cloud shadow in a high wind.

If only that top pattern could be gotten off from the under one! I mean to try it, little by little.

I have found out another funny thing, but I shan't tell it this time! It does not do to trust people too much.

There are only two more days to get this paper off, and I believe John is beginning to notice. I don't like the look in his eyes.

And I heard him ask Jennie a lot of professional questions about me. She had a very good report to give.

She said I slept a good deal in the daytime.

John knows I don't sleep very well at night, for all I'm so quiet!

He asked me all sorts of questions, too, and pre-tended to be very loving and kind.

As if I couldn't see through him!

Still, I don't wonder he acts so, sleeping under this paper for three months.

It only interests me, but I feel sure John and Jennie are secretly affected by it.

Hurrah! This is the last day, but it is enough. John is to stay in town over night, and won't be out until this evening.

Jennie wanted to sleep with me—the sly thing! But I told her I should undoubtedly rest better for a night all alone.

That was clever, for really I wasn't alone a bit! As soon as it was moonlight and that poor thing began to crawl and shake the pattern, I got up and ran to help her.

I pulled and she shook, I shook and she pulled, and before morning we had peeled off yards of that paper.

A strip about as high as my head and half around the room.

And then when the sun came and that awful pattern began to laugh at me, I declared I would finish it to-day!

We go away to-morrow, and they are moving all my furniture down again to leave things as they were before.

Jennie looked at the wall in amazement, but I told her merrily that I did it out of pure spite at the vicious thing.

She laughed and said she wouldn't mind doing it herself, but I must not get tired.

How she betrayed herself that time!

But I am here, and no person touches this paper but me—not *alive!*

She tried to get me out of the room—it was too patent! But I said it was so quiet and empty and clean now that I believed I would lie down again and sleep all I could, and not to wake me even for dinner—I would call when I woke.

So now she is gone, and the servants are gone, and the things are gone, and there is nothing left but that great bedstead nailed down, with the canvas mattress we found on it.

We shall sleep downstairs to-night, and take the boat home tomorrow.

I quite enjoy the room, now it is bare again.

How those children did tear about here!

This bedstead is fairly gnawed!

But I must get to work.

I have locked the door and thrown the key down into the front path.

I don't want to go out, and I don't want to have anybody come in, till John comes.

I want to astonish him.

I've got a rope up here that even Jennie did not find. If that woman does get out, and tries to get away, I can tie her!

But I forgot I could not reach far without anything to stand on!

This bed will *not* move!

I tried to lift and push it until I was lame, and then I got so angry I bit off a little piece at one corner—but it hurt my teeth.

Then I peeled off all the paper I could reach standing on the floor. It sticks horribly and the pattern just enjoys it! All those strangled heads and bulbous eyes and waddling fungus growths just shriek with derision!

I am getting angry enough to do something desperate. To jump out of the window would be admirable exercise, but the bars are too strong even to try.

Besides I wouldn't do it. Of course not. I know well enough that a step like that is improper and might be misconstrued.

I don't like to *look* out of the windows even—there are so many of those creeping women, and they creep so fast.

I wonder if they all come out of that wallpaper as I did?

But I am securely fastened now by my well-hidden rope—you don't get *me* out in the road there!

I suppose I shall have to get back behind the pattern when it comes night, and that is hard!

It is so pleasant to be out in this great room and creep around as I please!

I don't want to go outside. I won't, even if Jennie asks me to.

For outside you have to creep on the ground, and everything is green instead of yellow.

But here I can creep smoothly on the floor, and my shoulder just fits in that long smooch around the wall, so I cannot lose my way.

Why there's John at the door!

It is no use, young man, you can't open it!

How he does call and pound!

Now he's crying to Jennie for an axe.

It would be a shame to break down that beautiful door!

"John, dear!" said I in the gentlest voice, "the key is down by the front steps, under a plantain leaf!"

That silenced him for a few moments.

Then he said, very quietly indeed, "Open the door, my darling!"

"I can't," said I. "The key is down by the front door under a plantain leaf!"

And then I said it again, several times, very gently and slowly, and said it so often that he had to go and see, and he got it of course, and came in. He stopped short by the door.

"What is the matter?" he cried. "For God's sake, what are you doing!"

I kept on creeping just the same, but I looked at him over my shoulder.

"I've got out at last," said I, "in spite of you and Jane. And I've pulled off most of the paper, so you can't put me back!"

Now why should that man have fainted? But he did, and right across my path by the wall, so that I had to creep over him every time!

Background
to the Story

Through This

The dawn colors creep up my bedroom wall, softly, slowly.

Darkness, dim gray, dull blue, soft lavender, clear pink, pale yellow, warm gold—sunlight.

A new day.

With the great sunrise great thoughts come.

I rise with the world. I live. I can help. Here close at hand lie the sweet home duties through which my life shall touch the others! Through this man made happier and stronger by my living; through these rosy babies sleeping here in the growing light; through this small, sweet, well-ordered home, whose restful influence shall touch all comers; through me too, perhaps—there's the baker, I must get up, or this bright purpose fades.

How well the fire burns! Its swift kindling and gathering roar speak of accomplishment. The rich odor of coffee steals through the house.

John likes morning-glories on the breakfast table—scented flowers are better with lighter meals. All is ready—healthful, dainty, delicious.

The clean-aproned little ones smile milky-mouthed over their bowls of mush. John kisses me good-by so happily.

Through this dear work, well done, I shall reach. I shall help—but I must get the dishes done and not dream.

"Good morning! Soap, please, the same kind. Coffee, rice, two boxes of gelatine. That's all, I think. Oh—crackers! Good morning."

There, I forgot the eggs! I can make these go, I guess.

From *Kate Field's Washington*, 13 September 1893, 166.

Now to soak the tapioca. Now the beets on, they take so long. I'll bake the potatoes—they don't go in yet. Now babykins must have her bath and nap.

A clean hour and a half before dinner. I can get those little nightgowns cut and basted. How bright the sun is! Amaranth lies on the grass under the rosebush, stretching her paws among the warm, green blades. The kittens tumble over her. She's brought them three mice this week. Baby and Jack are on the warm grass too—happy, safe, well. Careful, dear! Don't go away from little sister!

By and by when they are grown, I can—O there! the bell!

Ah, well!—yes—I'd like to have joined. I believe in it, but I can't now. Home duties forbid. This is my work. Through this, in time, there's the bell again, and it waked the baby!

As if I could buy a sewing machine every week! I'll put out a bulletin, stating my needs for the benefit of the agents. I don't believe in buying at the door anyway, yet I suppose they must live. Yes, dear! Mamma's coming!

I wonder if torchon would look better, or Hamburg? It's softer but it looks older. Oh, here's that knit edging grandma sent me. Bless her dear heart!

There! I meant to have swept the bed-room this morning so as to have more time to-morrow. Perhaps I can before dinner. It does look dreadfully. I'll just put the potatoes in. Baked potatoes are so good! I love to see Jack dig into them with his little spoon.

John says I cook steak better than anyone he ever saw. Yes, dear?

Is that so? Why I should think they'd *know* better. Can't the people do anything about it?

Why no—not *personally*—but I should think *you* might. What are men for if they can't keep the city in order?

Cream on the pudding, dear?

That was a good dinner. I like to cook. I think housework is noble if you do it in a right spirit.

That pipe must be seen to before long. I'll speak to John about it. Coal's pretty low, too.

Guess I'll put on my best boots. I want to run down town for a few moments—in case mother comes and can stay with baby. I wonder if mother wouldn't like to join that—she has time enough. But she doesn't seem to be a bit interested in outside things. I ought to take baby out in her carriage, but it's so heavy with Jack, and yet Jack can't walk a great way. Besides, if mother comes I needn't. Maybe we'll all go in the car—but that's such an undertaking! Three o'clock.

Jack! Jack! Don't do that—here—wait a moment.

I ought to answer Jennie's letter. She writes such splendid things, but I don't go with her in half she says. A woman can't do that way and keep a family going. I'll write to her this evening.

Of course if one *could*, I'd like as well as anyone to be in those great live currents of thought and action. Jennie and I were full of it in school. How long ago that seems. But I never thought then of being so happy. Jennie isn't happy, I know—she can't be, poor thing, till she's a wife and mother.

O, there comes mother! Jack, deary, open the gate for Grandma! So glad you could come, mother dear! Can you stay awhile and let me go down town on a few errands?

Mother looks real tired. I wish she would go out more and have some outside interest. Mary and the children are too much for her, I think. Harry ought not to have brought them home. Mother needs rest. She's brought up one family.

There, I've forgotten my list, I hurried so. Thread, elastic, buttons; what was the other thing? Maybe I'll think of it.

How awfully cheap! How can they make them at that price! Three, please. I guess with these I can make the others last through the year. They're so pretty, too. How much are these? Jack's got to have a new coat before long—not to-day.

O dear! I've missed that car, and mother can't stay after five! I'll cut across and hurry.

Why the milk hasn't come, and John's got to go out early tonight. I wish election was over.

I'm sorry, dear, but the milk was so late, I couldn't make it. Yes, I'll speak to him. O, no, I guess not; he's a very reliable man, usually, and the milk's good. Hush, hush, baby! Papa's talking!

Good night, dear, don't be too late.

Sleep, baby, sleep!
The large stars are the sheep,
The little stars are the lambs, I guess.
And the fair moon is the shepherdess.
Sleep, baby, sleep!

How pretty they look! Thank God, they keep so well.

It's no use. I can't write a letter to-night—especially to Jennie. I'm too tired. I'll go to bed early. John hates to have me wait up for him late. I'll go now, if it is before dark—then get up early to-morrow and get the sweeping done. How loud the crickets are! The evening shades creep down my bedroom wall—softly—slowly.

Warm gold—pale yellow—clear pink—soft lavender—dull blue—dim gray—darkness.

Making a Change

"Wa-a-a-a-a: Waa-a-a-waa!"

Frank Gordins set down his coffee cup so hard that it spilled over into the saucer.

"Is there no way to stop that child crying?" he demanded.

"I do not know of any," said his wife, so definitely and politely that the words seemed cut off by machinery.

"I *do*," said his mother with even more definiteness, but less politeness.

Young Mrs. Gordins looked at her mother-in-law from under her delicate level brows, and said nothing. But the weary lines about her eyes deepened. She had been kept awake nearly all night, and for many nights.

So had he. So, as a matter of fact, had his mother. She had not the care of the baby—but lay awake wishing she had.

"There's no use talking about it," said Julia. "If Frank is not satisfied with the child's mother, he must say so—perhaps we can make a change."

This was ominously gentle. Julia's nerves were at the breaking point. Upon her tired ears, her sensitive mother's heart, the grating wail from the next room fell like a lash—burnt in like fire. Her ears were hypersensitive, always. She had been an ardent musician before her marriage, and had taught quite successfully on both piano and violin. To any mother a child's cry is painful; to a musical mother it is torment.

But if her ears were sensitive, so was her conscience. If her nerves were weak, her pride was strong. The child was

From *The Forerunner*, December 1911.

her child, it was her duty to take care of it, and take care of it she would. She spent her days in unremitting devotion to its needs and to the care of her neat flat; and her nights had long since ceased to refresh her.

Again the weary cry rose to a wail.

"It does seem to be time for a change of treatment," suggested the older woman acidly.

"Or a change of residence," offered the younger, in a deadly quiet voice.

"Well, by Jupiter! There'll be a change of some kind, and p.d.q.!" said the son and husband, rising to his feet.

His mother rose also, and left the room, holding her head high and refusing to show any effects of that last thrust.

Frank Gordins glared at his wife. His nerves were raw, too. It does not benefit anyone in health or character to be continuously deprived of sleep. Some enlightened persons use that deprivation as a form of torture.

She stirred her coffee with mechanical calm, her eyes sullenly bent on her plate.

"I will not stand having Mother spoken to like that," he stated with decision.

"I will not stand having her interfere with my methods of bringing up children."

"Your methods! Why, Julia, my mother knows more about taking care of babies than you'll ever learn! She has the real love of it—and the practical experience. Why can't you let her take care of the kid—and we'll all have some peace!"

She lifted her eyes and looked at him; deep inscrutable wells of angry light. He had not the faintest appreciation of her state of mind. When people say they are "nearly crazy" from weariness, they state a practical fact. The old phrase which describes reason as "tottering on her throne" is also a clear one.

Julia was more near the verge of complete disaster than the family dreamed. The conditions were so simple, so usual, so inevitable.

Here was Frank Gordins, well brought up, the only son of a very capable and idolatrously affectionate mother. He had fallen deeply and desperately in love with the exalted beauty and the fine mind of the young music teacher, and his mother had approved. She too loved music and admired beauty.

Her tiny store in the savings bank did not allow of a separate home, and Julia had cordially welcomed her to share in their household.

Here was affection, propriety, and peace. Here was a noble devotion on the part of the young wife, who so worshipped her husband that she used to wish she had been the greatest musician on earth—that she might give it up for him! She had given up her music, perforce, for many months, and missed it more than she knew.

She bent her mind to the decoration and artistic management of their little apartment, finding her standards difficult to maintain by the ever-changing inefficiency of her help. The musical temperament does not always include patience, nor, necessarily, the power of management.

When the baby came, her heart overflowed with utter devotion and thankfulness; she was his wife—the mother of his child. Her happiness lifted and pushed within till she longed more than ever for her music, for the free-pouring current of expression, to give forth her love and pride and happiness. She had not the gift of words.

So now she looked at her husband, dumbly, while wild visions of separation, of secret flight—even of self-destruction—swung dizzily across her mental vision. All she said was, "All right, Frank. We'll make a change. And you shall have—some peace."

"Thank goodness for that, Jule! You do look tired, girlie—let Mother see to His Nibs, and try to get a nap, can't you?"

"Yes," she said, "Yes . . . I think I will." Her voice had a peculiar note in it. If Frank had been an alienist, or even a general physician, he would have noticed it. But his work lay in electric coils, in dynamos and copper wiring—not in women's nerves—and he did not notice it.

He kissed her and went out, throwing back his shoulders and drawing a long breath of relief as he left the house behind him and entered his own world.

"This being married—and bringing up children—is not what it's cracked up to be." That was the feeling in the back of his mind. But it did not find full admission, much less expression.

When a friend asked him, "All well at home?" he said,

"Yes, thank you—pretty fair. Kid cries a good deal—but that's natural, I suppose."

He dismissed the whole matter from his mind and bent his faculties to a man's task—how he can earn enough to support a wife, a mother, and a son.

At home his mother sat in her small room, looking out of the window at the ground-glass one just across the "well," and thinking hard.

By the disorderly little breakfast table his wife remained motionless, her chin in her hands, her big eyes staring at nothing, trying to formulate in her weary mind some reliable reason why she should not do what she was thinking of doing. But her mind was too exhausted to serve her properly.

Sleep—sleep—sleep—that was the one thing she wanted. Then his mother could take care of the baby all she wanted to, and Frank could have some peace. . . . Oh, dear! It was time for the child's bath.

She gave it to him mechanically. On the stroke of the hour, she prepared the sterilized milk and arranged the little one comfortably with his bottle. He snuggled down, enjoying it, while she stood watching him.

She emptied the tub, put the bath apron to dry, picked up all the towels and sponges and varied appurtenances of the elaborate performance of bathing the first-born, and then sat staring straight before her, more weary than ever, but growing inwardly determined.

Greta had cleared the table, with heavy heels and hands, and was now rattling dishes in the kitchen. At every slam, the young mother winced, and when the girl's high voice began a sort of doleful chant over her work, young Mrs. Gordins rose to her feet with a shiver and made her decision.

She carefully picked up the child and his bottle, and carried him to his grandmother's room.

"Would you mind looking after Albert?" she asked in a flat, quiet voice, "I think I'll try to get some sleep."

"Oh, I shall be delighted," replied her mother-in-law. She said it in a tone of cold politeness, but Julia did not notice. She laid the child on the bed and stood looking at him in the same dull way for a little while, then went out without another word.

Mrs. Gordins, senior, sat watching the baby for some

long moments. "He's a perfectly lovely child!" she said softly, gloating over his rosy beauty. "There's not a *thing* the matter with him! It's just her absurd ideas. She's so irregular with him! To think of letting that child cry for an hour. He is nervous because she is. And of course she couldn't feed him till after his bath—of course not!"

She continued in these sarcastic meditations for some time, taking the empty bottle away from the small wet mouth, that sucked on for a few moments aimlessly and then was quiet in sleep.

"I could take care of him so that he'd *never* cry!" she continued to herself, rocking slowly back and forth. "And I could take care of twenty like him—and enjoy it! I believe I'll go off somewhere and do it. Give Julia a rest. Change of residence, indeed!"

She rocked and planned, pleased to have her grandson with her, even while asleep.

Greta had gone out on some errand of her own. The rooms were very quiet. Suddenly the old lady held up her head and sniffed. She rose swiftly to her feet and sprang to the gas jet—no, it was shut off tightly. She went back to the dining room—all right there.

"That foolish girl has left the range going and it's blown out!" she thought, and went to the kitchen. No, the little room was fresh and clean, every burner turned off.

"Funny! It must come in from the hall." She opened the door. No, the hall gave only its usual odor of diffused basement. Then the parlor—nothing there. The little alcove called by the renting agent "the music room," where Julia's closed piano and violin case stood dumb and dusty—nothing there.

"It's in her room—and she's asleep!" said Mrs. Gordins, senior; and she tried to open the door. It was locked. She knocked—there was no answer; knocked louder—shook it—rattled the knob. No answer.

Then Mrs. Gordins thought quickly. "It may be an accident, and nobody must know. Frank mustn't know. I'm glad Greta's out. I *must* get in somehow!" She looked at the transom, and the stout rod Frank had himself put up for the portieres Julia loved.

"I believe I can do it, at a pinch."

She was a remarkably active woman of her years, but no memory of earlier gymnastic feats could quite cover the exercise. She hastily brought the step-ladder. From its top she could see in, and what she saw made her determine recklessly.

Grabbing the pole with small strong hands, she thrust her light frame bravely through the opening, turning clumsily but successfully, and dropping breathlessly and somewhat bruised to the floor, she flew to open the windows and doors.

When Julia opened her eyes she found loving arms around her, and wise, tender words to soothe and reassure.

"Don't say a thing, dearie—I understand. I *under-stand*. I tell you! Oh, my dear girl—my precious daughter! We haven't been half good enough to you, Frank and I! But cheer up now—I've got the *loveliest* plan to tell you about! We *are* going to make a change! Listen now!"

And while the pale young mother lay quiet, petted and waited on to her heart's content, great plans were discussed and decided on.

Frank Gordins was pleased when the baby "outgrew his crying spells." He spoke of it to his wife.

"Yes," she said sweetly. "He has better care."

"I knew you'd learn," said he, proudly.

"I have!" she agreed. "I've learned—ever so much!"

He was pleased, too, vastly pleased, to have her health improve rapidly and steadily, the delicate pink come back to her cheeks, the soft light to her eyes; and when she made music for him in the evening, soft music, with shut doors—not to waken Albert—he felt as if his days of courtship had come again.

Greta the hammer-footed had gone, and an amazing French matron who came in by the day had taken her place. He asked no questions as to this person's peculiarities, and did not know that she did the purchasing and planned the meals, meals of such new delicacy and careful variance as gave him much delight. Neither did he know that her wages were greater than her predecessor's. He turned over the same sum weekly, and did not pursue details.

He was pleased also that his mother seemed to have taken a new lease of life. She was so cheerful and brisk, so full of little jokes and stories—as he had known her in his boyhood; and above all she was so free and affectionate with Julia, that he was more than pleased.

"I tell you what it is!" he said to a bachelor friend. "You fellows don't know what you're missing!" And he brought one of them home to dinner—just to show him.

"Do you do all that on thirty-five a week?" his friend demanded.

"That's about it," he answered proudly.

"Well, your wife's a wonderful manager—that's all I can say. And you've got the best cook I ever saw, or heard of, or ate of—I suppose I might say—for five dollars."

Mrs. Gordins was pleased and proud. But he was neither pleased nor proud when someone said to him, with displeasing frankness, "I shouldn't think you'd want your wife to be giving music lessons, Frank!"

He did not show surprise nor anger to his friend, but saved it for his wife. So surprised and so angry was he that he did a most unusual thing—he left his business and went home early in the afternoon. He opened the door of his flat. There was no one in it. He went through every room. No wife; no child; no mother; no servant.

The elevator boy heard him banging about, opening and shutting doors, and grinned happily. When Mr. Gordins came out, Charles volunteered some information.

"Young Mrs. Gordins is out, sir; but old Mrs. Gordins and the baby—they're upstairs. On the roof, I think."

Mr. Gordins went to the roof. There he found his mother, a smiling, cheerful nursemaid, and fifteen happy babies.

Mrs. Gordins, senior, rose to the occasion promptly.

"Welcome to my baby-garden, Frank," she said cheerfully. "I'm so glad you could get off in time to see it."

She took his arm and led him about, proudly exhibiting her sunny roof-garden, her sand-pile and big, shallow, zinc-lined pool, her flowers and vines, her seesaws, swings, and floor mattresses.

"You see how happy they are," she said. "Celia can manage very well for a few moments." And then she exhibited to him the whole upper flat, turned into a convenient place for many little ones to take their naps or to play in if the weather was bad.

"Where's Julia?" he demanded first.

"Julia will be in presently," she told him, "by five o'clock anyway. And the mothers come for the babies by then, too. I have them from nine or ten to five."

He was silent, both angry and hurt.

"We didn't tell you at first, my dear boy, because we knew you wouldn't like it, and we wanted to make sure it would go well. I rent the upper flat, you see—it is forty dollars a month, same as ours—and pay Celia five dollars a week, and pay Dr. Holbrook downstairs the same for looking over my little ones every day. She helped me to get them, too. The mothers pay me three dollars a week each, and don't have to keep a nursemaid. And I pay ten dollars a week board to Julia, and still have about ten of my own."

"And she gives music lessons?"

"Yes, she gives music lessons, just as she used to. She loves it, you know. You must have noticed how happy and well she is now—haven't you? And so am I. And so is Albert. You can't feel very badly about a thing that makes us all happy, can you?"

Just then Julia came in, radiant from a brisk walk, fresh and cheery, a big bunch of violets at her breast.

"Oh, Mother," she cried, "I've got tickets and we'll all go to hear Melba—if we can get Celia to come in for the evening."

She saw her husband, and a guilty flush rose to her brow as she met his reproachful eyes.

"Oh, Frank!" she begged, her arms around his neck. "Please don't mind! Please get used to it! Please be proud of us! Just think, we're all so happy, and we earn about a hundred dollars a week—all of us together. You see, I have Mother's ten to add to the house money, and twenty or more of my own!"

They had a long talk together that evening, just the two of them. She had told him, at last, what a danger had hung over them—how near it came.

"And Mother showed me the way out, Frank. The way to have my mind again—and not lose you! She is a different woman herself now that she has her heart and hands full of babies. Albert does enjoy it so! And *you've* enjoyed it—till you found it out!

"And dear—my own love—don't mind it now at all! I love my home, I love my work, I love my mother, I love you. And as to children—I wish I had six!"

He looked at her flushed, eager, lovely face, and drew her close to him.

"If it makes all of you as happy as that," he said, "I guess I can stand it."

And in after years he was heard to remark, "This being married and bringing up children is as easy as can be—when you learn how!"

The "Nervous Breakdown" of Women

Time was when women died in childbirth before they were old enough to die of anything else; or lived to some degree of age in such domestic obscurity that their state of health had no more than strictly local notice. Women who succeeded in living to be old, and who had no families in which to conceal themselves, were apt to be regarded with disfavor, even to the charge—and punishment—of being witches.

But now, in the steadily increasing prominence and serviceability of women, their state of health and length of life becomes more prominent. This has not only a genuine importance through the change in their feminine, domestic, economic and political activities, but is also given a fictitious notoriety because this change is under constant discussion.

Our self-conscious and voluble race has always been mightily concerned about its own growth, and made a prodigious noise over it; but instead of the excusable pride of a child in his new shoes, or a boy in his new razor, we find humanity always objecting to each step of progress. Every change in government, in religion, in methods of education, industry, art, or of economic relation has met with criticism and opposition, so we need not wonder that so universal a movement as that of half the human race should be as universally discussed.

In this limelight the faults and virtues, charms and failings, strength and weakness of women are being continually discussed, and one of the favorites of the disputants is the last named subject—woman's physical weakness. By those who deprecate the change in the position of women, their unques-

---

From *The Forerunner*, July–August 1916, 202–206.

tioned endurance, which has enabled them to work their lives long at the ceaseless cares and labors of housework, with the cares and labors of maternity as well, is held to belong only to those special tasks; and the "nervous breakdown," which is more conspicuous when the sufferer is in business, is assumed to be a consequence of that business.

If the breakdown occurs in the home, it is then alleged to be due to the pressure of "outside interests" conflicting with the "natural" domestic ones; if it happens to a young woman, with no domestic cares as yet, it is credited to "overstudy"; the only puzzling instance, from this point of view, is when the wholly domestic and maternal farmer's wife gives way. That she does, and frequently, is known to her friends, but as this woman lives in the privacy of the home and in rural seclusion, does not appear in public, or belong to clubs, and is seldom literary, her case is not prominent.

What is prominent, the general condition which calls for careful study, is the prevalence of "nervous breakdown" among American women of all classes at the present time.

Of course it occurs among men, but that is always accounted for on quite other grounds. We seldom hear it advanced that the nerve-weakness of women is similar to that of men, and due to similar causes. Still less is it shown that the special conditions of women's lives are such that there is reason for a much greater amount of neurasthenia than we see; and that the ability of women to sustain their present condition as well as they do, shows a high degree of nerve power.

Full nervous serenity depends on the smooth adjustment of the two interacting parts of every living thing—the body and the spirit. The creature must be satisfied with itself; it must do what it likes to do, and like to do what it does. Any caged animal shows the result on the nervous system of interference with natural physical habits. There are very few of us, men or women, who can have the peace of that perfect adjustment. No man who spends his whole time in an office; no woman who spends her whole time in a kitchen can maintain that equipose of soul and body, unless—and here comes in one of our human superiorities—unless the individual is consciously convinced that the work he is doing is necessary and right. If that fact is clearly established, fully accepted, then the nerve-force which would otherwise demand different expression is used to keep the machine steady, to hold the nose firmly to the supposedly necessary and beneficial grindstone.

Let it once enter the mind which is behind the nose that grindstones are not necessary—much less beneficial—and the position becomes irksome. It may be impossible to change it for many compelling reasons, but if the individual no longer contentedly accepts his "lot"—or hers—the effect on the nervous system is disastrous.

Even if the physico-psychic balance is perfect, there remains another necessity for peace of mind; that is the adjustment between the individual and the environment.

The result of such perfect adjustment is shown in any animal species, and to a less degree in human beings of certain classes living under fixed conditions for many generations, such as an agricultural peasantry in China, or any long-descended hereditary aristocracy.

The contented aristocrat, though quite at peace within himself, if suddenly transferred to a new economic environment, however healthy, would show nerve strain in the effort at adjustment.

This cause is acting upon the whole American public, in varying degree, and to a less pronounced extent is seen in other "advanced" races. Our conditions change faster than we do; we do not have time to become adapted to one kind of environment before another kind sets in. We in America have been hustled from farms to towns, from towns to cities, from normal cities to the acromegalous monstrosities so many of us now live—and die—in. Our homes have changed over our heads from the four-square farm house, with sunlight and fresh wind on every side, to those dark lairs with cramped and cell-like rooms we call "flats."

Our ears, for many ages used to comparative silence, and to sounds understood and attended to, must now attune themselves to definite disuse—a steady effort not to hear the roaring meaningless discord about us. Some of us live, and some of us die, but to all of us living is more of a strain.

These causes operate equally upon men and women, producing various degrees of nervous distress and injury; these causes have been recognized to a considerable degree, especially in their effect on men; but when the case of women comes up, other and different causes are postulated.

There are special causes, operating upon women; but there are also further causes affecting both men and women, of which we will speak first.

The greatest general cause of nerve strain to-day with the more "civilized" peoples is this: We have reached, through our social progress, a stage of human development which is adapted to a far higher, smoother, more beautiful standard of living; while at the same time we are withheld by the slow movement, the reactionary attitude of our minds, from attaining that standard.

With our moral advance, with our educational advance, with our economic advance, we are quite capable of living and functioning contentedly in a world of peace, plenty, beauty and happiness. We are not only capable of it, but our natures demand it. Yet because our still dominant ideas have not kept up with the facts of life; and further because we do not freely accept and act upon even such ideas as are proper to our times; we are twentieth century people living in an artificially preserved environment many centuries out of date. Our life does not fit us—that is the large main cause of our "nervous diseases."

Children are not treated worse than they used to be; on the contrary there is much improvement in their status, but the children of today resent what would have been peacefully accepted in 1600 or 1700. Men do not sustain more oppression and exploitation than was formerly the case, but they resent it more, because they are not fitted for far higher conditions. "Britons never will be slaves" is now sung, but they were once, and did not object any more than any other people. We were quite satisfied to be colonies, once, but would not be now.

All this strain of rapidly improving life against slowly improving conditions, wears heavily upon the nerve force of the race. We need a different environment, and we shall never come into smooth, peaceful, richly productive life until we have it.

Meanwhile, women, bearing their share of this world-stress, have a heavy additional pressure upon them, both as a sex and as an industrial class. We are so used to assuming the industrial position of women to be part of their sex abilities and disabilities, that it surprises us to have them dissociated; yet there is no essential connection between the two.

Even if we should remove every legal and political discrimination against women; even if we should accept their true dignity and power as a sex; so long as their universal business is private housework they remain, industrially, at the level of private domestic hand labor, and economically a nonproductive, dependent class—servants of the other sex.

No paeans of praise are sung about the "noble" duties of butlers, footmen or man-cooks. No one calls his manservant a "partner," however ably he may serve his master's interests. But with women we have so long confounded feminine functions with domestic industry that we assume them to be identical.

They are not. The relation of wife to husband may be perfectly sustained though the contracting parties be a pair of homeless wanderers, a king and a queen, a ship captain and his wife, or a pair of competent schoolteachers or doctors. Similarly a woman may be a mother and a good mother, too, even if she really gives all her time to it. The father might hire a full list of servants and a competent housekeeper without injuring the mother as a mother. Mating and parentage are not at all in the same class with domestic industry.

In this vexing period of ours, while the great wheel of social change rolls on, the special changes in the woman's dual position roll even faster, and the wonder is not that so many women break down, but so few.

In the matter of sex, its duties, pleasures and responsibilities, a part of the present movement affects both men and women—namely, the growing feeling that our standard of indulgence is excessive. This applies to the pleasures, rather than the duties and responsibilities. It may be said to demand more denial of men than of women, but it may also be said that fewer men than women are influenced by it, thus practically equalling the pressure of required change.

In the matter of duties and responsibilities, however, the man is in a measure relieved. Less the being required of him as a "provider" in proportion as the woman becomes economically independent; less in legal exaction, as the wife emerges from the position of "femme couverte" and becomes a recognized individual. A little more is required of him as a father, by some earnest thinkers, but there is small evidence of any wide response to such requisition.

But the woman, instead of the old simple subservience, degrading perhaps, but calling for no mental exercise, is now expected to stand on her own feet, use her own judgment and conscience and decide for herself how far it is right: (a) to indulge her own desires, and (b) to gratify his.

As to motherhood, which is the larger and more important part of her sex nature, she is being hurled forward from a happy or unhappy acceptance of maternity as "the will of God," to the serious consideration of how many children she ought to have; of whether she has a right to refuse motherhood altogether; of the absolute duty of refusing it to an unfit father, as one intoxicated or diseased; of the duty of denying herself the great privilege in case she is similarly unfitted; of her right to become a mother at her own expense (and the child's) without marriage; of the social duty of restricting parentage among the unfit. This last, of course, calls for his consideration as well as hers.

But the present-day mother, quite beyond these matters, is called upon to reconsider her whole range of mother duty after the child is born. Her ancient instinctive methods and hereditary habits are under sharp criticism. She is charged with incompetence—and the charge is proven. An exacting new standard of preparedness is set before her. It is as if a vast multitude of cheerfully primitive farmers were suddenly confronted with the requirements of the highest grade of intensive agriculture.

Moreover, even beyond the insistence upon improved personal methods, comes that appalling new proposition of a collectively responsible motherhood. Never before have women as a class been called upon to assume the care of children as a class. That "a good mother," whose own children are undeniably well reared, should be blamed for her indifference to the condition of a thousand, yes, of millions of children not her own, is something new. Untrained, overworked, already smarting under the charge of personal unfitness, this vast new "cry of the children" is now ringing in the ears of women with a call that is not to be denied. It is as if a tired mother, who had at last fed her six children and put them comfortably to bed, should hear outside the ailing of six hundred tired babies who had no beds nor suppers.

Some women deny the larger responsibility; some indeed do not feel it, but thousands do feel it and it grows more insistent.

This is no question of extra personal effort, such as the adoption of a child or two; it is a question of a new grade of effort, of organized effort in motherhood, a thing absolutely new to woman.

As if this were not enough to tax the adaptability of women, they must face at the same time the educational, economic and political changes which apply to them as a class, beyond those which affect both sexes. Not only are both men and women required to learn more than formerly, but women are required to learn more in proportion. That they do so, eagerly, gladly, does not minimize the fact that it is a new demand.

Then comes the crashing swiftness of the economic change which has forced the contented—or discontented— domestic worker out into the specialized labor of the general market. In so far as women, as human beings, possess human faculties equally with men, this is not a difficulty but a joy; in so far as women as females feel the impulses and limitations of their long sex-training, it is harder for a given woman to hold the same industrial position than for a given man, even though the personal qualifications are equal.

Similarly a man, though possessing all the personal qualifications to make him an efficient and contented "chambermaid," would feel it a strain to hold such a position owing to his strictly masculine impulses and limitations. Sex-prejudice is a thing of long establishment; it is not to be dis-established in one lifetime without an appreciable tax on the individual.

Further yet comes the sudden enormous opening of political responsibility. This submerged half of the race, this sex of whom in the past we have required but one virtue and two duties; now stands like Balboa, facing a new ocean.

It is not a question of unfitness, of incapacity. She is fit. She is capable. She is even now happier, more alive, more hopeful, because of her larger life. But as an instance of sudden, sweeping, exacting change of conditions, it is the most impressive in history. Some parallel may be seen in the freeing of slaves in our country; a race but a few generations from savagery, first jerked from Africa to America, from comparative idleness to enforced labor, and then catapaulted into full enfranchisement, with a very rapid increase of insanity as one result, the nervous system failing to accommodate itself in many cases to such sudden change.

Those who look down upon the negro and condemn his shortcomings should compare his present rate of progress with our own when we were at the same starting point. Of course he has had us to help him, but also to hinder!

So women, as a class, hurtled forward on these waves of social advancement, have men, as a class, to help them, and to hinder. Being equally capable, as members of the same race, their race-inheritance being a far larger and stronger thing than their sex-inheritance, they do not have to develop new faculties, but merely to unpack them, as it were. Also they come into a degree of civilization, the mechanical advancement of which removes many of the previous difficulties of life and progress.

But as a hindrance they have to meet something which men have never met—the cold and cruel opposition of the other sex. In every step of their long upward path men have had women with them, never against them. In hardship, in privation, in danger, in the last test of religious martyrdom, in the pains and terrors of warfare, in rebellions and revolutions, men have had women with them. Individual women have no doubt been a hindrance to individual men, and the economic dependence of women is a drag upon men's freedom of action; but at no step of man's difficult advance has he had to meet the scorn, the neglect, the open vilification of massed womanhood.

No one has seemed to notice the cost of this great artificial barrier to the advance of women, the effect upon her nervous system of opposition and abuse from the quarter where nature and tradition had taught her to expect aid and comfort. She has had to keep pace with him in meeting the demands of our swiftly changing times. She has had to meet

the additional demands of her own even more swiftly changing conditions. And she has had to do this in the face not only
of the organized opposition of the other sex, entrenched in
secure possession of all the advantageous positions of church
and state, buttressed by law and custom, fully trained and experienced, and holding all the ammunition—the "sinews of
war"—the whole money power of the world; but besides this
her slow, difficult, conscientious efforts to make the changes
she knew were right, or which were forced upon her by conditions, have too often cost her man's love, respect and good will.

This is a heavy price to pay for progress.

We should be more than gentle with the many women
who cannot yet meet it.

We should be more than grateful for those strong men
who are more human than male, who can feel, think and act
above the limitations of their sex, and who have helped women
in their difficult advance.

Also we should deeply honor those great women of the
last century, who met all demands, paid every exaction, faced
all opposition and made the way easier for us now.

But we should not be surprised at the "nervous breakdown" of some women, nor attribute it to weakness.

Only the measureless strength of the mother sex could
have enabled women to survive the sufferings of yesterday and
to meet the exactions of to-day.

☐ CARROLL SMITH-ROSENBERG ■

The Hysterical Woman: Sex Roles and Role Conflict in Nineteenth-Century America

Hysteria was one of the classic diseases of the nineteenth century. It was a protean ailment characterized by such varied symptoms as paraplegia, aphonia, hemi-anaesthesia, and violent epileptoid seizures. Under the broad rubric of hysteria, nineteenth-century physicians gathered cases which might today be diagnosed as neurasthenia, hypochondriasis, depression, conversion reaction, and ambulatory schizophrenia. It fascinated and frustrated some of the century's most eminent clinicians; through its redefinition Freud rose to international fame, while the towering reputation of Charcot suffered a comparative eclipse. Psychoanalysis can historically be called the child of the hysterical woman.

Not only was hysteria a widespread and—in the intellectual history of medicine—significant disease, it remains to this day a frustrating and ever-changing illness. What was diagnosed as hysteria in the nineteenth century is not necessarily related to the hysterical character as defined in the twentieth century, or again to what the Greeks meant by hysteria when they christened the disease millennia ago. The one constant in this varied history has been the existence in

From *Social Research* 39:4 (1972), 653–678.

This project was supported in part by grant No. 7 FO2 HD48800-01A1 from the National Institutes of Health and by a grant from the Grant Foundation, New York.

virtually every era of Western culture of some clinical entity called hysteria; an entity which has always been seen as peculiarly relevant to the female experience, and one which has almost always carried with it a pejorative implication.

For the past half century and longer, American culture has defined hysteria in terms of individual psychodynamics. Physicians and psychologists have seen hysteria as "neurosis" or character disorder, the product of an unresolved Oedipal complex. Hysterical women, fearful of their own sexual impulses—so the argument went—channeled that energy into psychosomatic illness. Characteristically, they proved unable to form satisfying and stable relationships.[1] More recently psychoanalysts such as Elizabeth Zetzel have refined this Freudian hypothesis, tracing the roots of hysteria to a woman's excessively ambivalent preoedipal relation with her mother and to the resulting complications of oedipal development and resolution.[2] Psychologist David Shapiro has emphasized the hysterical woman's impressionistic thought pattern.[3] All such interpretations focus exclusively on individual psychodynamics and relations within particular families.

Yet hysteria is also a socially recognized behavior pattern and as such exists within the larger world of cultural values and role relationships. For centuries hysteria has been seen as characteristically female—the hysterical woman the embodiment of a perverse or hyper femininity.[4] Why has this been so? Why did large numbers of women "choose" the character traits of hysteria as their particular mode of expressing malaise, discontent, anger or pain?[5] To begin to answer this question, we must explore the female role and role socialization. Clearly not all women were hysterics; yet the parallel between the hysteric's behavior and stereotypic femininity is too close to be explained as mere coincidence. To examine hysteria from this social perspective means necessarily to explore the complex relationships that exist between cultural norms and individual behavior, between behavior defined as disease and behavior considered normal.

Using nineteenth-century America as a case study,[6] I propose to explore hysteria on at least two levels of social interaction. The first involves an examination of hysteria as a social role within the nineteenth-century family. This was a period when, it has been argued, social and structural change had created stress within the family and when, in addition, individual domestic role alternatives were few and rigidly defined. From this perspective hysteria can be seen as an alternate role option for particular women incapable of accepting their life situation. Hysteria thus serves as a valuable indicator both of domestic stress and of the tactics through which some individuals sought to resolve that stress. By analyzing the function of hysteria within the family and the interaction of the hysteric, her family, and the interceding—yet interacting—physician, I also hope to throw light upon the role of women and female-male relationships within the larger world of nineteenth-century American society. Secondly, I will attempt to raise some questions concerning female role socialization, female personality options, and the nature of hysterical behavior.[7]

I

It might be best to begin with a brief discussion of three relatively well known areas: first, the role of women in nineteenth-century American society; second, the symptoms which hysterical women presented and which established the definition of the disease, and lastly, the response of male physicians to their hysterical patients.

The ideal female in nineteenth-century America was expected to be gentle and refined, sensitive and loving. She was the guardian of religion and spokeswoman for morality. Hers was the task of guiding the more worldly and more frequently tempted male past the maelstroms of atheism and uncontrolled sexuality. Her sphere was the hearth and the nursery; within it she was to bestow care and love, peace and joy. The American girl was taught at home, at school, and in the literature of the period, that aggression, independence, self-assertion and curiosity were male traits, inappropriate for the weaker sex and her limited sphere. Dependent throughout her life, she was to reward her male protectors with affection and submission. At no time was she expected to achieve in any area considered important by men and thus highly valued by society. She was, in essence, to remain a child-woman, never developing the strengths and skills of adult autonomy. The stereotype of the middle class woman as emotional, pious, passive and nurturant was to become increasingly rigid throughout the nineteenth century.[8]

There were significant discontinuities and inconsistencies between such ideals of female socialization and the real world in which the American woman had to live. The first relates to a dichotomy between the ideal woman and the ideal mother. The ideal woman was emotional, dependent and gentle—a born follower. The ideal mother, then and now, was expected to be strong, self-reliant, protective, an effective caretaker in relation to children and home. She was to manage the family's day-to-day finances, prepare foods, make clothes, compound drugs, serve as family nurse—and, in rural areas, as physician as well.[9] Especially in the nineteenth century, with its still primitive obstetrical practices and its high child mortality rates, she was expected to face severe bodily pain, disease and death—and still serve as the emotional support and strength of her family.[10] As S. Weir Mitchell, the eminent Philadelphia neurologist, wrote in the 1880s, "We may be sure that our daughters will be more likely to have to face at some time the grim question of pain than the lads who grow up beside them. . . . To most women . . . there comes a time when pain is a grim presence in their lives." Yet, as Mitchell pointed out, it was boys whom society taught from early childhood on to bear pain stoically, while girls were encouraged to respond to pain and stress with tears and expectations of elaborate sympathy.[11]

Contemporaries noted routinely in the 1870s, 1880s and 1890s that middle-class American girls seemed ill-prepared to assume the responsibilities and trials of marriage, motherhood and maturation. Frequently women, especially married women with children, complained of isolation, loneliness, and depression. Physicians reported a high incidence of nervous disease and hysteria among women who felt overwhelmed by the burdens of frequent pregnancies, the demands of children, the daily exertions of housekeeping and family management.[12] The realities of adult life no longer permitted them to elaborate and exploit the role of fragile, sensitive and dependent child.

Not only was the Victorian woman increasingly ill-prepared for the trials of childbirth and childrearing, but changes were also at work within the larger society which were to make her particular socialization increasingly inappropriate. Reduced birth and mortality rates, growing population concentration in towns, cities and even in rural areas, a new, highly mobile economy, as well as new patterns of middle class aspiration—all reached into the family, altering that institution, affecting domestic relations and increasing the normal quantity of infrafamilial stress.[13] Women lived longer; they married later and less often. They spent less and less time in the primary processing of food, cloth and clothing. Increasingly, both middle and lower class women took jobs outside the home until their marriages—or permanently if unable to secure a husband.[14] By the post-Civil War years, family limitation—with its necessary implication of altered domestic roles and relationships—had become a real option within the decision-making processes of every family.[15]

Despite such basic social, economic and demographic changes, however, the family and gender role socialization remained relatively inflexible. It is quite possible that many women experienced a significant level of anxiety when forced to confront or adapt in one way or another to these changes. Thus hysteria may have served as one option or tactic offering particular women otherwise unable to respond to these changes a chance to redefine or restructure their place within the family.

So far this discussion of role socialization and stress has emphasized primarily the malaise and dissatisfaction of the middle class woman. It is only a covert romanticism, however, which permits us to assume that the lower class or farm woman, because her economic functions within her family were more vital than those of her decorative and economically secure urban sisters, escaped their sense of frustration, conflict or confusion. Normative prescriptions of proper womanly behavior were certainly internalized by many poorer women. The desire to marry and the belief that a woman's social status came not from the exercise of her own talents and efforts but from her ability to attract a competent male protector were as universal among lower class and farm women as among middle and upper class urban women. For some of these women—as for their urban middle class sisters—the traditional female role proved functional, bringing material and psychic rewards. But for some it did not. The discontinuity between the child and adult female roles, along with the failure to develop substantial ego strengths, crossed class and geographic barriers—as did hysteria itself. Physicians connected with almshouses, and later in the century with urban hospitals and dispensaries, often reported hysteria among immigrant and tenement house women.[16] Sex differentiation and class distinctions both play a role in American social history, yet hysteria seems to have followed a psychic fault line corresponding more to distinctions of gender than to those of class.

Against this background of possible role conflict and discontinuity, what were the presenting symptoms of the female hysteric in nineteenth-century America? While physicians agreed that hysteria could afflict persons of both sexes and of all ages and economic classes (the male hysteric was an accepted clinical entity by the late nineteenth century), they reported that hysteria was most frequent among women between the ages of 15 and 40 and of the urban middle and upper middle classes. Symptoms were highly varied. As early as the seventeenth century, indeed, Sydenham had remarked that "the frequency of hysteria is no less remarkable than the multiformity of the shapes it puts on. Few maladies are not imitated by it; whatever part of the body it attacks, it will create the proper symptom of that part."[17] The nineteenth-century physician could only concur. There were complaints of nervousness, depression, the tendency to tears and chronic fatigue, or of disabling pain. Not a few women thus afflicted showed a remarkable willingness to submit to long-term, painful therapy—to electric shock treatment, to blistering, to multiple operations, even to amputations.[18]

The most characteristic and dramatic symptom, however, was the hysterical "fit." Mimicking an epileptic seizure, these fits often occurred with shocking suddenness. At other times they "came on" gradually, announcing their approach with a general feeling of depression, nervousness, crying or lassitude. Such seizures, physicians generally agreed, were precipitated by a sudden or deeply felt emotion—fear, shock, a sudden death, marital disappointment— or by physical trauma. It began with pain and tension, most frequently in the "uterine area." The sufferer alternately sobbed and laughed violently, complained of palpitations of the heart, clawed her throat as if strangling and, at times, abruptly lost the power of hearing and speech. A death-like trance might follow, lasting hours, even days. At other times violent convulsions—sometimes accompanied by hallucinations—seized her body.[19] "Let the reader imagine," New York physician E. H. Dixon wrote in the 1840s,

> the patient writhing like a serpent upon the floor, rending her garments to tatters, plucking out handsful of hair, and striking her person with violence—with contorted and swollen countenance and fixed eyes resisting every effort of bystanders to control her . . .[20]

Finally the fit subsided; the patient, exhausted and sore, fell into a restful sleep.

During the first half of the nineteenth century physicians described hysteria principally though not exclusively in terms of such episodes. Symptoms such as paralysis and contracture were believed to be caused by seizures and categorized as infraseizure symptoms. Beginning in mid-century, however, physicians became increasingly flexible in their diagnosis of hysteria and gradually the fit declined in significance as a pathognomonic symptom.[21] Dr. Robert Carter, a widely-read British authority on hysteria, insisted in 1852 that at least one hysterical seizure must have occurred to justify a diagnosis of hysteria. But, he admitted, this seizure might be so minor as to have escaped the notice even of the patient herself; no subsequent seizures were necessary.[22] This was clearly a transitional position. By the last third of the nineteenth century the seizure was no longer the central phenomenon defining hysteria; physicians had categorized hysterical symptoms which included virtually every known human ill. They ranged from loss of sensation in part, half or all of the body, loss of taste, smell, hearing, or vision, numbness of the skin, inability to swallow, nausea, headaches, pain in the breast, knees, hip, spine or neck, as well as contracture or paralysis of virtually any extremity.[23]

Hysterical symptoms were not limited to the physical. An hysterical female character gradually began to emerge in the nineteenth-century medical literature, one based on interpretations of mood and personality rather than on discrete physical symptoms—one which grew closely to resemble twentieth-century definitions of the "hysterical personality." Doctors commonly described hysterical women as highly impressionistic, suggestible, and narcissistic. Highly labile, their moods changed suddenly, dramatically, and for seemingly inconsequential reasons. Doctors complained that the hysterical woman was egocentric in the extreme, her involvement with others consistently superficial and tangential. While the hysterical woman might appear to physicians and relatives as quite sexually aroused or attractive, she was, doctors cautioned, essentially asexual and not uncommonly frigid.[24]

Depression also appears as a common theme. Hysterical symptoms not infrequently followed a death in the family, a miscarriage, some financial setback which forced the patient to become self-supporting; or they were seen by the patient as related to some long-term, unsatisfying life situation—a tired school teacher, a mother unable to cope with the demands of a large family.[25] Most of these women took to their beds because of pain, paralysis or general weakness. Some remained there for years.

The medical profession's response to the hysterical woman was at best ambivalent. Many doctors—and indeed a significant proportion of society at large—tended to be caustic, if not punitive towards the hysterical woman. This resentment seems rooted in two factors: first, the baffling and elusive nature of hysteria itself, and second, the relation which existed in the physicians' minds between their categorizing of hysteria as a disease and the role women were expected to play in society. These patients did not function as women were expected to function, and, as we shall see, the physician who treated them felt threatened both as a professional and as a rejected male. He was the therapist thwarted, the child untended, the husband denied nurturance and sex.

During the second half of the nineteenth century, the

newly established germ theory and discoveries by neurologists and anatomists for the first time made an insistence on disease specificity a *sine qua non* for scientific respectability. Neurology was just becoming accepted as a speciality, and in its search for acceptance it was particularly dependent on the establishment of firm, somatically-based disease entities.[26] If hysteria *was* a disease, and not the imposition of self-pitying women striving to avoid their traditional roles and responsibilities—as was frequently charged—it must be a disease with a specific etiology and a predictable course. In the period 1870 to 1900, especially, it was felt to be a disease rooted in some specific organic malfunction.

Hysteria, of course, lacked all such disease characteristics. Contracture or paralysis could occur without muscular atrophy or change in skin temperature. The hysteric might mimic tuberculosis, heart attacks, blindness or hip disease, while lungs, heart, eyes and hips remained in perfect health.[27] The physician had only his patient's statement that she could not move or was wracked with pain. If concerned and sympathetic, he faced a puzzling dilemma. As George Preston wrote in his 1897 monograph on hysteria:

> In studying the . . . disturbances of hysteria, a very formidable difficulty presents itself in the fact that the symptoms are purely subjective. . . . There is only the bald statement of the patient. . . . No confirming symptoms present themselves . . . and the appearance of the affected parts stands as contradictory evidence against the patient's words.[28]

Equally frustrating and medically inexplicable were the sudden changes in the hysteric's symptoms. Paralysis or anaesthesia could shift from one side of the body to the other, from one limb to another. Headaches would replace contracture of a limb, loss of voice, the inability to taste. How could a physician prescribe for such ephemeral symptoms? "Few practitioners desire the management of hysterics," one eminent gynecologist, Samuel Ashwell, wrote in 1833. "Its symptoms are so varied and obscure, so contradictory and changeable, and if by chance several of them, or even a single one be relieved, numerous others almost immediately spring into existence."[29] Half a century later, neurologist Charles K. Mills echoed Ashwell's discouraging evaluation. "Hysteria is pre-eminently a chronic disease," he warned. "Deceptive remissions in hysterical symptoms often mislead the unwary practitioner. Cures are sometimes claimed where simply a change in the character of the phenomena has taken place. It is a disease in which it is unsafe to claim a conquest."[30]

Yet physicians, especially newly established neurologists with urban practices, were besieged by patients who appeared to be sincere, respectable women sorely afflicted with pain, paralysis or uncontrollable "nervous fits." "Looking at the pain evoked by ideas and beliefs," S. Weir Mitchell, America's leading expert on hysteria, wrote in 1885, "we are hardly wise to stamp these pains as non-existent."[31] Despite the tendency of many physicians to contemptuously dismiss the hysterical patient when no organic lesions could be found, neurologists such as Mitchell, George M. Beard, or Charles L. Dana sympathized with these patients and sought to alleviate their symptoms.

Such pioneer specialists were therefore in the position of having defined hysteria as a legitimate disease entity, and the hysterical woman as sick, when they were painfully aware that no organic etiology had yet been found. Cautiously, they sought to formally define hysteria in terms appropriately mechanistic. Some late nineteenth-century physicians, for example, still placing a traditional emphasis on hysteria's uterine origins, argued that hysteria resulted from "the reflex effects of utero-ovarian irritation."[32] Others, reflecting George M. Beard's work on neurasthenia, defined hysteria as a functional disease caused either by "metabolic or nutritional changes in the cellular elements of the central nervous system." Still others wrote in terms of a malfunction of the cerebral cortex.[33] All such explanations were but hypothetical gropings for an organic explanation—still a necessity if they were to legitimate hysteria as a disease.[34]

The fear that hysteria might after all be only a functional or "ideational" disease—to use a nineteenth-century term—and therefore not really a disease at all, underlies much of the writing on hysteria as well as the physicians' own attitudes toward their patients. These hysterical women might after all be only clever frauds and sensation-seekers—morally delinquent and, for the physician, professionally embarrassing.

Not surprisingly, a compensatory sense of superiority and hostility permeated many physicians' discussions of the nature and etiology of hysteria. Except when called upon to provide a hypothetical organic etiology, physicians saw hysteria as caused either by the indolent, vapid and unconstructive life of the fashionable middle and upper class woman, or by the ignorant, exhausting and sensual life of the lower or working class woman. Neither were flattering etiologies. Both denied the hysteric the sympathy granted to sufferers from unquestionably organic ailments.

Any general description of the personal characteristics of the well-to-do hysteric emphasized her idleness, self-indulgence, her deceitfulness and "craving for sympathy." Petted and spoiled by her parents, waited upon hand and foot by servants, she had never been taught to exercise self-control or to curb her emotions and desires.[35] Certainly she had not been trained to undertake the arduous and necessary duties of wife and mother. "Young persons who have been raised in luxury and too often in idleness," one late-nineteenth-century physician lectured, "who have never been called upon to face the hardships of life, who have never accustomed themselves to self-denial, who have abundant time and opportunity to cultivate the emotional and sensuous, to indulge the sentimental side of life, whose life purpose is too often an indefinite and self-indulgent idea of pleasure, these are the most frequent victims of hysteria."[36] Sound education, outside interests such as charity and good works, moral training, systematic outdoor exercise and removal from an overly sympathetic family were among the most frequent forms of treatment recommended. Mothers, consistently enough, were urged to bring up daughters with a strong sense of self-discipline, devotion to family needs, and a dread of uncontrolled emotionality.[37]

Emotional indulgence, moral weakness and lack of will power characterized the hysteric in both lay and medical thought. Hysteria, S. Weir Mitchell warned, occurred in women who had never developed habitual restraint and "rational endurance"—who had early lost their power of "self rule."[38] "The mind and body are deteriorated by the force of evil habit," Charles Lockwood wrote in 1895, "morbid thought and morbid impulse run through the poor, weak, unresisting brain, until all mental control is lost, and the poor sufferer is . . . at the mercy of . . . evil and unrestrained passions, appetites and morbid thoughts and impulses."[39]

In an age when will, control, and hard work were fundamental social values, this hypothetical etiology necessarily implied a negative evaluation of those who succumbed to hysteria. Such women were described as weak, capricious and, perhaps most important, morbidly suggestible.[40] Their intellectual abilities were meager, their powers of concentration eroded by years of self-indulgence and narcissistic introspection.[41] Hysterical women were, in effect, children, and ill-behaved, difficult children at that. "They have in fact" Robert Carter wrote, "all the instability of childhood, joined to the vices and passions of adult age."[42]

Many nineteenth-century critics felt that this emotional regression and instability was rooted in woman's very nature. The female nervous system, doctors argued, was physiologically more sensitive and thus more difficult to subject to the will. Some physicians assumed as well that woman's blood was "thinner" than man's, causing nutritional inadequacies in the central nervous system and an inability to store nervous energy—a weakness, Mary Putnam Jacobi stressed, women shared with children. Most commonly, a woman's emotional states generally, and hysteria in particular, were believed to have the closest ties to her reproductive cycle.[43] Hysteria commenced with puberty and ended with menopause, while ailments as varied as menstrual pain and irregularity, prolapsed or tipped uterus, uterine tumor, vaginal infections and discharges, sterility, could all—doctors were certain—cause hysteria. Indeed, the first question routinely asked hysterical women was "are your courses regular?"[44] Thus a woman's very physiology and anatomy predisposed her to hysteria: it was, as Thomas Laycock put it, "the natural state" in a female, a "morbid state" in the male.[45] In an era when a sexual perspective implied conflict and ambivalence, hysteria was perceived by physician and patient as a disease both peculiarly female and peculiarly sexual.

Hysteria could also result from a secret and less forgivable form of sexuality. Throughout the nineteenth century, physicians believed that masturbation was widespread among America's females and a frequent cause of hysteria and insanity. As early as 1846, E. H. Dixon reported that masturbation caused hysteria "among females even in society where physical and intellectual culture would seem to present the strongest barriers against its incursions." Other physicians concurred, reporting that harsh public and medical reactions to hysterical women were often based on the belief that masturbation was the cause of their behavior.[46]

Masturbation was only one form of sexual indulgence. A number of doctors saw hysteria among lower class women as originating in the sensuality believed to characterize their class. Such tenement-dwelling females, doctors reported, "gave free reign to . . . 'passions of the baser sort,' not feeling the necessity of self-control because they have to a pitiably small degree any sense of propriety or decency." Hysteria, another physician reported, was found commonly among prostitutes, while virtually all physicians agreed that even within marriage sexual excess could easily lead to hysteria.[47]

Expectedly, conscious anger and hostility marked the response of a good many doctors to their hysterical patients. One New York neurologist called the female hysteric a willful, self-indulgent and narcissistic person who cynically manipulated her symptoms. "To her distorted vision," he complained, "there is but one commanding personage in the universe—herself—in comparison with whom the rest of mankind are nothing." Doctors admitted that they were frequently tempted to use such terms as "willful" and "evil," "angry" and "impatient" when describing the hysteric and her symptoms.[48] Even the concerned and genteel S. Weir Mitchell, confident of his remarkable record in curing hysteria, described hysterical women as "the pests of many households, who constitute the despair of physicians, and who furnish those annoying examples of despotic selfishness, which wreck the constitutions of nurses and devoted relatives, and in unconscious or half-conscious self-indulgence destroy the comfort of everyone about them." He concluded by quoting Oliver Wendell Holmes' acid judgment that "a hysterical girl is a vampire who sucks the blood of the healthy people about her."[49]

Hysteria as a chronic, dramatic and socially accepted sick role could thus provide some alleviation of conflict and tension, but the hysteric purchased her escape from the emotional—and frequently—from the sexual demands of her life only at the cost of pain, disability, and an intensification of woman's traditional passivity and dependence. Indeed a complex interplay existed between the character traits assigned women in Victorian society and the characteristic symptoms of the nineteenth-century hysteric: dependency, fragility, emotionality, narcissism. (Hysteria has, after all, been called in that century and this a stark caricature of femininity.) Not surprisingly the hysteric's peculiar passive aggression and her exploitive dependency often functioned to cue a corresponding hostility in the men who cared for her or lived with her. Whether father, husband, or physician, they reacted with ambivalence and in many cases with hostility to her aggressive and never-ending demands.

II

What inferences concerning woman's role and female-male relationships can be drawn from this description of nineteenth-century hysteria and of medical attitudes toward the female patient? What insights does it allow into patterns of stress and resolution within the traditional nuclear family?

Because traditional medical wisdom had defined hysteria as a disease, its victims could expect to be treated as sick and thus to elicit a particular set of responses—the right to be seen and treated by a physician, to stay in bed and thus be relieved of their normal day-to-day responsibilities, to enjoy the special prerogatives, indulgences, and sympathy the sick role entailed. Hysteria thus became one way in which conventional women could express—in most cases unconsciously—dissatisfaction with one or several aspects of their lives.

The effect of hysteria upon the family and traditional sex role differentiation was disruptive in the extreme. The hysterical woman virtually ceased to function within the family. No longer did she devote herself to the needs of others, acting as self-sacrificing wife, mother, or daughter. Through her hysteria she could and in fact did force others to assume those functions. Household activities were reoriented to answer the hysterical woman's importunate needs. Children were hushed, rooms darkened, entertaining suspended, a devoted nurse recruited. Fortunes might be spent on medical bills or for drugs and operations. Worry and concern bowed the husband's shoulders; his home had suddenly become a hospital and he a nurse. Through her illness, the bedridden woman came to dominate her family to an extent that would have been considered inappropriate—indeed shrewish—in a healthy woman. Taking to one's bed, especially when suffering from dramatic and ever-visible symptoms, might also have functioned as a mode of passive aggression, especially in a milieu in which weakness was rewarded and in which women had since childhood been taught not to express overt aggression. Consciously or unconsciously, she had thus opted out of her traditional role.

Women did not accomplish this redefinition of domestic roles without the aid of the men in their family. Doctors commented that the hysteric's husband and family often, and unfortunately, rewarded her symptoms with elaborate sympathy. "The hysteric's credit is usually first established," as one astute mid-century clinician pointed out, "by those who have, at least, the wish to believe them."[50] Husbands and fathers were not alone in their cooperation; the physician often played a complex and in a sense emotionally compromising role in legitimizing the female hysteric's behavior. As an impartial and professionally skilled observer, he was empowered to judge whether or not a particular woman had the right to withdraw from her socially allotted duties. At the same time, these physicians accepted as correct, indeed as biologically inevitable, the structure of the Victorian family and the division of sex roles within it. He excused the woman only in the belief that she was ill and that she would make every effort to get well and resume her accustomed role. It was the transitory and unavoidable nature of the sick role that made it acceptable to family and physician as an alternate mode of female behavior.[51]

The doctor's ambivalence toward the hysterical woman, already rooted as we have seen in professional and sexual uncertainties, may well have been reinforced by his complicitory role within the family. It was for this reason that the disease's erratic pattern, its chronic nature, its lack of a determinable organic etiology, and the patient's seeming failure of will, so angered him. Even if she were not a conscious malingerer, she might well be guilty of self-indulgence and moral delinquency. By diagnosing her as ill, he had in effect created or permitted the hysterical woman to create a bond between himself and her. Within the family configuration he had sided with her against her husband or other male family members—men with whom he would normally have identified.[52]

The quintessential sexual nature of hysteria further complicated the doctor's professional stance. As we have already seen, the hysterical patient in her role as woman may well have mobilized whatever ambivalence towards sex a particular physician felt. In a number of cases, moreover, the physician also played the role of oedipal father figure to the patient's child-woman role, and in such instances his complicity was not only moral and intellectual but sexual as well. These doctors had become part of a domestic triangle—a husband's rival, the fatherly attendant of a daughter. This intra-family role may therefore go far to explain the particularly strident and suspicious tone which characterized much of the clinical discussion of hysteria. The physician had, by his alertness to deception and self-indulgence and by his therapeutic skills, to prevent the hysterical woman from using her disease to avoid her feminine duties—and from making him an unwitting accomplice in her deviant role. While tied to her as physician and thus legitimizer of her sick role, he had also to preserve his independence.

Although much of this interpretation must remain speculative, both the tone and substance of contemporary medical reaction to the female hysteric tends to confirm these inferences. Physicians were concerned with—and condemned—the power which chronic illness such as hysteria gave a woman over her family. Many women, doctors noted with annoyance, enjoyed this power and showed no inclination to get well: it is hardly coincidental that most late-nineteenth-century authorities agreed that removal from her family was a necessary first step in attempting to cure the hysterical patient.[53]

Not only did the physician condemn the hysteric's power within her family, he was clearly sensitive to her as a threat to his own prestige and authority. It is evident from their writings that many doctors felt themselves to be locked in a power struggle with their hysterical patients. Such women, doctors claimed, used their symptoms as weapons in asserting autonomy in relation to their physician; in continued illness was their victory. Physicians perceived hysterical women as unusually intractable and self-assertive. Although patients and women, they reserved the right to judge and approve their male physician's every action. Indeed, much of the medical literature on hysteria is devoted to providing doctors with the means of winning this war of wills. Physicians felt that they must dominate the hysteric's will; only in this way, they wrote, could they bring about her permanent cure. "Do not flatter yourselves . . . that you will gain an easy victory," Dr. L. C. Grey told a medical school class in 1888:

> On the contrary, you must expect to have your temper, your ingenuity, your nerves tested to a degree that cannot be surpassed even by the greatest surgical operations. I maintain that the man who has the nerve and the tact to conquer some of these grave cases of hysteria has the nerve and the tact that will make him equal to the great emergencies of life. Your patient must be taught day by day . . . by steady resolute, iron-willed determination and tact—that combination which the French . . . call "the iron hand beneath the velvet glove."[54]

"Assume a tone of authority which will of itself almost compel submission," Robert Carter directed. "If a patient . . . interrupts the speaker, she must be told to keep silence and to listen; and must be told, moreover, not only in a voice that betrays no impatience and no anger, but in such a manner as to convey the speaker's full conviction that the command will be immediately obeyed."[55]

Much of the treatment prescribed by physicians for hysteria reflects, in its draconic severity, their need to exert control—and, when thwarted, their impulse to punish. Doctors frequently recommended suffocating hysterical women until their fits stopped, beating them across the face and body with wet towels, ridiculing and exposing them in front of family and friends, showering them with icy water. "The mode

adopted to arrest this curious malady," a physician connected
with a large mental hospital wrote,

> consists in making some strong and sudden impression on
> the mind through . . . the most potent of all impressions,
> fear. . . . Ridicule to a woman of sensitive mind, is a powerful
> weapon . . . but there is no emotion equal to fear and the
> threat of personal chastisement. . . . They will listen to the
> voice of authority.[56]

When, on the other hand, the hysterical patient proved
tractable, gave up her fits or paralyses and accepted the physician as saviour and moral guide, he no longer had to appear
in the posture of chastising father. He could respond to his
hysterical patient with fondness, sympathy, and praise. No
longer was she thwarting him with "temper, tears, tricks, and
tantrums"—as one doctor chose to title a study of hysteria.[57]
Her cure demonstrated that he had mastered her will and
body. The successful father-like practitioner had restored another wayward woman to her familial duties. Thomas Addis
Emmett, pioneer gynecological specialist, recalled with in-
genuous candor his mode of treating hysterics:

> the patient . . . was a child in my hands. In some respects the
> power gained was not unlike that obtained over a wild beast
> except that in one case the domination would be due to fear,
> while with my patient as a rule, it would be the desire to
> please me and to merit my approval from the effort she would
> make to gain her self-control. I have at times been depressed
> with the responsibility attending the blind influence I have
> often been able to gain over the nervous women under my
> influence.[58]

Not surprisingly, S. Weir Mitchell ended one of his treatises
on hysteria with the comment that doctors, who knew and
understood all women's petty weaknesses, who could govern
and forgive them, made the best husbands.[59] Clearly the male
physician who treated the hysterical woman was unable to

escape the sex role relations that existed within nineteenth-century society generally.

III

The hysterical female thus emerges from the essentially male medical literature of the nineteenth century as a "child-woman," highly impressionable, labile, superficially sexual, exhibitionistic, given to dramatic body language and grand gestures, with strong dependency needs and decided ego weaknesses. She resembled in many ways the personality type referred to by Guze in 1967 as a "hysterical personality," or by Kernberg in 1968 as an "infantile personality."[60] But in a very literal sense these characteristics of the hysteric were merely hypertrophied versions of traits and behavior commonly reinforced in female children and adolescents. At a time when American society accepted egalitarian democracy and free will as transcendent social values, women, as we have seen, were nevertheless routinely socialized to fill a weak, dependent and severely limited social role. They were sharply discouraged from expressing competition or mastery in such "masculine" areas as physical skill, strength and courage, or in academic or commercial pursuits, while at the same time they were encouraged to be coquettish, entertaining, non-threatening and nurturant. Overt anger and violence were forbidden as unfeminine and vulgar. The effect of this socialization was to teach women to have a low evaluation of themselves, to significantly restrict their ego functions to low prestige areas, to depend on others and to altruistically wish not for their own worldly success, but for that of their male supporters.

In essence, then, many nineteenth-century women reached maturity with major ego weaknesses and with narrowly limited compensatory ego strengths, all of which implies, I think, a generic relationship between this pattern of socialization and the adoption of hysterical behavior by particular individuals. It seems plausible to suggest that a certain percentage of nineteenth-century women faced with stress developing out of their own peculiar personality needs or because of situational anxieties might well have defended themselves against such stress by regressing towards the childish hyper-femininity of the hysteric. The discontinuity between the roles of courted woman and pain-bearing, self-sacrificing wife and mother, the realities of an unhappy marriage, the loneliness and chagrin of spinsterhood may all have made the petulant infantilism and narcissistic self-assertion of the hysteric a necessary alternative to women who felt unfairly deprived of their promised social role and who had few strengths with which to adapt to a more trying one. Society had indeed structured this regression by consistently reinforcing those very emotional traits characterized in the stereotype of the female—and caricatured in the symptomatology of the hysteric. At the same time, the nineteenth-century female hysteric also exhibited a significant level of hostility and aggression—rage—which may have led in turn to her depression and to her self-punishing psychosomatic illnesses. In all these ways, then, the hysterical woman can be seen as both product and indictment of her culture.

I must conclude with a caution. The reasons why individuals displayed that pattern of behavior called by nineteenth-century physicians "hysteria" must in individual cases remain moot. What this paper has sought to do is to suggest why certain symptoms were available and why women, in particular, tended to resort to them. It has sought as well to use the reactions of contemporaries to illuminate female-male and intrafamilial role realities. As such it has dealt with hysteria as a social role produced by and functional within a specific set of social circumstances.

☐ Notes ■

1. For a review of the recent psychiatric literature on hysteria see Aaron Lazare, "The Hysterical Character in Psychoanalytic Theory: Evolution and Confusion," *Archives of General Psychiatry* XXV (August, 1971), pp. 131–137; Barbara Ruth Easser and S. R. Lesser, "Hysterical Personality: A Reevaluation," *Psychoanalytic Quarterly* XXXIV (1965), pp. 390–405, and Marc H. Hollander, "Hysterical Personality," *Comments on Contemporary Psychiatry* I (1971), pp. 17–24.

2. Elizabeth Zetzel, *The Capacity for Emotional Growth. Theoretical and Clinical Contributions to Psychoanalysis, 1943–1969* (London: Hogarth Press, 1970), Chap. 1–f, "The So-Called Good Hysteric."

3. David Shapiro, *Neurotic Styles* (New York: Basic Books, 1965).

4. The argument can be made that hysteria exists among men and therefore is not exclusively related to the female experience; the question is a complex one, and I am presently at work on a parallel study of male hysteria. There are, however, four brief points concerning male hysteria that I would like to make. First, to this day hysteria is still believed to be principally a female "disease" or behavior pattern. Second, the male hysteric is usually seen by physicians as somehow different. Today it is a truism that hysteria in males is found most frequently among homosexuals; in the nineteenth century men diagnosed as hysterics came almost exclusively from a lower socio-economic status than their physicians—immigrants, especially "new immigrants," miners, railroad workers, blacks. Third, since it was defined by society as a female disease, one may hypothesize that there was some degree of female identification among the men who assumed a hysterical role. Lastly, we must recall that a most common form of male hysteria was battle fatigue and shell shock. I should like to thank Erving Goffman for the suggestion that the soldier is in an analogous position to women regarding autonomy and power.

5. The word choose, even in quotes, is value-laden. I do not mean to imply that hysterical women consciously chose their behavior. I feel that three complex factors interacted to make hysteria a real behavioral option for American women: first, the various experiences that caused a woman to arrive at adulthood with significant ego weaknesses; second, certain socialization patterns and cultural values which made hysteria a readily available alternate behavior pattern for women, and third, the secondary gains conferred by the hysterical role in terms of enhanced power within the family. Individual cases presumably each represented their own peculiar balance of these factors, all of which will be discussed in this paper.

6. Nineteenth-century hysteria has attracted a good number of students: two of the most important are Henri F. Ellenberger, *The Discovery of the Unconscious* (New York: Basic Books, 1970), and Ilza Veith, *Hysteria: The History of a Disease* (Chicago: University

of Chicago Press, 1965). Ellenberger and Veith approach hysteria largely from the framework of intellectual history. For a review of Veith see Charles E. Rosenberg, "Historical Sociology of Medical Thought," *Science* CL (October 15, 1965), p. 330. For two studies which view nineteenth-century hysteria from a more sociological perspective see Esther Fischer-Homberger, "Hysterie und Misogynie: Ein Aspekt der Hysteriegeschichte," *Gesnerus* XXVI (1969) pp. 117–127, and Marc H. Hollander, "Conversion Hysteria: A Post-Freudian Reinterpretation of Nineteenth-Century Psychosocial Data," *Archives of General Psychiatry* XXVI (1972), pp. 311–314.

7. I would like to thank Renée Fox, Cornelia Friedman, Erving Goffman, Charles E. Rosenberg and Paul Rosenkrantz for having read and criticized this paper. I would also like to thank my clinical colleagues Philip Mechanick, Henry Bachrach, Ellen Berman, and Carol Wolman of the Psychiatry Department of the University of Pennsylvania for similar assistance. Versions of this paper were presented to the Institute of the Pennsylvania Hospital, the Berkshire Historical Society, and initially, in October 1971, at the Psychiatry Department of Hannehmann Medical College, Philadelphia.

8. This summary of woman's role and role socialization is drawn from a larger study of male and female gender roles and gender role socialization in the United States from 1785 to 1895 on which I am presently engaged. This research has been supported by both the Grant Foundation, New York City and the National Institute of Child Health and Human Development, N.I.H. It is difficult to refer succinctly to the wide range of sources on which this paragraph is based. Such a role model appears in virtually every nineteenth-century woman's magazine, in countless guides to young women and young wives and in etiquette books. For a basic secondary source see Barbara Welter, "The Cult of True Womanhood," *American Quarterly* XVIII (1966), pp. 151–174. For an excellent over-all history of women in America see Eleanor Flexner, *Century of Struggle,* (Cambridge, Massachusetts: Harvard University Press, 1959).

9. For the daily activities of a nineteenth-century American housewife see, for example, *The Maternal Physician: By an American Matron* (New York: Isaac Riley, 1811. Reprinted New York: Arno Press, 1972); Hugh Smith, *Letters to Married Ladies* (New York: Bliss, White and G. & C. Carville, 1827); John S. C. Abbott, *The Mother at Home* (Boston: Crocker and Brewster, 1833); Lydia H. Sigourney, *Letters to Mothers* (New York: Harper & Brothers, 1841);

Mrs. C. A. Hopkinson, *Hints for the Nursery or the Young Mother's Guide* (Boston: Little, Brown & Company, 1836); Catherine Beecher and Harriet Beecher Stowe, *The American Woman's Home* (New York: J. B. Ford & Company, 1869). For an excellent secondary account of the southern woman's domestic life see Anne Firor Scott, *The Southern Lady* (Chicago: University of Chicago Press, 1970).

10. Nineteenth-century domestic medicine books, gynecological textbooks, and monographs on the diseases of women provide a detailed picture of women's diseases and health expectations.

11. S. Weir Mitchell, *Doctor and Patient* (Philadelphia: J. B. Lippincott Company, 1887), pp. 84, 92.

12. See among others Edward H. Dixon, *Woman and Her Diseases* (New York: Charles H. Ring, 1846), pp. 135–136; Alice Stockham, *Tokology: A Book for Every Woman* (Chicago: Sanitary Publishers, 1887), p. 83; Sarah A. Stevenson, *Physiology of Women*, 2nd edn. (Chicago: Cushing, Thomas & Co., 1881), p. 91; Henry Pye Chavasse, *Advice to a Wife and Counsel to a Mother* (Philadelphia: J. B. Lippincott, 1891), p. 97. A Missouri physician reported the case of a twenty-eight year old middle class woman with two children. Shortly after the birth of her second child, she missed her period, believed herself to be pregnant for a third time and succumbed to hysterical symptoms: depression, headaches, vomiting and seizures. Her doctor concluded that she had uterine disease, exacerbated by pregnancy. He aborted her and reported a full recovery the following day. George J. Engelmann, "A Hystero-Psychosis Epilepsy Dependent upon Erosions of the Cervix Uteri," *St. Louis Clinic Record* (1878), pp. 321–324. For similar cases, see A. B. Arnold, "Hystero-Hypochondriasis," *Pacific Medical Journal* XXXIII (1890), pp. 321–324, and George J. Engelmann, "Hystero-neurosis," *Transactions of the American Gynecological Association* II (1877), pp. 513–518.

13. For a study of declining nineteenth-century American birth rates see Yasukichi Yasuba, *Birth Rates of the White Population in the United States, 1800–1860* (Baltimore: Johns Hopkins University Press, 1962) and J. Potter, "American Population in the Early National Period," in *Proceedings of Section V of the Fourth Congress of the International Economic History Association*, Paul Deprez, ed. (Winnipeg, 1970), pp. 55–69.

14. For a useful general discussion of women's changing roles see Eleanor Flexner, *Century of Struggle*.

15. For a discussion of birth control and its effect on domestic

relations see Carroll Smith-Rosenberg and Charles E. Rosenberg, "The New Woman and the Troubled Man: Medical and Biological Views of Women in Nineteenth-century America," *Journal of American History* (in press).

16. William A. Hammond, *On Certain Conditions of Nervous Derangement* (New York: G. P. Putnam's Sons, 1881), p. 42; S. Weir Mitchell, *Lectures on the Diseases of the Nervous System, Especially in Women,* 2nd ed. (Philadelphia: Lea Brothers & Co., 1885), pp. 114, 110; Charles K. Mills, "Hysteria," in *A System of Practical Medicine by American Authors,* William Pepper, ed., assisted by Louis Starr, vol. V. "Diseases of the Nervous System" (Philadelphia: Lea Brothers & Co., 1883), p. 213; Charles E. Lockwood, "A Study of Hysteria and Hypochondriasis," *Transactions of the New York State Medical Association* XII (1895), pp. 340–351. E. H. Van Deusen, Superintendent of the Michigan Asylum for the Insane reported that nervousness, hysteria and neurasthenia were common among farm women and resulted, he felt, from the social and intellectual deprivation of their isolated lives. Van Deusen, "Observations on a Form of Nervous Prostration," *American Journal of Insanity* XXV (1869), p. 447. Significantly most English and American authorities on hysteria were members of a medical elite who saw the wealthy in their private practices and the very poor in their hospital and dispensary work. Thus the observation that hysteria occurred in different social classes was often made by the very same clinicians.

17. Thomas Sydenham, "Epistolary Dissertation," in *The Works of Thomas Sydenham, M.D. . . . with a Life of the Author,* R. G. Latham, ed., 2 vols. (London: New Sydenham Society, 1850), II, p. 85.

18. Some women diagnosed as hysterics displayed quite bizarre behavior—including self-mutilation and hallucinations. Clearly a certain percentage of these women would be diagnosed today as schizophrenic. The majority of the women diagnosed as hysterical, however, did not display such symptoms, but rather appear from clinical descriptions to have had a personality similar to that considered hysterical by mid-twentieth-century psychiatrists.

19. For three typical descriptions of such seizures, see Buel Eastman, *Practical Treatise on Diseases Peculiar to Women and Girls* (Cincinnati: C. Cropper & Son, 1848), p. 40; Samuel Ashwell, *A Practical Treatise on the Diseases Peculiar to Women* (London: Samuel Highley, 1844), pp. 210–212; William Campbell, *Introduc-*

tion to the Study and Practice of Midwifery and the Diseases of Children (London: Longman, Rees, Orme, Brown, Green & Longman, 1833), pp. 440–442.

20. E. H. Dixon, op. cit., p. 133.

21. For examples of mid-nineteenth-century hysterical symptoms see Colombat de L'Isère, *A Treatise on the Diseases and Special Hygiene of Females,* trans. with additions by Charles D. Meigs (Philadelphia: Lea and Blanchard, 1845), pp. 522, 527–530; Gunning S. Bedford, *Clinical Lectures on the Diseases of Women and Children* (New York: Samuel S. & W. Wood, 1855), p. 373.

22. Robert B. Carter, *On the Pathology and Treatment of Hysteria* (London: John Churchill, 1853), p. 3.

23. See, for example, F. C. Skey, *Hysteria* (New York: A. Simpson, 1867), pp. 66, 71, 86; Mary Putnam Jacobi, "Hysterical Fever," *Journal of Nervous and Mental Disease* XV (1890), pp. 373–388; Landon Carter Grey, "Neurasthenia: Its Differentiation and Treatment," *New York Medical Journal* XLVIII (1888), p. 421.

24. See, for example, George Preston, *Hysteria and Certain Allied Conditions,* (Philadelphia: P. Blakiston, Son & Co., 1897), pp. 31, 53; Charles E. Lockwood, p. 346; Buel Eastman, p. 39; Thomas More Madden, *Clinical Gynecology* (Philadelphia: J. B. Lippincott, 1895), p. 472.

25. See W. Symington Brown, *A Clinical Handbook on the Diseases of Women* (New York: William Wood & Company, 1882); Charles L. Dana, "A Study of the Anaesthesias of Hysteria," *American Journal of the Medical Sciences* (October, 1890), p. 1; William S. Playfair, *The Systematic Treatment of Nerve Prostration and Hysteria* (Philadelphia: Henry C. Lea's Son & Co., 1883), p. 29.

26. For a discussion of the importance of creating such organic etiologies in the legitimization of an increasingly large number of such "functional" ills, see Charles E. Rosenberg, "The Place of George M. Beard in Nineteenth-Century Psychiatry," *Bulletin of the History of Medicine* XXXVI (1962), pp. 245–259. See also Owsei Temkin's discussion in his classic history of epilepsy, *The Falling Sickness,* 2nd ed., rev. (Baltimore: Johns Hopkins University Press, 1971).

27. William Campbell, pp. 440–441; Walter Channing, *Bed Case: Its History and Treatment* (Boston: Ticknor and Fields, 1860), pp. 41–42, 49. Charles L. Mix, "Hysteria: Its Nature and Etiology," *New York Medical Journal* LXXII (August, 1900), pp. 183–189.

28. George Preston, pp. 96–97.

29. Samuel Ashwell, p. 226.

30. Charles K. Mills, p. 258.

31. S. Weir Mitchell, *Lectures on the Diseases of the Nervous System,* p. 66.

32. Thomas More Madden, p. 474. The uterine origin of hysteria was by far the most commonly held opinion throughout the eighteenth and nineteenth centuries. Some believed it to be the exclusive cause, others to be among the most important causes. For three typical examples see: Alexander Hamilton, *A Treatise on the Management of Female Complaints and of Children in Early Infancy* (Edinburgh: Peter Hill, 1792), pp. 51–53; George J. Engelmann, "Hystero-Neurosis," note 12; Augustus P. Clarke, "Relations of Hysteria to Structural Changes in the Uterus and its Adnexa," *American Journal of Obstetrics* XXXIII (1894), pp. 477–483. The uterine theory came under increasing attack during the late nineteenth century. See Hugh J. Patrick, "Hysteria; Neurasthenia," *International Clinics* III (1898), pp. 183–184; F. C. Skey, p. 68.

33. Robert Barnes, *Medical and Surgical Diseases of Women* (Philadelphia: H. C. Lea, 1874), p. 101; S. D. Hopkins, "A Case of Hysteria Simulating Organic Disease of the Brain," *Medical Fortnightly* XI (July 1897), p. 327; C. K. Mills, p. 218; J. Leonard Corning, *A Treatise on Hysteria and Epilepsy* (Detroit: George S. Davis, 1888), p. 2; August A. Eshner, "Hysteria in Early Life," read before the Philadelphia County Medical Society, June 23, 1897.

34. For examples of such concern and complexity, see A. A. King, "Hysteria," *The American Journal of Obstetrics* XXIV (May, 1891), pp. 513–515; Marshall Hall, *Commentaries Principally on the Diseases of Females* (London: Sherwood, Gilbert and Piper, 1830), p. 118; C. L'Isère, p. 530.

35. Robert B. Carter, p. 140; J. L. Corning, p. 70; Mills, p. 218.

36. Preston, p. 36.

37. See, for example: Mitchell, *Lectures on the Diseases of the Nervous System,* p. 170; Rebecca B. Gleason, M.D., of Elmira, New York, quoted by M. L. Holbrook, *Hygiene of the Brain and Nerves and the Cure of Nervousness* (New York: M. L. Holbrook & Company, 1878), pp. 270–271.

38. S. Weir Mitchell, *Fat and Blood* (Philadelphia: J. B. Lippincott, 1881), pp. 30–31.

39. Lockwood, pp. 342–343; virtually every authority on hysteria echoed these sentiments.

40. Alexander Hamilton, p. 52; Dixon, pp. 142–143; Ashwell, p. 217; Mills, p. 230.

41. Walter Channing, p. 28.

42. Robert B. Carter, p. 113.

43. Mary P. Jacobi, pp. 384–388; M. E. Dirix, *Woman's Complete Guide to Health* (New York: W. A. Townsend & Adams, 1869), p. 24; E. B. Foote, *Medical Common Sense* (New York: Published by the author, 1864), p. 167.

44. Reuben Ludlum, *Lectures, Clinical and Didactic, on the Diseases of Women* (Chicago: C. S. Halsey, 1872), p. 87; Robert Barnes, p. 247. In 1847, the well-known Philadelphia gynecologist, Charles D. Meigs, had asked his medical school class the rhetorical question: "What is her erotic state? What the protean manifestations of the life force developed by a reproductive irritation which you call hysteria." Meigs, *Lectures on the Distinctive Characteristics of the Female,* delivered before the Class of Jefferson Medical College, January 5, 1847 (Philadelphia: T. K. & P. G. Collins, 1847), p. 20.

45. Thomas Laycock, *Essay on Hysteria,* pp. 76, 103, 105. See also Graham J. Barker-Benfield, "The Horrors of the Half-Known Life" (unpublished Ph.D. thesis, University of California at Los Angeles, 1969) and Ann Douglas Wood, "The Fashionable Diseases: Women's Complaints and Their Treatment in Nineteenth-Century America," *Journal of Interdisciplinary History* (in press) for a speculative psychoanalytic approach to gynecological practice in nineteenth-century America.

46. Dixon, p. 134; J. Leonard Corning, p. 70; William Murray, *A Treatise on Emotional Disorders of the Sympathetic System of the Nerves,* (London: John Churchill, 1866). An extensive nineteenth-century masturbation literature exists. See, for example, Samuel Gregory, *Facts and Important Information for Young Women on the Self-Indulgence of the Sexual Appetite* (Boston: George Gregory, 1857), and Calvin Cutter, *The Female Guide: Containing Facts and Information upon the Effects of Masturbation* (West Brookfield, Mass.: Charles A. Mirick, 1844). Most general treatises on masturbation refer to its occurrence in females.

47. Preston, p. 37; Carter, pp. 46, 90. Nineteenth-century physicians maintained a delicate balance in their view of the sexual etiology of hysteria. Any deviation from moderation could cause hys-

teria or insanity: could cause habitual masturbation, extended virginity, overindulgence, prostitution, or sterility.

48. Skey, p. 63.

49. Mitchell, *Lectures on the Diseases of the Nervous System,* p. 266; S. Weir Mitchell, *Fat and Blood,* p. 37.

50. Carter, p. 58.

51. For an exposition of this argument see Erving Goffman, "Insanity of Place," *Psychiatry* XXXII (1969), pp. 357–388.

52. Such complaints are commonplace in the medical literature. See Mitchell, *Lectures* p. 67; Mitchell, *Doctor and Patient,* p. 117; Robert Thornton, *The Hysterical Women: Trials, Tears, Tricks and Tantrums,* (Chicago: Donohue & Henneberry, 1893), pp. 97–98; Channing, pp. 35–37; L'Isère, p. 534.

53. The fact that the physician was at the same time employed and paid by the woman or her family— in a period when the profession was far more competitive and economically insecure than it is in mid-twentieth century—implied another level of stress and ambiguity.

54. Channing, p. 22; Thomas A. Emmett, *Principles and Practices of Gynecology* (Philadelphia: H. C. Lea, 1879), p. 107; L. C. Grey, "Clinical Lecture," p. 132.

55. Carter, p. 119; Ashwell, p. 227.

56. Skey, p. 60.

57. Robert Thornton, *The Hysterical Women.*

58. Thomas A. Emmett, *Incidents of My Life* (New York: G. P. Putnam's Sons, 1911), p. 210. These are Emmett's recollections at the end of a long life. It is interesting that decades earlier Emmett, in discussing treating hysterical women, had confessed in hostile frustration that "in fact the physician is helpless. . . ." Emmett, *Principles and Practices,* p. 107.

59. Mitchell, *Doctor and Patient,* pp. 99–100.

60. Samuel Guze, "The Diagnosis of Hysteria: What are We Trying to Do," *American Journal of Psychiatry* CXXIV (1967), pp. 494–498; Otto Kernberg, "Borderline Personality Organization," *Journal of the American Psychoanalytical Assocation* XV (1967), pp. 641–685. For a critical discussion of the entire problem of diagnosis, see Henry Bachrach. "In Defense of Diagnosis," *Psychiatry* (in press).

Selections from *Fat and Blood, Wear and Tear,* and *Doctor and Patient*

The following excerpts are from the writings of
Dr. S. Weir Mitchell, the Philadelphia physician who
in 1887 treated Charlotte Perkins Stetson for "nervous
prostration" following the birth of her daughter.
Considered the most prominent American neurologist
of his day, Mitchell's "rest cure" was internationally
accepted and acclaimed. Whatever his medical success,
however, his condescending attitude and patronizing
manner toward women leave little doubt that for
someone of Gilman's constitution his methods of medical
treatment were destructive.

From Fat and Blood: An Essay on
the Treatment of Certain Forms
of Neurathenia and Hysteria

As a rule, no harm is done by rest, even in such people as give
us doubts about whether it is or is not well for them to exert
themselves. There are plenty of these women who are just
well enough to make it likely that if they had motive enough
for exertion to cause them to forget themselves they would
find it useful. In the doubt I am rather given to insisting on
rest, but the rest I like for them is not at all their notion of rest.
To lie abed half the day, and sew a little and read a little, and
be interesting as invalids and excite sympathy, is all very well,
but when they are bidden to stay in bed a month, and neither

Philadelphia: J. B. Lippincott, 1877.

to read, write, nor sew, and to have one nurse,—who is not a relative,— then repose becomes for some women a rather bitter medicine, and they are glad enough to accept the order to rise and go about when the doctor issues a mandate which has become pleasantly welcome and eagerly looked for. I do not think it easy to make a mistake in this matter unless the woman takes with morbid delight to the system of enforced rest, and unless the doctor is a person of feeble will. I have never met myself with any serious trouble about getting out of bed any woman for whom I thought rest needful, but it has happened to others, and the man who resolves to send any nervous woman to bed must be quite sure that she will obey him when the time comes for her to get up.

I have, of course, made use of every grade of rest for my patients, from insisting upon repose on a lounge for some hours a day up to entire rest in bed. In carrying out my general plan of treatment in extreme cases it is my habit to ask the patient to remain in bed from six weeks to two months. At first, and in some cases for four or five weeks, I do not permit the patient to sit up, or to sew or write or read, or to use the hands in any active way except to clean the teeth. Where at first the most absolute rest is desirable, I arrange to have the bowels and water passed while lying down, and the patient is lifted on to a lounge for an hour in the morning and again at bedtime, and then lifted back again into the newly-made bed. In most cases of weakness, treated by rest, I insist on the patient being fed by the nurse, and, when well enough to sit up in bed, I insist that the meats shall be cut up, so as to make it easier for the patient to feed herself.

In many cases I allow the patient to sit up in order to obey the calls of nature, but I am always careful to have the bowels kept reasonably free from costiveness, knowing well how such a state and the efforts it gives rise to enfeeble a sick person.

The daily sponging bath is to be given by the nurse, and should be rapidly and skilfully done. It may follow the first food of the day, the early milk, or cocoa, or coffee, or, if preferred, may be used before noon, or at bedtime, which is found in some cases to be best and to promote sleep.

For some reason, the act of bathing, or even the being bathed, is mysteriously fatiguing to certain invalids, and if so I have the general sponging done for a time but thrice a week.

Most of these patients suffer from use of the eyes, and this makes it needful to prohibit reading and writing, and to have all correspondence carried on through the nurse. But many neurasthenic people also suffer from being read to, or, in other words, from any prolonged effort at attention. In these cases it will be found that if the nurse will read the morning paper, and as she does so relate such news as may be of interest, the patient will bear it very well, and will by degrees come to endure the hearing of such reading as is already more or less familiar.

Usually, after a fortnight I permit the patient to be read to,—one to three hours a day,—but I am daily amazed to see how kindly nervous and anæmic women take to this absolute rest, and how little they complain of its monotony. In fact, the use of massage and the battery, with the frequent comings of the nurse with food, and the doctor's visits, seem so to fill up the day as to make the treatment less tiresome than might be supposed. And, besides this, the sense of comfort which is apt to come about the fifth or sixth day,—the feeling of ease, and the ready capacity to digest food, and the growing hope of final cure, fed as it is by present relief,—all conspire to make most patients contented and tractable.

The intelligent and watchful physician must, of course, know how far to enforce and when to relax these rules. When it is needful, as it sometimes is, to prolong the state of rest to two or three months, the patient may need at the close occupation of some kind, and especially such as, while it does not tax the eyes, gives the hands something to do, the patient being, we suppose, by this time able to sit up in bed during a part of the day.

The moral uses of enforced rest are readily estimated. From a restless life of irregular hours, and probably endless drugging, from hurtful sympathy and over-zealous care, the patient passes to an atmosphere of quiet, to order and control, to the system and care of a thorough nurse, to an absence of drugs, and to simple diet. The result is always at first, whatever it may be afterwards, a sense of relief, and a remarkable and often a quite abrupt disappearance of many of the nervous symptoms with which we are all of us only too sadly familiar.

All the moral uses of rest and isolation and change of habits are not obtained by merely insisting on the physical conditions needed to effect these ends. If the physician has the force of character required to secure the confidence and respect of his patients, he has also much more in his power, and should have the tact to seize the proper occasions to direct the thoughts of his patients to the lapse from duties to others, and to the selfishness which a life of invalidism is apt to bring about. Such moral medication belongs to the higher sphere of the doctor's duties, and, if he means to cure his patient permanently, he cannot afford to neglect them. Above all, let him be careful that the masseuse and the nurse do not talk of the patient's ills, and let him by degrees teach the sick person how very essential it is to speak of her aches and pains to no one but himself.

• • •

"Let us think, then, when we put a person in bed, that we are lessening the heart-beats some twenty a minute, nearly a third; that we are causing the tardy blood to linger in the by-ways of the blood-round, for it has its by-ways; that rest in bed binds the bowels, and tends to destroy the desire to eat; and that muscles at rest too long get to be unhealthy and shrunken in substance. Bear these ills in mind, and be ready to meet them, and we shall have answered the hard question of how to help by rest without hurt to the patient."

When I first made use of this treatment I allowed my patients to get up too suddenly, and in some cases I thus brought on relapses and a return of the feeling of painful fatigue. I also saw in some of these cases what I still see at times under like circumstances,—a rapid loss of flesh.

I now begin by permitting the patient to sit up in bed, then to feed herself, and next to sit up out of bed a few minutes at bedtime. In a week, she is desired to sit up fifteen minutes twice a day, and this is gradually increased until, at the end of six to twelve weeks, she rests on the bed only three to five hours daily. Even after she moves about and goes out, I insist

108

for two months on absolute repose at least two or three hours daily.

The use of a hammock is found by some people to be a very agreeable change from the bed during a part of the day.

From Wear and Tear

If the mothers of a people are sickly and weak, the sad inheritance falls upon their offspring, and this is why I must deal first, however briefly, with the health of our girls, because it is here, as the doctor well knows, that the trouble begins. Ask any physician of your acquaintance to sum up thoughtfully the young girls he knows, and to tell you how many in each score are fit to be healthy wives and mothers, or in fact to be wives and mothers at all. I have been asked this question myself very often, and I have heard it asked of others. The answers I am not going to give, chiefly because I should not be believed—a disagreeable position, in which I shall not deliberately place myself. Perhaps I ought to add that the replies I have heard given by others were appalling.

Next, I ask you to note carefully the expression and figures of the young girls whom you may chance to meet in your walks, or whom you may observe at a concert or in the ballroom. You will see many very charming faces, the like of which the world cannot match—figures somewhat too spare of flesh, and especially south of Rhode Island, a marvellous littleness of hand and foot. But look further, and especially among New England young girls: you will be struck with a certain hardness of line in form and feature which should not be seen between thirteen and eighteen, at least; and if you have an eye which rejoices in the tints of health, you will too often miss them on the cheeks we are now so daringly criticising. I do not want to do more than is needed of this ungracious talk: suffice it to say that multitudes of our young girls are merely pretty to look at, or not that; that their destiny is the shawl and the sofa, neuralgia, weak backs, and the varied

---

Philadelphia: J. B. Lippincott, 1872.

forms of hysteria,—that domestic demon which has produced untold discomfort in many a household, and, I am almost ready to say, as much unhappiness as the husband's dram. My phrase may seem outrageously strong, but only the doctor knows what one of the self-made invalids can do to make a household wretched.

. . .

It were better not to educate girls at all between the ages of fourteen and eighteen, unless it can be done with careful reference to their bodily health. To-day, the American woman is, to speak plainly, too often physically unfit for her duties as woman, and is perhaps of all civilized females the least qualified to undertake those weightier tasks which tax so heavily the nervous system of man. She is not fairly up to what nature asks from her as wife and mother. How will she sustain herself under the pressure of those yet more exacting duties which nowadays she is eager to share with the man?

While making these stringent criticisms, I am anxious not to be misunderstood. The point which above all others I wish to make is this, that owing chiefly to peculiarities of climate, our growing girls are endowed with organizations so highly sensitive and impressionable that we expose them to needless dangers when we attempt to overtax them mentally. In any country the effects of such a course must be evil, but in America I believe it to be most disastrous.

From Doctor and Patient

Wise women choose their doctors and trust them. The wisest ask the fewest questions. The terrible patients are nervous women with long memories, who question much where answers are difficult, and who put together one's answers from time to time and torment themselves and the physician with the apparent inconsistencies they detect. Another form of trouble arises with the woman whose standards are of un-

---

Philadelphia: J. B. Lippincott, 1886.

earthly altitude. This is the woman who thinks herself deceived if she does not know what you are giving her, or who, if without telling her you substitute an innocent drug for a hurtful one which she may have learned to take too largely, thinks that you are untruthful in the use of such a method.

❑ Critical Essays

☐ SANDRA M. GILBERT and SUSAN GUBAR ■

From *The Madwoman in the Attic*

Dramatizations of imprisonment and escape are so all-pervasive in nineteenth-century literature by women that we believe they represent a uniquely female tradition in this period. Interestingly, though works in this tradition generally begin by using houses as primary symbols of female imprisonment, they also use much of the other paraphernalia of "woman's place" to enact their central symbolic drama of enclosure and escape. Ladylike veils and costumes, mirrors, paintings, statues, locked cabinets, drawers, trunks, strong-boxes, and other domestic furnishing appear and reappear in female novels and poems throughout the nineteenth century and on into the twentieth to signify the woman writer's sense that, as Emily Dickinson put it, her "life" has been "shaven and fitted to a frame," a confinement she can only tolerate by believing that "the soul has moments of escape/When bursting all the doors/She dances like a bomb abroad."[1] Significantly, too, the explosive violence of these "moments of escape" that women writers continually imagine for themselves returns us to the phenomenon of the mad double so many of these women have projected into their works. For it is, after all, through the violence of the double that the female author enacts her own raging desire to escape male houses and male texts, while at the same time it is through the double's violence that this anxious author articulates for herself the costly destructiveness of anger repressed until it can no longer be contained.

As we shall see, therefore, infection continually breeds

From *The Madwoman in the Attic: The Woman Writer and the Nineteenth-Century Literary Imagination* (New Haven: Yale University Press, 1979), 85–92.

in the sentences of women whose writing obsessively enacts this drama of enclosure and escape. Specifically, what we have called the distinctively female diseases of anorexia and agoraphobia are closely associated with this dramatic/thematic pattern. Defining themselves as prisoners of their own gender, for instance, women frequently create characters who attempt to escape, if only into nothingness, through the suicidal self-starvation of anorexia. Similarly, in a metaphorical elaboration of bulimia, the disease of overeating which is anorexia's complement and mirror-image (as Marlene Boskind-Lodahl has recently shown),[2] women writers often envision an "outbreak" that transforms their characters into huge and powerful monsters. More obviously, agoraphobia and its complementary opposite, claustrophobia, are by definition associated with the spatial imagery through which these poets and novelists express their feelings of social confinement and their yearning for spiritual escape. The paradigmatic female story, therefore— the story such angels in the house of literature as Goethe's Makarie and Patmore's Honoria were in effect "forbidden" to tell—is frequently an arrangement of the elements most readers will readily remember from Charlotte Brontë's *Jane Eyre*. Examining the psychosocial implications of a "haunted" ancestral mansion, such a tale explores the tension between parlor and attic, the psychic split between the lady who submits to male dicta and the lunatic who rebels. But in examining these matters the paradigmatic female story inevitably considers also the equally uncomfortable spatial options of expulsion into the cold outside or suffocation in the hot indoors, and in addition it often embodies an obsessive anxiety both about starvation to the point of disappearance and about monstrous inhabitation.

Many nineteenth-century male writers also, of course, used imagery of enclosure and escape to make deeply felt points about the relationship of the individual and society. Dickens and Poe, for instance, on opposite sides of the Atlantic, wrote of prisons, cages, tombs, and cellars in similar ways and for similar reasons. Still, the male writer is so much more comfortable with his literary role that he can usually elaborate upon his visionary theme more consciously and objectively than the female writer can. The distinction between male and female images of imprisonment is—and always has been—a distinction between, on the one hand, that which is both metaphysical and metaphorical, and on the other hand, that which is social and actual. Sleeping in his coffin, the seventeenth-century poet John Donne was piously rehearsing the constraints of the grave in advance, but the nineteenth-century poet Emily Dickinson, in purdah in her white dress, was anxiously living those constraints in the present. Imagining himself buried alive in tombs and cellars, Edgar Allan Poe was letting his mind poetically wander into the deepest recesses of his own psyche, but Dickinson, reporting that "I do not cross my Father's ground to any house in town," was recording a real, self-willed, self-burial. Similarly, when Byron's Prisoner of Chillon notes that "my very chains and I grew friends," the poet himself is making an epistemological point about the nature of the human mind, as well as a political point about the tyranny of the state. But when Rose Yorke in *Shirley* describes Caroline Helstone as living the life of a toad enclosed in a block of marble, Charlotte Brontë is speaking through her about her own deprived and constricted life, and its real conditions.[3]

Thus, though most male metaphors of imprisonment have obvious implications in common (and many can be traced back to traditional images used by, say, Shakespeare and Plato), such metaphors may have very different aesthetic functions and philosophical messages in different male literary works. Wordsworth's prison-house in the "Intimations" ode serves a purpose quite unlike that served by the jails in Dickens's novels. Coleridge's twice-five miles of visionary greenery ought not to be confused with Keats's vale of soul-making, and the escape of Tennyson's Art from her Palace should not be identified with the resurrection of Poe's Ligeia. Women authors, however, reflect the literal reality of their own confinement in the constraints they depict, and so all at least begin with the same unconscious or conscious purpose in employing such spatial imagery. Recording their own distinctively female experience, they are secretly working through and within the conventions of literary texts to define their own lives.

While some male authors also use such imagery for implicitly or explicitly confessional projects, women seem forced to live more intimately with the metaphors they have created

117

to solve the "problem" of their fall. At least one critic does deal not only with such images but with their psychological meaning as they accrue around houses. Noting in *The Poetics of Space* that "the house image would appear to have become the topography of our inmost being," Gaston Bachelard shows the ways in which houses, nests, shells, and wardrobes are in us as much as we are in them.[4] What is significant from our point of view, however, is the extraordinary discrepancy between the almost consistently "felicitous space" he discusses and the negative space we have found. Clearly, for Bachelard the protective asylum of the house is closely associated with its maternal features, and to this extent he is following the work done on dream symbolism by Freud and on female inner space by Erikson. It seems clear too, however, that such symbolism must inevitably have very different implications for male critics and for female authors.

Women themselves have often, of course, been described or imagined as houses. Most recently Erik Erikson advanced his controversial theory of female "inner space" in an effort to account for little girls' interest in domestic enclosures. But in medieval times, as if to anticipate Erikson, statues of the Madonna were made to open up and reveal the holy family hidden in the Virgin's inner space. The female womb has certainly, always and everywhere, been a child's first and most satisfying house, a source of food and dark security, and therefore a mythic paradise imaged over and over again in sacred caves, secret shrines, consecrated huts. Yet for many a woman writer these ancient associations of house and self seem mainly to have strengthened the anxiety about enclosure which she projected into her art. Disturbed by the real physiological prospect of enclosing an unknown part of herself that is somehow also not herself, the female artist may, like Mary Shelley, conflate anxieties about maternity with anxieties about literary creativity. Alternatively, troubled by the anatomical "emptiness" of spinsterhood, she may, like Emily Dickinson, fear the inhabitations of nothingness and death, the transformation of womb into tomb. Moreover, conditioned to believe that as a house she is herself owned (and ought to be inhabited) by a man, she may once again but for yet another reason see herself as inescapably an object. In other words, even if she does

118

not experience her womb as a kind of tomb or perceive her child's occupation of her house/body as depersonalizing, she may recognize that in an essential way she has been defined simply by her purely biological usefulness to her species.

To become literally a house, after all, is to be denied the hope of that spiritual transcendence of the body which, as Simone de Beauvoir has argued, is what makes humanity distinctively human. Thus, to be confined in childbirth (and significantly "confinement" was the key nineteenth-century term for what we would now, just as significantly, call "delivery") is in a way just as problematical as to be confined in a house or prison. Indeed, it might well seem to the literary woman that, just as ontogeny may be said to recapitulate phylogeny, the confinement of pregnancy replicates the confinement of society. For even if she is only metaphorically denied transcendence, the woman writer who perceives the implications of the house/body equation must unconsciously realize that such a trope does not just "place" her in a glass coffin, it transforms her into a version of the glass coffin herself. There is a sense, therefore, in which, confined in such a network of metaphors, what Adrienne Rich has called a "thinking woman" might inevitably feel that now she has been imprisoned within her own alien and loathsome body.[5] Once again, in other words, she has become not only a prisoner but a monster.

As if to comment on the unity of all these points—on, that is, the anxiety-inducing connections between what women writers tend to see as their parallel confinements in texts, houses, and maternal female bodies—Charlotte Perkins Gilman brought them all together in 1890 in a striking story of female confinement and escape, a paradigmatic tale which (like *Jane Eyre*) seems to tell *the* story that all literary women would tell if they could speak their "speechless woe." "The Yellow Wallpaper," which Gilman herself called "a description of a case of nervous breakdown," recounts in the first person the experiences of a woman who is evidently suffering from a severe postpartum psychosis.[6] Her husband, a censorious and paternalistic physician, is treating her according to methods by which S. Weir Mitchell, a famous "nerve specialist," treated Gilman herself for a similar problem. He has confined her to a large garret room in an "ancestral hall" he has rented, and he has forbidden her to touch pen to paper until she is well again, for he feels, says the narrator, "that with my imaginative power and habit of story-making, a nervous weakness like mine is sure to lead to all manner of excited fancies, and that I ought to use my will and good sense to check the tendency."

The cure, of course, is worse than the disease, for the sick woman's mental condition deteriorates rapidly. "I think sometimes that if I were only well enough to write a little it would relieve the press of ideas and rest me," she remarks, but literally confined in a room she thinks is a one-time nursery because it has "rings and things" in the walls, she is literally locked away from creativity. The "rings and things," although reminiscent of children's gymnastic equipment, are really the paraphernalia of confinement, like the gate at the head of the stairs, instruments that definitively indicate her imprisonment. Even more tormenting, however, is the room's wallpaper: a sulphurous yellow paper, torn off in spots, and patterned with "lame uncertain curves" that "plunge off at outrageous angles" and "destroy themselves in unheard of contradictions." Ancient, smoldering, "unclean" as the oppressive structures of the society in which she finds herself, this paper surrounds the narrator like an inexplicable text, censorious and overwhelming as her physician husband, haunting as the "hereditary estate" in which she is trying to survive. Inevitably she studies its suicidal implications—and inevitably, because of her "imaginative power and habit of story-making," she revises it, projecting her own passion for escape into its otherwise incomprehensible hieroglyphics. "This wall-paper," she decides, at a key point in her story,

> has a kind of sub-pattern in a different shade, a particularly irritating one, for you can only see it in certain lights, and not clearly then.
>
> But in the places where it isn't faded and where the sun is just so—I can see a strange, provoking, formless sort of figure, that seems to skulk about behind that silly and conspicuous front design.

As time passes, this figure concealed behind what corresponds (in terms of what we have been discussing) to the facade of the patriarchal text becomes clearer and clearer. By moonlight the pattern of the wallpaper "becomes bars! The outside pattern I mean, and the woman behind it is as plain as can be." And eventually, as the narrator sinks more deeply into what the world calls madness, the terrifying implications of both the paper and the figure imprisoned behind the paper begin to permeate—that is, to *haunt*—the rented ancestral mansion in which she and her husband are immured. The "yellow smell" of the paper "creeps all over the house," drenching every room in its subtle aroma of decay. And the woman creeps too—through the house, in the house, and out of the house, in the garden and "on that long road under the trees." Sometimes, indeed, the narrator confesses, "I think there are a great many women" both behind the paper and creeping in the garden,

> and sometimes only one, and she crawls around fast, and her crawling shakes [the paper] all over. . . . And she is all the time trying to climb through. But nobody could climb through that pattern—it strangles so; I think that is why it has so many heads.

Eventually it becomes obvious to both reader and narrator that the figure creeping through and behind the wallpaper is both the narrator and the narrator's double. By the end of the story, moreover, the narrator has enabled this double to escape from her textual/architectural confinement: "I pulled and she shook, I shook and she pulled, and before morning we had peeled off yards of that paper." Is the message of the tale's conclusion mere madness? Certainly the righteous Doctor John—whose name links him to the anti-hero of Charlotte Brontë's *Villette*—has been temporarily defeated, or at least momentarily stunned. "Now why should that man have fainted?" the narrator ironically asks as she creeps around her attic. But John's unmasculine swoon of surprise is the least of the triumphs Gilman imagines for her madwoman. More significant are the madwoman's own imaginings and creations, mirages of health and freedom with which her author endows her like a fairy godmother showering gold on a sleeping heroine. The woman from behind the wallpaper creeps away, for instance, creeps fast and far on the long road, in broad day-light. "I have watched her sometimes away off in the open country," says the narrator, "creeping as fast as a cloud shadow in a high wind."

Indistinct and yet rapid, barely perceptible but inexo-rable,the progress of that cloud shadow is not unlike the prog-ress of nineteenth-century literary women out of the texts defined by patriarchal poetics into the open spaces of their own authority. That such an escape from the numb world be-hind the patterned walls of the text was a flight from dis-ease into health was quite clear to Gilman herself. When "The Yel-low Wallpaper" was published she sent it to Weir Mitchell, whose strictures had kept her from attempting the pen during her own breakdown, thereby aggravating her illness, and she was delighted to learn, years later, that "he had changed his treatment of nervous prostration since reading" her story. "If that is a fact," she declared, "I have not lived in vain."[7] Be-cause she was a rebellious feminist besides being a medical iconoclast, we can be sure that Gilman did not think of this triumph of hers in narrowly therapeutic terms. Because she knew, with Emily Dickinson, that "Infection in the sentence breeds," she knew that the cure for female despair must be spiritual as well as physical, aesthetic as well as social. What "The Yellow Wallpaper" shows she knew, too, is that even when a supposedly "mad" woman has been sentenced to im-prisonment in the "infected" house of her own body, she may discover that, as Sylvia Plath was to put it seventy years later, she has "a self to recover, a queen."[8]

☐ Notes ■

1. J. 512 ("The Soul has Bandaged moments—") in *The Poems of Emily Dickinson,* ed. Thomas Johnson, 3 vols. (Cambridge, Mass.: The Belknap Press of Harvard University Press, 1955).

2. Marlene Boskind-Lodahl, "Cinderella's Stepsisters: A Femi-nist Perspective on Anorexia Nervosa and Bulimia," *Signs* 2, no. 2 (Winter 1976): 342–356.

3. *The Letters of Emily Dickinson,* ed. Thomas Johnson, 3 vols. (Cambridge, Mass.: The Belknap Press of Harvard University

Press, 1958), 2: 460; Byron, "The Prisoner of Chillon," lines 389–893; Brontë, *Shirley* (New York: Dutton, 1970), p. 316.

4. Gaston Bachelard, *The Poetics of Space,* trans. Maria Jolas (Boston: Beacon, 1970), p. xxxii.

5. *Adrienne Rich's Poetry,* ed. Barbara Charlesworth Gelpi and Albert Gelpi (New York: Norton, 1975), p. 12: "A thinking woman sleeps with monsters. The beak that grips her, she becomes" ("Snapshots of a Daughter-in-Law,"#3).

6. Charlotte Perkins Gilman, *The Yellow Wallpaper* (Old Westbury: The Feminist Press, 1973).

7. *The Living of Charlotte Perkins Gilman* (New York: Harper and Row, 1975), p. 121.

8. "Stings," *Ariel* (New York: Harper and Row, 1966), p. 62.

☐ CONRAD SHUMAKER ■

"Too Terribly Good to Be Printed": Charlotte Gilman's "The Yellow Wallpaper"

In 1890 William Dean Howells sent a copy of "The Yellow Wallpaper" to Horace Scudder, editor of the *Atlantic Monthly*. Scudder gave his reason for not publishing the story in a short letter to its author, Charlotte Perkins Stetson (later to become Charlotte Perkins Gilman): "Dear Madam, Mr. Howells has handed me this story. I could not forgive myself if I made others as miserable as I have made myself!"[1] Gilman persevered, however, and eventually the story, which depicts the mental collapse of a woman undergoing a "rest cure" at the hands of her physician husband, was printed in the *New England Magazine* and then later in Howells's own collection, *Great Modern American Stories,* where he introduces it as "terrible and too wholly dire," and "too terribly good to be printed."[2] Despite (or perhaps because of) such praise, the story was virtually ignored for over fifty years until Elaine Hedges called attention to its virtues, praising it as "a small literary masterpiece."[3] Today the work is highly spoken of by those who have read it, but it is not widely known and has been slow to appear in anthologies of American literature.

Some of the best criticism attempts to explain this neglect as a case of misinterpretation by audiences used to "traditional" literature. Annette Kolodny, for example, points out that though nineteenth-century readers had learned to "follow

From *American Literature* 57 : 4 (1985): 588–599.

the fictive processes of aberrant perception and mental break-down" by reading Poe's tales, they were not prepared to understand a tale of mental degeneration in a middle-class mother and wife. It took twentieth-century feminism to place the story in a "nondominant or subcultural" tradition which those steeped in the dominant tradition could not understand.[4] Jean F. Kennard suggests that the recent appearance of feminist novels has changed literary conventions and led us to find in the story an exploration of women's role instead of the tale of horror or depiction of mental breakdown its original audience found.[5] Both arguments are persuasive, and the feminist readings of the story that accompany them are instructive. With its images of barred windows and sinister bedsteads, creeping women and domineering men, the story does indeed raise the issue of sex roles in an effective way, and thus anticipates later feminist literature.

Ultimately, however, both approaches tend to make the story seem more isolated from the concerns of the nineteenth-century "dominant tradition" than it really is, and since they focus most of our attention on the story's polemical aspect, they invite a further exploration of Gilman's artistry—the way in which she molds her reformer concerns into a strikingly effective work of literature. To be sure, the polemics are important. Gilman, an avowed feminist and a relative of Harriet Beecher Stowe, told Howells that she didn't consider the work to be "literature" at all, that everything she wrote was for a purpose, in this case that of pointing out the dangers of a particular medical treatment. Unlike Gilman's other purposeful fictions, however, "The Yellow Wallpaper" transcends its author's immediate intent, and my experience teaching it suggests that it favorably impresses both male and female students, even before they learn of its feminist context or of the patriarchal biases of nineteenth-century medicine. I think the story has this effect for two reasons. First, the question of women's role in the nineteenth century is inextricably bound up with the more general question of how one perceives the world. Woman is often seen as representing an imaginative or "poetic" view of things that conflicts with (or sometimes complements) the American male's "common sense" approach to reality. Through the characters of the "rational" doctor and the "imaginative" wife, Gilman explores a question that was—and in many ways still is—central both to American literature and to the place of women in American culture: What happens to the imagination when it's defined as feminine (and thus weak) and has to face a society that values the useful and the practical and rejects anything else as nonsense? Second, this conflict and the related feminist message both arise naturally and effectively out of the action of the story because of the author's skillful handling of the narrative voice.

One of the most striking passages in Gilman's autobiography describes her development and abandonment of a dream world, a fantasy land to which she could escape from the rather harsh realities of her early life. When she was thirteen, a friend of her mother warned that such escape could be dangerous, and Charlotte, a good New England girl who considered absolute obedience a duty, "shut the door" on her "dear, bright, glittering dreams."[6] The narrator of "The Yellow Wallpaper" has a similar problem: from the beginning of the story she displays a vivid imagination. She wants to imagine that the house they have rented is haunted, and as she looks at the wallpaper, she is reminded of her childhood fancies about rooms, her ability to "get more entertainment and terror out of blank walls and plain furniture than most children could find in a toy store." Her husband has to keep reminding that she "must not give way to fancy in the least" as she comments on her new surroundings. Along with her vivid imagination she has the mind and eye of an artist. She begins to study the wallpaper in an attempt to make sense of its artistic design, and she objects to it for aesthetic reasons: it is "one of those sprawling, flamboyant patterns committing every artistic sin." When her ability to express her artistic impulses is limited by her husband's prescription of complete rest, her mind turns to the wallpaper, and she begins to find in its tangled pattern the emotions and experiences she is forbidden to record. By trying to ignore and repress her imagination, in short, John eventually brings about the very circumstance he wants to prevent.

Though he is clearly a domineering husband who wants to have absolute control over his wife, John also has other reasons for forbidding her to write or paint. As Gilman points out in her autobiography, the "rest cure" was designed for "the business man exhausted from too much work, and the society woman exhausted from too much play."[7] The treatment is intended, in other words, to deal with physical symptoms of overwork and fatigue, and so is unsuited to the narrator's more complex case. But as a doctor and an empiricist who "scoffs openly at things not to be felt and seen and put down in figures," John wants to deal only with physical causes and effects: if his wife's symptoms are nervousness and weight loss, the treatment must be undisturbed tranquility and good nutrition. The very idea that her "work" might be beneficial to her disturbs him; indeed, he is both fearful and contemptuous of her imaginative and artistic powers, largely because he fails to understand them or the view of the world they lead her to.

Two conversations in particular demonstrate his way of dealing with her imagination and his fear of it. The first occurs when the narrator asks him to change the wallpaper. He replies that to do so would be dangerous, for "nothing was worse for a nervous patient than to give way to such fancies." At this point, her "fancy" is simply an objection to the paper's ugliness, a point she makes clear when she suggests that they move to the "pretty rooms" downstairs. John replies by calling her a "little goose" and saying "he would go down to the cellar if she wished and have it whitewashed into the bargain." Besides showing his obviously patriarchal stance, his reply is designed to make her aesthetic objections seem nonsense by fastening on concrete details—color and elevation—and ignoring the real basis of her request. If she wants to go downstairs away from yellow walls, he will take her to the cellar and have it whitewashed. The effect is precisely what he intends: he makes her see her objection to the paper's ugliness as "just a whim." The second conversation occurs after the narrator has begun to see a woman behind the surface pattern of the wallpaper. When John catches her getting out of bed to examine the paper more closely, she decides to ask him to take her away. He refuses, referring again to concrete details: "You are gaining flesh and color, your appetite is better, I feel really much better about you." When she implies that her physical condition isn't the real problem, he cuts her off in midsentence: "I beg of you, for my sake and for our child's sake, as well as for your own, that you will never for one instant let that idea enter your mind! There is nothing so dangerous, so fascinating, to a temperament like yours. It is a false and foolish fancy." For John, mental illness is the inevitable result of using one's imagination, the creation of an attractive "fancy" which the mind then fails to distinguish from reality. He fears that because of her imaginative "temperament" she will create the fiction that she is mad and come to accept it despite the evidence—color, weight, appetite—that she is well. Imagination and art are subversive because they threaten to undermine his materialistic universe.

Ironically, despite his abhorrence of faith and superstition, John fails because of his own dogmatic faith in materialism and empiricism, a faith that will not allow him even to consider the possibility that his wife's imagination could be a positive force. In a way John is like Aylmer in Hawthorne's "The Birthmark": each man chooses to interpret a characteristic of his wife as a defect because of his own failure of imagination, and each attempts to "cure" her through purely physical means, only to find he has destroyed her in the process. He also resembles the implied villain in many of Emerson's and Thoreau's lectures and essays, the man of convention who is so taken with "common sense" and traditional wisdom that he is blind to truth. Indeed, the narrator's lament that she might get well faster if John were not a doctor and her assertion that he can't understand her "because he is so wise" remind one of Thoreau's question in the first chapter of *Walden:* "How can he remember his ignorance—which his growth requires—who has so often to use his knowledge?" John's role as a doctor and an American male requires that he use his "knowledge" continuously and doggedly, and he would abhor the appearance of imagination in his own mind even more vehemently than in his wife's.

The relationship between them also offers an insight into how and why this fear of the imagination has been institutionalized through assigned gender roles. By defining his wife's artistic impulse as a potentially dangerous part of her feminine "temperament," John can control both his wife and a facet of human experience which threatens his comfortably materialistic view of the world. Fear can masquerade as calm authority when the thing feared is embodied in the "weaker sex." Quite fittingly, the story suggests that America is full of Johns: the narrator's brother is a doctor, and S. Weir Mitchell—"like John and my brother only more so!"—looms on the horizon if she doesn't recover.

As her comments suggest, the narrator understands John's problem yet is unable to call it his problem, and in many ways it is this combination of insight and naiveté, of resistance and resignation, that makes her such a memorable character and gives such power to her narrative. The story is in the form of a journal which the writer knows no one will read—she says she would not criticize John to "a living soul, of course, but this is dead paper"—yet at the same time her occasional use of "you," her questions ("What is one to do?" she asks three times in the first two pages), and her confidential tone all suggest that she is attempting to reach or create the listener she cannot otherwise find. Her remarks reveal that her relationship with her husband is filled with deception on her part, not so much because she wants to hide things from him but because it is impossible to tell him things he does not want to acknowledge. She reveals to the "dead paper" that she must pretend to sleep and have an appetite because that is what John assumes will happen as a result of his treatment, and if she tells him that she isn't sleeping or eating he will simply contradict her. Thus the journal provides an opportunity not only to confess her deceit and explain its necessity but also to say the things she really wants to say to John and would say if his insistence on "truthfulness," i.e., saying what he wants to hear, didn't prevent her. As both her greatest deception and her attempt to be honest, the journal embodies in its very form the absurd contradictions inherent in her role as wife.

At the same time, however, she cannot quite stop deceiving herself about her husband's treatment of her, and her descriptions create a powerful dramatic irony as the reader gradually puts together details the meaning of which she doesn't quite understand. She says, for instance, that there is "something strange" about the house they have rented, but her description reveals bit by bit a room that has apparently been used to confine violent mental cases, with bars on the windows, a gate at the top of the stairs, steel rings on the walls, a nailed-down bedstead, and a floor that has been scratched and gouged. When she tries to explain her feelings about the house to John early in the story, her report of the conversation reveals her tendency to assume that he is always right despite her own reservations:

> . . . there is something strange about the house—I can feel it.
>
> I even said so to John one moonlight evening, but he said what I felt was a *draught,* and shut the window.
>
> I get unreasonably angry with John sometimes. I'm sure I never used to be so sensitive. I think it is due to this nervous condition.

As usual, John refuses to consider anything but physical details, but the narrator's reaction is particularly revealing here. Her anger, perfectly understandable to us, must be characterized, even privately, as "unreasonable," a sign of her condition. Whatever doubts she may have about John's methods, he represents reason, and it is her own sensitivity that must be at fault. Comments such as these reveal more powerfully than any direct statement could the way she is trapped by the conception of herself which she has accepted from John and the society whose values he represents. As Paula A. Treichler has pointed out, John's diagnosis is a "sentence," a "set of linguistic signs whose representational claims are authorized by society," and thus it can "control women's fate, whether or not those claims are valid." The narrator can object to the terms of the sentence, but she cannot question its authority, even in her own private discourse. [8]

To a great extent, the narrator's view of her husband is colored by the belief that he really does love her, a belief that provides some of the most striking and complex ironies in the story. When she says, "it is hard to talk to John about my case because he is so wise, and because he loves me so," it is tempting to take the whole sentence as an example of her naiveté. Obviously he is not wise, and his actions are not what we would call loving. Nevertheless, the sentence is in its way powerfully insightful. If John were not so wise—so sure of his own empirical knowledge and his expertise as a doctor—and so loving—so determined to make her better in the only way he knows—then he might be able to set aside his fear of her imagination and listen to her. The passage suggests strikingly the way both characters are doomed to act out their respective parts of loving husband and obedient wife right to the inevitably disastrous end.

Gilman's depiction of the narrator's decline into madness has been praised for the accuracy with which it captures the symptoms of mental breakdown and for its use of symbolism.[9] What hasn't been pointed out is the masterly use of associations, foreshadowing, and even humor. Once the narrator starts attempting to read the pattern of the wallpaper, the reader must become a kind of psychological detective in order to follow and appreciate the narrative. In a sense, he too is viewing a tangled pattern with a woman behind it, and he must learn to revise his interpretation of the pattern as he goes along if he is to make sense of it. For one thing, the narrator tells us from time to time about new details in the room. She notices a "smooch" on the wall "low down, near the mopboard," and later we learn that the bedstead is "fairly gnawed." It is only afterwards that we find out that she is herself the source of these new marks as she bites the bedstead and crawls around the room, shoulder to the wallpaper. If the reader has not caught on already, these details show clearly that the narrator is not always aware of her own actions or in control of her thoughts and so is not always reliable in reporting them. They also foreshadow her final separation for her wifely self, her belief that she is the woman who has escaped from behind the barred pattern of the wallpaper.

But the details also invite us to reread earlier passages, to see if the voice which we have taken to be a fairly reliable though naive reporter has not been giving us unsuspected hints of another reality all along. If we do backtrack we find foreshadowing everywhere, not only in the way the narrator reads the pattern on the wall but in the pattern of her own narrative, the way in which one thought leads to another. One striking example occurs when she describes John's sister, Jen-

nie, who is "a dear girl and so careful of me," and who therefore must not find out about the journal.

> She is a perfect and enthusiastic housekeeper, and hopes for
> no better profession. I verily believe she thinks it is the writ-
> ing which made me sick!
>
> But I can write when she is out, and see her a long way
> off from these windows.
>
> There is one that commands the road, a lovely shaded
> winding road, and one that just looks off over the country. A
> lovely country too, full of great elms and velvet meadows.
>
> This wallpaper has a kind of sub-pattern in a different
> shade, a particularly irritating one, for you can only see it in
> certain lights, and not clearly then.
>
> But in the places where it isn't faded and where the sun
> is just so—I can see a strange, provoking, formless sort of
> figure, that seems to skulk about behind that silly and con-
> spicuous front design.
>
> There's sister on the stairs!

The "perfect and enthusiastic housekeeper" is, of course, the
ideal sister for John, whose view of the imagination she shares.
Thoughts of Jennie lead to the narrator's assertion that she
can "see her a long way off from these windows," foreshadowing later passages in which the narrator will see a creeping
woman, and then eventually many creeping women from the
same windows, and the association suggests a connection between the "enthusiastic housekeeper" and those imaginary
women. The thought of the windows leads to a description of
the open country and suggests the freedom that the narrator
lacks in her barred room. This, in turn, leads her back to the
wallpaper, and now she mentions for the first time the "sub-
pattern," a pattern which will eventually become a woman
creeping behind bars, a projection of her feelings about herself
as she looks through the actual bars of the window. The train
of associations ends when John's sister returns, but this time
she's just "sister," as if now she's the narrator's sister as well,
suggesting a subconscious recognition that they both share
the same role, despite Jennie's apparent freedom and content-
ment. Taken in context, this passage prepares us to see the

connection between the pattern of the wallpaper, the actual bars on the narrator's windows, and the "silly and conspicuous" surface pattern of the wifely role behind which both women lurk.

We can see just how Gilman develops the narrator's mental collapse if we compare the passage quoted above to a later one in which the narrator once again discusses the "subpattern," which by now has become a woman who manages to escape in the daytime.

> I think that woman gets out in the daytime!
>
> And I'll tell you why—privately—I've seen her!
>
> I can see her out of every one of my windows!
>
> It is the same woman, I know, for she is always creeping, and most women do not creep by daylight.
>
> I see her on that long road under the trees, creeping along, and when a carriage comes she hides under the blackberry vines.
>
> I don't blame her a bit. It must be very humiliating to be caught creeping by daylight!
>
> I always lock the door when I creep by daylight!

Here again the view outside the window suggests a kind of freedom, but now it is only a freedom to creep outside the pattern, a freedom that humiliates and must be hidden. The dark humor that punctuates the last part of the story appears in the narrator's remark that she can recognize the woman because "most women do not creep by daylight," and the sense that the journal is an attempt to reach a listener becomes clear through her emphasis on "privately." Finally, the identification between the narrator and the woman is taken a step further and becomes more nearly conscious when the narrator reveals that she too creeps, but only behind a locked door. If we read the two passages in sequence, we can see just how masterfully Gilman uses her central images—the window, the barred pattern of the paper, and the woman—to create a pattern of associations which reveals the source of the narrator's malady yet allows the narrator herself to remain essentially unable to verbalize her problem. At some level, we see, she understands what has rendered her so thoroughly powerless and confused, yet she is so completely trapped in her role that she can express that knowledge only indirectly in a way that hides it from her conscious mind.

In the terribly comic ending, she has destroyed both the wallpaper and her own identity: now she is the woman from behind the barred pattern, and not even Jane—the wife she once was—can put her back. Still unable to express her feelings directly, she acts out both her triumph and her humiliation symbolically, creeping around the room with her shoulder in the "smooch," passing over her fainting husband on every lap. Loralee MacPike suggests that the narrator has finally gained her freedom,[10] but that is true only in a very limited sense. She is still creeping, still inside the room with a rope around her waist. She has destroyed only the front pattern, the "silly and conspicuous" design that covers the real wife, the creeping one hidden behind the facade. As Treichler suggests, "her triumph is to have sharpened and articulated the nature of women's condition,"[11] but she is free only from the need to deceive herself and others about the true nature of her role. In a sense, she has discovered, bit by bit, and finally revealed to John, the wife he is attempting to create—the woman without illusions or imagination who spends all her time creeping.

The story, then, is a complex work of art as well as an effective indictment of the nineteenth-century view of the sexes and the materialism that underlies that view. It is hard to believe that readers familiar with the materialistic despots created by such writers as Hawthorne, Dickens, and Browning could fail to see the implications. Indeed, though Howells' comment that the story makes him "shiver" has been offered as evidence that he saw it as a more or less conventional horror story, I would assert that he understood quite clearly the source of the story's effect. He originally wrote to Gilman to congratulate her on her poem "Women of Today," a scathing indictment of women who fear changing sexual roles and fail to realize that their view of themselves as mothers, wives, and housekeepers is a self-deception. In fact, he praises that poem in terms that anticipate his praise of the story, calling it "dreadfully true."[12] Perhaps the story was unpopular because it was, at least on some level, understood all too clearly, because it struck too deeply and effectively at traditional ways of seeing the world and woman's place in it. That, in any case, seems to be precisely what Howells implies in his comment that it is "too terribly good to be printed."

The clearest evidence that John's view of the imagination and art was all but sacred in Gilman's America comes, ironically, from the author's own pen. When she replied to Howells' request to reprint the story by saying that she did not write "literature," she was, of course, denying that she was a mere imaginative artist, defending herself from the charge that Hawthorne imagines his Puritan ancestors would lay at his doorstep: "A writer of story-books!—what mode of glorifying God, or being serviceable to mankind in his day and generation—may that be? Why, the degenerate fellow might as well have been a fiddler!"[13] One wonders what this later female scion of good New England stock might have done had she been able to set aside such objections. In any case, one hopes that this one work of imagination and art, at least, will be restored to the place that Howells so astutely assigned it, alongside stories by contemporaries such as Mark Twain, Henry James, and Edith Wharton.

☐ Notes ■

1. Quoted in Charlotte Perkins Gilman, *The Living of Charlotte Perkins Gilman: An Autobiography* (1935; rpt. New York: Arno, 1972), p. 119.

2. *The Great Modern American Stories: An Anthology* (New York: Boni and Liveright, 1920), p. vii.

3. Afterword, *The Yellow Wallpaper* (Old Westbury, N.Y.: Feminist Press, 1973), p. 37.

4. "A Map for Rereading: Or, Gender and the Interpretation of Literary Texts," *New Literary History* 11 (1980), 455–456.

5. "Convention Coverage or How to Read Your Own Life," *New Literary History* 13 (1981): 73–74.

6. Gilman, *Living*, p. 24.

7. *Living*, p. 95.

8. "Escaping the Sentence: Diagnosis and Discourse in 'The Yellow Wallpaper,'" *Tulsa Studies in Women's Literature* 3 (1984): 74.

9. See Beate Schöpp-Schilling, "'The Yellow Wallpaper': A Rediscovered 'Realistic' Story," *American Literary Realism* 8 (1975): 284–286; Loralee MacPike, "Environment as Psychopathological Symbolism in 'The Yellow Wallpaper,'" *American Literary Realism* 8 (1975): 286–88.

10. MacPike, p. 288.

11. Treichler, p. 74.

12. Quoted in Gilman, *Living,* p. 113.

13. *The Scarlet Letter* (Columbus: Ohio State University Press, 1962), p. 10.

☐ JULIANN E. FLEENOR ■

The Gothic Prism: Charlotte Perkins Gilman's Gothic Stories and Her Autobiography

Fictional forms can sometimes pervade the manner in which women shape their autobiographies. A case in point is the Gothic, a literary genre popular with female readers and authors for nearly two centuries. Identified as women's fiction and analyzed by feminist critics for evidence of women's experiences, it has been suggested that the Gothic has been used to voice rebellion and anger over the status of women; its themes of madness and disintegration have been analyzed for proof of women's victimization. The female experience, it has been suggested, is that of victim in an androcentric society, and the Gothic form with its ambivalent female symbolism and its psychological effect has been congenial for expressing that ambivalent experience for both readers and writers. In particular, the Gothic has been a form which has expressed women's need for and fear of maternity. Women writers have used the Gothic to convey a fear of maternity and its consequent dependent mother/infant relationship as well as a fear of the mother and a quest for maternal approval.

I would like to propose in the following discussion that the Gothic form is one framework through which Charlotte Perkins Gilman shaped her autobiography as well as general-

From *The Female Gothic*, ed. Juliann E. Fleenor (Montreal: Eden Press, 1983), 227–241.

ized about the female experience. Its use is both limiting and yet revealing—limiting in that it reduces Gilman's life to that of a victim; revealing in that its use suggests that the major conflict in Gilman's life was with her female self, with her mother, and with the very act of creation. Nancy K. Miller has suggested that women's fiction has been about the plots of fiction and not about life.[1] Might it also be possible that women's autobiography, at least in this instance, is about the plots of fiction *and* about life? In an attempt to answer that question, let me first discuss the nature of autobiography and the nature of women's autobiographies.

Whatever division existed between fiction and autobiography has been disappearing for some time, if it ever existed at all.[2] Once, autobiography was commonly assumed to be real and fiction unreal. Increasingly, critics of autobiography have been seeking form, shape, and unity, all common to literary forms. But that literary basis has been difficult to discover or define. Some critics have suggested that autobiographical form is determined by the writer's desire to discover one identity based on one facet of the personality.[3] Reality is simplified, and a pattern is imposed on the writer's life with a coherent story. On the other hand, Francis Hart has maintained that writers have complicated and shifting intentions which account for autobiography as a changing and varied form within the same work.[4] William Spengemann has attempted to synthesize these two poles by asserting that:

> we must view autobiography historically, not as one thing that writers have done again, and again, but as the pattern described by the various things they have done in response to changing ideas about the nature of the self, the ways in which the self may be apprehended, and the proper methods of reporting these apprehensions.[5]

In his study, *The Forms of Autobiography*, Spengemann examines fiction and autobiography by men, claiming that autobiography has been found "to assume fictive forms in the modern era."[6] The questions Spengemann asks about autobiography are, how does the self know the self, and how is the self to be reconciled with the absolute. He concludes: "What makes *Sartor Resartus* and *David Copperfield* autobiographies . . . is not the inclusion of autobiographical materials but their efforts to discover, through a fictive action, some ground upon which conflicting aspects of the writer's own nature might be reconciled in complete being."[7]

Spengemann's conclusions have only limited application to women's autobiographies. Estelle Jelinek suggests that women's autobiographies differ generally from those written by men. She points out these three characteristics: an emphasis in male autobiographies on the public life, while women write about their personal lives; understatement in women's autobiographies as women camouflage their feelings and distance themselves from their lives; and irregular narratives in women's autobiographies rather than an orderly linear chronology.[8] The first two appear contradictory; the emphasis upon the personal leads a reader to expect that women would reveal their feelings; yet distancing occurs. Gilman's autobiography only partially fits these general characteristics. She writes consistently about her public life, stressing her commitment to the social welfare rather than the private. She writes of her personal experience; but it is always generalized to the plight of other women. Finally, her narrative is linear, beginning with her early life and proceeding chronologically to her death.

Spengemann has suggested that fiction and autobiography seek a reconciliation of the writer's nature into what might be construed as an absolute, a quest for completeness. Women's autobiographies have for the most part ignored that quest by keeping to the private sphere, not the public one. Thus, the female identity has been defined through its relationships with others, not by its own dimensions. Gilman's autobiography fits this definition.

Spengemann's approach to fiction through autobiography, however, is intriguing.[9] I would suggest that if fiction can be analyzed through autobiography, then autobiography might in turn be analyzed through a literary form, the Gothic, The Gothic paradigm has been and continues to be an important vehicle for women writers. If he is correct, and if autobiography is the thing that writers "have done in response to changing ideas about the nature of self," then the form might not be so fluid and changing in relation to women's autobiographies.

The Gothic form can be used to suggest that the nature of the female self has not been fluid and changing, but limited within a patriarchal culture. Women's autobiography could be described as the Gothic has been, as ambivalent and concerned with women's lives in the private sphere. In this instance *The Living of Charlotte Perkins Gilman* offers a unique opportunity to relate Gilman's puzzling autobiography to her Gothic stories. This analysis also reveals that she wrote in response to the ideas of the nature of woman and woman as mother. Such a study gives an opportunity to move between fiction and autobiography and perhaps further define the nature of women writers and the nature of the mother-author conflict women face.

Moving between Gilman's short story, "The Yellow Wallpaper," and her autobiography is not a novel suggestion. Readers have consistently connected Gilman's story and her life. Perhaps the popularity of the Gothic itself has also prepared women readers for this connection, for the story graphically describes the nervous breakdown of a woman after she is confined to her country home by her physician-husband and told not to work but to rest. Since Gilman herself experienced a similar breakdown, readers have generally accepted her assertion that the story was a literal transcription of her life. She writes in her autobiography that:

> the real purpose of the story was to reach Dr. S. Weir Mitchell, and to convince him of the error of his ways. I sent him a copy as soon as it came out, but got no response. However, many years later, I met someone who knew close friends of Dr. Mitchell's who said he had told them that he had changed his treatment of nervous prostration since reading "The Yellow Wallpaper." If that is a fact, I have not lived in vain. [10]

Ann Douglas, Gail Parker, Patricia Meyer Spacks, and Elaine Hedges have all accepted Gilman's statements and have interpreted the story accordingly as "the form of her life," as the story of Gilman's "blighted, damaged" yet "transcendent" life, and as the story of "a woman who is denied the right to be an adult." [11] These feminist critics move, as Gilman intended, from the story to the autobiography and back again. Her journals and letters support this interpretation as well. Sandra Gilbert and Susan Gubar have recently suggested that Gilman's story is a tale of all literary women trapped in a house which rapidly becomes the narrator's own body.[12]

Although it is not generally known, Gilman wrote at least two other Gothic stories around the same time as "The Yellow Wallpaper." All three were published in the *New England Magazine*. At the time that "The Rocking Chair" and "The Giant Wistaria" were written, Gilman and her young daughter, Katherine, were living in the warmth of Pasadena, separated from her husband, Charles Walter Stetson. Gilman later noted in her papers: "'The Yellow Wallpaper' was written in two days, with the thermometer at one hundred and three in Pasadena, Ca."[13] Her husband was living on the east coast, and, perhaps coincidentally, all three stories appear to be set in a nameless eastern setting, one urban and two rural. All three display similar themes, and all three are evidence that the conflict, central to Gilman's Gothic fiction and later to her autobiography, was a conflict with the mother, with motherhood, and with creation.

In all three stories women are confined within the home; it is their prison, their insane asylum, even their tomb. A sense of the female isolation which Gilman felt, of exclusion from the public world of work and of men, is contained in the anecdote related by Zona Gale in her introduction to Gilman's autobiography. After watching the approach of several locomotives to a train platform in a small town in Wisconsin, Gilman said, "'All that, . . . and women have no part in it. Everything done by men, working together, while women worked on alone within their four walls!'"[14] Female exclusion, women denied the opportunity to work, or their imprisonment behind four walls, led to madness. Her image, interestingly, does not suggest a female subculture of women working together; Gilman was working against her own culture's definition of women, and her primary antagonists were women like her own mother.

"The Rocking Chair" perhaps suggests conflict with an androcentric society. A beautiful, golden-haired girl sits in a clumsy, brass rocking chair, "something from the old country."[15] She is visible to two young men, but only from a distance. They describe her in terms of a feminine enigma: "Hers was a strange beauty, infinitely attractive, yet infinitely perplexing." They can never see her while they too are in the house, only while they are outside. The chair and its origins represent the effect that an androcentric tradition has upon women and men. The fact that she cannot be seen except from a distance indicates how the man relates to the woman. In this case she is in a rocking chair rather than on a pedestal. Originally the story was called "Inanimate," with the adjective modifying perhaps the girl, perhaps the chair. Her existence is created by the two men. They are doubles of each other, together since childhood, at school, as college roommates, and now as hack journalists. They "are organisms so mutually adapted that they never seem to weary each other." But that is not true of their relation to the unnamed girl.

The chair the girl occupies is described by Maurice, the narrator: "I never saw a chair so made to hurt as that one. It was large and heavy and ill-balanced, and every joint and corner so shod with brass." When asked about its origin, the landlady, whom they call Mrs. Sphynx, replies, "It is Spanish . . . Spanish oak, Spanish leather, Spanish brass, Spanish—." Maurice describes it in detail:

> It was a strange ill-balanced thing that chair, though so easy and comfortable to sit in. The rockers where long and sharp behind, always lying in wait for the unwary, but cut short off in front; and the back was so high and so heavy on top that what with its weight and the shortness of the front rockers, it tipped over forward with an ease and a violence equally astounding.
>
> This I knew from experience, as it had plunged over upon me during some of our frequent encounters with it. Hal also was a sufferer, but in spite of our manifold bruises, neither of us would have had the chair moved, for did not she sit in it, evening after evening, and rock there in the light of the setting sun?

Each man sees the other in the chair with the girl in his arms, and each claims to be sitting in the chair alone. Consequently, each grows suspicious of the other; they quarrel and end their friendship. Gilman appears to be satirizing the male proclivity to worship of a non-existent woman.

In the manuscript the landlady is identified as the girl's mother. There is also the assertion that the mother/landlady keeps the girl away from the two men and the neighbors. The neighbors pity the daughter because the mother refuses to be sociable and keeps the daughter from being so. Neither leaves the house; the narrator notes: "Of course we made covert inquiries in the neighborhood, but nothing new could be elicited. That there was a pretty daughter, often seen in the window, that the mother was reserved and disagreeable neither calling nor returning calls, and that everybody pitied the daughter—that was all." The implication is that the mother imprisoned the girl. However, this description is eliminated from the published story, leaving it much tighter in focus. The omission of the neighbor's account makes the existence of the girl and the mother less possible.

Gilman could not or would not draw the mother/daughter relationship with any sense of reality. There are no conversations between them in either the manuscript or the published version. The narration is restricted to the male point of view. In fact, although the landlady is identified as the mother, at one point she denies it. All this takes place in an empty house in an unnamed city, where the light is usually shut out. The narrator describes the scene: "A waving spot of sunshine, a bright signal light, that caught the eye at once on a waste of commonplace houses and all the dreariness of a narrow city street. Across some low roof that made a gap in the wall of masonry, shot a level brilliant beam of the just setting sun, and struck directly on the golden head of a girl in an upper window." Nature is kept out of this place, except when it enters through one "brief signal light" which ends on the non-existent girl.

There are similarities between "The Rocking Chair" and "The Yellow Wallpaper" other than those mentioned above. The men beg at the door for the young woman to open it, as does the husband in "The Yellow Wallpaper." They search for her:

> Door after door I knocked at, tried and opened; room after room I entered and searched thoroughly—in all that house, from cellar to garret, was no furnished room but ours, no sign of human occupancy. Dust, dust and cobwebs every-where—nothing else.

The house is empty, actually having never been occupied, and they discover they are the only occupants. The girl here becomes one of the figures behind the wallpaper in the later story, and the landlady/mother becomes the woman outside of the wallpaper.

The friends are separated by this vision, one dies, killed with the same kind of slashes left by the rocking chair. The narrator returns to his room:

> The room was empty, both rooms utterly devoid of all life. Yes all, for with the love of a whole lifetime surging up in my heart I sprang to where Hal lay beneath the window and found him cold and dead.
>
> Dead, and most horribly dead—those heavy merciless blows—those deep three-cornered gashes—I started to my feet—even the chair had gone.
>
> And again that whispered laugh!

With that nearly comic image of the rocking chair inflicting mortal wounds Gilman ends her Gothic tale, one which combines satire with horror, as she satirizes the male need to create charming young women to pursue even when that pursuit leads to the death of a best friend, or perhaps a part of themselves.

The setting in "The Rocking Chair" is the city; in "The Giant Wistaria," it is the country. "The Giant Wistaria," however, is similar to "The Yellow Wallpaper" in that both have as a theme the punishment of women, by both women and men, for being women. In fact, women are punished for having babies because doing so imprisons them in the social structure symbolized by the house. The house is again employed as a major symbol; it is haunted, as is the manor house in "The Yellow Wallpaper," by female vulnerability and the sin of maternity.

146

The young woman in "The Giant Wistaria" has had an illegitimate child, given to a servant by her parents. The woman wears a carnelian cross, one of agate, which could be either flesh colored or deep red. Like Hester Prynne, she wears a symbol of her adultery. Unlike "The Rocking Chair," however, the maternal conflict is explicit here: the mother tells the daughter "Meddle not with my new vine child! See! Thou has already broken the tender shoot! Never needle or distaff for thee, and yet thou wilt not be quiet!" The parents even lock her in her room, binding her to keep her there.

A hundred years later, after the death of all those involved, four young people—two women and two men—visit the house and find a huge wistaria vine covering the house. Nature now runs wild:

> The old lilacs and laburnums, the pires and syringa, nodded against the second-story windows. What garden plants survived were great ragged bushes or great shapeless beds. A huge wistaria covered the whole front of the house. The trunk, it was too large to call a stem, rose at the corner of the porch by the high steps, and had once climbed its pillars; but now the pillars were wrenched from their places and held rigid and helpless by tightly wound and knotted arms.
>
> It fended in all the upper story of the porch with a knitted wall of stem and leaf; it ran along the eaves, holding up the gutter that once supported it; it shaded every window with a heavy green; and the drooping, fragrant blossoms made a waving sheet of purple from roof to ground.

Like the house in Shirley Jackson's novel, *We Have Always Lived in the Castle,* nature has reclaimed the house. Like "The Yellow Wallpaper," the four visitors begin to see female figures throughout the grounds, even though the house is unoccupied. A group of trees look like "a crouching, haunted figure" of a woman picking huckleberries. For one of the visitors the vine itself takes on human form and appears as "'a writhing body—cringing—beseeching!'" One of the men begins to dream of the young mother, and soon they discover that she has been buried under the porch in the roots of the giant wistaria. The woman, through the vine has held the house in her arms, and her baby—dead at the age of a month—lay in the old well in the basement. Thus, pregnancy leads first to ostracism and then to death for both mother and child.

This fate might be construed as apt punishment for illegitimacy, but no such confusion exists in "The Yellow Wallpaper." Diseased maternity is explicit in Gilman's third Gothic story. The yellow wallpaper symbolizes more than confinement, victimization, and the inability to write. It suggests a disease within the female self. When the narrator peels the wallpaper off, "It sticks horribly and the pattern just enjoys it! All those strangled heads and bulbous eyes and the waddling fungus growths just shriek with derision." This passage describes more than the peeling of wallpaper: the "strangled heads and bulbous eyes and waddling fungus" imply something strange and terrible about birth and death conjoined, about female procreation, and about female physiology. Nature is perverted here, too. The narrator thinks of "old foul, bad yellow things." The smell "creeps all over the house." She finds it "hovering in the dining-room, skulking in the parlor, hiding in the hall, lying in wait for me on the stairs." Finally, "it gets into my hair."

The paper stains the house in a way that suggests the effect of afterbirth.[16] The house, specifically this room, becomes more than a symbol of a repressive society; it represents the physical self of the narrator as well. She is disgusted, perhaps awed, perhaps frightened of her own bodily processes. The story establishes a sense of fear and disgust, the skin crawls and grows clammy with the sense of physiological fear that Ellen Moers refers to as the Female Gothic.[17]

My contention that one of the major themes in the story, punishment for becoming a mother (as well as punishment for being female), is supported by the absence of the child. The child is taken away from the mother, almost in punishment, as was the child in "The Giant Wistaria." This differs from Gilman's experience; she had been told to keep her child with her at all times. In both the story and in Gilman's life, a breakdown occurs directly after the birth of a child. The narrator is confined as if she had committed a crime. Maternity—the creation of a child—is combined with writing—the creation of writing—in a way that suggests they are interre-

148

lated and perhaps symbiotic, as are the strange toadstools behind the wallpaper.

The pathological nature of both experiences is not surprising, given the treatment Gilman received, and given the fact that maternity reduced women to mothers and not writers. Childbirth has long been a rite of passage for women. But the question is, where does that passage lead? Becoming a mother leads to a child-like state. The narrator becomes the absent child.

All three of these stories have similar themes related to the Gothic as it is used by women. All depict women trapped and driven insane in a patriarchal society. They illustrate a conflict with the mother or with maternity itself, for all are about the act of creating a narrative; they are all processes of discovery. In "The Rocking Chair" the young man pieces together the story for the reader; in "The Giant Wistaria" the two couples discover through intuition, dreams, and finally the removal of the old porch, the secret of the house; and in "The Yellow Wallpaper" the narrator—this time nameless— reads the wallpaper, creating figures and a diseased nature from its faded surfaces.

Imagination is diseased in these stories, like the overgrown gardens in "The Giant Wistaria," like the abandoned garden in "The Yellow Wallpaper," and like the darkened city street where one beam of sunlight reaches the head of the young woman. In two of these stories the creation of an infant is related to the creation of the narrative. In both the infants are conspicuous by their absence, further evidence of a diseased female imagination. In the hands of a female writer, diseased imagination and madness become diseased maternity; for literary creation is directly related to the creation of a child. How these themes relate to Gilman's autobiography, written some twenty-five years later, is the subject of the remainder of this essay.

When Gilman begins her autobiography she makes her mental breakdown the most significant event in her life. Her daughter, Katherine, or perhaps Zona Gale, or both, chose to end the biography with her suicide note, thus, making the breakdown and the suicide important. Readers have since been making a similar emphasis. For example, Ann J. Lane, in her recent edition of Gilman's fiction, chooses to begin her introduction with Gilman's suicide. Lane presents it as an indication of "the struggle and the triumph of her life."[18] Seeing it as a "choice," "an act of will, of rationality, of affirmation," Lane sets it within the shape of Gilman's life, as described by Gilman. Perhaps Lane is correct in asserting that Gilman's death was a rational act, and it certainly agrees with the persona described by Gilman in her autobiography—the woman who reasoned everything out and then acted solely on reason. The problem is not one of truth but of choice and emphasis. The problem is also one of reading an autobiography as a factual transcription of a life rather than as a literary form.

While Gilman's suicide might seem both heroic and rational, it is also a familiar ending in fiction by women. Madness, death, and suicide have predominated in women's fiction, and the Gothic form, with its themes of madness and disintegration, pervades the fiction of such writers as Shirley Jackson, Doris Lessing, Charlotte and Emily Brontë, and Sylvia Plath, not to mention the endings of such works as *The Awakening, Wuthering Heights,* and *The Mill on the Floss.* Here is an instance of autobiography being conceptualized as literary form and perhaps with the aid of literary form. I am not suggesting that Gilman's life was conflict-free and that art and fiction shaped her life. No, Gilman's autobiography was written within the context of the conflict with her society. She was repeatedly labeled an outcast. We need not rely upon her autobiography for testimony to that fact. The California newspapers reported unfairly upon her divorce from Walter Stetson, for example, making her a notorious woman. Surely this conflict shaped her autobiography. Even if conflict had not been so open and so frequent throughout her life, such conflict frequently molds the writing of women's autobiographies. As Norine Voss observes: "The act of writing autobiography reawakens and exacerbates the autobiographer's life-long conflict between rigid definitions of femininity and her need for self-esteem and a vocation. The conflicts between egoism and unselfishness, self-love and self-effacement can affect the narrative mode and the form of autobiography."[19] While Voss is writing about women autobiographers in general, her observation has particular relevance to Gilman. Certainly she had a life-long conflict between what she termed "service" and her role as a woman and mother, and between her egotism and her desire to be unselfish.

Yet that conflict was not as great as one might expect, for Gilman's feminism is, of course, not the feminism of 1982. Like her contemporaries, she apparently believed that women were morally superior to men and the role of social reformer adapted itself well to this belief. Building on Lester Ward's theory that woman is the basis of society and man only the appendage and upon Social Darwinism, Gilman wrote the following passages in *Women and Economics* (1898):

> The naturally destructive tendencies of the male have been gradually subverted to the conservative tendencies of the female, and this is so palpably that the process is plainly to be observed throughout history. Into the male have been bred, by natural selection and unbroken training, the instincts and habits of the female, to his immense improvement.
> • • •
> With a full knowledge of the initial superiority of her sex and the sociological necessity for its temporary subversion, woman should feel only a deep and tender pride in the long patient ages during which she has waited and suffered, that man might slowly rise to full racial equality with her. She could afford to wait. She could afford to suffer.
> • • •
> In her subordinate position, under every disadvantage, through the very walls of her prison, the constructive force of woman has made man its instrument, and worked for the upbuilding of the world.
> • • •
> Women can well afford their period of subjection for the sake of a conquered world, a civilized man.
> • • •
> The woman's movement rests not alone on her larger personality, with its tingling sense of revolt against injustice, but on the wide, deep sympathy of women for one another.
> • • •
> A society whose economic unity is a sex-union can no more develop beyond a certain point industrially than a society like

the patriarchal, whose political unit was a sex-union, could develop beyond a certain point politically.[20]

In these excerpts Gilman expounds the theory of the innate superiority of the female based on the nineteenth-century doctrine of the spheres. This position made the work of Jane Addams and her contemporaries possible; it did not limit them. So the conflict that Gilman felt was not over the definition of femininity but the definition of motherhood.[21]

It is this conflict, over her abandonment of her daughter to her father, viewed by her contemporaries as "unnatural" that most concerns her. It is this conflict which causes her to suggest that she is a mortally wounded woman, scarred for life, and that continues to shape her life and autobiography. Also, it is not surprising to find that it surfaces most in her Gothic stories and in her autobiography. As Lynn Z. Bloom has noted, women autobiographers assume the maternal role in the act of writing their life stories; they become their own mothers. The woman autobiographer "becomes the recreator of her maternal parent and the controlling adult in their literary relationship."[22] Such a role must surely result not in control but in excess and pathos when an autobiographer such as Gilman is trying to atone for what she considers her guilt. In addition, since she so completely rejected the role her mother had played—that of the submissive, long-suffering wife—the autobiography is also a self-justification for this rejection. But, as I pointed out above, others were doing similar service to their society and fitting it within the prescribed role; however, Gilman was unique; she was a mother, and she had rejected that role soundly and publicly.

Thus it is not surprising to find that as in her Gothic stories where women are punished for being women and for having children, in Gilman's autobiography she, too, is punished for having a child. Gilman suggests in the autobiography that Mitchell, the male physician, is punishing her as a woman. She writes, "He had a prejudice against the Beechers, 'I've had two women of your blood here already,' he told me scornfully."[23] After his treatment of her for hysteria fails, she descends into madness. Furthermore, her description of that madness consists of a rejection of her child: "I made a rag baby, hung it on a doorknob and played with it. I would crawl into remote closets and under beds—to hide from the grinding pressure of that profound distress." By hanging the baby on the doorknob, she figuratively destroys it; or she retreats into closets or under beds—to escape even that representative. Gilman needs to build a very strong case for the loss of her daughter, and she does so by claiming that the mental breakdown scarred her permanently, breaking her mind at the age of twenty-four:

> The result has been a lasting loss of power, total in some direction, partial in others; the necessity for a laboriously acquired laziness foreign to both temperament and conviction, a crippled life. . . . After the debacle I could read nothing—instant exhaustion preventing. As years passed there was some gain in this line; if a story was short and interesting and I was feeling pretty well I could read a little while.

Yet letters to her second husband, Houghton Gilman, indicate that she read voraciously and even that he planned readings for her (much as her father had sent her reading lists years before).[24]

Further proof of my contention that Gilman's central conflict was with the role of mother and not woman is found in her description of her mother, Mary Fitch Perkins. Gilman complains about her mother's long-suffering passivity and describes herself positively as recreating herself—Athena-like—out of her own intellect and will. Her dissatisfaction with her mother's performance as a mother is clear in the autobiography. She argues that motherhood requires rationalism, discipline, and independence, not "devotion to duty, sublime self-sacrifice." Gilman attacks the traditional belief that a maternal instinct exists and that every woman can be a mother simply because she has a womb. This attack arises from her argument that knowledge is to be acquired; it is not innate; nor is moral judgment innate. This position is in direct conflict with the one she took in *Women and Economics*. There, as pointed out above, she maintained that women were innately superior. Here she maintains that women must be taught motherhood. Yet, in her biography of Gilman, Mary Hill has

153

pointed out that Gilman, who had no education to be a mother, regarded herself as a superior parent.[25] This contradiction appears to be necessary in order for her to argue that she had to give up her child on a logical basis, not because she could not stand the responsibility and self-sacrifice required of a mother.

Rejecting her mother and her actions in the autobiography, Gilman searches for mother figures, women she hoped would give her the approval and love she needed but could not herself give. She creates a sense of a female community which needs and supports the rational and independent self of the autobiography. The support and admiration of women nurtures the Gilman of the autobiography to the point that Gilman de-emphasizes her dependence upon men, particularly her long (and apparently happy) relationship with Houghton. This is consonant with her comment in *Women and Economics* that the woman's movement rests "on the wide, deep sympathy of women for one another."[26] Yet these relationships are misrepresented. Gilman is frequently the preacher, not the teacher, and her relationships with women, particularly her two love-relationships, are not warm and sustaining but at times sharp and bitter. In her autobiography she is particularly bitter about her relationship with the anonymous "Dora," a woman she lived with while still separated from Stetson and living on the west coast.[27] She also does not admit to the rifts between herself and Grace Channing, the woman who later married Stetson and raised Katherine for some years.

Since the purpose of this paper is to draw a relationship between the Female Gothic and Gilman's conflict with motherhood and creation, I will not dwell on the contradictions, omissions and misrepresentations concerning her relationships with women that appear throughout Gilman's biography. That Gilman tied the two together is clear, both in her autobiography and in her Gothic stories. Once approval was denied to Gilman, rage, depression and guilt followed. Her letters to Houghton [her second husband] give a graphic account of the psychological wounds she suffered. Yet she was able to write numerous books, begin her own publishing company (Charlton) with Houghton, and write her own journal, *The Forerunner*. All of this was accomplished even though she claims in the autobiography that:

> When I am forced to refuse invitations, to back out of work
> that seems easy, to own that I cannot read a heavy book,
> apologetically alleging his weakness of mind, friends gibber
> amiably, "I wish I had your mind!" I wish they had, for a
> while, as a punishment for doubting my word. What confuses
> them is the visible work I have been able to accomplish. They
> see activity, achievement, they do not see blank months of
> idleness; nor can they see what the work would have been if
> the powerful mind I had to begin with had not been broken
> at twenty-four.[28]

Gilman, the unsuccessful mother, becomes the unsuccessful
or suffering mother. Maternity and creation become thus in-
tertwined in a most destructive and painful way. Contrary to
her many claims, woman as author is depicted in the autobiography not as the forceful, decisive woman she intended, but
as a wounded woman in constant torment.

Because of this conviction the autobiography does not
end on the positive note one would expect from a woman
stressing her long and successful life. Suicide in the context of this life is not an affirmation. The result is that the
heroine of this work is damaged, controlled by others—male
and female, permanently scarred, and not the logical, self-
supporting, and successful woman she appeared to others.

She was undoubtedly both Gilmans—the highly emotional self and the logical self. She does try to draw for her
readers the successful, creative Gilman, even to the point of
omitting or misrepresenting some events. Yet the heroine of
the autobiography is an injured woman, wounded in part by
being female and most certainly by maternity. Her search for
a mother to save and to guide her is a fruitless one. Precisely
because of this search, this conflict, and these ambiguities, I
would maintain that her autobiography resembles a literary
form, one she was familiar with, and one congenial to expressing such ambivalences and such conflict, the Gothic.

The autobiography bears a startlingly close relationship
to Gilman's Gothic stories. On the surface these stories, like
her autobiography, convey her continued rebellion and anger
over the treatment women received in a patriarchal society.
On closer examination, however, they also reveal an ambiva-

155

lent relationship with the mother, one that is duplicated in the autobiography. And, finally, they reveal an ambivalence about the capacity of female imagination and female creativity. Gilman's autobiography was shaped, like the stories, through a Gothic prism.[29] We see a woman at odds with her society, at odds with those of her own sex, and primarily at odds with herself. In her lifelong attempt to redefine American motherhood—not American womanhood—Gilman was singularly out of step with her contemporaries. Constantly under attack—both provoked and unprovoked—she lived her life as a Gothic heroine might: impetuously, righteously, and reasonably. Yet she insisted that she lived it virtually alone. The Gothic prism had become the Gothic prison.

☐ Notes ■

1. Nancy K. Miller, "Emphasis Added: Plots and Plausibilities in Women's Fiction," *PMLA* 96 (January 1981), 46. Miller notes: "The point is . . . that the plots of women's literature are not about 'life' and solutions in any therapeutic sense, nor should they be. They are about the plots of literature itself, about the constraints of rendering a female life in fiction."

2. Earlier biography had been used to interpret fiction, a practice discarded in the practice of modern literary criticism. The attempt to link fiction and autobiography is a different endeavor and recognizes that autobiography, like fiction, has literary form and tradition.

3. For a full discussion of the many problems in defining autobiography, see William C. Spengemann, *Forms of Autobiography: Episodes in the History of a Literary Genre* (New Haven and London: Yale University Press, 1980), pp. 183–189.

4. Frances R. Hart, "Notes for an Anatomy of Modern Autobiography," *New Literary History* 1 (1970), 485–511.

5. Spengemann, *Forms of Autobiography,* p. xiii.

6. Ibid.

7. Ibid., p. 132.

8. Estelle C. Jelinek, "Introduction: Women's Autobiography and the Male Tradition," in *Women's Autobiography: Essays in*

Criticism, ed. Estelle C. Jelinek (Bloomington: Indiana University Press, 1980), pp. 1–20.

9. For Spengemann autobiography is a changing form, "an idea that changes with every new statement about it" (p. 84). This essay does not attempt to generalize about women's autobiographies and the Gothic form, only to speculate on the connection of the two in the case of Charlotte Perkins Gilman.

10. Charlotte Perkins Gilman, *The Living of Charlotte Perkins Gilman*, foreword by Zona Gale (1935; rpt., New York: Harper and Row, 1975), p. 121.

11. Gail Parker, "Introduction," in *The Oven Birds: American Women on Womanhood, 1820–1920*, ed. Gail Parker (Garden City, N.Y.: Doubleday, 1972), pp. 52–53; Patricia Meyer Spacks, *The Female Imagination* (1972; rpt., New York: Avon Books, 1976), pp. 268–269; and Elaine Hedges, "Afterword," to "The Yellow Wallpaper" (Old Westbury, N.Y.: The Feminist Press, 1973), pp. 37–63.

12. Sandra M. Gilbert and Susan Gubar, *The Madwoman in the Attic: The Woman Writer and the Nineteenth-Century Literary Imagination* (New Haven and London: Yale University Press, 1979), pp. 88–89.

13. Folder 222, The Charlotte Perkins Gilman Collection, Schlesinger Library, Radcliffe College.

14. *The Living of Charlotte Perkins Gilman*, p. xxiv.

15. All quotations from "The Rocking Chair" and "The Giant Wistaria" have been taken from the published and manuscript copies of these stories on file at Schlesinger Library.

16. See Ellen Moers' discussion of *Frankenstein in Literary Women* (Garden City, N.Y.: Anchor Books, 1977), pp. 140 and 142.

17. Ibid., p. 138.

18. Ann J. Lane, *The Charlotte Perkins Gilman Reader* (New York: Pantheon Books, 1980), p. [ix].

19. Norine Voss, "'Saying the Unsayable': An Introduction to Women's Autobiography," in *First Labor: An Interdisciplinary Women's Studies Journal*, ed. by Graduate Women in English (Bloomington, Indiana: Hysteria Press, 1980), p. 106.

20. Charlotte Perkins Gilman, *Women and Economics: The Economic Factor Between Men and Women as a Factor in Social Evolution* (1898; rpt., New York: Harper and Row, 1966), pp. 128, 129, 133, 134, 139, and 144.

21. Jill Conway points out that "Once Addams had met Les-

ter Ward at Hull-House in the decade of the 1890s, she accepted Ward's assumption that the female was the prototype of the human being and the most highly evolved of the two sexes" ("Women Reformers and American Culture, 1870–1930," originally printed in the *Journal of Social History* 5 [Winter 1971–1972], 164–177; rpt. in *Our American Sisters: Women in American Life and Thought,* ed. Jean E. Friedman and William G. Shade, Second Edition [Boston: Allyn & Bacon, 1976], pp. 307–308). This acceptance by Addams, Lillian Wald, and Charlotte Perkins Gilman left these female reformers unable to cope with the later popularized Freudian stereotypes of women. In fact, as Conway points out, they may have contributed to the Twenties' frenzy over the flapper by never challenging the sexual stereotypes in their culture.

22. Lynn Z. Bloom, "Heritages: Dimensions of Mother-Daughter Relationships in Women's Autobiographies," in *The Lost Tradition: Mothers and Daughters in Literature,* ed. Cathy N. Davidson and E. M. Broner (New York: Frederick Ungar, 1980), p. 292.

23. *The Living of Charlotte Perkins Gilman,* p. 95.

24. Letters to Houghton Gilman on file in the Charlotte Perkins Gilman Collection, Schlesinger Library, Radcliffe College.

25. Mary A. Hill, *Charlotte Perkins Gilman: The Making of a Radical Feminist* (Philadelphia: Temple University Press, 1980), pp. 230–231.

26. Gilman's autobiography demonstrates her lifelong search for mother figures and for women who would love and approve of her unconventional life.

27. The woman is identified in Gilman's papers as Adeline E. Knapp. For a discussion of this relationship see Hill, pp. 189–194.

28. *The Living of Charlotte Perkins Gilman,* p. 98.

29. The title of this essay was suggested by the collection of essays, *The Prism of Sex: Essays in the Sociology of Knowledge,* ed. Julia A. Sherman and Evelyn Torton Beck (Madison, Wisconsin: The University of Wisconsin Press, 1979).

A Map for Rereading: Or, Gender and the Interpretation of Literary Texts

Appealing particularly to a generation still in the process of divorcing itself from the New Critics' habit of bracketing off any text as an entity in itself, as though "it could be read, understood, and criticized entirely in its own terms,"[1] Harold Bloom has proposed a dialectical theory of influence between poets and poets, as well as between poems and poems which, in essence, does away with the static notion of a fixed or knowable text. As he argued in *A Map of Misreading* in 1975, "a poem is a response to a poem, as a poet is a response to a poet, or a person to his parent." Thus, for Bloom, "poems . . . are neither about 'subjects' nor about 'themselves.' They are necessarily about *other poems*."[2]

To read or to know a poem,[1] according to Bloom, engages the reader in an attempt to map the psychodynamic relations by which the poet at hand has willfully misunderstood the work of some precursor (either single or composite) in order to correct, rewrite, or appropriate the prior poetic vision as his own. As first introduced in *The Anxiety of Influence* in 1973, the resultant "wholly different practical criticism . . . give[s] up the failed enterprise of seeking to 'understand' any single poem as an entity in itself" and "pursue[s] instead the quest of learning to read any poem as its poet's deliberate misinterpretation, *as a poet*, of a precursor poem or of poetry

From *New Literary History* 11 (1980): 451–467.

in general."[3] What one deciphers in the process of reading, then, is not any discrete entity but, rather, a complex relational event, "itself a synecdoche for a larger whole including other texts."[4] "Reading a text is necessarily the reading of a whole system of texts," Bloom explains in *Kabbalah and Criticism*, "and meaning is always wandering around between texts" (*KC*, 107–108).

To help purchase assent for this "wholly different practical criticism," Bloom asserted an identity between critics and poets as coequal participants in the same "belated and all-but-impossible act" of reading (which, as he hastens to explain in *A Map of Misreading*, "if strong is always a misreading," p. 3). As it is a drama of epic proportions, in Bloom's terms, when the ephebe poet attempts to appropriate and then correct a precursor's meaning, so, too, for the critic, his own inevitable misreadings or *misprisions* are no less heroic—nor any the less creative. "Poets' misinterpretations or poems" may be "more drastic than critics' misinterpretations or criticism," Bloom admits, but since he recognizes no such thing as "interpretations but only misinterpretations . . . all criticism" is necessarily elevated to a species of "prose poetry" (*AI*, 94–95). The critic's performance, thereby, takes place as one more "act of misprision [which] displaces an earlier act of misprision"—presumably the poet's or perhaps that of a prior critic; and, in this sense, the critic participates in that same act of "defensive warfare" before his own critical forebears, or even before the poet himself, as the poet presumably enacted before his poetic father/precursor (*KC*, 125, 104, 108). Their legacy, whether as poetry or as "prose poetry" criticism, consequently establishes the strong survivors of these psychic battles as figures whom others, in the future, will need to overcome in their turn: "A poet is strong because poets after him must work to evade him. A critic is strong if his readings similarly provoke other readings."[5] It is unquestionably Bloom's most brilliant rhetorical stroke, persuading not so much by virtue of the logic of his argument as by the pleasure his (intended and mostly male) readership will take in the discovery that their own activity replicates the psychic adventures of The Poet, every critic's *figura* of heroism.[6]

What is left out of account, however, is the fact that

whether we speak of poets and critics "reading" texts or writers "reading" (and thereby recording for us) the world, we are calling attention to interpretive strategies that are learned, historically determined, and thereby necessarily gender-inflected. As others have elsewhere questioned the adequacy of Bloom's paradigm of poetic influence to explain the production of poetry by women,[7] so now I propose to examine analogous limitations in his model for the reading—and hence critical—process (since both, after all, derive from his revisionist rendering of the Freudian family romance). To begin with, to locate that "meaning" which "is always wandering around between texts" (*KC,* 107–8), Bloom assumes a community of readers (and, thereby, critics) who know that same "whole system of texts" within which the specific poet at hand has enacted his *misprision.* The canonical sense of a shared and coherent literary tradition is thereby essential to the utility of Bloom's paradigm of literary influence as well as to his notions of reading (and misreading). "What happens if one tries to write, or to teach, or to think or even to read without the sense of a tradition?" Bloom asks in *A Map of Misreading.* "Why," as he himself well understands, "nothing at all happens, just nothing. You cannot write or teach or think or even read without imitation, and what you imitate is what another person has done, that person's writing or teaching or thinking or reading. Your relation to what informs that person *is* tradition, for tradition is influence that extends past one generation, a carrying-over of influence" (*MM,* 32).

So long as the poems and poets he chooses for scrutiny participate in the "continuity that began in the sixth century B.C. when Homer first became a schoolbook for the Greeks" (*MM,* 33–34), Bloom has a great deal to tell us about the carrying over of literary influence; where he must remain silent is where carrying over takes place among readers and writers who in fact have been, or at least have experienced themselves as, cut off and alien from that dominant tradition. Virginia Woolf made the distinction vividly over a half-century ago, in *A Room of One's Own,* when she described being barred entrance, because of her sex, to a "famous library" in which was housed, among others, a Milton manuscript. Cursing the "Oxbridge" edifice, "venerable and calm, with all its treasures safe locked within its breast," she returns to her room at the inn later that night, still pondering "how unpleasant it is to be locked out; and I thought how it is worse perhaps to be locked in; and, thinking of the safety and prosperity of the one sex and of the poverty and insecurity of the other and of the effect of tradition and of the lack of tradition upon the mind of a writer."[8] And, she might have added, on the mind of a reader as well. For while my main concern here is with reading (albeit largely and perhaps imperfectly defined), I think it worth noting that there exists an intimate interaction between readers and writers in and through which each defines for the other what s/he is about. "The effect . . . of the lack of tradition upon the mind of a writer" will communicate itself, in one way or another, to her readers; and, indeed, may respond to her readers' sense of exclusion from high (or highbrow) culture.

An American instance provides perhaps the best example. Delimited by the lack of formal or classical education, and constrained by the social and aesthetic norms of their day to conceptualizing "authorship as a profession rather than a calling, as work and not art,"[9] the vastly popular women novelists of the so-called feminine fifties often enough, and somewhat defensively, made a virtue of their sad necessities by invoking an audience of readers for whom aspirations to "literature" were as inappropriate as they were for the writer. As Nina Baym remarks in her recent study *Woman's Fiction,* "often the women deliberately and even proudly disavowed membership in an artistic fraternity." "'Mine is a story for the table and arm-chair under the reading lamp in the livingroom, and not for the library shelves,'" Baym quotes Marion Harland from the introduction to Harland's autobiography; and then, at greater length, Baym cites Fanny Fern's dedicatory pages to her novel *Rose Clark:*

> When the frost curtains the windows, when the wind whistles fiercely at the key-hole, when the bright fire glows, and the tea-tray is removed, and father in his slippered feet lolls in his arm-chair; and mother with her nimble needle "makes auld claes look amaist as weel as new," and grandmamma draws closer to the chimney-corner, and Tommy with his

plate of chestnuts nestles contentedly at her feet; then let my unpretending story be read. For such an hour, for such an audience, was it written.

Should any *dictionary on legs* rap inopportunely at the door for admittance, send him away to the groaning shelves of some musty library, where "literature" lies embalmed, with its stony eyes, fleshless joints, and ossified heart, in faultless preservation. [10]

If a bit overdone, prefaces like these nonetheless point up the self-consciousness with which writers like Fern and Harland perceived themselves as excluded from the dominant literary tradition and as writing for an audience of readers similarly excluded. To quote Baym again, these "women were expected to write specifically for their own sex and within the tradition of their woman's culture rather than within the Great Tradition. They never presented themselves as followers in the footsteps of Milton or Spenser." [11]

On the one hand, of course, increased literacy (if not substantially improved conditions of education) marked the generations of American women at midcentury, opening a vast market for a literature which would treat the contexts of their lives—the sewing circle rather than the whaling ship, the nursery instead of the lawyer's office—as functional symbols of the human condition. [12] On the other hand, while this vast new audience must certainly be credited with shaping the features of what then became popular women's fiction, it is also the case that the writers in their turn both responded to and helped to formulate their readers' tastes and habits. And both together, I would suggest, found this a means of accepting (or at least coping with) the barred entryway that was to distress Virginia Woolf so in the next century. But these facts of our literary history also suggest that from the 1850s on, in America at least, the meanings "wandering around between texts" were wandering around somewhat different groups of texts where male and female readers were concerned. [13] So that with the advent of women "who wished to be regarded as artists rather than careerists," [14] toward the end of the nineteenth century, there arose the critical problem with which we are still plagued and which Bloom so determinedly ignores:

the problem of reading any text as "a synecdoche for a larger whole including other texts" when that necessarily assumed "whole system of texts" in which it is embedded is foreign to one's reading knowledge.

The appearance of Kate Chopin's novel *The Awakening* in 1899, for example, perplexed readers familiar with her earlier (and intentionally "regional") short stories not so much because it turned away from themes or subject matter implicit in her earlier work, nor even less because it dealt with female sensuality and extramarital sexuality, but because her elaboration of those materials deviated radically from the accepted norms of women's fiction out of which her audience so largely derived its expectations. The nuances and consequences of passion and individual temperament, after all, fairly define the focus of most of her preceding fictions. "That the book is strong and that Miss Chopin has a keen knowledge of certain phases of feminine character will not be denied," wrote the anonymous reviewer for the Chicago *Times-Herald*. What marked an unacceptable "new departure" for this critic, then, was the impropriety of Chopin's focus on material previously edited out of the popular genteel novels by and about women which, somewhat inarticulately, s/he translated into the accusation that Chopin had "enter[ed] the overworked field of sex fiction." [15]

Charlotte Perkins Gilman's initial difficulty in seeing "The Yellow Wallpaper" into print repeated the problem, albeit in a somewhat different context: for her story located itself not as any deviation from a previous tradition of women's fiction but, instead, as a continuation of a genre popularized by Poe. And insofar as Americans had earlier learned to follow the fictive processes of aberrant perception and mental breakdown in *his* work, they should have provided Gilman, one would imagine, with a ready-made audience for *her* protagonist's progressively debilitating fantasies of entrapment and liberation. As they had entered popular fiction by the end of the nineteenth century, however, the linguistic markers for those processes were at once heavily male-gendered and highly idiosyncratic, having more to do with individual temperament than with social or cultural situations per se. As a result, it would appear that the reading strategies by which cracks in

164

ancestral walls and suggestions of unchecked masculine will-fulness were immediately noted as both symbolically and se-mantically relevant did not, for some reason, necessarily *carry over* to "the nursery at the top of the house" with its windows barred, nor even less to the forced submission of the woman who must "take great pains to control myself before" her phy-sician husband.

A reader today seeking meaning in the way Harold Bloom outlines that process might note, of course, a fleeting resemblance between the upstairs chamber in Gilman—with its bed nailed to the floor, its windows barred, and metal rings fixed to the walls—and Poe's evocation of the dungeon cham-bers of Toledo; in fact, a credible argument might be made for reading "The Yellow Wallpaper" as Gilman's willful and purposeful misprision of "The Pit and the Pendulum." Both stories, after all, involve a sane mind entrapped in an insanity-inducing situation. Gilman's "message" might then be that the equivalent revolution by which the speaking voice of the Poe tale is released to both sanity and freedom is unavailable to her heroine. No *deus ex machina,* no General Lasalle trium-phantly entering the city, no "outstretched arm" to prevent Gilman's protagonist from falling into her own internal "abyss" is conceivable, given the rules of the social context in which Gilman's narrative is embedded. When gender is taken into account, then, so this interpretation would run, Gilman is say-ing that the nature of the trap envisioned must be understood as qualitatively different, and so too the possible escape routes.

Contemporary readers of "The Yellow Wallpaper," how-ever, were apparently unprepared to make such connections. Those fond of Poe could not easily transfer their sense of men-tal derangement to the mind of a comfortable middle-class wife and mother; and those for whom the woman in the home was a familiar literary character were hard-pressed to compre-hend so extreme an anatomy of the psychic price she paid. Horace Scudder, the editor of *The Atlantic Monthly* who first rejected the story, wrote only that "I could not forgive myself if I made others as miserable as I have made myself!" And even William Dean Howells, who found the story "chilling" and admired it sufficiently to reprint it in 1920, some twenty-eight years after its first publication (in the *New England*

Magazine of May 1892), like most readers, either failed to notice or neglected to report "the connection between the insanity and the sex, or sexual role, of the victim." For readers at the turn of the century, then, that "meaning" which "is always wandering around between texts" had as yet failed to find connective pathways linking the fanciers of Poe to the devotees of popular women's fiction, or the shortcut between Gilman's short story and the myriad published feminist analyses of the ills of society (some of them written by Gilman herself). Without such connective contexts, Poe continued as a well-traveled road, while Gilman's story, lacking the possibility of further influence, became a literary dead-end.

In one sense, by hinting at an audience of male readers as ill-equipped to follow the symbolic significance of the narrator's progressive breakdown as was her doctor-husband to diagnose properly the significance of his wife's fascination with the wallpaper's patternings; and by predicating a female readership as yet unprepared for texts which mirrored back, with symbolic exemplariness, certain patterns underlying their empirical reality, "The Yellow Wallpaper" anticipated its own reception. For insofar as writing and reading represent linguistically-based interpretive strategies—the first for the recording of a reality (that has, obviously, in a sense, already been "read") and the second for the deciphering of that recording (and thus also the further decoding of a prior imputed reality)—the wife's progressive descent into madness provides a kind of commentary upon, indeed is revealed in terms of, the sexual politics inherent in the manipulation of those strategies. We are presented at the outset with a protagonist who, ostensibly for her own good, is denied both activities and who, in the course of accommodating herself to that deprivation, comes more and more to experience her self as a text which can neither get read nor recorded.

In his doubly authoritative role as both husband and doctor, John not only appropriates the interpretive processes of reading—diagnosing his wife's illness and thereby selecting what may be understood of her "meaning"; reading to her, rather than allowing her to read for herself—but, as well, he determines what may get written and hence communicated. For her part, the protagonist avers, she does not agree with her husband's ideas: "Personally, I believe that congenial work, with excitement and change, would do me good." But given the fact of her marriage to "a physician of high standing" who "assures friends and relatives that there is really nothing the matter with one but temporary nervous depression—a slight hysterical tendency—what is one to do?" she asks. Since her husband (and by extension the rest of the world) will not heed what she says of herself, she attempts instead to communicate it to "this . . . dead paper . . . a great relief to my mind." But John's insistent opposition gradually erodes even this outlet for her since, as she admits, "it *does* exhaust me a good deal—having to be so sly about it, or else meet with heavy opposition." At the sound of his approach, following upon her first attempt to describe "those sprawling flamboyant patterns" in the wallpaper, she declares, "There comes John, and I must put this away,—he hates to have me write a word."

Successively isolated from conversational exchanges, prohibited free access to pen and paper, and thus increasingly denied what Jean Ricardou has called "the local exercise of syntax and vocabulary,"[16] the protagonist of "The Yellow Wallpaper" experiences the extreme extrapolation of those linguistic tools to the processes of perception and response. In fact, it follows directly upon a sequence in which: (1) she acknowledges that John's opposition to her writing has begun to make "the effort . . . greater than the relief"; (2) John refuses to let her "go and make a visit to Cousin Henry and Julia"; and (3) as a kind of punctuation mark to that denial, John carries her "upstairs and laid me on the bed, and sat by me and read to me till it tired my head." It is after these events, I repeat, that the narrator first makes out the dim shape lurking "behind the outside pattern" in the wallpaper: "it is like a woman stooping down and creeping."

From that point on, the narrator progressively gives up the attempt to *record* her reality and instead begins to *read* it—as symbolically adumbrated in her compulsion to discover a consistent and coherent pattern amid "the sprawling outlines" of the wallpaper's apparently "pointless pattern." Selectively emphasizing one section of the pattern while repressing others, reorganizing and regrouping past impressions into

167

newer, more fully realized configurations—as one might with any complex formal text—the speaking voice becomes obsessed with her quest for meaning, jealous even of her husband's or his sister's momentary interest in the paper. Having caught her sister-in-law "with her hand on it once," the narrator declares, "I know she was studying that pattern, and I am determined that nobody shall find it out but myself!" As the pattern changes with the changing light in the room, so too do her interpretations of it. And what is not quite so apparent by daylight becomes glaringly so at night: "At night in any kind of light, in twilight, candle light, lamplight, and worst of all by moonlight, it becomes bars! The outside pattern I mean, and the woman behind it is as plain as can be." "By daylight," in contrast (like the protagonist herself), "she is subdued, quiet."

As she becomes wholly taken up with the exercise of these interpretative strategies, so, too, she claims, her "life is very much more exciting now than it used to be. You see I have something more to expect, to look forward to, to watch." What she is watching, of course, is her own psyche writ large; and the closer she comes to "reading" in the wallpaper the underlying if unacknowledged patterns of her real-life experience, the less frequent becomes that delicate oscillation between surrender to or involvement in and the more distanced observation of developing meaning. Slowly but surely the narrative voice ceases to distinguish itself from the woman in the wallpaper pattern, finally asserting that "I don't want anybody to get that woman out at night but myself," and concluding with a confusion of pronouns that merges into a grammatical statement of identity:

> As soon as it was moonlight and that poor thing began to crawl and shake the pattern, I got up and ran to help her.
>
> *I* pulled and *she* shook, and *I* shook and *she* pulled, and before morning *we* had peeled off yards of that paper. [my italics]

She is, in a sense, now totally surrendered to what is quite literally her own text—or, rather, her self as text. But in decoding its (or her) meaning, what she has succeeded in doing is

168

discovering the symbolization of her own untenable and un-acceptable reality. To escape that reality she attempts the destruction of the paper which seemingly encodes it: the pattern of bars entrapping the creeping woman. "'I've got out at last,' said I, 'in spite of you and Jane. I've pulled off most of the paper, so you can't put me back!'" Their paper pages may be torn and moldy (as is, in fact, the smelly wallpaper), but the meaning of texts is not so easily destroyed. Liberation here is liberation only into madness: for in decoding her own projections onto the paper, the protagonist had managed merely to reencode them once more, and now more firmly than ever, within.

With the last paragraphs of the story, John faints away—presumably in shock at his wife's now totally delusional state. He has repeatedly misdiagnosed, or misread, the heavily edited behavior with which his wife has presented herself to him; and never once has he divined what his wife sees in the wallpaper. But given his freedom to read (or, in this case, misread) books, people, and the world as he chooses, he is hardly forced to discover for himself so extreme a text. To exploit Bloom's often useful terminology once again, then, Gilman's story represents not so much an object for the recurrent mis-readings, or misprisions, of readers and critics (though this, of course, continues to occur) as an exploration, within itself, of the gender-inflected interpretive strategies responsible for our mutual misreadings, and even horrific misprisions, across sex lines. If neither male nor female reading audiences were prepared to decode properly "The Yellow Wallpaper," even less, Gilman understood, were they prepared to comprehend one another.

It is unfortunate that Gilman's story was so quickly relegated to the backwaters of our literary landscape because, coming as it did at the end of the nineteenth century, it spoke to a growing concern among American women who would be serious writers: it spoke, that is, to their strong sense of writing out of nondominant or subcultural traditions (both literary and otherwise), coupled with an acute sensitivity to the fact that since women and men learn to read different worlds, different groups of texts are available to their reading and writing strategies. Had "The Yellow Wallpaper" been able to stand as a potential precursor for the generation of subsequent corrections and revisions, then, as in Bloom's paradigm, it might have made possible a form of fiction by women capable not only of commenting upon but even of overcoming that impasse. That it did not—nor did any other woman's fiction become canonical in the United States[17]—meant that, again and again, each woman who took up the pen had to confront anew her bleak premonition that, both as writers and as readers, women too easily became isolated islands of symbolic significance, available only to, and decipherable only by, one another.[18] If any Bloomian "meaning" wanders around between women's texts, therefore, it must be precisely this shared apprehension.

On the face of it such statements should appear nothing less than commonsensical, especially to those most recent theorists of reading who combine an increased attentiveness to the meaning-making role of the reader in the deciphering of texts with a recognition of the links between our "reading" of texts and our "reading" of the world and one another. Among them, Bloom himself seems quite clearly to understand this when, in *Kabbalah and Criticism,* he declares: "That which you are, that only can you read" (*KC,* 96). Extrapolating from his description of the processes involved in the reading of literary texts to a larger comment on our ability to take in or decipher those around us, Wolfgang Iser has lately theorized that "we can only make someone else's thought into an absorbing theme for ourselves, provided the virtual background of our own personality can adapt to it."[19] Anticipating such pronouncements in almost everything they have been composing for over a hundred years now, the women who wrote fiction, most especially, translated these observations into the structures of their stories by invoking that single feature which critics like Iser and Bloom still manage so resolutely to ignore: and that is, the crucial importance of the *sex* of the "interpreter" in that process which Nelly Furman has called "the active attribution of significance to formal signifiers."[20] Antedating both Bloom and Iser by over fifty years, for example, Susan Keating Glaspell's 1917 short story "A Jury of Her Peers" explores the necessary (but generally

ignored) gender marking which *must* constitute any definition of "peers" in the complex process of unraveling truth or
meaning. [21]

The opening paragraph of Glaspell's story serves, essentially, to alert the reader to the significations to follow: Martha
Hale, interrupted at her kitchen chores, must drop "everything right where it was" in order to hurry off with her husband and the others. In so doing, "her eye made a scandalized
sweep of her kitchen," noting with distress "that her kitchen
was in no shape for leaving: her bread all ready for mixing,
half the flour sifted and half unsifted." The point, of course, is
that highly unusual circumstances demand this of her, and "it
was no ordinary thing that called her away." When she seats
herself "in the big two-seated buggy" alongside her impatient
farmer husband, the sheriff and his wife, and the county attorney, the story proper begins.

All five drive to a neighboring farm where a murder has
been committed—the farmer strangled, his wife already ar-
rested. The men intend to seek clues to the motive for the
crime, while the women are, ostensibly, simply to gather together the few necessities required by the wife incarcerated in
the town jail. Immediately upon approaching the place, however, the very act of perception becomes sex-coded: the men
look at the house only to talk "about what had happened,"
while the women note the geographical topography which
makes it, repeatedly in the narrative, "a lonesome-looking
place." Once inside, the men "'go upstairs first—then out to
the barn and around there'" in their search for clues (even
though the actual crime took place in the upstairs master
bedroom), while the women are left to the kitchen and parlor. Convinced as they are of "the insignificance of kitchen
things," the men cannot properly attend to what these might
reveal and, instead, seek elsewhere for "'a clue to the motive,'"
so necessary if the county attorney is to make his case. Indeed,
it is the peculiar irony of the story that although the men never
question their attribution of guilt to Minnie Foster, they nonetheless cannot meaningfully interpret this farm wife's world—
her kitchen and parlor. And, arrogantly certain that the women
would not even "'know a clue if they did come upon it,'" they

thereby leave the discovery of the clues, and the consequent unraveling of the motive, to those who do, in fact, command the proper interpretive strategies.

Exploiting the information sketched into the opening, Glaspell has the neighbor, Mrs. Hale, and the sheriff's wife, Mrs. Peters, note, among the supposedly insignificant kitchen things, the unusual, and on a farm unlikely, remnants of kitchen chores left "half done," denoting an interruption of some serious nature. Additionally, where the men could discern no signs of "'anger—or sudden feeling'" to substantiate a motive, the women comprehend the implications of some "fine, even sewing" gone suddenly awry, "'as if she didn't know what she was about!'" Finally, of course, the very drabness of the house, the miserliness of the husband to which it attests, the old and broken stove, the patchwork that has become Minnie Foster's wardrobe—all these make the women uncomfortably aware that to acknowledge fully the meaning of what they are seeing is "'to get her own house to turn against her!'" Discovery by discovery, they destroy the mounting evidence—evidence which the men, at any rate, cannot recognize as such; and, sealing the bond between them as conspirators in saving Minnie Foster, they hide from the men the canary with its neck broken, the penultimate clue to the strangling of a husband who had so systematically destroyed all life, beauty, and music in his wife's environment.

Opposing against one another male and female realms of meaning and activity—the barn and the kitchen—Glaspell's narrative not only invites a semiotic analysis but, indeed, performs that analysis for us. If the absent Minnie Foster is the "transmitter" or "sender" in this schema, then only the women are competent "receivers" or "readers" of her "message," since they alone share not only her context (the supposed insignificance of kitchen things) but, as a result, the conceptual patterns which make up her world. To those outside the shared systems of quilting and knotting, roller towels and bad stoves, with all their symbolic significations, these may appear trivial, even irrelevant to meaning; but to those within the system, they comprise the totality of the message: in this case, a reordering of who in fact has been murdered and, with that, what has constituted the real crime in the story.

For while the two women who visit Minnie Foster's house slowly but surely decipher the symbolic significance of her action—causing her husband's neck to be broken because he had earlier broken her canary's neck—the narrative itself functions, for the reader, as a further decoding of what that symbolic action says about itself. The essential crime in the story, we come to realize, has been the husband's inexorable strangulation, over the years, of Minnie Foster's spirit and personality; and the culpable criminality is the complicity of the women who had permitted the isolation and the loneliness to dominate Minnie Foster's existence: "'I wish I had come over to see Minnie Foster sometimes,'" declares her neighbor guiltily. "'I can see now—' She did not put it into words."

> "I wish you'd seen Minnie Foster," [says Mrs. Hale to the sheriff's wife] "when she wore a white dress with blue ribbons, and stood up there in the choir and sang."
>
> The picture of that girl, the fact that she had lived neighbor to that girl for twenty years, and had let her die for lack of life, was suddenly more than she could bear.
>
> "Oh, I *wish* I'd come over here once in a while!" she cried. "That was a crime! That was a crime! Who's going to punish that?"

The recognition is itself, of course, a kind of punishment. With it comes, as well, another recognition, as Mrs. Peters reveals experiences in her own life of analogous isolation, desperate loneliness, and brutality at the hands of a male. Finally they conclude: "'We all go through the same things—it's all just a different kind of the same thing! If it weren't—why do you and I *understand*? Why do we *know*—what we know this minute?'" By this point the narrative emphasis has shifted: To understand why it is that they know what they now know is for these women to recognize the profoundly sex-linked world of meaning which they inhabit; to discover how specialized is their ability to read that world is to discover anew their own shared isolation within it.

While neither the Gilman nor the Glaspell story necessarily excludes the male as reader—indeed, both in a way are directed specifically at educating him to become a better reader—they do, nonetheless, insist that, however inadvertently, he is a *different kind* of reader and that, where women are concerned, he is often an inadequate reader. In the first instance, because the husband cannot properly diagnose his wife or attend to her reality, the result is horrific: the wife descends into madness. In the second, because the men cannot even recognize as such the very clues for which they search, the ending is a happy one: Minnie Foster is to be set free, no motive having been discovered by which to prosecute her. In both, however, the same point is being made: lacking familiarity with the women's imaginative universe, that universe within which their acts are signs,[22] the men in these stories can neither read nor comprehend the meanings of the women closest to them—and this in spite of the apparent sharing of a common language. It is, in short, a fictive rendering of the dilemma of the woman writer. For while we may all agree that in our daily conversational exchanges men and women speak more or less meaningfully and effectively with one another, thus fostering the illusion of a wholly shared common language, it is also the case that where figurative usage is invoked—that usage which often enough marks the highly specialized language of literature—it "can be inaccessible to all but those who share information about one another's knowledge, beliefs, intentions, and attitudes."[23] Symbolic representations, in other words, depend on a fund of shared recognitions and potential inference. For their intended impact to *take hold* in the reader's imagination, the author simply must, like Minnie Foster, be able to call upon a shared context with her audience; where she cannot, or dare not, she may revert to silence, to the imitation of male forms, or, like the narrator in "The Yellow Wallpaper," to total withdrawal and isolation into madness.

It may be objected, of course, that I have somewhat stretched my argument so as to conflate (or perhaps confuse?) *all* interpretive strategies with language processes, specifically *reading*. But in each instance, it is the survival of the *woman*

as text—Gilman's narrator and Glaspell's Minnie Foster—that
is at stake; and the competence of her reading audience alone
determines the outcome. Thus, in my view, both stories intentionally function as highly specialized language acts (called
"literature") which examine the difficulty inherent in deciphering other highly specialized realms of meaning—in this
case, women's conceptual and symbolic worlds. And further,
the intended emphasis in each is the inaccessibility of female
meaning to male interpretation.[24] The fact that in recent years
each story has increasingly found its way into easily available
textbooks, and hence into the Women's Studies and American
Literature classroom, to be read and enjoyed by teachers and
students of both sexes happily suggests that their fictive premises are attributable not so much to necessity as to contin-
gency.[25] Men can, after all, learn to apprehend the meanings
encoded in texts by and about women—just as women have
learned to become sensitive readers of Shakespeare and Milton, Hemingway and Mailer.[26] Both stories function, in effect,
as a prod to that very process by alerting the reader to the
fundamental problem of "reading" correctly within cohabiting
but differently structured conceptual worlds.

To take seriously the implications of such relearned
reading strategies is to acknowledge that we are embarking
upon a revisionist rereading of our entire literary inheritance
and, in that process, demonstrating the full applicability of
Bloom's second formula for canon-formation. "You are or become what you read" (*KC*, 96). To set ourselves the task of
learning to read a wholly different set of texts will make of us
different kinds of readers (and perhaps different kinds of people
as well). But to set ourselves the task of doing this in a public
way, on behalf of women's texts specifically, engages us—as
the feminists among us have learned—in a challenge to the
inevitable issue of "*authority* . . . in all questions of canon-
formation" (*KC*, 100). It places us, in a sense, in a position
analogous to that of the narrator of "The Yellow Wallpaper,"
bound, if we are to survive, to challenge the (accepted and
generally male) authority who has traditionally wielded the
power to determine what may be written and how it shall be
read. It challenges fundamentally not only the shape of our

canon of major American authors but, indeed, that very "continuity that began in the sixth century B.C. when Homer first became a schoolbook for the Greeks" (*MM*, 33–34).

It is no mere coincidence, therefore, that readers as diverse as Adrienne Rich and Harold Bloom have arrived by various routes at the conclusion that *re-vision* constitutes the key to an ongoing literary history. Whether functioning as ephebe/poet or would-be critic, Bloom's reader, as "revisionist," "strives to *see* again, so as to esteem and *estimate* differently, so as then to *aim* 'correctively'" (*MM*, 4). For Rich, "re-vision" entails "the act of looking back, of seeing with fresh eyes, of entering an old text from a new critical direction."[27] And each, as a result—though from different motives—strives to make the "literary tradition . . . the captive of the revisionary impulse" (*MM*, 36). What Rich and other feminist critics intended by that "re-visionism" has been the subject of this essay: not only would such revisionary rereading open new avenues for comprehending male texts but, as I have argued here, it would, as well, allow us to appreciate the variety of women's literary expression, enabling us to take it into serious account for perhaps the first time rather than, as we do now, writing it off as caprice or exception, the irregularity in an otherwise regular design. Looked at this way, feminist appeals to revisionary rereading, as opposed to Bloom's, offer us all a potential enhancing of our capacity to read the world, our literary texts, and even one another, anew.

To end where I began, then, Bloom's paradigm of poetic history, when applied to women, proves useful only in a negative sense: for by omitting the possibility of poet/mothers from his psychodynamic of literary influence (allowing the feminine only the role of Muse—as composite whore and mother), Bloom effectively masks the fact of an *other* tradition entirely—that in which women taught one another how to read and write about and out of their own unique (and sometimes isolated) contexts. In so doing, however, he points up not only the ignorance informing our literary history as it is currently taught in the schools, but, as well, he pinpoints (however unwittingly) what must be done to change our skewed perceptions: all readers, male and female alike, must be taught first to recognize the existence of a significant body of writing by women in America and, second, they must be encouraged to learn how to read it within its own unique and informing contexts of meaning and symbol. *Re-visionary rereading,* if you will. No more must we impose on future generations of readers the inevitability of Norman Mailer's "terrible confession . . .—I have nothing to say about any of the talented women who write today. . . . I do not seem able to read them."[28] Nor should Bloom himself continue to suffer an inability to express useful "judgment upon . . . the 'literature of Women's Liberation.'"[29]

Notes ■

1. Albert William Levi, "*De Interpretatione:* Cognition and Context in the History of Ideas," *Critical Inquiry* 3, No. 1 (Autumn 1976), 164.

2. Harold Bloom, *A Map of Misreading* (New York, 1975), p. 18 (hereafter cited as *MM*).

3. Bloom, *The Anxiety of Influence: A Theory of Poetry* (New York, 1973), p. 43 (hereafter cited as *AI*).

4. Bloom, *Kabbalah and Criticism* (New York, 1975), p. 106 (hereafter cited as *KC*). This concept is further refined in his *Poetry and Repression: Revisionism from Blake to Stevens* (New Haven, 1976), p. 26, where Bloom describes poems as "defensive processes in constant change, which is to say that poems themselves are *acts of reading.* A poem is . . . a fierce, proleptic debate *with itself,* as well as with precursor poems."

5. *KC*, p. 125; by way of example, and with a kind of Apollonian modesty. Bloom demonstrates his own propensities for misreading, placing himself amid the excellent company of those other Super Misreaders, Blake, Shelley, C. S. Lewis, Charles Williams, and T. S. Eliot (all of whom misread Milton's Satan), and only regrets the fact "that the misreading of Blake and Shelley by Yeats is a lot stronger than the misreading of Blake and Shelley by Bloom" (pp. 125–126).

6. In *Poetry and Repression,* p. 18, Bloom explains that "by 'reading' I intend to mean the work both of poet and of critic, who themselves move from dialectic irony to synecdochal representation as they confront the text before them."

177

7. See, for example, Joanne Feit Diehl's attempt to adapt the Bloomian model to the psychodynamics of women's poetic production in "'Come Slowly—Eden': An Exploration of Women Poets and Their Muse," *Signs* 3, No. 3 (Spring 1978), 572–587; and the objections to that adaptation raised by Lillian Faderman and Louise Bernikow in their Comments, *Signs* 4, No. 1 (Autumn 1978), 188–191 and 191–195, respectively. More recently, Sandra M. Gilbert and Susan Gubar have tried to correct the omission of women writers from Bloom's male-centered literary history in *The Madwoman in the Attic: The Woman Writer and the Nineteenth-Century Literary Imagination* (New Haven, 1979).

8. Virginia Woolf, *A Room of One's Own* (1928; rpt. Harmondsworth, 1972), pp. 9–10, 25–26.

9. Nina Baym, *Woman's Fiction: A Guide to Novels By and About Women in America, 1820–1870* (Ithaca, 1978), p. 32.

10. See Baym, *Woman's Fiction*, pp. 32–33.

11. *Ibid.*, p. 178.

12. I paraphrase rather freely here from some of Baym's acutely perceptive and highly suggestive remarks, p. 14.

13. The problem of audience is complicated by the fact that in nineteenth-century America distinct classes of so-called highbrow and lowbrow readers were emerging, cutting across sex and class lines; and, for each sex, distinctly separate "serious" and "popular" reading materials were also being marketed. Full discussion, however, is beyond the scope of this essay. In its stead, I direct the reader to Henry Nash Smith's clear and concise summation in the introduction chapter to his *Democracy and the Novel: Popular Resistance to Classic American Writers* (New York, 1978), pp. 1–15.

14. Baym, p. 178.

15. From "Books of the Day," Chicago *Times-Herald* (1 June 1899), p. 9; excerpted in Kate Chopin, *The Awakening*, ed. Margaret Culley (New York, 1976), p. 149.

16. Jean Ricardou, "Composition Discomposed," tr. Erica Freiberg, *Critical Inquiry* 3, No. 1 (Autumn 1976), 90.

17. The possible exception here is Harriet Beecher Stowe's *Uncle Tom's Cabin; or, Life Among the Lowly* (1852).

18. If, to some of the separatist advocates in our current wave of New Feminism, this sounds like a wholly acceptable, even happy circumstance, we must nonetheless understand that, for earlier generations of women artists, acceptance within male precincts

conferred the mutually understood marks of success and, in some quarters, vitally needed access to publishing houses, serious critical attention, and even financial independence. That this was *not* the case for the writers of domestic fictions around the middle of the nineteenth century was a fortunate but anomalous circumstance. Insofar as our artist-mothers were separatist, therefore, it was the result of impinging cultural contexts and not (often) of their own choosing.

19. Wolfgang Iser, *The Implied Reader: Patterns of Communication in Prose Fiction from Bunyan to Beckett* (Baltimore, 1974), p. 293.

20. Nelly Furman, "The Study of Women and Language: Comment on Vol. 3, No. 3." *Signs* 4, No. 1 (Autumn 1978), 184.

21. First published in *Every Week* (15 March 1917), the story was then collected in *Best Short Stories of 1917,* ed. Edward O'Brien (London, 1917). My source for the text is Mary Anne Ferguson's *Images of Women in Literature* (Boston, 1973), pp. 370–385; for some reason the story was dropped from Ferguson's 1975 revised edition but, as will be indicated below, it is elsewhere collected. Since there are no textual difficulties involved, I have omitted page references to any specific reprinting.

22. I here paraphrase Clifford Geertz, *The Interpretation of Cultures* (New York, 1973), p. 13, and specifically direct the reader to the parable from Wittgenstein quoted on that same page.

23. Ted Cohen, "Metaphor and the Cultivation of Intimacy," *Critical Inquiry* 5, No. 1 (Autumn 1978), 78.

24. It is significant, I think, that the stories do not suggest any difficulty for the women in apprehending the men's meanings. On the one hand this simply is not relevant to either plot; and on the other, since in each narrative the men clearly control the public realms of discourse, it would, of course, have been incumbent upon the women to learn to understand them. Though masters need not learn the language of their slaves, the reverse is never the case: for survival's sake, oppressed or subdominant groups always study the nuances of meaning and gesture in those who control them.

25. For example, Gilman's "The Yellow Wallpaper" may be found, in addition to the Feminist Press reprinting, in *The Oven Birds: American Women on Womanhood, 1820–1920,* ed. Gail Parker (Garden City, 1972), pp. 317–334; and Glaspell's "A Jury of Her Peers" is reprinted in *American Voices, American Women,* ed. Lee R. Edwards and Arlyn Diamond (New York, 1973), pp. 359–381.

26. That women may have paid a high psychological and emotional price for their ability to read men's texts is beyond the scope of this essay, but I enthusiastically direct the reader to Judith Fetterley's provocative study of the problem in her *The Resisting Reader: A Feminist Approach to American Fiction* (Bloomington, 1978).

27. Adrienne Rich, "When We Dead Awaken: Writing as Re-Vision," *College English* 34, No. 1 (October 1972), 18; rpt. in *Adrienne Rich's Poetry,* ed. Barbara Charlesworth Gelpi and Albert Gelpi (New York, 1975), p. 90.

28. Norman Mailer, "Evaluations—Quick and Expensive Comments on the Talent in the Room," collected in his *Advertisements for Myself* (New York, 1966), pp. 434–435.

29. *MM,* p. 36. What precisely Bloom intends by the phrase is nowhere made clear; for the purposes of this essay, I have assumed that he is referring to the recently increased publication of new titles by women writers.

☐ JUDITH FETTERLEY ■

Reading about Reading:
"The Yellow Wallpaper"

In her "Afterword" to the 1973 Feminist Press Edition of Charlotte Perkins Gilman's "The Yellow Wallpaper," Elaine Hedges
claims that until recently "no one seems to have made the
connection between the insanity and the sex, or sexual role,
of the victim." Nevertheless, it seems likely, as she also suggests, that the content of the story has provided the reason for
its negative reception, outright rejection, and eventual oblit-
eration by a male-dominated literary establishment. Though
not, I would argue, as determinedly instructive as [Susan
Glaspell's] "A Jury of Her Peers," neither, I would equally propose, is "The Yellow Wallpaper" susceptible of a masculinist
reading as, for example, is "The Murders in the Rue Morgue."
That it has taken a generation of feminist critics to make Gilman's story a "classic" bears out the truth of Glaspell's thesis.

Gilman opens her story with language evocative of Poe:
"It is very seldom that mere ordinary people like John and myself secure ancestral halls for the summer." Here we have
echoes of the "scenes of mere household events" which the
narrator of "The Black Cat" wishes "to place before the world,
plainly, succinctly, and without comment." Poe's ancestral
halls serve as image and symbol of the mind of his narrator,
and they serve as analogue for the texts men write and read.
These halls/texts are haunted by the ghosts of women buried
alive within them, hacked to death to produce their effect,

From *Gender and Reading: Essays on Readers, Texts, and Contexts*, ed. Elizabeth A. Flynn and Patrocinio P. Schweickart (Baltimore: Johns Hopkins University Press, 1986), 158–164.

killed by and in the service of the necessities of male art: "The death, then, of a beautiful woman is, unquestionably, the most poetical topic in the world—and equally is it beyond doubt that the lips best suited for such topic are those of a bereaved lover." Die, then, women must so that men may sing. If such self-knowledge ultimately drives Roderick Usher mad, nevertheless as he goes down he takes self and text and sister with him; no other voice is heard, no alternate text remains. No doubt the madness of Poe's narrators reflects that masculine anxiety mentioned earlier, the fear that solipsism, annihilation, nothingness, will be the inevitable result of habitually silencing the other. Yet apparently such anxiety is preferable to the loss of power and control which would accompany giving voice to that other.

Gilman's narrator recognizes that she is in a haunted house, despite the protestations of her John, who is far less up-front than Poe's Roderick. Writing from the point of view of a character trapped in that male text—as if the black cat or Madeline Usher should actually find words and speak—Gilman's narrator shifts the center of attention away from the male mind that has produced the text and directs it instead to the consequences for women's lives of men's control of textuality. For it is precisely at this point that "The Yellow Wallpaper" enters this discussion of the connections between gender and reading. In this text we find the analysis of why who gets to tell the story and what story one is required, allowed, or encouraged to read matter so much, and therefore why in a sexist culture the practice of reading follows the theory proposed by Glaspell. Gilman's story makes clear the connection between male control of textuality and male dominance in other areas, and in it we feel the force behind what is usually passed off as a casual accident of personal preference or justified by invoking "absolute" standards of "universal" value: these are just books I happen to like and I want to share them with you; these are our great texts and you must read them if you want to be literate. As man, husband, and doctor, John controls the narrator's life. That he chooses to make such an issue out of what and how she reads tells us what we need to know about the politics of reading.

In "The Yellow Wallpaper," Gilman argues that male

control of textuality constitutes one of the primary causes of women's madness in a patriarchal culture. Forced to read men's texts, women are forced to become characters in those texts. And since the stories men tell assert as fact what women know to be fiction, not only do women lose the power that comes from authoring; more significantly, they are forced to deny their own reality and to commit in effect a kind of psychic suicide. For Gilman works out in considerable detail the position implicit in "A Jury of Her Peers"—namely, that in a sexist culture the interests of men and women are antithetical, and, thus, the stories each has to tell are not simply alternate versions of reality, they are, rather, radically incompatible. The two stories cannot coexist; if one is accepted as true, then the other must be false, and vice versa. Thus, the struggle for control of textuality is nothing less than the struggle for control over the definition of reality and hence over the definition of sanity and madness. The nameless narrator of Gilman's story has two choices. She can accept her husband's definition of reality, the prime component of which is the proposition that for her to write her own text is "madness" and for her to read his text is "sanity"; that is, she can agree to become a character in his text, accept his definition of sanity, which is madness for her, and thus commit psychic suicide, killing herself into his text to serve his interests. Or she can refuse to read his text, refuse to become a character in it, and insist on writing her own, behavior for which John will define and treat her as mad. Though Gilman herself was able to choose a third alternative, that of writing "The Yellow Wallpaper," she implicitly recognizes that her escape from this dilemma is the exception, not the rule. Though the narrator chooses the second alternative, she does as a result go literally mad and, thus, ironically fulfills the script John has written for her. Nevertheless, in the process she manages to expose the fact of John's fiction and the implications of his insistence on asserting his fiction as fact. And she does, however briefly, force him to become a character in her text.

An appropriate title for the story the narrator writes, as distinct from the story Gilman writes, could well be "John Says." Though the narrator attempts to confide to "dead" paper her alternative view of reality, she is, at least initially, careful to present John's text as well. Thoroughly subject to his control, she writes with the distinct possibility of his discovering her text and consequently escalating her punishment for refusing to accept his text—punishment that includes, among other things, solitary confinement in an attic nursery. She rightly suspects that the treason of a resisting author is more serious than that of a resisting reader; for this reason, in part, she turns the wallpaper into her primary text: what she writes on this paper can not be read by John.

Gilman, however, structures the narrator's reporting of John's text so as to expose its madness. John's definition of sanity requires that his wife neither have nor tell her own story. Presumably the narrator would be released from her prison and even allowed to write again were John sure that she would tell only "true" stories and not "fancies"; "John has cautioned me not to give way to fancy in the least. He says that with my imaginative power and habit of story-making, a nervous weakness like mine is sure to lead to all manner of excited fancies, and that I ought to use my will and good sense to check the tendency. So I try." But, of course, what John labels "fancies" are the narrator's facts: "Still I will proudly declare that there is something queer about it. Else, why should it be let so cheaply? And why have stood so long untenanted? John laughs at me, of course, but one expects that in marriage. John is practical in the extreme"; "that spoils my ghostliness, I am afraid, but I don't care—there is something strange about the house—I can feel it." John's laughter, like that of the husbands in "A Jury of Her Peers," is designed to undermine the narrator's belief in the validity of her own perceptions and to prevent her from writing them down and thus claiming them as true. Indeed, John is "practical in the extreme."

Conversely, John's facts appear rather fanciful. In John's story, he "loves" his wife and everything he does is for her benefit: "He said we came here solely on my account, that I was to have perfect rest and all the air I could get." Yet he denies her request for a room on the first floor with access to the air outside, and confines her instead to the attic, where she can neither sleep nor rest. Later, when she asks to have the attic wallpaper changed, he "took me in his arms and called me a blessed little goose, and said he would go down to the cellar, if I wished, and have it whitewashed into the bargain." Yet while he may be willing to whitewash the cellar, he won't change the attic because "I don't care to renovate the house for a three months' rental." For a three months' confinement, though, John has been willing to rearrange the furniture so as to make her prison ugly: "The furniture in this room is no worse than inharmonious, however, for we had to bring it all from downstairs." Though the narrator is under steady pressure to validate the fiction of John's concern for her—"He is very careful and loving . . . he takes all care from me, and so I feel basely ungrateful not to value it more"—she nevertheless intuits that his "love" is part of her problem: "It is so hard to talk with John about my case, because he is so wise, and because he loves me so." And, in fact her narrative reveals John to be her enemy whose "love" will destroy her.

John's definition of sanity for the narrator, however, includes more than the requirement that she accept his fiction as fact and reject her facts as fancy. In effect, it requires nothing less than she eliminate from herself the subjectivity capable of generating an alternate reality from his. Thus, "John says that the very worst thing I can do is think about my condition," and he designs a treatment calculated to pressure the narrator into concluding that her self not him is the enemy, and calculated also to force her to give her self up. She is denied activity, work, conversation, society, even the opportunity to observe the activity of others. She is to receive no stimulus that might lead to the development of subjectivity. Indeed, one might argue that the narrator overinterprets the wallpaper, the one stimulus in her immediate environment, as a reaction against this sensory deprivation. Nor is the narrator allowed access to her feelings: "I get unreasonably angry with John sometimes. . . . But John says I feel so, I shall neglect proper self-control, so I take plans to control myself." By "proper self-control," John means control to the point of eliminating the self that tells a different story from his. If the narrator learns the exercise of this kind of self-control, John need no longer fear her writing.

The more the narrator "rests," the more exhausted she becomes. Her exhaustion testifies to the energy she devotes to repressing her subjectivity and to the resistance she offers to that effort. In this struggle, "dead" paper provides her with her only vital sign. It constitutes her sole link with her embattled self. Yet because she is imprisoned in John's house and text and because his text has infected her mind, she experiences anxiety, contradiction, and ambivalence in the act of writing. Forced to view her work from the perspective of his text, to see it not as *work* but "work"—the denigrating quotation marks reflecting John's point of view—she finds it increasingly difficult to put pen to paper. Blocked from expressing herself *on* paper, she seeks to express herself *through* paper. Literally, she converts the wall*paper* into her text. Initially the narrator identifies the wallpaper with her prison and reads the text as enemy. The wallpaper represents the condition she is not to think about as she is being driven into it. It is ugly, "one of those sprawling flamboyant patterns committing every artistic sin," disorderly, confusing, and full of contradictions. In struggling to organize the paper into a coherent text, the narrator establishes her artistic self and maintains her link with subjectivity and sanity. Yet the narrator at some level identifies with the wallpaper, as well. Just as she recognizes that John's definition of madness is her idea of sanity, so she recognizes in the wallpaper elements of her own resisting self. Sprawling, flamboyant, sinful, irritating, provoking, outrageous, unheard of—not only do these adjectives describe a female self intolerable to the patriarchy, they are also code words that reflect the masculinist response to the perception of female subjectivity per se. In identifying with the wallpaper and in seeing herself in it, the narrator lets herself out; increasingly, her behavior becomes flamboyant and outrageous. Getting out through the text of the wallpaper, she not surprisingly gets in to the subtext within the text that presents the story of a woman trying to get out.

Possessed by the need to impose order on the "impertinence" of row after row of unmatched breadths and to retain, thus, a sense of the self as orderly and ordering, and at the same time identifying with the monstrously disruptive self implicit in the broken necks and bulbous eyes, the narrator continues to elaborate and revise her text. Her descriptions of the

wallpaper become increasingly detailed and increasingly feminine, reflecting the intuition that her disintegration derives
from the "condition" of being female: "Looked at in one way
each breadth stands alone, the bloated curves and flourishes—
a kind of 'debased Romanesque' with *delirium tremens*—go
waddling up and down in isolated columns of fatuity." Yet the
"delirium tremens" of "isolated columns of fatuity" can serve
as a metaphor for the patterns conventionally assigned to
women's lives and for the "sanity" conventionally prescribed
for women. In the "pointless pattern," the narrator senses the
patriarchal point. Thus, the narrator concentrates on her subtext, "a thing nobody seems to notice but myself," on the pattern behind the pattern, the woman who wants out.

At the end of "The Yellow Wallpaper," we witness a war
between texts. The patriarchal text is a formidable foe; it has
an enormous capacity for maintaining itself: "there are always
new shoots on the fungus"; and its influence is pervasive: "I
find it hovering in the dining-room, skulking in the parlor, hiding the hall, lying in wait for me on the stairs. It gets into my
hair. . . . I thought seriously of burning the house—to reach
the smell." Its repressive power is equally large: "But nobody
could climb through that pattern—it strangles so." Nevertheless, the narrator is sure that her woman "gets out in the daytime." And she is prepared to help her: "I pulled and she
shook, I shook and she pulled, and before morning we had
peeled off yards of that paper."

Despite the narrator's final claim that she has, like the
woman in the paper, "got out at last, " she does not in fact
escape the patriarchal text. Her choice of literal madness may
be as good as or better than the "sanity" prescribed for her by
John, but in going mad she fulfills his script and becomes a
character in his text. Still, going mad gives the narrator temporary sanity. It enables her to articulate her perception of reality and, in particular, to cut through the fiction of John's
love: "He asked me all sorts of questions, too, and pretended
to be very loving and kind. As if I couldn't see through him!"
It also enables her to contact her feelings, the heart of the
subjectivity that John seeks to eliminate. She no longer needs
to project her rage onto the imaginary children who occupied

her prison before her, gouging the floor, ripping the paper, gnawing the bedstead, for she is now herself "angry enough to do something desperate." Angry, she is energized; she has gotten through to and found her work. If the effort to be sane has made her sick, her madness makes her feel "ever so much better."

This relief, however, is only temporary, for the narrator's solution finally validates John's fiction. In his text, female madness results from work that engages the mind and will; from the recognition and expression of feelings, and particularly of anger; in a word, from the existence of a subjectivity capable of generating a different version of reality from his own. And, indeed, the onset of the narrator's literal madness coincides precisely with her expression of these behaviors. More insidious still, through her madness the narrator does not simply become the character John already imagines her to be as part of his definition of feminine nature; she becomes a version of John himself. Mad, the narrator is manipulative, secretive, dishonest; she learns to lie, obscure, and distort. Further, she masters the art of sinister definition; she claims normalcy for herself, labels John "queer," and determines that he needs watching. This desire to duplicate John's text but with the roles reversed determines the narrator's choice of an ending. Wishing to drive John mad, she selects a denouement that will reduce him to a woman seized by a hysterical fainting fit. Temporary success, however, exacts an enormous price, for when John recovers from his faint, he will put her in a prison from which there will be no escape. John has now got his story, the story, embedded in a text like *Jane Eyre,* of the victimized and suffering husband with a mad wife in the attic. John will tell his story, and there will be no alternate text to expose him.

Gilman, however, has exposed John. And in analyzing how men drive women mad through the control of textuality, Gilman has escaped the fate of her narrator and created a text that can help the woman reader to effect a similar escape. The struggle recorded in the text has its analogue in the struggle around and about the text, for nothing less than our sanity and survival is at stake in the issue of what we read.

188

❑ *Note* ∎

In conceptualizing this essay, I have been enormously helped by the work of Annette Kolodny, in particular her "A Map for Rereading: Or, Gender and the Interpretation of Literary Texts" and of Jean E. Kennard in "Convention Coverage, or How to Read Your Own Life." In writing, revising, and rewriting, I owe a large debt to the following readers and writers: Judith Barlow, Susan Kress, Margorie Pryse, Joan Schulz, Patsy Schweickart.

☐ JANICE HANEY-PERITZ ■

Monumental Feminism and Literature's Ancestral House: Another Look at "The Yellow Wallpaper"

In 1973, the Feminist Press brought forth a single volume edition of Charlotte Perkins Gilman's "The Yellow Wallpaper," a short story which had originally appeared in the May 1892 issue of *New England Magazine.* Since William Dean Howells included Gilman's story in his 1920 collection of *Great Modern American Stories,* it can not be said that between 1892 and 1973 "The Yellow Wallpaper" was completely ignored. What can be said, however, is that until 1973, the story's feminist thrust had gone unremarked; even Howells, who was well aware not only of Gilman's involvement in the women's movement but also of her preference for writing "with a purpose," had nothing to say about the provocative feminism of Gilman's text.[1] In the introduction to his 1920 collection, Howells notes the story's chilling horror and then falls silent.[2]

Although brief, Howells's response does place him in a long line of male readers, a line that includes the following: M.D., the anonymous doctor who in an 1892 letter to the Boston *Transcript* complained about the story's morbidity and called for its censure; Horace Scudder, the editor of *The Atlantic Monthly* who in a letter to Gilman claimed to have been made so miserable by the story that he had no other choice than to reject it for publication; Walter Stetson, Gilman's first husband who informed her that he found the story utterly ghastly, more

From *Women's Studies* 12 (1986): 113–128.

horrifying than even Poe's tales of terror;[3] John, the physician-husband of "The Yellow Wallpaper's" narrator who in coming face to face with his mad wife is so astonished that he faints; and last but not least, Milton's Adam, the 'first' man who is represented as being both chilled and horrified by a woman's story-telling:

> Thus *Eve* with Count'nance blithe her story told;
> But in her Cheek distemper flushing glow'd.
> On th'other side, *Adam,* soon as he heard
> The fatal Trespass done by *Eve,* amaz'd,
> Astonied stood and Blank, while horror chill
> Ran through his veins, and all his joints relax'd.[4]

It is this male line of response that the 1973 edition of "The Yellow Wallpaper" seeks to disrupt and displace, implicitly by affixing to the text the imprint of the Feminist Press and explicitly by appending to the text an afterword in which Elaine Hedges reads the story as a "feminist document," as "one of the rare pieces of literature we have by a nineteenth-century woman which directly confronts the sexual politics of the male-female, husband-wife relationship."[5] So effective has this disruption and displacement been that it is not much of an exaggeration to say that during the last ten years, Gilman's short story has assumed monumental proportions, serving at one and the same time the purposes of a memorial and a boundary marker. As a memorial, "The Yellow Wallpaper" is used to remind contemporary readers of the enduring import of the feminist struggle against patriarchal domination; while as a boundary marker, it is used to demarcate the territory appropriate to a feminist literary criticism.[6] Although I am interested in pointing out some of the more troubling implications of a literary criticism in which Gilman's story functions as a feminist monument, before doing so, it is necessary to take another look at "The Yellow Wallpaper" itself.

From beginning to end, "The Yellow Wallpaper" presents itself as the writing of a woman who along with her physician-husband John and her sister-in-law Jennie is spending the summer in what she calls an "ancestral hall," a home away from home which has been secured in the hope that it will prove beneficial to the narrator's health and well-being. In ten diary-like entries that span her three-month stay in this ancestral hall, the narrator not only recounts her interactions with John and Jennie but also describes in detail the yellow wallpaper that covers the walls of a large upstairs room, a room which at one time seems to have been a nursery and, at another, a gymnasium; this summer, however, it has become the master bedroom, a place where the narrator spends much of her time, drawn in, it seems, by the very yellow wallpaper which so repels her.

However, before her attention becomes focused on the wallpaper, the narrator attempts to grasp her situation by naming the kind of place in which she finds herself as well as the kind of place she would like it to be. In the opening lines of her text, she refers to the place as both a "colonial mansion" and an "hereditary estate"; however what she would like to believe is that the place is really a "haunted house." According to the narrator, a haunted house would be "the height of romantic felicity," a place more promising that that which "fate" normally assigns to "mere ordinary people like John and [herself]." Since haunted houses are a peculiarly literary kind of architecture, the narrator's desire for such a place may be associated not only with her desire for writing but also with her interest in the wallpaper; in all cases, what is at issue is the displacement of a colonial inheritance that fate seems to have decreed as her lot.

But even though a haunted house may be desired, the possibility of realizing that desire is seriously in doubt. Not only does John find his wife's desire laughable but in the beginning, the narrator also demurs, afraid that at this point, she is demanding too much too soon of either fate or John. As the narrator sees it, the problem is that John scoffs at "talk of things not to be felt and seen and put down in figures." To John, the narrator's haunted house is nothing; however, so too is her feeling that she is not well. Nevertheless, at the same time that he assures his wife that there is really nothing the matter with her, John also prescribes a regimen which will help her get well; she is not to think about haunted houses or her condition; nor, given her habit of fanciful story-making, is she to write. Instead, she is to eat well, exercise in moderation, and rest as much as she can in the airy upstairs room, the master bedroom.

Ironically, it is precisely because the narrator is patient enough to follow some of the doctor's orders that she finds it necessary to deal with the yellow wallpaper which covers the walls of the master bedroom. At first glance, that wallpaper appears to be nothing more than an error in taste—"one of those sprawling, flamboyant patterns committing every artistic sin"; at second glance, however, more troubling possibilities emerge, for as the narrator notes, the wallpaper's pattern "is dull enough to confuse the eye in following, *pronounced* enough to constantly irritate and provoke study, and when you follow the lame uncertain curves for a little distance they suddenly commit suicide—plunge off at outrageous angles, destroy themselves in *unheard of contradictions*" (emphasis added). Although commentators have seen in this description of the wallpaper a general representation of "the oppressive structures of the society in which [the narrator] finds herself" (*Madwoman,* p. 90), the word "pronounced" as well as the phrase "unheard of contradictions" suggest that the specific oppressive structure at issue is discourse. Furthermore, since we have just been treated to an account of John's discourse on his wife's condition, a discourse based on the unspoken and therefore "unheard of contradiction" that somehow she is both well and ill, we may want to be even more specific and say that the oppressive structure at issue is a man's prescriptive discourse about a woman.

However, as it is described by the narrator, the yellow wallpaper also resembles the text we are reading—that is, it resembles the narrator's own writing. In part, this resemblance can be attributed to the fact that the narrator's writing not only recounts John's prescriptive discourse but also relies on the very binary oppositions which structure that discourse—oppositions like sick and well, the real and the fanciful, order and anarchy, self and other, and male and female. Thus, it is not surprising to find that the narrator's reflections produce a text in which one line of thinking after another "suddenly commits suicide—plung[ing] off at outrageous angles, [and] destroy[ing itself] in unheard of contradictions." For example, although the narrator claims that writing would do her good, she also says that it tires her out. Worse yet, at the very moment that she is writing, she expresses a wish that she were well enough to write. Such contradictions not only betray the narrator's dependence on the oppressive discursive structure we associate with John but also help us to understand why she jumps from one thing to another, producing paragraphs that are usually no more than a few lines in length. Since a discursive line of reasoning based on binary oppositions like sick and well is bound to "destroy" itself in "unheard-of contradictions,"[7] one way the narrator can continue to produce a text that has some pretence to being reasonable is quickly to change the subject, say from her condition to the house or from the wallpaper to John.

If the resemblance between the narrator's writing and John's discourse is disturbing—so much so that it often goes unremarked—it may be because what we want of woman's writing is something different, a realization of that *écriture féminine* which figures so significantly in many contemporary attempts to specify what makes a woman's writing distinctive.[8] However, if we repress this resemblance, we may forget to pose what Luce Irigaray calls "the first question": that is, "how can women analyze their exploitation, [and] inscribe their claims, within an order prescribed by the masculine?" Having posed this first question, Irigaray suggests that one answer might be for a woman "to play with mimesis," to deliberately "resubmit herself to 'ideas,' notably about her, elaborated in/by a masculine logic." Although such miming runs the risk of reproducing a discursive system in which woman as Other is repressed, according to Irigaray, it may also have the uncanny effect of making "'visible' . . . what should have remained hidden: the recovery of a possible operation of the feminine in language."[9]

In "The Yellow Wallpaper," the narrator's labor of miming does seem to produce just some such uncanny effect, for not only does her writing expose the "unheard of contradictions" in a man's prescriptive logic but in dealing with those contradictory impasses by jumping from one thing to another, it also makes the reader aware of gaps in that discursive structure. Furthermore, since the narrator occasionally notes what she might have said but didn't, those gaps can also be read as "unheard of contradictions"; that is, they can be read as the places where the narrator might have contradicted John's prescriptions, if only the woman had a voice to do so. Lacking such a voice, the narrator partially recoups her loss in a writing that is punctuated by the "unsaid," by what remains muted in a discourse which at this point seems to be what matters most.

To the extent that the narrator's writing does indeed display discourse to be what is really the matter, then we can not presume that the text's "hereditary estate" is built on or out of the bedroom of a real anatomical difference between the sexes. However, if the ancestral hall is not to be considered a real "hereditary estate," neither is it to be considered a real "colonial mansion," a place defined by the non-discursive social relations between masters and slaves. Instead the ancestral house must be thought of as in and of what Lacan has called the symbolic order, the order of Language.[10] By committing herself to a writing about discourse and by focusing her attention on the yellow wallpaper as a discursive structure, the narrator has turned what seemed to be a real hereditary and colonial estate into an uncanny place in which no-body is or can be at home—no matter what s/he might say to the contrary.

If "The Yellow Wallpaper" ended at this point, we might consider it a Poesque text, for as Joseph Riddel has convincingly argued, what Poe introduces into American literature is the theme of "de-constructed architecture," a theme which later American writers obsessively repeat.[11] By locating man's ancestral house within the symbolic order, Poe produces a writing that disrupts all non-textual origins which might once have made the house of man seem sufficient to have stood its ground. "The Yellow Wallpaper," however, does not end at this point—the point of deconstructed architecture—for in the text's crucial third section, the narrator discerns something "like a woman stooping down and creeping about behind [the wallpaper's] pattern" and with this vision, the register of the narrator's reading and writing begins to shift from the symbolic to the imaginary.

The possibility of such a shift was foreshadowed in the text's second movement wherein the narrator counterpointed her description of Jennie as the perfect housekeeper with a remark that the wallpaper had some kind of sub-pattern—a "formless sort of figure that seems to skulk about behind that silly and conspicuous front design." However, at this point no explicit splitting of the subject occurred, for the narrator still appeared to be both willing and able to comprehend this nascent imaginary figure within the symbolic order. Instead of apprehending the formless figure as a really different body, the narrator merely noted that from one perspective, the paper's design seemed to be composed of "bloated curves and flourished . . . [which] go waddling up and down in isolated columns of fatuity."

By the end of the third movement, however, the imaginary does emerge as a distinctly different way of seeing and an explicit splitting of the subject does indeed take place. This crisis of sorts seems to be precipitated by a failure of intercourse; first, there is the narrator's unsuccessful attempt to have a "real earnest reasonable talk" with John; then, there is a prohibition—John's refusal to countenance his wife's proposed visit to Henry and Julia; and finally, there is a breakdown in the master bedroom itself as John reads to his wife until her head tires. The scene is now set for the emergence of something different; as the moonlight creeps into the darkened bedroom, something *"like* a woman" is seen "creeping about" behind the wallpaper's outer pattern. Although this vision initiates the shift in register from the symbolic to the imaginary, the explicit splitting of the subject only takes place after the awakened John resolutely dismisses his wife's apprehensions by reminding her that as a doctor, he is the one who really knows. From this point on, the narrator sees things otherwise; now the wallpaper's "outside pattern" is perceived to be bars, while its sub-pattern is perceived to *be* a woman rather than something *"like* a woman."

With the emergence of the imaginary over the symbolic, the narrator's writing takes a different tack than that of a Poe text in which a haunted house is revealed to be nothing more nor less mysterious than a house of fiction. Unable to rest secure in the no-place of such a deconstructed architecture, the narrator of "The Yellow Wallpaper" turns a symbolic house into the haunted house she initially feared might be too much to demand of fate. But even though this haunted house may seem to promise "the height of romantic felicity"—that is, the realization of a self—we should not forget that it is located within and constituted by what Lacan calls the Imaginary.[12]

In Lacanian psychoanalysis, the Imaginary is specified not only by its assimilation to a dual relation between on the one hand, a subject and an image and on the other, a subject and an other but also by the absence or repression of a symbolic mediation between the subject and its doubles. Without mediation, a subject has no access to the symbolic dimension of his or her experience and is therefore driven to establish the imaginary in the real. As a result of this realization, a complicated interplay between the eroticism and aggression characteristic of unmediated dual relations surfaces, as does a child-like transitivism.

In "The Yellow Wallpaper," the emergence of the imaginary as well as its assimilation to an unmediated dual relation first produces a clarity of perception and purpose which temporarily obscures the transitivism the story's ending exposes. As the shadow-woman becomes as "plain as can be," the narrator finds that it is possible to distinguish clearly day from night, sleep from waking, and most importantly, "me" from them. Now the woman who had earlier wondered what one was to do when caught in a contradictory situation knows exactly what she must do: she must free the shadow-woman from the paper-pattern that bars her full self-realization and through identification, bind that woman to herself. However, since this process of identification necessitates the alienation of the subject by and in an image, it engenders not only an implicitly ambivalent relation between the narrator and her imaginary double but also an explicit rivalry between the narrator and John. Perceiving John to be her other, the narrator acts as though she could only win a place for herself at his expense; hence, when she undertakes the realization of her imaginary double, she does so with the express intention of "astonish[ing]." Apparently, the narrator wants to amaze John as Eve did Adam and as the Medusa did many a man.

If at one level this desire seems aggressive, then at another it appears erotic, for what is involved is a transitivism in which it is unclear exactly who is doing what to whom. In-

198

deed, if it can be said that by becoming another woman, the narrator realizes herself in spite of John, then it can also be said the self she realizes is not "her" self but a self engendered by John's demands and desires. On the one hand, the narrator seems to have become the child John has always demanded she be, for like a child, she crawls around the perimeter of the master bedroom, bound by an umbilical cord that keeps her firmly in place. On the other hand, however, the narrator's identification with the wallpaper's shadow-woman seems to have turned her into the woman of John's dreams, for not only did the shadow-woman first appear while John was sleeping, but the narrator also suspects that when all is said and done, she is what John really desires, the secret he would reveal if he were given the opportunity to do so.

In the final words of "The Yellow Wallpaper," the narrator describes how she must crawl over John's astonished body. Like the transitivism of the narrator's 'self-realization,' this closing image displays a conjunction of erotic and aggressive impulses, a conjunction which once again suggests that by identifying herself with the wallpaper's shadow-woman, the narrator has firmly installed herself in the realm of the imaginary, the realm of haunted houses.

Although the text of "The Yellow Wallpaper" ends at this point, the story does not, for it has been repeated by a number of important feminist critics who have seen in "The Yellow Wallpaper" not only an accurate representation of the situation of woman in patriarchal culture but also a model for their own reading and writing practices. While Elaine Hedges can be said to have begun this repetition in her influential afterword to the Feminist Press's edition of the text, it is Sandra Gilbert and Susan Gubar who turn repetition into monumentalism. In their magesterial work, *The Madwoman in the Attic*, Gilbert and Gubar not only repeat the story but also present it as a paradigm, as "*the* story that all literary women would tell if they could speak their 'speechless woe.'" According to Gilbert and Gubar, that woe begins when like the narrator of "The Yellow Wallpaper," a woman writer senses her "parallel confinements" in patriarchal texts, paternal houses, and maternal bodies; and it ends when like the narrator of "The Yellow Wallpaper," the woman writer "escape[s] from her textual/architectual confinement." The way to this end, however, is fraught with difficulty for like the narrator of "The Yellow Wallpaper," the woman writer must engage in a revisionary reading of the handwriting on the wall; only then will she discover her double, the other woman whose passion for escape demands recognition. By identifying with this other woman, the writer effects her liberation from disease into health and thereby finds that she has entered a new space, "the open space of [her] own authority."

Although my reading of "The Yellow Wallpaper" makes me doubt that an imaginary revision and identification can indeed free women from either textual or architectural confinement, at this point I am less interested in questioning the specifics of Gilbert and Gubar's interpretation and more interested in pointing out some of the side-effects such a monumental reading may have on feminist literary criticism. These side effects are particularly evident in two recently published essays that attempt to delineate the nature and function of contemporary Anglo-American feminist literary criticism.

In her 1980 essay entitled "A Map for Re-Reading: Or, Gender and the Interpretation of Literary Texts," Annette Kolodny continues the story of "The Yellow Wallpaper" more or less along the feminist lines set down by Hedges, Gilbert and Gubar. However, since Kolodny is interested in explaining why this feminist story was not recognized as such in its own time, her essay can also help us towards an understanding of what is involved when "The Yellow Wallpaper" is turned into a feminist monument. According to Kolodny, "The Yellow Wallpaper" was unreadable in its own time because neither men nor women readers had access to a tradition or shared context which would have made the "female meaning" of the text clear. Men readers may have been familiar with Poe but Poe would not have prepared them for a woman narrator whose problems are socio-cultural rather than idiosyncratic. On the other hand, women readers may have been familiar with domestic fiction but such fiction would not have prepared them for a narrator whose home life is psychologically disturbing. Although Kolodny contends that Gilman uses the breakdown in communication between the narrator and John to prefigure her story's unreadability, she also declares this unreadability to be historically contingent. Nowadays, it seems, we have the wherewithal to read the story "correctly," for nowadays we have the shared context, if not the tradition we need to identify what she calls the story's "female meaning."

In an attempt to be more precise about how we know what we now know about female meaning, Jean Kennard takes up the story of "The Yellow Wallpaper" once again in her 1981 essay entitled "Convention Coverage or How to Read Your Own Life." Linking the feminism of the 1970s and 1980s with a massive reversal of both literary and non-literary conventions. Kennard claims that a new and explicitly feminist set of interpretive conventions has made it possible to agree on the following ideas: that the oppressive use of power by a male is an instance of patriarchy; that a patriarchal culture's socialization of women makes them ill; that a woman's discomfort in ancestral halls indicates a healthy desire for a room of her own; and that both a revisionary reading of texts and a descent into madness are creditable ways for a woman to find and therefore free herself. Although Kennard shows how all these ideas engender a reading of "The Yellow Wallpaper" as the story of woman's quest for identity within an oppressive patriarchal culture, what I find particularly valuable about her essay is its explicit linking of a certain kind of feminism, a certain kind of feminist literary criticism, and a certain reading of "The Yellow Wallpaper."

But what, we might wonder, accounts for this linking? Here too Kennard may be of assistance, for to some extent she realizes that even before new conventions can be used to engender this feminist reading of "The Yellow Wallpaper," the contemporary critic must recognize and accept the narrator as a double with whom she can identify. However, in so doing, the contemporary critic can be said to repeat the move the narrator of "The Yellow Wallpaper" makes when she discovers and identifies herself with an imaginary woman, the woman behind the wallpaper's pattern. As I see it, this repetition accounts for a number of similarities between the narrator's imaginary mode of conceiving and representing her situation and the seemingly 'new' conventions that support a certain kind of feminist literary criticism which might also be called imaginary. Like the narrator of "The Yellow Wallpaper," some contemporary feminist critics see in literature a really distinctive body which they seek to liberate through identification. Although this body goes by many names, including the woman's story, female meaning, *écriture féminine,* and the maternal subtext, it is usually presented as essential to a viable feminist literary criticism and celebrated as something so distinctive that it shakes, if it does not destroy, the very foundations of patriarchal literature's ancestral house.[13]

However, if it is at all accurate to say that in repeating the story of "The Yellow Wallpaper," this kind of modern feminist criticism displays itself as imaginary, then it seems to me that it behooves us to be more skeptical about what appears to be "the height of romantic felicity."[14] Although inspiring, imaginary feminism is locked into a rivalry with an other, a rivalry that is both erotic and aggressive. As I see it, the transitivism of this dual relation belies not only claims to having identified the woman's story or female meaning but perhaps more importantly, assurances that identification is liberating. Just as we can't be sure who engenders the shadow-woman of "The Yellow Wallpaper," neither can we be sure that the story we're reading is the woman's story; indeed, it may be the case that in reading "The Yellow Wallpaper," we are reading the story of John's demands and desires rather than something distinctively female. If so, then the assurance that identification is liberating becomes highly problematic, for it too appears to be an assurance generated and sanctioned by the very ancestral structure that feminists have found so confining.[15]

In "The Yellow Wallpaper," the narrator does not move out into open country; instead, she turns an ancestral hall into a haunted house and then encrypts herself therein as a fantasy figure.[16] If we wish to consider the result of this turn to be a feminist monument, then perhaps it would be better to read such a monument as a *memento mori* that signifies the death of (a) woman rather than as a memorial that encloses the body essential to a viable feminist literary criticism. Unlike a memorial, a *memento mori* would provoke sympathy rather than identification and in so doing, would encourage us to apprehend the turn to the imaginary not as a model of liberation but as a sign of what may happen when a possible operation of the feminine in *language* is repressed.

If such an apprehension seems an uninspiring alternative for those of us committed to feminism, then I suggest that we look to Gilman rather than to the narrator of "The Yellow Wallpaper" for the inspiration we seek. By representing the narrator as in some sense mad, Gilman can be said to have preferred sympathy to identification, a preference which becomes all the more significant once we recall that much of "The Yellow Wallpaper" is based on Gilman's personal experience. However, Gilman did more than sympathize, for as Dolores Hayden has documented, she also involved herself in efforts to change the material conditions of social existence through the construction of kitchenless houses and feminist apartment hotels—new architectural spaces in which alternative social and discursive relations might emerge.[17] Although those of us interested in literature may find Gilman's concern for the material conditions of social life a troubling defection,[18] it is also quite possible to consider that concern a thoughtful deferral based on a recognition that the prevailing social structure made it idealistic, if not dangerously presumptuous to lay claim to having identified either the woman's story or female meaning. Indeed, it may just be that what Gilman learned in writing and reading "The Yellow Wallpaper" was that as yet, a woman could only *imagine* that she had found herself, for until the material conditions of social life were radically changed, there would be no 'real' way out of mankind's ancestral mansion of many apartments.

☐ Notes ∎

1. When Howells requested permission to include "The Yellow Wallpaper" in his collection, Gilman responded that the story "was no more 'literature' than [her] other stuff, being definitely written with a purpose." See *The Living of Charlotte Perkins Gilman: An Autobiography.* (New York: D. Appleton-Century Company, 1935), p. 121. For evidence of Howells's familiarity with Gilman's interest in the woman question, see p. 113.

2. William Dean Howells, ed., *The Great Modern American Stories* (New York: Boni & Liveright, 1920), p. vii.

3. For the letters by M. D. and Horace Scudder, see *The*

Living of Charlotte Perkins Gilman, cited above, pp. 119–120. For Gilman's account of Walter Stetson's response, see Mary A. Hill, *Charlotte Perkins Gilman: The Making of a Radical Feminist 1860–1896* (Philadelphia: Temple University Press, 1980), p. 186.

4. John Milton, *Paradise Lost,* ed. Merrit Y. Hughes (Indianapolis: Odyssey Press, 1962), p. 226. To my knowledge, no critic has yet noted in print the connection between *Paradise Lost* and the ending of "The Yellow Wallpaper." That connection rests not only on John's response to his 'mad' wife but also on the narrator's statement to John that the "key" to the room is to be found in the garden under a "plantain leaf." In *Paradise Lost,* Eve tells Adam that she first "espi'd" him, "fair indeed and tall/Under a Plantan" (Book IV, 11.477–8). Although a plantain leaf is not exactly the same as a Plantan or plane tree, there is a sound resemblance between the two words as well as an etymological connection by way of *plátano, plátano,* the Spanish words for plane tree. Since I am interested in other matters, I do not deal at length with the connection between "The Yellow Wallpaper" and *Paradise Lost;* nevertheless, I trust that the reader will keep the connection in mind, for it does have a bearing on both my interpretation of the story and my response to critics who read the story as a feminist monument.

5. Elaine Hedges, "Afterword" to Charlotte Perkins Gilman's *The Yellow Wallpaper* (New York: The Feminist Press, 1973), p. 39.

6. Although much of this monumentalizing occurs within classes devoted to women's studies or women's literature, at least three influential publications treat the story as both a memorial and a boundary marker: Sandra Gilbert and Susan Gubar, *The Madwoman in the Attic: The Woman Writer and the Nineteenth-Century Literary Imagination* (New Haven: Yale University Press, 1979), pp. 89–92; Annette Kolodny, "A Map for Rereading: Or, Gender and the Interpretation of Literary Texts," *NLH* 11 (1980), 451–67; and Jean Kennard. "Convention Coverage or How to Read Your Own Life." *NLH* 13 (1981), 69–88. Hereafter, Gilbert and Gubar's book will be cited as *Madwoman.*

7. For a more theoretical explanation of why and how a discourse based on binary oppositions is bound to destroy itself in unheard of contradictions, see the work of Jacques Derrida, especially *Of Grammatology,* trans. Gavatri Spivak (Baltimore: Johns Hopkins University Press, 1976).

8. The term *écriture féminine* names the desired or hypo-

204

thetical specificity of woman's writing: as a concept, it underwrites the work of certain French feminists, most importantly Helene Cixous' "The Laugh of the Medusa," trans. Keith and Paula Cohen, *Signs* 1 (1976), 875–893 and Luce Irigaray's *Ce sexe qui n'en est pas un* (Paris: Minuit, 1977). Portions of Irigaray's text have been translated and printed in *New French Feminisms,* ed. Elaine Marks and Isabelle de Courtivron (Amherst: University of Massachusetts Press, 1980). In both France and America, the concept of *écriture féminine* has occasioned much debate: for a French questioning of the appeal to *écriture féminine,* see "Variations sur des themes communs" in *Questions feministes,* 1 (1977), trans. Yvonne Rochette-Ozzeilo as "Variations on Common Themes" in *New French Feminisms,* pp. 212–230, for Anglo-American responses to the postulated *écriture féminine,* see the following: Ann Rosalind Jones, "Writing the Body: Toward an Understanding of L'Ecriture Feminine." *Feminist Studies* 7 (1981), 247–263; Helene Vivienne Wenzel, "The Text as Body/ Politics: An Appreciation of Monique Wittig's Writings in Context," *Feminist Studies* 7 (1981), 264–287; Carolyn Burke, "Irigaray Through the Looking Glass," *Feminist Studies* 7 (1981), 288–306; Elaine Showalter, "Feminist Criticism in the Wilderness," in *Writing and Sexual Difference,* ed. Elizabeth Abel (Chicago: University of Chicago Press, 1982), pp. 9–35; Mary Jacobus, "The Question of Language: Men and Maxims and *The Mill on the Floss,*" in *Writing and Sexual Difference,* pp. 37–52; and *The Future of Difference,* ed. Hester Eisenstein and Alice Jardine (Boston: G. J. Hall & Co., 1980). As this essay indicates, I am both sympathetic to the utopian political impulse that underwrites appeals to *écriture féminine* and wary of various and sundry claims to having produced or identified a demonstrably feminine writing. Like Mary Jacobus, I think such claims too often "founder on the rock of essentialism (the text as body) [or] gesture towards an avant-garde practice which turns out not to be specific to women"; see Jacobus's essay cited above, p. 37.

9. Luce Irigaray, *Ce sexe qui n'en est pas un,* p. 78 and p. 74 respectively; I am using Mary Jacobus's translation of these passages in her essay "The Question of Language: Men and Maxims and *The Mill on the Floss,*" p. 37 and p. 40 respectively.

10. Although the significance of the Symbolic order is best apprehended in terms of its relationship to what Lacan calls the Imaginary and the Real, it is possible to describe the Symbolic as if it were a determinate space in which the relations between subject and

sign as well as subject and other are mediated by the law of the signifier or the structure of Language. This triadic relation in which the subject is alienated in and by the symbolic mediations of language rests on a necessary separation of the paternal role from the biological father, a separation effected by the subject's awakening not only to the "Name-of-the-Father" but also the general naming function of language. It is this separation which allows me to claim that discourse is a structure in which no-body is or can be at-home; by (dis)placing the subject in a chain of signifiers, the symbolic institutes a double disruption between on the one hand, biological need and articulate demand and on the other, articulate demand and unconscious desire. For a more detailed exposition of the Symbolic order, see the following texts: Jacques Lacan, *The Language of the Self,* trans. Anthony Wilden (New York: Dell, 1968); Jacques Lacan, *Ecrits* (Paris: Editions du Seuil, 1966); jacques Lacan, *Ecrits: A Selection,* translated by Alan Sheridan (New York: W. W. Norton, 1982); Jacques Lacan, *The Four Fundamental Concepts of Psycho-analysis,* ed. Jacques-Alain Miller, trans. Alan Sheridan (New York: W. W. Norton, 1978); Anika Lemaire, *Jacques Lacan,* trans. David Macey (London: Routledge & Kegan Paul, 1977); Samuel Ysseling, "Structuralism and Psychoanalysis in the Work of Jacques Lacan," *International Philosophical Quarterly* 10 (1970), 102–117; Martin Thom, "The Unconscious structured like a language" in *Economy and Society* 5 (1976), 435–469; Fredric Jameson, "Imaginary and Symbolic in Lacan: Marxism, Psychoanalytic Criticism, and the Problem of the Subject." *YFS* 55–56 (1977), 338–395; Richard Wolheim, "The Cabinet of Dr. Lacan," *NYRB* 25 (January 1979), 36–45; Juliet Mitchell, *Psychoanalysis and Feminism* (New York: Random House, 1975), pp. 382–398; Jane Gallop, *The Daughter's Seduction: Feminism and Psychoanalysis* (Ithaca: Cornell University Press, 1982), pp. 1–55; and Juliet Mitchell and Jacqueline Rose, eds., *Feminine Sexuality: Jacques Lacan and the Ecole Freudienne,* trans. Jacqueline Rose (New York: W. W. Norton, 1982).

11. Joseph Riddel, "The Crypt of Edgar Poe," *Boundary* 2, 7 (1979) 117–144; the reference to "de-constructed architecture" appears on p. 125.

12. Although the significance of the Imaginary is best apprehended in terms of its relationship to what Lacan calls the Symbolic and the Real, it is possible to describe the Imaginary as if it were a specific kind of psychic space wherein bodies or forms are related to

one another by means of such basic oppositions as inside-outside and container/contained. Developmentally speaking, the Imaginary originates in what Lacan calls the "mirror stage," that period between six and eighteen months during which the infant becomes aware of its image in the mirror, thereby fixing the self in a line of fiction, a line of imaginary doubles. Although this doubling is the precondition of primary narcissism, it is also the source of human aggression, for in both cases there is a transitivistic substitution of images, an indifferentiation of subject and object which leads the child who hits to imagine that s/he is being hit. For more on the Imaginary, see the works cited in note 10.

13. For the appeal to "the woman's story," see Gilbert and Gubar, *Madwoman;* for the appeal to "female meaning," see not only Annette Kolodny's "A Map to Rereading: Or, Gender and the Interpretation of Literary Texts" but also her more controversial essay, "Dancing Through the Minefield: Some Observations on the Theory, Practice and Politics of a Feminist Literary Criticism," *Feminist Studies* 6 (1980), 1–25; for the appeal to *écriture féminine* as a body, see Helene Cixous's "The Laugh of the Medusa"; for the appeal to a maternal subtext, see Judith Kegan Gardiner's "On Female Identity and Writing by Women," in *Writing and Sexual Difference,* ed. Elizabeth Abel (Chicago: University of Chicago Press, 1982), pp. 177–191. In "Feminist Criticism in the Wilderness," Elaine Showalter distinguishes between feminist critics who appeal to the difference of the woman's body and feminist critics who appeal to the difference of a woman's language, psychology, or culture; in practice, however, much feminist criticism belies the theoretical distinction Showalter makes, for the identification of a woman's language, psychology, or culture is often presented as though it were the discovery of a distinctly feminine body, even though that body may now be defined structurally rather than biologically.

14. Since the imaginary is associated with pre-oedipal relations with the mother, the thrust of Lacanian psychoanalysis is to value the symbolic over the imaginary. Like many other feminists, I do not accept wholeheartedly this value judgment; however, I also do not believe that a simple reversal wherein the imaginary is valued over the symbolic suffices. Thus, I ask for skepticism rather than either denigration or celebration of the imaginary. For a more detailed exploration of the claims of the imaginary and the symbolic as well as an account of Julia Kristeva's attempt to effect a semiotic displace-

ment of the Lacanian Imaginary, see Jane Gallop's *The Daughter's Seduction: Feminism and Psychoanalysis.*

15. Although identity is often considered to be one of the key benefits of the women's liberation movement, it seems to me that the relationship between identity and liberation is much more problematic than we sometimes care to admit. To the extent that identity means being at-one with oneself, then it necessitates the repression of a difference within, a repression which Jacques Derrida sees as characteristic of the phallologocentric discourse of the West. However, even though I am not willing to equate identity with liberation, neither am I willing to claim that it is either possible or desirable to forgo identity again. I ask only for a more skeptical approach to the issue of identity, an approach that refuses to accept wholeheartedly the notion that identity is liberating.

16. For a meditation on crypts and encrypting, especially as they relate to the psychoanalytic processes of introjection and incorporation, see Jacques Derrida's "Fors," trans. Barbara Johnson, *The Georgia Review* 31 (1977), 64–116.

17. Dolores Hayden. *The Grand Domestic Revolution: A History of Feminist Designs for American Homes, Neighborhoods, and Cities* (Cambridge: MIT Press, 1981), pp. 182–277.

18. Some such discomfort may account for Gilbert and Gubar's defensive insistence that "we can be sure that Gilman . . . knew that the cure for female despair must be spiritual as well as physical, aesthetic as well as social" (*Madwoman,* p. 92).

Gendered Doubleness and the "Origins" of Modernist Form

Modernism is an ideal literary territory for the feminist critic to rechart. Pioneering work by critics such as Shari Benstock, Carolyn Burke, Rachel Blau DuPlessis, Susan Stanford Friedman, Sandra Gilbert and Susan Gubar, Jane Marcus, Alicia Ostriker, and Bonnie Kime Scott has given us female modernism: a separate, previously buried or discredited tradition (or anti-tradition) of modernist writing by women that is radically different in many ways from "high canonical male modernism."[1] The important figures so far in this emerging tradition are Djuna Barnes, Isak Dinesen, H.D., Zora Neale Hurston, Amy Lowell, Mina Loy, Katherine Mansfield, Marianne Moore, Jean Rhys, Dorothy Richardson, Gertrude Stein, and, of course, Virginia Woolf. It is characteristic of this female modernism that H. D., in *Trilogy* and *Helen in Egypt,* rejects the pessimistic turn toward hierarchical mythologies in the works of many male modernists, offering instead "the unwritten volume of the new" (*Tribute to the Angels*) and a revisionist, egalitarian mythology in place of the modernist vision of culture we customarily accept as inevitable—the rough beast (Sweeney, Bella/o Cohen), its hour come round at last, slouching through the Waste Land with Achilles, Prufrock, Kurtz, Birkin, Stephen Dedalus, and Quentin Compson toward a scene of monstrous childbirth (made monstrous, of course, by the repression of the mother's body).

From *Tulsa Studies in Women's Literature* 8:1 (Spring 1989): 19–21, 28–35.

The delineation of the (anti-)tradition of female modernism is an invaluable contribution to the work of recharting the modernist territory, as is the analysis of male-female conflict ("the battle of the sexes") and its importance to the history of gender in modernism that Gilbert and Gubar develop in *No Man's Land*.[2] What I would like to offer in this essay, however, is an analysis of two female-signed modernist texts; rather than focusing on a separate female tradition or locating itself in relation to the conflict between male and female modernists, this analysis will consider the ways in which some aspects of modernist *form* common to all (or most) works we would consider modernist—the invention of which we are accustomed to crediting to James, Yeats, Conrad, Pound, Joyce— were just as much birthed by female writers as they were invented by male writers.

I am *not* arguing that female modernists preceded male modernists; I do not think such a competitive model is helpful. Rather, I am arguing that female writers fashioned modernist narrative forms at the same time as the customarily accredited male proto-modernists and modernist originators. Specifically, I will argue that *The Awakening* (1899)* and *The Yellow Wallpaper* (1891),[3] texts not associated with either proto-modernism or the high modernist canon, deploy features of modernist form—decentered subjectivity, rupture of linearity in plot and temporal structure, foregrounding of pre-Oedipal, presymbolic language, stylistic indeterminacy, multiplicity, fragmentation (Woolf's "breaking the sentence" and "breaking the sequence"[4] and Malcolm Bradbury and James McFarlane's "the shock, the violation of expected continuities, the element of decreation and crisis"[5]). Chopin and Gilman use these devices, however, for the purposes of a female modernism in which the ambivalence toward "making it new" involved not a fear of the loss of hegemony, as in the work of the male modernists,[6] but a fear of punishment for a desire for the new, a desire felt to be unallowable.

The problem of definition inevitably arises: What do I

---

*The discussion of *The Awakening* has been omitted with the author's permission.

mean by "modernist form"; what do I mean by "modernism"? I doubt that we can arrive at firm consensual definitions for either term, not only because of the broad diversity of modernist writing and in critical approaches to it, but also because modernist texts typically evade attempts at definition. As Irving Howe says, "modernism does not establish a prevalent style of its own; or if it does, it *denies itself,* thereby ceasing to be modern."[7] I cite Howe here because his statement so pungently deploys the trope of doubleness characteristically invoked by definers of modernism.[8] Maurice Merleau-Ponty's analysis of "Cézanne's Doubt" might stand as a general formulation of this doubleness in both descriptions of modernist form and in modernist form itself:

> His painting was paradoxical: he was pursuing reality without giving up the sensuous surface, with no other guide than the immediate impression of nature, without following the contours, with no outline to enclose the color, with no perspectival or pictorial arrangement. This is what Bernard called Cézanne's suicide: aiming for reality while *denying himself* the means to attain it.[9]

In his own characteristically modernist formulation, Howe suggests that modernism is inevitably inconsistent with itself. I would extend Howe's statement as follows: modernism's "prevalent" or characteristic style is defined by the fact that it continually denies itself, as in modernism's simultaneous assertion and denial of rebellious impulses. The modernist historical moment (approximately 1890 to World War II) was a time in which a radically new order of both gender and class relations, represented by feminist and socialist militancy, appeared possible and, in the early modernist period, perhaps likely.[10] This new order was simultaneously alluring and terrifying—alluring to male modernists in its promise to destroy bankrupt bourgeois culture and to female modernists in its promise, simply, of freedom and autonomy; terrifying to male modernists in its threat to destroy their privileges and to female modernists in its potential for bringing on retribution from a still-empowered patriarchy.

At the same time, just as bourgeois patriarchal capitalism coexisted with and generated the real possibility of its own destruction and replacement, hegemonic bourgeois-patriarchal ideology had a strong hold over both the politics and the modes of representation of the modernists even as they fashioned alternatives to it.[11] The juxtaposed use and transformation of nineteenth-century modes of representation, which characterizes modernist form overall, corresponds, in short, to a simultaneity of desire to "make it new" and fear of what the "new" might be, an ambivalence freighted in opposite ways for male and female modernists (hence "*gendered* doubleness"). This ambivalence—not the dehistoricized "paradox," "tension," or "ambiguity" of the New Criticism, resolved, contained, or unified by an organically coherent form, but a simultaneity of irresolvable contradictions—permeates the language and structures of modernist writing. . . .

"The Yellow Wallpaper," though written earlier than *The Awakening,* represents even more violently the doubleness of female modernism; it moves further from nineteenth-century realist convention toward a Kafkaesque, proto-Surrealist formal stylization that deploys the great power of dream structure to enact self-contradiction. Charlotte Perkins Gilman's narrator is placed by her husband/father in a children's nursery, which has barred windows and "rings and things in the walls," a Kafkaesque detail suggesting a dungeon torture chamber.[12] In the room is a heavy bedstead nailed to the floor, and there is a gate at the head of the stairs. These details are planted among effusions about the beauty of the house and garden, the airiness of the nursery, and the kindness of sinister husband John. Gilman makes heavily sure that we get the point about husband John immediately:

> John laughs at me, of course, but one expects that in marriage. . . . I sometimes fancy that in my condition if I had less opposition and more society and stimulus—but John says the very worst thing I can do is think about my condition, and I confess it always makes me feel bad.

The "opposition" she has, in place of "society and stimulus," is that of her husband and brother, both doctors, to her writing. The writing of the narrative is itself the narrator's most successful act of rebellion. But she cannot feel successful: "I did write for a while in spite of them; but it *does* exhaust me a good deal—having to be so sly about it, or else meet with heavy opposition." The fact that she "disagree[s] with their ideas" and "believe[s] that congenial work, with excitement and change, would do [her] good" does not help her combat that "exhaustion" any more than it alleviates the "bad feeling" induced by thinking about her "condition." They are the exhaustion and bad feeling of self-destructive internal conflict—of needs and impulses pushed back by frightened repression.

Like Edna [in *The Awakening*], Gilman's narrator has internalized the punitive, constraining voices of paternalism so successfully that the story's battle is primarily her own against herself. Unlike Gilman's narrator, Edna does manage to move away from her husband's house. But Edna does not repudiate Léonce openly. She attains whatever freedom she has by regressing to a childish state of irresponsibility. Her suicide, for all its overtones of rebirth and of swimming far out where no woman had swum before, parallels the madness of the narrator in "The Yellow Wallpaper." Edna's move toward freedom, her swimming as far out as she can, only means that she will drown. The similar move of Gilman's narrator, her "breaking out" from behind the "bars" of the wallpaper's "front pattern," means that she is "free" to crawl or, as she puts it, creep around and around the nursery of her imprisonment where, like Edna, she has been forced by her impasse into a state of infantile helplessness. "The Yellow Wallpaper," in its double modernist structure, enacts the same ambivalence as *The Awakening*.[13]

Gilman represents that ambivalence—with an inventiveness, a wealth of detail, and a power of compression that have been insufficiently appreciated—by means of the narrator's symbolic projections onto the wallpaper. When Gilman first mentions the wallpaper, it is already a figure not only of the narrator's repressed anger, sexuality, and desire for freedom, but a figure of that repression itself. The narrator introduced the wallpaper to the reader by calling it "one of those sprawling flamboyant patterns committing every artistic sin." Its color is a "smouldering unclean yellow, strangely faded by the slow-turning sunlight. It is a dull yet lurid orange in some places, a sickly sulphur tint in others." The yellow-orange of anger and sexuality, the patternlessness and flamboyance of freedom are alienated and contaminated for the narrator by her fear of them: the color is "unclean," "repellent, almost revolting"—dangerously angry and sexual—but it is also "faded," "dull," "sickly," nearly extinguished by repression. The "sprawling flamboyant pattern" is "dull enough to confuse the eye in following, pronounced enough to constantly irritate and provoke study": in the very act of condemning the wallpaper's freedom, the narrator cannot help but express her fascination. But expressing it immediately brings on a fit of self-repressive fear. Just after she says the pattern is "pronounced enough to constantly irritate and provoke study," she goes on to say, "and when you follow the lame uncertain curves for a little distance they suddenly commit suicide—plunge off at outrageous angles, destroy themselves in unheard of contradictions." The "sprawling and flamboyant" pattern has suddenly become "lame" and "uncertain." Its dangerous perspectives—its "outrageous angles"—can only "destroy themselves" in the "suicide" of "unheard of contradictions": at once a description of modernist doubleness and a foreshadowing of the story's deadlocked end.

The theme of self-destructive repression is elaborated in the wallpaper's next appearance. The narrator has been lamenting the strictures her husband places on her freedom, just as she had before her first mention of the wallpaper. He has told her she must curb her "imaginative power and habit of story-making"; in other words, her creativity, her impulse to write. She moves from an expression of capitulation to John's strictures—"He says . . . I ought to use my will and good sense to check the tendency. So I try"—to, in rapid sequence, expressions of rebellion, frustration, defeat, and denial:

> I think sometimes that if I were only well enough to write a little it would relieve the press of ideas and rest me.
> But I find I get pretty tired when I try.
> It is so discouraging not to have any advice and companionship about my work. . . .
> I wish I could get well faster.
> But I must not think about that.

The moment she voices that final denial—"I must not think about that"—the narrator turns to the wallpaper: "This paper looks to me as if it *knew* what a vicious influence it had!" The "vicious influence" of her own dangerously rebellious feelings—the feelings that prevent her from "getting well" in a way that will satisfy her husband—combats repression through projection onto the wallpaper. The personified wallpaper's guilty knowledge of its "vicious influence" is, of course, the narrator's own knowledge of both her anger and her fear. The anger and fear combine to impel her to elaborate the theme of suicide (as in *The Awakening*, the ultimate self-cancellation), initiated in the first passage about the wallpaper, now clarified as death by strangulation: "There is a recurrent spot where the pattern lolls like a broken neck and two bulbous eyes stare at you upside down." By the end of the story, the narrator has actually made an unsuccessful attempt to hang herself: "I've got a rope up here that even Jennie did not find. . . . But I forgot I could not reach far without anything to stand on!"

The eyes staring upside down are a wonderful invention. They stare at her, as projections of her own knowledge, but they are dead, both denying that knowledge and killed by it. Further, they are grotesquely "bulbous," swollen with the pressure of unallowable feeling. Knowledge and feeling together have been killed by strangulation, and they are upside down, inverted, products of denial and displacement.

The narrator's relation to the wallpaper progresses as her "condition" deteriorates:

> I don't feel as if it was worth while to turn my hand over for anything, and I'm getting dreadfully fretful and querulous.
> I cry at nothing, and cry most of the time. . . .
> I am alone a good deal just now. . . .
> I'm getting really fond of the room in spite of the wall-paper. Perhaps *because* of the wall-paper.
> It dwells in my mind so!

Only in the wallpaper, which, quite literally, "dwells *in* [her] mind," can she allow herself a displaced representation of her desire for freedom from repressive "laws": "I know a little of the principle of design, and I know this thing was not arranged on any laws of radiation, or alternation, or repetition, or symmetry, or anything else that I ever heard of." She must, of course, separate herself from this representation in a desperate attempt both to check or contain her defiance and to allow it to play itself out: "I determine for the thousandth time that I *will* follow that pointless pattern to some sort of a conclusion." The disapproval evident in her tone here becomes suffused with the disgust attendant on denied sexual feeling. Again, she sees the wallpaper as "bloated," presumably by the pressure of that repressed desire:

> Looked at in one way each breadth stands alone, the bloated curves and flourishes—a kind of "debased Romanesque" with *delirium tremens*—go waddling up and down in isolated columns of fatuity.
> But, on the other hand, they connect diagonally, and the sprawling outlines run off in great slanting waves of optic horror, like a lot of wallowing seaweeds in full chase.

Beneath the surface tone of conventional sarcasm, Gilman's diction develops the narrator's dilemma. "Delirium tremens" suggests madness resulting from excess, revealing again the narrator's fear of her feelings (if she "lets them loose," they will both elude control and become addictive, like liquor to the alcoholic). "Waddling," "sprawling," and "wallowing" suggest female sexual self-disgust. "Debased" and "isolated" describe the narrator's condition itself.

As the narrator's torment intensifies, the wallpaper can no longer provide her release. She is losing the battle against her desire, against herself. The wallpaper's "lack of sequence," its "defiance of law," is now "a constant irritant to a normal mind." She is becoming desperate because she knows she can rely less and less on the defenses she has constructed against what she has projected onto that lawless wallpaper:

> The color is hideous enough, and unreliable enough, and infuriating enough, but the pattern is torturing.
> You think you have mastered it, but just as you get well underway in following, it turns a back-somersault and there

you are. It slaps you in the face, knocks you down, and tramples upon you. It is like a bad dream.

The mastery provided by denial is defeated—slapped, knocked down, and trampled—by the projected "bad dream" her desire has become, which in its "back-somersault" refuses to remain repressed.

The imagery Gilman uses to represent that repressed desire continues to point as often to sexuality as to liberation from repressive "laws." The pattern, in an image that combines both phallic and vaginal suggestions with terrifyingly uncontrolled fecundity, has become a "toadstool in joints, and interminable string of toadstools, budding and sprouting in endless convolutions." Finally, the wallpaper acquires a foul, "yellow" smell, which "creeps all over the house. I find it hovering in the dining-room, skulking in the parlor, hiding in the hall, lying in wait for me on the stairs." The yellow smell of the narrator's sexual disgust is described in the same terms—in its creeping, hovering, skulking, and hiding—as the "woman behind bars," the "back pattern" of the wallpaper, which Gilman has been developing throughout the story in tandem with the "front pattern" of similarly denied desire.[14]

The caged woman first appears as a "kind of sub-pattern in a different shade, a particularly irritating one . . . a strange, provoking, formless sort of figure, that seems to skulk about behind the silly and conspicuous front design." This "sub-pattern" is visible only in "certain lights." At its next appearance, the "sub-pattern" has become, dimly or faintly but unmistakably, "a woman stooping down and creeping about," who only appears in moonlight and who seems to "shake the pattern, just as if she wanted to get out." The moonlight and its effect on the narrator are described in the same terms as the caged woman herself: "I hate to see it sometimes, it creeps so slowly. . . . I kept still and watched the moonlight on that undulating wall-paper till I felt creepy."

Almost immediately—the narrator's deterioration has accelerated—the sub-pattern becomes as constitutive of the wallpaper as the outside pattern. She connects the outside pattern to the male sun and the sub-pattern, again, to the female moon:

There is one marked peculiarity about this paper, a thing nobody seems to notice but myself, and that is that it changes as the light changes.

When the sun shoots in through the east window—I always watch for that first long, straight ray—it changes so quickly that I never can quite believe it.

That is why I watch it always.

By moonlight—the moon shines in all night when there is a moon—I wouldn't know it was the same paper.

At night in any kind of light, in twilight, candle light, lamplight, and worst of all by moonlight, it becomes bars! The outside pattern I mean, and the woman behind it is as plain as can be.

I didn't realize for a long time what the thing was that showed behind, that dim sub-pattern, but now I am quite sure it is a woman.

By daylight she is subdued, quiet. I fancy it is the pattern that keeps her so still. It is so puzzling. It keeps me quiet by the hour.

By the end of the story, the narrator has "resolved" her dilemma by separating entirely from the rebellious self she had projected onto the front pattern and *becoming* the caged woman of the sub-pattern:

I think that woman gets out in the daytime!

And I'll tell you why—privately—I've seen her!

I can see her out of every one of my windows!

It is the same woman, I know, for she is always creeping, and most women do not creep by daylight. . . .

I always lock the door when I creep by daylight.

The ending depicts the narrator's "success" in "freeing" herself, the caged woman, from the prison of the wallpaper, so that she can creep around and around the nursery, tied, presumably, to the nailed-down nursery/marriage bed by her suicide rope:

I don't like to *look* out of the windows even—there are so many of those creeping women, and they creep so fast.

> I wonder if they all come out of that wall-paper as I did?
> But I am securely fastened now by my well-hidden rope—
> you don't get *me* out in the road there!

Superficially, any move to free oneself from behind bars would appear to be a positive step, and the story tempts the reader to see the narrator as having in some way liberated herself. Our sympathy for the caged woman is irresistible. However, everything else in the story negates that reading. The "front pattern," which becomes the prison bars, is in fact (the potential for) the narrator's adult, autonomous self, denied and displaced under extreme duress. That (potential) self becomes a prison for her only when she has lost all hope of attaining it, and any reminder of it, however displaced, torments the defeated, mad, bound, creeping woman she has become instead. It is impossible to think of that creeping woman as any embodiment of liberation, even though she has ripped away "bars" and even though her creeping circuit takes her over, again and again, her husband's fallen body. She has defeated him and his world of anti-female laws at far too great a cost to herself, precisely as Edna "defeated" a similar husband and the same laws by means of her suicide.

To be male, the sun/moon imagery tells us, is to "shoot . . . a long straight ray"; to be female is to creep. Women skulk in their prisons as anyone in prison might, but when they are freed they simply go on skulking, no different outside the bars than within. Gilman has constituted in the remarkable figure of the wallpaper a self-defeating duality of prison and prisoner. Even the narrator hints at the spuriousness of that duality when she says she "lay there for hours trying to decide whether that front pattern and the back pattern really did move together or separately." In our empathy with the narrator, we want her to succeed in "freeing" the woman of the subpattern, who shakes the bars of her prison as if she wants to get out. That image of shaking the bars and coming out from behind them is so compelling that it can make us forget what the bars actually are. There is some indication that Gilman forgets too, since she allows the narrator to connect the front pattern with the male sun. Gilman seems to be participating in the narrator's increasing hopelessness about taking possession of anything that she has projected onto the wallpaper, seeing health and freedom as available only to men. No wonder she finds the front pattern's imprisonment of the back pattern's woman, her hopeless dilemma, "so puzzling"—a statement, in its modesty, of unbearable pathos.

The self-division inscribed in the wallpaper is the story's double figure of ambivalence about female freedom. The front pattern and the back pattern are one—they do "move together" as the narrator suspects. They are the twin offspring of the narrator's internalization of her own oppression. The self stifled by the husband's law erupts onto the wallpaper. When that projection of denied anger, sexuality, and self-assertion becomes too threatening to the self that participates in the stifling, the eruption itself becomes ironically the "prison" whose bars must be pulled down. The woman it imprisons, the victor who escapes from behind the bars, is in fact also the victim—the self-jailer that her capitulation to her husband has made her. The impulse toward freedom invents the wallpaper; the fear of freedom divides it into front and back patterns and sets them at war against one another. Like Chopin, Gilman could write her narrative only by arriving at modernist form.

☐ *Notes* ■

1. Shari Benstock, *Women of the Left Bank: Paris, 1900–1940* (Austin: University of Texas Press, 1986); Carolyn Burke, "Getting Spliced: Modernist Poetry and Sexual Difference," *American Quarterly* 39 (Spring 1987), 98–121, and "Supposed Persons: Modernist Poetry and the Female Subject," *Feminist Studies* 11, No. 1 (1985), 131–48; Rachel Blau DuPlessis, *Writing Beyond the Ending: Narrative Strategies of Twentieth-Century Women Writers* (Bloomington: Indiana University Press, 1985); Susan Stanford Friedman, *Psyche Reborn: The Emergence of H. D.* (Bloomington: Indiana University Press, 1981); Sandra Gilbert and Susan Gubar, *No Man's Land: The Place of the Woman Writer in the Twentieth Century*, Vol. I (New Haven: Yale University Press, 1987); Jane Marcus, *Virginia Woolf and the Languages of Patriarchy* (Bloomington: Indiana University Press, 1987); Alicia Ostriker, *Stealing the Language: The*

Emergence of Women's Poetry in America (Boston: Beacon, 1986); Bonnie Kime Scott, ed., *The Gender of Modernism* (Bloomington: Indiana University Press, 1990).

This is a partial list. For more works on individual women modernists, see the "Selected Bibliographies" in Sandra Gilbert and Susan Gubar, eds., *The Norton Anthology of Literature by Women: The Tradition in English* (New York: Norton, 1985), pp. 2391–430. This selection of modernist women writers has also been influential in confirming the female modernist (anti-)tradition; see "Contents, Modernist Literature," pp. xiii–xvii.

2. Gilbert and Gubar, *No Man's Land*, Chs. 1–2, pp. 3–121.

3. Kate Chopin, *The Awakening: An Authoritative Text, Contexts, Criticism,* ed. Margaret Culley (New York: Norton, 1976); Charlotte Perkins Gilman, *The Yellow Wallpaper* (Old Westbury, New York: Feminist Press, 1973), pp. 37–63. Future references to these editions will appear in the text. I have chosen to discuss *The Awakening and The Yellow Wallpaper* because they are central to the feminist canon. Clearly, these two texts have become crucial to feminist criticism, perhaps more so than any others except *Jane Eyre* and *A Room of One's Own*. We teach them and write about them almost obsessively. Jane Marcus suggested to me that this is the case at least in part because these narratives of rebellion-suicide and rebellion-madness represent for us our divided feelings about our own dangerous enterprise.

I have also chosen these texts because they were written early enough in modernist time (1891 and 1899) to be immune to the charge of merely having adapted a preexisting form, a charge less easy to dismiss for the women modernists of the twenties and thirties. As their dates show, these fictions were written contemporaneously with many of the "seminal" works by men (except, of course, the crucial pre-modernist works by Poe, the Symbolists, Flaubert, and James's work of the nineties, which everyone had access to—Flaubert was particularly important for Chopin, and Gilman's text is clearly indebted to Poe).

In my book in progress on gender, history, and modernism, I develop more fully, especially in its theoretical and historical dimensions, the notion of irresolvable doubleness as a general characteristic of modernist form. For the purposes of this essay, I give that notion more or less the status of a working hypothesis, hoping that it justifies itself in the light it sheds on these texts.

4. Virginia Woolf, *A Room of One's Own* (New York: Harcourt, 1929), p. 141.

5. Malcolm Bradbury and James McFarlane, "The Name and Nature of Modernism," in Bradbury and McFarlane, eds., *Modernism* (New York and Harmondsworth: Penguin, 1976), p. 24.

6. See Sandra Gilbert, "Costumes of the Mind: Transvestism as Metaphor in Modern Literature," *Critical Inquiry* 7, No. 2 (1980), 391–417; see also Gilbert and Gubar, *No Man's Land.*

7. Irving Howe, "The Idea of the Modern," in Howe, ed., *The Idea of the Modern in Literature and the Arts* (New York: Horizon, 1967), p. 13 (emphasis added).

8. For the key theoretical discourse on this use of "doubleness," see Jacques Derrida, *Positions,* trans. Alan Bass (Chicago: University of Chicago Press, 1981):

> Therefore we must proceed using a double gesture, according to a unity that is both systematic and in an of itself divided, a double writing. . . . By means of this double, and precisely stratified, dislodged and dislodging, writing, we must also mark the interval between inversion, which brings low what was high, and the irruptive emergence of a new "concept," a concept that can no longer be, and never could be, included in the previous regime. . . . Neither/nor, that is, *simultaneously* either *or.* . . . (pp. 41–43)

I urge the reader interested in this issue to read the entire passage from pages 41 to 44, to which the above excerpt, selected to emphasize the key ideas and phrases, does not begin to do justice.

9. Maurice Merleau-Ponty, "Cézanne's Doubt," in *Sense and Non-Sense,* trans. Hubert L. Dreyfus and Patricia Allen Dreyfus (Evanston: Northwestern University Press, 1964), p. 12 (emphasis added).

10. I am discussing modernism here in its stricter or Anglo-American sense, therefore bounded approximately by 1890 and World War II (as defined, for example, by Bradbury and McFarlane, though their terminating year is 1930).

11. For some sources of this (highly condensed) analysis, which, in greatly expanded form, is central to my book in progress on gender, history, and modernism, see Theodor Adorno, *Aesthetic Theory,* trans. C. Lenhardt (London and New York: Routledge and Kegan Paul, 1984); Perry Anderson, et al., eds., *Aesthetics and Politics* (London: New Left Books, 1977), which contains key documents

in the Adorno-Benjamin and Brecht-Lukács debates on the politics of modernism; Perry Anderson, "Modernity and Revolution," in Cary Nelson and Lawrence Grossberg, eds., *Marxism and the Interpretation of Culture* (Urbana and Chicago: University of Illinois Press, 1988), pp. 317–33; Fredric Jameson, *The Political Unconscious: Narrative as a Socially Symbolic Act* (Ithaca: Cornell University Press, 1981); Eugene Lunn, *Marxism and Modernism: An Historical Study of Lukács, Brecht, Benjamin and Adorno* (Berkeley: University of California Press, 1982).

12. See Sandra Gilbert and Susan Gubar, *The Madwoman in the Attic: The Woman Writer and the Nineteenth-Century Literary Imagination* (New Haven: Yale University Press, 1979), p. 90.

13. For other (partly congruent, partly divergent) feminist analyses of "The Yellow Wallpaper," see Gillian Brown, "The Empire of Agoraphobia," *Representations* 20 (Fall 1987), 134–57; Gilbert and Gubar, *Madwoman*, pp. 89–92; Janice Haney-Peritz, "Monumental Feminism and Literature's Ancestral House: Another Look at 'The Yellow Wallpaper,'" *Women's Studies* 12, No. 2 (1986), 113–28; Elaine R. Hedges, Afterword, in Gilman, *The Yellow Wallpaper;* Jean E. Kennard, "Convention Coverage or How to Read Your Own Life," *New Literary History* 8, No. 1 (1981), 69–88; and Annette Kolodny, "A Map for Rereading: Or, Gender and the Interpretation of Literary Texts," *New Literary History* 11, No. 3 (1980), 451–67.

14. The "back pattern," in its position "underneath" or "behind" the masculinist "front pattern," is suggestive of alienated feminine sexuality: the narrator links her negated sexuality to her defeated victimhood, "freeing" the "front pattern" altogether from contaminating feminine embodiment.

Additionally, Gillian Brown, in "The Empire of Agoraphobia," analyzing the story in relation to domesticity and the market economy, also finds that the front and back patterns "move together" for the narrator: "The protagonist of 'The Yellow Wallpaper' withdraws into the world she sees in the wallpaper; oblivious to all else, she becomes indistinguishable from the paper *and* the woman she imagines behind it" (p. 138, emphasis added).

☐ SUSAN S. LANSER ■

Feminist Criticism, "The Yellow Wallpaper," and the Politics of Color in America

> "The difference between mad people and sane people,"
> Brave Orchid explained to the children, "is that sane
> people have variety when they talk-story. Mad people
> have only one story that they talk over and over."
> —MAXINE HONG KINGSTON, *The Woman Warrior:*
> *Memoirs of a Girlhood among Ghosts*

In 1973, a new publishing house with the brave name of The Feminist Press reprinted in a slim volume Charlotte Perkins Gilman's "The Yellow Wallpaper," first published in 1892 and out of print for half a century. It is the story of an unnamed woman confined by her doctor-husband to an attic nursery with barred windows and a bolted-down bed. Forbidden to write, the narrator-protagonist becomes obsessed with the room's wallpaper, which she finds first repellent and then riveting; on its chaotic surface she eventually deciphers an imprisoned woman whom she attempts to liberate by peeling the paper off the wall. This brilliant tale of a white, middle-class wife driven mad by a patriarchy controlling her "for her own good" has become an American feminist classic; in 1987, the Feminist Press edition numbered among the ten best-selling works of fiction published by a university press.[1]

The canonization of "The Yellow Wallpaper" is an obvious sign of the degree to which contemporary feminism has

From *Feminist Studies* 15:3 (Fall 1989): 415–441.

transformed the study of literature. But Gilman's story is not simply one to which feminists have "applied" ourselves; it is one of the texts through which white, American academic feminist criticism has constituted its terms.[2] My purpose here is to take stock of this criticism through the legacy of "The Yellow Wallpaper" in order to honor the work each has fostered and to call into question the status of Gilman's story—and the story of academic feminist criticism—as sacred texts.[3] In this process I am working from the inside, challenging my own reading of "The Yellow Wallpaper," which had deepened but not changed direction since 1973.

My inquiry will make explicit use of six well-known studies of "The Yellow Wallpaper," but I consider these six to articulate an interpretation shared by a much larger feminist community. The pieces I have in mind are written by Elaine Hedges, Sandra Gilbert and Susan Gubar, Annette Kolodny, Jean Kennard, Paula Treichler, and Judith Fetterley, respectively, and their publication dates span from 1973 to 1986.[4] Reading these essays as a body, I am struck by a coherence that testifies to a profound unity in white, American feminist criticism across apparent diversity.[5] That is, although Hedges is concerned primarily with biography, Gilbert and Gubar with female authorship, Treichler with textual form, and Fetterley, Kolodny, and Kennard with interpretation, and although each discussion illuminates the text in certain unique ways, the six readings are almost wholly compatible, with one point of difference which is never identified as such and to which I will return. I will also return later to the significance of this redundancy and to the curiously unchallenged, routine elision from nearly all the discussion of one of the story's key tropes.

The theoretical positions that "The Yellow Wallpaper" helped to shape and perhaps to reify may be clearer if we recall some of the critical claims with which U.S. academic feminist criticism began. In the late sixties and early seventies, some academic women, most of them trained in Anglo-American methods and texts, began to take a new look at those works by men and a few white women that comprised the standard curriculum. The earliest scholarship—Kathryn Rogers's *The Troublesome Helpmate* (1966), Mary Ellmann's *Thinking about Women* (1968), Kate Millett's *Sexual Politics* (1970),

226

Elaine Showalter's "Women Writers and the Double Standard" (in *Woman in Sexist Society,* 1971)—was asserting against prevailing New Critical neutralities that literature is deeply political, indeed steeped in (patriarchal) ideology. Ideology, feminists argued, makes what is cultural seem natural and inevitable, and what had come to seem natural and inevitable to literary studies was that its own methods and great books transcended ideology.[6]

This conception of literature as a privileged medium for universal truths was defended by the counterclaim that those who found a work's content disturbing or offensive were letting their "biases" distract them from the aesthetic of literature.[7] Feminist criticism was bound to challenge this marginalization of social content and to argue that literary works both reflect and constitute structures of gender and power. In making this challenge, feminist criticism was implying that canonical literature was not simply *mimesis,* a mirror or the way things are or the way men and women are, but *semiosis*—a complex system of conventional (androcentric) tropes. And by questioning the premises of the discipline, feminists were of course arguing that criticism, too, is political, that no methodology is neutral, and that literary practice is shaped by cultural imperatives to serve particular ends.[8] Although the word "deconstruction" was not yet in currency, these feminist premises inaugurated the first major opposition to both (old) scholarly and (New) critical practices, generating what has become the most widespread deconstructive imperative in the American academy.

Yet the feminist project involved, as Gayle Greene and Coppélia Kahn have put it, not only "deconstructing dominant male patterns of thought and social practice" but also "reconstructing female experience previously hidden or overlooked."[9] In the early 1970s, the rediscovery of "lost" works like "The Yellow Wallpaper," Kate Chopin's *The Awakening,* and Susan Glaspell's "A Jury of Her Peers" offered not only welcome respite from unladylike assaults on patriarchal practices and from discouraging expositions of androcentric "images of women in literature" but also an exhilarating basis for reconstructing literary theory and literary history. The fact that these works which feminists now found so exciting and powerful had been denounced, ignored, or suppressed seemed virtual proof of the claim that literature, criticism, and history were political. The editor of the *Atlantic Monthly* had rejected "The Yellow Wallpaper" because "I could not forgive myself if I made others as miserable as I have made myself!"[10] Even when William Dean Howells reprinted Gilman's story in 1920 he wrote that it was "terrible and too wholly dire," "too terribly good to be printed."[11] Feminists could argue convincingly that Gilman's contemporaries, schooled on the "terrible" and "wholly dire" tales of Poe, were surely balking at something more particular: the "graphic" representation of "raving lunacy" in a middle-class mother and wife that revealed the rage of the woman on a pedestal.[12]

As a tale openly preoccupied with questions of authorship, interpretation, and textuality, "The Yellow Wallpaper" quickly assumed a place of privilege among rediscovered feminist works, raising basic questions about writing and reading as gendered practices. The narrator's double-voiced discourse—the ironic understatements, asides, hedges, and negations through which she asserts herself against the power of John's voice—came for some critics to represent "women's language" or the "language of the powerless."[13] With its discontinuities and staccato paragraphs Gilman's narrative raised the controversial question of a female aesthetic; and the "lame uncertain curves," "outrageous angles," and "unheard of contradictions" of the wallpaper came for many critics to symbolize both Gilman's text and, by extension, the particularity of female form.[14] The story also challenged theories of genius that denied the material conditions—social, economic, psychological, and literary—that make writing (im)possible, helping feminists to turn questions like "Where is your Shakespeare?" back upon the questioners. Gilbert and Gubar, for example, saw in the narrator's struggles against censorship "*the* story that all literary women would tell if they could speak their 'speechless woe.'"[15]

"The Yellow Wallpaper" has been evoked most frequently, however, to theorize about reading through the lens of a "female" consciousness. Gilman's story has been a particularly congenial medium for such a re-vision not only because the narrator herself engages in a form of feminist interpretation when she tries to read the paper on her wall but also because turn-of-the-century readers seem to have ignored or avoided the connection between the narrator's condition and patriarchal politics, instead praising the story for its keenly accurate "case study" of a presumably inherited insanity. In the contemporary feminist reading, on the other hand, sexual oppression is evident from the start: the phrase "John says" heads a litany of "benevolent" prescriptions that keep the narrator infantilized, immobilized, and bored literally out of her mind. Reading or writing her self upon the wallpaper allows the narrator, as Paula Treichler puts it, to "escape" her husband's "sentence" and to achieve the limited freedom of madness which, virtually all these critics have agreed, constitutes a kind of sanity in the face of the insanity of male dominance.

This reading not only recuperated "The Yellow Wallpaper" as a feminist text but also reconstituted the terms of interpretation itself. Annette Kolodny theorized that emerging feminist consciousness made possible a new, female-centered interpretive paradigm that did not exist for male critics at the turn of the century. Defining that paradigm more specifically, Jean Kennard maintained that the circulation of feminist conventions associated with four particular concepts—"patriarchy, madness, space, quest"—virtually ensured the reading that took place in the 1970s. Furthermore, the premise that "we engage not texts but paradigms,"[16] as Kolodny puts it in another essay, explodes the belief that we are reading what is "there." Reading becomes the product of those conventions or strategies we have learned through an "interpretive community"—Stanley Fish's term to which Kolodny and Kennard give political force; to read is to reproduce a text according to this learned system or code.

These gender-based and openly ideological theories presented a radical challenge to an academic community in which "close reading" has remained the predominant critical act. A theory of meaning grounded in the politics of reading destabilizes assumptions of interpretive validity and shifts the emphasis to the contexts in which meanings are produced. A text like "The Yellow Wallpaper" showed that to the extent that we remain unaware of our interpretive conventions, it is difficult to distinguish "*what* we read" from "*how* we have learned to read it."[17] We experience meaning as given in "the text itself." When alternative paradigms inform our reading, we are able to read texts differently or, to put it more strongly, to read different texts. This means that traditional works may be transformed through different interpretive strategies into new literature just as patriarchy's "terrible" and repellent "Yellow Wallpaper" was dramatically transformed into feminism's endlessly fascinating tale.

It is, I believe, this powerful theoretical achievement occasioned by "The Yellow Wallpaper" that has led so much critical writing on the story to a triumphant conclusion despite the narrator's own unhappy fate. I have found it striking that discussions of the text so frequently end by distinguishing the doomed and "mad" narrator, who could not write her way out of the partriarchal prisonhouse, from the same survivor Charlotte Perkins Gilman, who could.[18] The crucial shift from narrator to author, from story to text, may also serve to wrest readers from an unacknowledged overidentification with the narrator-protagonist. For just as the narrator's initial horror at the wallpaper is mirrored in the earlier critics' horror at Gilman's text, so now-traditional feminist rereadings may be reproducing the narrator's next move: her relentless pursuit of a single meaning on the wall. I want to go further still and suggest that feminist criticism's own persistent return to the "Wallpaper"—indeed, to specific aspects of the "Wallpaper"— signifies a somewhat uncomfortable need to isolate and validate a particular female experience, a particular relationship between reader and writer, and a particular notion of subjectivity as bases for the writing and reading of (women's) texts. Fully acknowledging the necessity of the feminist reading of "The Yellow Wallpaper" which I too have produced and perpetuated for many years, I now wonder whether many of us have repeated the gesture of the narrator who "*will* follow that pointless pattern to some sort of conclusion"—who will read until she finds what she is looking for—no less and no more. Although—or because—we have read "The Yellow Wallpaper" over and over, we may have stopped short, and our readings, like the narrator's, may have reduced the text's complexity to what we need most: our own image reflected back to us.

Let me return to the narrator's reading of the paper in order to clarify this claim. The narrator is faced with an unreadable text, a text for which none of her interpretive strategies is adequate. At first she is confounded by its contradictory style: it is "flamboyant" and "pronounced," yet also "lame," "uncertain," and "dull." Then she notices different constructions in different places. In one "recurrent spot" the pattern "lolls," in another place "two breadths didn't match," and elsewhere the pattern is torn off. She tries to organize the paper geometrically but cannot grasp its laws: it is marked vertically by "bloated curves and flourishes," diagonally by "slanting waves of optic horror like a lot of wallowing seaweeds in full chase," and horizontally by an order she cannot even figure out. There is even a centrifugal pattern in which "the interminable grotesques seem to form around a common centre and rush off in headlong plunges of equal distraction." Still later, she notices that the paper changes and moves according to different kinds of light. And it has a color and smell that she is never able to account for. But from all this indecipherability, from this immensely complicated text, the narrator—by night, no less—finally discerns a single image, a woman behind bars, which she then expands to represent the whole. This is hardly a matter of "correct" reading, then, but of fixing and reducing possibilities, finding a space of text on which she can locate whatever self-projection will enable her to move from "John says" to "I want." The very excess of description of the wallpaper, and the fact that it continues after the narrator has first identified the woman behind the bars, actually foregrounds the reductiveness of her interpretive act. And if the narrator, having liberated the paper woman, can only imagine tying her up again, is it possible that our reading too has freed us momentarily only to bind us once more?

Most feminist analyses of "The Yellow Wallpaper" have in fact recognized this bind without pursuing it. Gilbert and Gubar see the paper as "otherwise incomprehensible hieroglyphics" onto which the narrator projects "her own passion for escape."[19] Treichler notes that the wallpaper "remains indeterminate, complex, unresolved, disturbing."[20] Even Fetterley, who seems least to question the narrator's enterprise, speaks of the narrator's "need to impose order on the 'imper-

tinence' of row after row of unmatched breadths."[21] Kolodny
implicates all critical practice when she says that the narrator
obsessively and jealously "emphasiz[es] one section of the pattern while repressing others, reorganiz[es] and regroup[s] past
impressions into newer, more fully realized configurations—
as one might with any complex formal text."[22] And Kennard
states openly that much more goes on in both the wallpaper
and the story than is present in the standard account and that
the feminist reading of "The Yellow Wallpaper" is far from the
final and "correct" one that replaces the patriarchal "misreading" once and for all. Still, Kennard's position in 1981 was that
"despite all these objections . . . it is the feminist reading I
teach my students and which I believe is the most fruitful";
although suggesting that a new interpretive community might
read this and other stories differently, she declined to pursue
the possibility on grounds of insufficient "space"—a term that
evokes the narrator's own confinement.[23] In light of these
more-or-less conscious recognitions that the wallpaper remains
incompletely read, the redundancy of feminist readings of Gilman's story might well constitute the return of the repressed.

I want to suggest that this repressed possibility of another reading reveals larger contradictions in white, academic
feminist theories and practices. Earlier I named as the two
basic gestures of U.S. feminist criticism "deconstructing dominant male patterns of thought and social practice" and "reconstructing female experience previously hidden or overlooked."
This formulation posits as oppositional an essentially false and
problematic "male" system beneath which essentially true and
unproblematic "female" essences can be recovered—just as
the figure of the woman can presumably be recovered from
beneath the patriarchal pattern on Gilman's narrator's wall (a
presumption to which I will return). In designating gender as
the foundation for two very different critical activities, feminist criticism has embraced contradictory theories of literature, proceeding as if men's writings were ideological sign
systems and women's writings were representations of truth,
reading men's or masculinist texts with resistance and
women's or feminist texts with empathy. If, however, we acknowledge the participation of women writers and readers in
"dominant . . . patterns of thought and social practice," then

perhaps our own patterns must also be deconstructed if we are to recover meanings still "hidden or overlooked." We would then have to apply even to feminist texts and theories the premises I described earlier: that literature and criticism are collusive with ideology, that texts are sign systems rather than simple mirrors, that authors cannot guarantee their meanings, that interpretation is dependent on a critical community, and that our own literary histories are also fictional. The consequent rereading of texts like "The Yellow Wallpaper" might, in turn, alter our critical premises.

It is understandably difficult to imagine deconstructing something one has experienced as a radically reconstructive enterprise. This may be one reason—though other reasons suggest more disturbing complicities—why many of us have often accepted in principle but ignored in practice the deconstructive challenges that have emerged from within feminism itself. Some of the most radical of these challenges have come from women of color, poor women, and lesbians, frequently with primary allegiances outside the university, who have exposed in what has passed for feminist criticism blindnesses as serious as those to which feminism was objecting. In 1977, for example, Barbara Smith identified racism in some of the writings on which feminist criticism had been founded; in 1980, Alice Walker told the National Women's Studies Association of her inability to convince the author of *The Female Imagination* to consider the imaginations of women who are Black; in 1978, Judy Grahn noted the "scathing letters" the Women's Press Collective received when it published Sharon Isabell's *Yesterday's Lessons* without standardizing the English for a middle-class readership; at the 1976 Modern Language Association meetings and later in *Signs,* Adrienne Rich pointed to the erasure of lesbian identity from feminist classrooms even when the writers being taught were in fact lesbians; in the early 1980s, collections like *This Bridge Called My Back: Writings by Radical Women of Color* and *Nice Jewish Girls: A Lesbian Anthology* insisted that not all American writers are Black or white; they are also Latina, Asian, Arab, Jewish, Indian.[24]

The suppression of difference has affected the critical canon as well. In 1980, for example, *Feminist Studies* published Annette Kolodny's groundbreaking "Dancing Through the Minefield: Some Observations on the Theory, Practice, and Politics of a Feminist Literary Criticism" to which my own elucidation of feminist premises owes a considerable and respectful debt. In Fall, 1982, *Feminist Studies* published three responses to Kolodny, criticizing the essay not only for classism, racism, and homophobia in the selection and use of women's texts but also for perpetuating patriarchal academic values and methodologies. One respondent, Elly Bulkin, identified as a crucial problem "the very social and ethical issue of *which* women get published by whom and why—of what even gets *recognized* as 'feminist literary criticism.'"[25] Bulkin might have been speaking prophetically, because none of the three responses was included when "Dancing Through the Minefield" was anthologized.[26]

All these challenges occurred during the same years in which the standard feminist reading of "The Yellow Wallpaper" was produced and reproduced. Yet none of us seems to have noticed that virtually all feminist discourse on "The Yellow Wallpaper" has come from white academics and that it has failed to question the story's status as a universal woman's text. A feminist criticism willing to deconstruct its own practices would reexamine our exclusive reading of "The Yellow Wallpaper," rethink the implications of its canonization, and acknowledge both the text's position in ideology and our own. That a hard look at feminism's "Yellow Wallpaper" is now possible is already evident by the publication in 1986 of separate essays by Janice Haney-Peritz and Mary Jacobus which use psychoanalytic theory to expose the limits of both the narrator's and feminist criticism's interpretive acts.[27] I believe we have also entered a moment not only of historical possibility but of historical urgency to stop reading a privileged, white, New England woman's text as simply—a woman's text. If our traditional gesture has been to repeat the narrator's own act of *under*reading, of seeing too little, I want now to risk *over*reading, seeing perhaps too much. My reading will make use of textual details that traditional feminist interpretations have tended to ignore, but I do not propose it as a coherent or final reading; I believe no such reading is either possible or desirable and that one important message of "The Yellow Wallpaper" is precisely that. At the same time, I concur with Chris Weedon when she insists that meanings, however provisional, "have real effects."[28]

One way back to "The Yellow Wallpaper" is through the yellow wallpaper itself: through what I mentioned earlier as the point of difference and the point of silence in the feminist interpretations I have been discussing here. I begin with the difference that occurs within and among otherwise consistent readings when critics try to identify just whose text or what kind of text the wallpaper represents. For Hedges and for Gilbert and Gubar, the wallpaper signifies the oppressive situation in which the woman finds herself; for Kolodny the paper is the narrator's "own psyche writ large"; for Treichler it is a paradigm of women's writing; and for Fetterley it is the husband's patriarchal text which, however, becomes increasingly feminine in form. Haney-Peritz alone confronts the contradiction, seeing the wallpaper as both John's and his wife's discourse, because the narrator "relies on the very binary oppositions" that structure John's text.[29]

It seems, then, that just as it is impossible for the narrator to get "that top pattern . . . off from the under one," so it is impossible to separate the text of a culture from the text of an individual, to free female subjectivity from the patriarchal text. Far from being antitheses, the patriarchal text and the woman's text are in some sense one. And if the narrator's text is also the text of her culture, then it is no wonder that the wallpaper exceeds her ability to decipher it. If, instead of grasping as she does for the single familiar and self-confirming figure in the text, we understand the wallpaper as a pastiche of disturbed and conflicting discourses, then perhaps the wallpaper's chaos represents what the narrator (and we ourselves) must refuse in order to construct the singular figure of the woman behind bars: the foreign and alien images that threaten to "knock [her] down, and trample upon [her]," images that as a white, middle-class woman of limited consciousness she may neither want nor know how to read. In avoiding certain meanings while "liberating" others from the text, in struggling for the illusion of a fully "conscious knowing, unified, rational subject,"[30] is the narrator going "mad" not only from confinement, or from the effort to interpret, but also from the effort to repress? In this case, are those of us who reproduce the narrator's reading also attempting to constitute an essential female subject by shunting aside textual meanings that expose feminism's own precarious and conflicted identity? If the narrator is reading in the paper the text of her own unconscious, an unconscious chaotic with unspeakable fears and desires, is not the unconscious, by the very nature of ideology, political?

If we accept the culturally contingent and incomplete nature of readings guaranteed only by the narrator's consciousness, then perhaps we can find in the yellow wallpaper, to literalize a metaphor of Adrienne Rich, "a whole new psychic geography to be explored."[31] For in privileging the questions of reading and writing as essential "woman questions," feminist criticism has been led to the paper while suppressing the politically charged adjective that colors it.[32] If we locate Gilman's story within the "psychic geography" of Anglo-America at the turn of the century, we locate it in a culture obsessively preoccupied with race as the foundation of character, a culture desperate to maintain Aryan superiority in the face of massive immigrations from Southern and Eastern Europe, a culture openly anti-Semitic, anti-Asian, anti-Catholic, and Jim Crow. In New England, where Gilman was born and raised, agricultural decline, native emigration, and soaring immigrant birth rates had generated "a distrust of the immigrant [that] reached the proportions of a movement in the 1880's and 1890's."[33] In California, where Gilman lived while writing "The Yellow Wallpaper," mass anxiety about the "Yellow Peril" had already yielded such legislation as the Chinese Exclusion Act of 1882. Across the United States, newly formed groups were calling for selective breeding, restricted entry, and "American Protection" of various kinds. White, Christian, American-born intellectuals—novelists, political scientists, economists, sociologists, crusaders for social reform—not only shared this racial anxiety but, as John Higham puts it, "blazed the way for ordinary nativists" by giving popular racism an "intellectual respectability."[34]

These "intellectual" writings often justified the rejection and exclusion of immigrants in terms graphically physical. The immigrants were "human garbage": "'hirsute, low-browed, big-faced persons of obviously low mentality,'" "'oxlike men'" who "'belong in skins, in wattled huts at the close of the Great Ice age,'" ready to "'pollute'" America with "'non-Aryan elements.'" Owen Wister's popular Westerns were built on the premise that the eastern United States was being ruined by the "'debased and mongrel'" immigrants, "'encroaching alien vermin, that turn our cities to Babels and our citizenship to a hybrid farce, who degrade our commonwealth from a nation into something half pawn-shop, half-broker's office.'" In the "'clean cattle country,'" on the other hand, one did not find "'many Poles or Huns or Russian Jews,'" because pioneering required particular Anglo-Saxon abilities. Jack London describes a Jewish character as "'yellow as a sick persimmon'" and laments America's invasion by "'the dark-pigmented things, the half-castes, the mongrel-bloods.'" Frank Norris ridicules the "half-breed" as an "amorphous, formless mist" and contrasts the kindness and delicacy of Anglo-Saxons with "'the hot, degenerated blood'" of the Spanish, Mexican, and Portuguese.[35]

Implicit or explicit in these descriptions is a new racial ideology through which "newcomers from Europe could seem a fundamentally different order" from what were then called "native Americans." The common nineteenth-century belief in three races—black, white, yellow—each linked to a specific continent, was reconstituted so that "white" came to mean only "Nordic" or Northern European, while "yellow" applied not only to the Chinese, Japanese, and light-skinned African-Americans but also to Jews, Poles, Hungarians, Italians, and even the Irish. Crusaders warned of "yellow inundation." The California chapter of the Protestant white supremacist Junior Order of United American Mechanics teamed up with the Asiatic Exclusion League to proclaim that Southern Europeans were "semi-Mongolian" and should be excluded from immigration and citizenship on the same basis as the Chinese; Madison Grant declared Jews to be "a Mongrel admixture . . . of Slavs and of Asiatic invaders of Russia"; and a member of Congress announced that "the color of thousands" of the new immigrants "differs materially from that of the Anglo-Saxon." The greatest dangers were almost always traced back to Asia; in a dazzling conflation of enemies, for example, Grant warned that "'in the guise of Bolshevism with Semitic leadership and

Chinese executioners, [Asia] is organizing an assault upon Western Europe.'" Lothrop Stoddard predicted that "'colored migration'" was yielding the "'very immediate danger that the white stocks may be swamped by Asiatic blood.'" Again and again, nativists announced that democracy "simply will not work among Asiatics," that "non-Aryans," especially Slavs, Italians, and Jews, were "impossible to Americanize." The threat of "Yellow Peril" thus had "racial implications" much broader than anxiety about a takeover of Chinese or Japanese: "in every section, the Negro, the Oriental, and the Southern European appeared more and more in a common light."[36] In such a cultural moment, "yellow" readily connoted inferiority, strangeness, cowardice, ugliness, and backwardness. "Yellow-belly" and "yellow dog" were common slurs, the former applied to groups as diverse as the Irish and the Mexicans. Associations of "yellow" with disease, cowardice, and worth-lessness, uncleanliness, and decay may also have become implicit associations of race and class.[37]

    If "The Yellow Wallpaper" is read within this discourse of racial anxiety, certain of its tropes take on an obvious political charge. The very first sentence constructs the narrator in class terms, imagining an America in which, through democratic self-advancement, common (British) Americans can enjoy upper-class (British) privileges. Although the narrator and John are "mere ordinary people" and not the rightful "heirs and coheirs," they have secured "a colonial mansion, a hereditary estate," in whose queerness she takes pride; this house with its "private wharf" stands "quite alone . . . well back from the road, quite three miles from the village" like "English places that you read about, for there are hedges and walls and gates that lock, and lots of separate little houses for the gardeners and people." I am reminded by this description of another neglected "gentleman's manor house" that people "read about"—Thornfield—in which another merely ordinary woman "little accustomed to grandeur" comes to make her home. Charlotte Brontë's Jane Eyre is given a room with "gay blue chintz window curtains" that resemble the "pretty old-fashioned chintz hangings" in the room Gilman's narrator wanted for herself; Jane is not banished to Thornfield's third floor, where "wide and heavy beds" are surrounded by outlandish wall-hangings that portray "effigies of strange flowers, and stranger birds, and strangest human beings—all of which would have looked strange, indeed, by the pallid gleam of moonlight"—and where, if Thornfield had ghosts, Jane tells us, these ghosts would haunt. Like Gilman's narrator, Jane longs for both the freedom to roam and the pleasures of human society, and her "sole relief" in those moments is to walk around the attic and look out at the vista of road and trees and rolling hills so much like the view the narrator describes from her nursery in the writing that is her own sole "relief." It is from her attic perch that Jane feels so keenly that women, like men, need "exercise for their faculties" and "suffer from too rigid a restraining,"[38] as in her attic Gilman's narrator lies on the "great immovable bed" and longs for company and exercise.

But the permanent, imprisoned inhabitant of Thornfield's attic is not Jane; she is a dark Creole woman who might well have been called "yellow" in Gilman's America. Is Gilman's narrator, who "thought seriously of burning the house" imagining Bertha Mason's fiery revenge? Does the figure in the paper with its "foul, bad yellow" color, its "strange, provoking, formless sort of figure," its "broken neck" and "bulbous eyes," resemble Bertha with her "bloated features" and her "discoloured face"? Surely the narrator's crawling about her room may recall Bertha's running "backwards and forwards . . . on all fours." And like Brontë's "mad lady," who would "let herself out of her chamber" at night "and go roaming about the house" to ambush Jane,[39] the "smouldering" yellow menace in Gilman's story gets out at night and "skulk[s] in the parlor, [hides] in the hall," and "[lies] in wait for me." When the narrator tells John that the key to her room is beneath a plantain leaf, is she evoking not only the North American species of that name but also the tropical plant of Bertha's West Indies? When she imagines tying up the freed woman, is she repeating the fate of Bertha, brought in chains to foreign shores? Finally, does the circulation of Brontë's novel in Gilman's text explain the cryptic sentence at the end of the story—possibly a slip of Gilman's pen—in which the narrator cries to her husband that "I've got out at last . . . in spite of you and Jane"?

Is the wallpaper, then, the political unconscious of a

culture in which an Aryan woman's madness, desire, and anger, repressed by the imperatives of "reason," "duty," and "proper self-control" are projected onto the "yellow" woman who is, however, also the feared alien? When the narrator tries to liberate the woman from the wall, is she trying to purge her of her color, to peel her from the yellow paper, so that she can accept this woman as herself? If, as I suggested earlier, the wallpaper is at once the text of patriarchy and the woman's text, then perhaps the narrator is both resisting and embracing the woman of color who is self and not-self, a woman who might need to be rescued from the text of patriarchy but cannot yet be allowed to go free. Might we explain the narrator's pervasive horror of a yellow color and smell that threaten to take over the "ancestral halls," "stain[ing] everything it touched," as the British-American fear of a takeover by "aliens"? In a cultural moment when immigrant peoples and African Americans were being widely caricatured in the popular press through distorted facial and bodily images, might the "interminable grotesques" of "The Yellow Wallpaper"—with their lolling necks and "bulbous eyes" "staring everywhere," with their "peculiar odor" and "yellow smell," their colors "repellent, almost revolting," "smouldering" and "unclean," "sickly" and "particularly irritating," their "new shades of yellow" erupting constantly—figure the Asians and Jews, the Italians and Poles, the long list of "aliens" whom the narrator (and perhaps Gilman herself) might want at once to rescue and to flee?

For if anxieties about race, class, and ethnicity have inscribed themselves as a political unconscious upon the yellow wallpaper, they were conscious and indeed obsessive problems for Gilman herself, as I discovered when, disturbed by my own reading of "The Yellow Wallpaper," I turned to Gilman's later work.[40] Despite her socialist values, her active participation in movements for reform, her strong theoretical commitment to racial harmony, her unconventional support of interracial marriages, and her frequent condemnation of America's racist history,[41] Gilman upheld white Protestant supremacy; belonged for a time to eugenics and nationalist organizations; opposed open immigration; and inscribed racism, nationalism, and classism into her proposals for social change. In *Concern-*

240

ing Children (1900), she maintains that "a sturdy English baby would be worth more than an equally vigorous young Fuegian. With the same training and care, you could develop higher faculties in the English specimen than in the Fuegian specimen, because it was better bred."[42] In the same book, she argues that American children made "better citizens" than "the more submissive races" and in particular that "the Chinese and the Hindu, where parents are fairly worshipped and blindly obeyed," were "not races of free and progressive thought and healthy activity." Gilman advocated virtually compulsory enlistment of Blacks in a militaristic industrial corps, even as she opposed such regimentation for whites. In *The Forerunner,* the journal she produced single-handedly for seven years, "yellow" groups are singled out frequently and gratuitously: Gilman chides the "lazy old orientals" who consider work a curse, singles out Chinatown for "criminal conditions," and uses China as an example of various unhealthy social practices. And she all but justifies anti-Semitism by arguing, both in her "own" voice and more boldly through her Herlandian mouthpiece Ellador, that Jews have not yet "'passed the tribal stage'" of human development, that they practice an "'unethical'" and "'morally degrading'" religion of "'race egotism'" and "'concentrated pride,'" which has unfortunately found its way through the Bible into Western literature, and that in refusing to intermarry they "'artifically maintain characteristics which the whole world dislikes, and then complain of race prejudice.'"[43]

Like many other "nativist" intellectuals, Gilman was especially disturbed by the influx of poor immigrants to American cities and argued on both race and class grounds that these "undesirables" would destroy America. Although she once theorized that immigrants could be "healthier grafts upon our body politic," she wrote later that whatever "special gifts" each race had, when that race was transplanted, "their 'gift' is lost."[44] While proclaiming support for the admission of certain peoples of "assimilable stock," she declared that even the best of "Hindus . . . would make another problem" like the existing "problem" of African Americans, and that an "inflow" of China's "'oppressed'" would make it impossible to preserve the American "national character." This "character," it is clear, requires that "Americans" be primarily people "of native born parentage," who "should have a majority vote *in their own country.*"[45] Surprisingly perhaps for a socialist, but less surprisingly for a woman whose autobiography opens with a claim of kinship with Queen Victoria,[46] Gilman seems to equate class status with readiness for democracy. Repeatedly she claims to favor immigration so long as the immigrants are of "better" stock. In her futurist utopia, *Moving the Mountain,* for instance, a character remembers the "old" days when "'we got all the worst and lowest people'"; in the imaginary new America, immigrants may not enter the country until they "come up to a certain standard" by passing a "microscopic" physical exam and completing an education in American ways. It is surely no accident that the list of receiving gates Gilman imagines for her immigrant groups stops with Western Europe: "'There's the German Gate, and the Spanish Gate, the English Gate, and the Italian Gate—and so on.'"[47]

Classism, racism, and nationalism converge with particular virulence when Ellador, having established her antiracist credentials by championing the rights of Black Americans, observes that "'the poor and oppressed were not necessarily good stuff for a democracy'" and declares, in an extraordinary reversal of victim and victimizer to which even her American partner Van protests, that "'it is the poor and oppressed who make monarchy and despotism.'"[48] Ellador's triumph is sealed with the graphic insistence that you cannot "'put a little of everything into a melting-pot and produce a good metal,'" not if you are mixing "'gold, silver, copper and iron, lead, radium, pipe, clay, coal dust, and plain dirt.'" Making clear the racial boundaries of the melting pot, Ellador challenges Van, "'And how about the yellow? Do they 'melt'? Do you want them to melt? Isn't your exclusion of them an admission that you think some kinds of people unassimilable? That democracy must pick and choose a little?'" Ellador's rationale—and Gilman's—is that "'the human race is in different stages of development, and only some of the races—or some individuals in a given race—have reached the democratic stage.'" Yet she begs the question and changes the subject when Van asks, "'But how could we discriminate?'"[49]

The aesthetic and sensory quality of this horror at a pol-

242

luted America creates a compelling resemblance between the narrator's graphic descriptions of the yellow wallpaper and Gilman's graphic descriptions of the cities and their "swarms of jostling aliens."[50] She fears that America has become "bloated" and "verminous," a "dump" for Europe's "social refuse," "a ceaseless offense to eye and ear and nose,"[51] creating "multiforeign" cities that are "abnormally enlarged" and "swollen," "foul, ugly and dangerous," their conditions "offensive to every sense: assailing the eye with ugliness, the ear with noise, the nose with foul smells."[52] And when she complains that America has "stuffed" itself with "uncongenial material," with an "overwhelming flood of unassimilable characteristics," with "such a stream of non-assimilable stuff as shall dilute and drown out the current of our life," indeed with "'the most ill-assorted and unassimilable mass of human material that was ever held together by artificial means,'" Gilman might be describing the patterns and pieces of the wallpaper as well.[53] Her poem "The City of Death" (1913) depicts a diseased prison "piped with poison, room by room,"

> Whose weltering rush of swarming human forms,
> Forced hurtling through foul subterranean tubes
> Kills more than bodies, coarsens mind and soul.
> • • •
> And steadily degrades our humanness . . .[54]

Such a city is not so different from the claustrophic nursery which finally "degrades" the "humanness" of "The Yellow Wallpaper's" protagonist.

The text of Gilman's imagining, then, is the text of an America made as uninhabitable as the narrator's chamber, and her declaration that "children ought to grow up in the country, all of them,"[55] recalls the narrator's relief that her baby does not have to live in the unhappy prison at the top of the house. Clearly Gilman was recognizing serious social problems in her concern over the ghettos and tenements of New York and Chicago—she herself worked for a time at Hull House, although she detested Chicago's "noisome" neighborhoods. But her conflation of the city with its immigrant peoples repeats her own racism even as her nostalgia about the country harks back to a New England in the hands of the New English themselves.[56] These "'little old New England towns'" and their new counterparts, the "'fresh young western ones,'" says Ellador, "'have more of America in them than is possible—could ever be possible—in such a political menagerie as New York,'" whose people really "'belong in Berlin, in Dublin, in Jerusalem.'"[57]

It is no accident that some of the most extreme of Gilman's anti-immigrant statements come from the radical feminist Ellador, for race and gender are not separate issues in Gilman's cosmology, and it is in their intersection that a fuller reading of "The Yellow Wallpaper" becomes possible. For Gilman, patriarchy is a racial phenomenon: it is primarily non-Aryan "yellow" peoples whom Gilman holds responsible for originating and perpetuating patriarchal practices, and it is primarily Nordic Protestants whom she considers capable of change. In *The Man-Made World: or, Our Androcentric Culture,* Gilman associates the oppression of women with "the heavy millions of the unstirred East," and the "ancestor-worship[ping]" cultures of the "old patriarchal races" who "linger on in feudal Europe." The text singles out the behaviors of "savage African tribes," laments the customs of India, names the "Moslem" religion as "rigidly bigoted and unchanging," and dismisses "to the limbo of all outworn superstition that false Hebraic and grossly androcentric doctrine that the woman is to be subject to the man."[58] Elsewhere, Gilman declares that except for "our Pueblos," where "the women are comparatively independent and honored," nearly all "savages" are "decadent, and grossly androcentric."[59] In one of two essays in *The Forerunner* attacking Ida Tarbell, Gilman identifies Tarbell's "androcentrism" as "neither more nor less than the same old doctrine held by India, China, Turkey, and all the ancient races, held by all ignorant peasants the world over; held by the vast mass of ordinary, unthinking people, and by some quite intelligent enough to know better: that the business of being a woman is to bear and rear children, to 'keep house,' and nothing else."[60] The most progressive and dominant races" of the present day, she claims, are also "those whose women have most power and liberty; and in the feeblest and most backward races we find women most ill-treated

244

and enslaved." Gilman goes on to make clear that this is an explicitly Aryan accomplishment: "The Teutons and Scandinavian stocks seem never to have had that period of enslaved womanhood, that polygamous harem culture; their women never went through that debasement; and their men have succeeded in preserving the spirit of freedom which is inevitably lost by a race which has servile women."[61] That the "progressive and dominant races" Gilman lauds for not "enslaving" women were at that very moment invading and oppressing countries around the globe seems to present Gilman with no contradiction at all: indeed, imperialism might provide the opportunity, to paraphrase Gayatri Spivak, to save yellow women from yellow men.[62]

In this light, Gilman's wallpaper becomes not only a representation of patriarchy but also the projection of patriarchal practices onto non-Aryan societies. Such a projection stands, of course, in implicit tension with the narrative, because it is the modern-minded, presumably Aryan husband and doctor who constitute the oppressive force. But for Gilman, an educated, Protestant, social-democratic Aryan, America explicitly represented the major hope for feminist possibility. The superiority of this "wider and deeper" and "more human" of religions is directly associated with the fact that "in America the status of women is higher," for example, than in "Romanist" Spain.[63] Not all people are equally educable, after all, particularly if they belong to one of those "tribal" cultures of the East: "you could develop higher faculties in the English specimen than in the Fuegian." And Gilman's boast that "The Yellow Wallpaper" convinced S. Weir Mitchell to alter his practices suggests that like Van, the sociologist-narrator of two of Gilman's feminist utopias, educated, white Protestant men could be taught to change. The immigrant "invasion" thus becomes a direct threat to Gilman's program for feminist reform.

As a particular historical product, then, "The Yellow Wallpaper" is no more "*the* story that all literary women would tell" than the entirely white canon of *The Madwoman in the Attic* is *the* story of all women's writing or the only story those (white) texts can tell. "The Yellow Wallpaper" has been able to pass for a universal text only insofar as white, Western literatures and perspectives continue to dominate academic

American feminist practices even when the most urgent literary and political events are happening in Africa, Asia, and
Latin America, and among the new and old cultures of Color
in the United States. We might expand our theories of censorship, for example, if we read "The Yellow Wallpaper" in the
context of women's prison writings from around the world—
writings like Ding Ling's memoirs and Alicia Partnoy's *The
Little School: Tales of Disappearance and Survival in Argentina* and some of the stories of Bessie Head. We might have
something to learn about interpretation if we examined the
moment in Partnoy's narrative when her husband is tortured
because he gives the "wrong" reading of his wife's poems.[64]
We might better understand contemporary feminist racial
politics if we studied the complex but historically distanced
discourses of feminists a century ago.[65] Perhaps, like the
narrator of Gilman's story, white, American academic feminist criticism has sought in literature the mirror of its own
identity, erasing the literary equivalent of strange sights and
smells and colors so that we can have the comfort of reproducing, on a bare stage, that triumphant moment when a woman
recognizes her self. Perhaps white, American feminist practice too readily resembles that of Gilman, who deplores that
historically "we have cheated the Indian, oppressed the African, robbed the Mexican,"[66] and whose utopian impulses continue to insist that there is only "one race, the human race,"[67]
but for whom particular, present conditions of race and class
continue to be blindnesses justified on "other"—aesthetic, political, pragmatic—grounds.

"The Yellow Wallpaper" also calls upon us to recognize
that the white, female, intellectual-class subjectivity which
Gilman's narrator attempts to construct, and to which many
feminists have also been committed perhaps unwittingly, is a
subjectivity whose illusory unity, like the unity imposed on
the paper, is built on the repression of difference. This also
means that the conscious biographical experience which Gilman claims as the authenticating source of the story is but one
contributing element.[68] And if we are going to read this text in
relation to its author, we may have to realize that there are
dangers as well as pleasures in a feminist reading based on a
merging of consciousnesses.[69] Once we recognize Gilman as a

246

subject constituted in and by the contradictions of ideology, we might also remember that she acknowledges having been subjected to the narrator's circumstances but denies any relationship to the wallpaper itself—that is, to what I am reading as the site of a political unconscious in which questions of race permeate questions of sex. A recent essay by Ellen Messer-Davidow in *New Literary History* argues that literary criticism and feminist criticism should be recognized as fundamentally different activities, that feminist criticism is part of a larger interdisciplinary project whose main focus is the exploration of "ideas about sex and gender," that disciplinary variations are fairly insignificant differences of "medium," and therefore that feminist literary critics need to change their subject from "literature" to "ideas about sex and gender" as these happen to be expressed in literature.[70] I suggest that one of the messages of "The Yellow Wallpaper" is that textuality, like culture, is more complex, shifting, and polyvalent than any of the ideas we can abstract from it, that the narrator's reductive gesture is precisely to isolate and essentialize one "idea about sex and gender" from a more complex textual field.

Deconstructing our own reading of the wallpaper, then, means acknowledging that Adrienne Rich still speaks to feminist critics when she calls on us to "[enter] an old text from a new critical direction," to "take the work first of all as a clue to how we live . . . how we have been led to imagine ourselves, how our language has trapped as well as liberated us . . . and how we can begin to see and name—and therefore live—afresh," so that we do not simply "pass on a tradition but . . . break its hold over us."[71] Feminist critical theory offers the deconstructive principles for this continuing revision, so long as we require ourselves, as we have required our nonfeminist colleagues, to look anew at what have become old texts and old critical premises. Still, the revision I am proposing here would have been impossible without the first revision of "The Yellow Wallpaper" that liberated the imprisoned woman from the text. Adrienne Rich has addressed the poem "Heroines" to nineteenth-century white feminists who reflected racism and class privilege in their crusades for change. It is both to Gilman herself and to all of us whose readings of "The Yellow

Wallpaper" have been both transformative and limiting, that, in closing, I address the final lines of Rich's poem:

> How can I fail to love
> your clarity and fury
> how can I give you
> all your due
> take courage from your courage
> honor your exact
> legacy as it is
> recognizing
> as well
> that it is not enough?[72]

☐ Notes ■

For crucial advice at various stages of composition, I thank Evelyn Beck, Leona Fisher, Caren Kaplan, Joan Radner, Michael Ragussis, Jack Undank, audiences at Occidental College and the University of Maryland at College Park, and the students in my 1988 Literary Criticism Seminar at Georgetown University: Janet Auten, Jade Gorman, Claire McCusker, Jane Obenauer, Julie Rusnak, Xiomara Santamarina, and Nancy Shevlin.

1. In an 11 October 1987 *New York Times Book Review* listing of the best-selling works of university-press fiction for the past twenty-five years, "The Yellow Wallpaper" ranked seventh (145,000 copies) and Zora Neale Hurston's *Their Eyes Were Watching God* ranked fourth (240,000 copies). These figures are all the more astonishing, because these two books have been in print for considerably less than twenty-five years and "The Yellow Wallpaper" is also reprinted in several anthologies. The top entries are Eugene O'Neill's *Long Day's Journey into Night* (900,500 copies), Tom Clancy's *The Hunt for Red October* (358,000 copies), and Ovid's *Metamorphoses* (304,278 copies).

2. I use the term "American" here to refer not to the nationality of practitioners but to a set of practices that has dominated the discourse of feminist criticism in U.S. universities during the 1970s and into the 1980s. Elaine Showalter's *New Feminist Criticism* (New

248

York: Pantheon, 1985) offers a representative collection of this work. When I say "academic," I mean a criticism aligned predominantly with professional-class interests and produced primarily for academic settings: "scholarly" journals, university presses, classrooms, conferences, colloquia.

3. Janice Haney-Peritz and Mary Jacobus have also written critiques of feminism's "Yellow Wallpaper." I thank the anonymous reviewer of my essay for *Feminist Studies* for introducing me to Jacobus's essay, which I had not seen before submitting this paper. I will discuss the two essays more specifically below.

4. The six critical studies, in chronological order, are Elaine Hedges, "Afterword" to The Feminist Press edition of "The Yellow Wallpaper" (Old Westbury, N.Y.: The Feminist Press, 1973), 37–63; Sandra Gilbert and Susan Gubar, *The Madwoman in the Attic: The Woman Writer and the Nineteenth-Century Literary Imagination* (New Haven: Yale University Press, 1979), 89–92; Annette Kolodny, "A Map for Re-Reading: Or, Gender and the Interpretation of Literary Texts," *New Literary History* 11 (Spring 1980): 451–67; Jean Kennard, "Convention Coverage or How to Read Your Own Life," *New Literary History* 13 (Autumn 1981): 69–88; Paula Treichler, "Escaping the Sentence," *Tulsa Studies in Women's Literature* 3 (Spring/Fall 1984): 61–77; Judith Fetterley, "Reading about Reading: 'A Jury of Her Peers,' 'The Murderers in the Rue Morgue,' and 'The Yellow Wallpaper,'" in *Gender and Reading: Essays on Readers, Texts, and Contexts,* ed. Elizabeth Flynn and Patrocinio Schweikart (Baltimore: Johns Hopkins, 1986), 147–64. Similar, often briefer readings abound.

5. Kennard's essay is based precisely on this recognition of unity: she writes in 1981 that although her interpretation, Gilbert and Gubar's, Hedges's, and Kolodny's all "emphasize different aspects of the text, they do not conflict with each other" (p. 74).

6. Although "ideology" is now in currency through European theory, American feminism also used the term to designate what Catherine Belsey describes as the unacknowledged underpinnings of our social, political, intellectual, sexual, and emotional lives, our "imaginary relation" to real conditions, which presents "partial truths," smooths contradictions, and "appears to provide answers to questions which in reality it evades" (see her *Critical Practice* [London: Methuen, 1980], 57–58). For an early use of "ideology" as a feminist concept, see Sandra Bem and Daryl Bem, "Case Study of a

Nonconscious Ideology: Training a Woman to Know her Place," in *Beliefs, Attitudes, and Human Affairs,* ed. Daryl Bem (Brooks/Cole Publishing Company, 1970), 89–99.

7. Certainly these values linger. One of the most revealing defenses of the now-old New Criticism appeared in a 10 July 1988 letter by John W. Aldridge responding to *The New York Times Magazine's* essay of 5 June 1988, "The Battle of the Books":

> Our mission—if it had ever been defined—was to identify and promote the most artistically successful and esthetically satisfying works produced in that culture. It was also part of our mission to work as critics to try to educate public taste so as to be better able to make esthetic discriminations among contemporary works—in particular, to develop appreciation for neglected writers and to reexamine the work of those whose reputations had become overinflated. In the service of the first, we had Malcolm Cowley on Faulkner, Edmund Wilson on the early Hemingway, Cleanth Brooks on T. S. Eliot, and Eliot on the metaphysical poets. In the service of the second, we had Wilson on Kafka and murder mysteries, Dwight Macdonald on James Gould Cozzens, Norman Podhoretz on the Beats, and, in more recent years, if I may say so, myself writing negatively on John Updike, Mary McCarthy, William Styron, James Baldwin, and some others. . . .

8. In an essay that precedes Terry Eagleton's *Literary Theory* by a decade, for example, Fraya Katz-Stoker read in the agenda of New Criticism not only the attempt to hold poetry to a coherence absent in an era of fascism, McCarthyism, and world war but also an imposition on literature of the same political stance it sought to ignore. See "The Other Criticism: Feminism vs. Formalism," in *Images of Women in Fiction,* ed. Susan Koppelman Cornillon (Bowling Green, Ohio: Popular Press, 1972), 315–27.

9. Gayle Greene and Coppélia Kahn, "Feminist Scholarship and the Social Construction of Woman," in *Making a Difference: Feminist Literary Criticism,* ed. Gayle Greene and Coppélia Kahn (London: Methuen, 1985), 6.

10. Cited in Charlotte Perkins Gilman, *The Living of Charlotte Perkins Gilman* (New York: D. Appleton, 1935), 119.

11. The story was reprinted in *The Great Modern American Stories: An Anthology* (New York: Boni & Liveright, 1920), vii; William Dean Howells, cited in Conrad Shumaker, "'Too Terribly Good

to be Printed': Charlotte Gilman's 'The Yellow Wallpaper,'" *American Literature* 57 (December 1985): 588.

12. Anonymous letter to the Boston *Transcript,* cited in Gilman, *The Living of Charlotte Perkins Gilman,* 120.

13. On the difference between these terms, see William M. O'Barr and Bowman K. Atkins, "'Women's Language' or 'Powerless Language'?" in *Women and Language in Literature and Society,* ed. Sally McConnell-Ginet, Ruth Borker, and Nelly Furman (New York: Praeger, 1980), 93–110. On double-voiced "coding" strategies, see Joan Radner and Susan Lanser, "The Feminist Voice: Coding in Women's Folklore and Literature," *Journal of American Folklore* 100 (October 1987): 412–25.

14. Charlotte Perkins Gilman, *The Yellow Wallpaper* (Old Westbury, N.Y.: The Feminist Press, 1973), 13.

15. Gilbert and Gubar, 89.

16. Kennard, 74; Annette Kolodny, "Dancing through the Minefield: Some Observations on the Theory, Practice, and Politics of a Feminist Literary Criticism," *Feminist Studies* 6 (Spring 1980): 10.

17. Ibid., 12.

18. See, for example, Fetterley, 164; Gilbert and Gubar, 91–92; Hedges, 55; Treichler, 68–69.

19. Gilbert and Gubar, 90.

20. Treichler, 73.

21. Fetterley, 162.

22. Kolodny, "Map for Re-Reading," 458 (emphasis mine).

23. Kennard, 78, 84.

24. Barbara Smith, "Toward a Black Feminist Criticism," *Conditions Two* (October 1977): 29–30; rpt. in *The New Feminist Criticism,* 168–85; Alice Walker, "*One* Child of One's Own: A Meaningful Digression within the Work(s)," in *In Search of Our Mothers' Gardens: Womanist Prose* (New York: Harcourt Brace Jovanovich, 1983), 361–83; Judy Grahn, "Murdering the King's English," in *True to Life Adventure Stories* 2 vols. (Oakland: Diana Press, 1978), 1: 6–14; Adrienne Rich, "It Is the Lesbian in Us. . ." in *On Lies, Secrets, and Silence: Selected Prose, 1966–78* (New York: Norton, 1979), 199–202; and "Compulsory Heterosexuality and Lesbian Existence," *Signs* 5 (Summer 1980): 631–60; Cherríe Moraga and Gloria Anzaldúa, *This Bridge Called My Back: Writings by Radical Women of Color* (Watertown, Mass.: Persephone Press, 1981); and

Evelyn Torton Beck, *Nice Jewish Girls: A Lesbian Anthology* (Watertown, Mass.: Persephone Press, 1982). *This Bridge Called My Back* has been reprinted by Kitchen Table Press; *Nice Jewish Girls* appeared in 1989 in a revised third edition from Beacon Press.

25. Elly Bulkin, in Judith Kegan Gardiner, Elly Bulkin, Rena Grasso Patterson, and Annette Kolodny, "An Interchange on Feminist Criticism: On 'Dancing Through the Minefield,'" *Feminist Studies* 8 (Fall 1982): 636.

26. I am thinking in particular of Showalter's *New Feminist Criticism* (1985), which mentions the responses briefly in its introduction but does not discuss or excerpt them. Dale Spender's *Men's Studies Modified* (Oxford, England: Pergamon, 1981), which also reprints "Dancing Through the Minefield," was published before the responses to Kolodny appeared.

27. In "Monumental Feminism and Literature's Ancestral House: Another Look at 'The Yellow Wallpaper'" (*Women's Studies* 12 [December 1986]: 113–28), Janice Haney-Peritz argues from a Lacanian perspective that like the narrator, American feminist critics "see in literature a really distinctive body which they seek to liberate through identification" and which is "usually presented as essential to a viable feminist literary criticism and celebrated as something so distinctive that it shakes, if it does not destroy, the very foundations of patriarchal literature's ancestral house" (p. 123). In this process, says Haney-Peritz, gender hierarchies are not dismantled but merely reversed, and the material nature of feminist struggle is erased.

Mary Jacobus's "An Unnecessary Maze of Sign-Reading" (in *Reading Woman: Essays in Feminist Criticism* [New York: Columbia University Press, 1986], 229–48), was, as I said earlier, introduced to me by an anonymous reader for *Feminist Studies*. Although my interpretation of Gilman's story is very different from Jacobus's, our analyses of earlier feminist readings are strikingly similar, and we focus on some of the same key elements of the tale. Because all three readings seem to have been undertaken independently of one another, they clearly signify a new interpretive moment in both feminist criticism generally and criticism of "The Yellow Wallpaper" in particular.

28. Chris Weedon, *Feminist Practice and Poststructuralist Theory* (Oxford: Basil Blackwell, 1987), 86.

29. See Hedges, 51; Gilbert and Gubar, 90; Kolodny, "Map

for Re-Reading," 458; Treichler, 62ff; Fetterley, 162; Haney-Pertiz, 116.

30. Weedon, 21.

31. Adrienne Rich, "When We Dead Awaken: Writing As Re-Vision" (1971) in *On Lies, Secrets, and Silence*, 35.

32. Before 1986, only Jean Kennard had noted the degree to which "yellow" failed to figure in the standard feminist analysis (pp. 78–79). For other new readings of the long-unread trope of color, see Jacobus, 234ff, and William Veeder, "Who is Jane? The Intricate Feminism of Charlotte Perkins Gilman," *Arizona Quarterly* 44 (Autumn 1988): 40–79. Sometimes readers associate Gilman's paper with "yellow journalism," but that phrase was not coined until 1895.

33. Thomas F. Gossett, *Race: The History of an Idea in America* (Dallas: Southern Methodist University Press, 1975), 299.

34. John Higham, *Strangers in the Land: Patterns of American Nativism, 1860–1925*, 2d ed. (New York: Atheneum, 1975), 133, 39.

35. Ibid., 42; E. A. Ross, *The Old World and the New;* John W. Burgess, "The Ideal of the American Commonwealth"; Owen Wister, "The Evolution of the Cow Puncher"; and Jack London, *Burning Daylight,* all quoted in Gossett, 293, 307, and 219. See also Jack London's *Valley of the Moon,* quoted in Higham, 172; Frank Norris's *Collected Writings* and *The Octopus,* both quoted in Gossett, 219, 221–22.

36. Higham, 133. Roger Daniels and Harry Kitano, *American Racism: Exploration of the Nature of Prejudice* (Englewood Cliffs, N.J.: Prentice-Hall, 1970), 44; Higham, 174; Madison Grant, *The Conquest of a Continent* (New York: Scribners, 1933), 255; Higham, 168; Madison Grant, *The Passing of the Great Race* (1916), cited in Daniels and Kitano, 55; Lothrop Stoddard, cited in Daniels and Kitano, 55; Grant, *The Conquest of a Continent,* 356; and Higham, 166, 173.

37. See, for example, *Dictionary of American Slang,* ed. Harold Wentworth and Stuart Berg Flexner (New York: Thomas Y. Crowell, 1960). The association of the color yellow with artistic decadence, which Mary Jacobus also suggests (p. 234), may not be irrelevant to these other cultural practices.

38. Charlotte Brontë, *Jane Eyre,* Norton Critical Edition (New York: Norton, 1971), 86, 85, 92, 93, 96. Mary Jacobus also

discusses briefly resonances between "The Yellow Wallpaper" and *Jane Eyre*.

39. Brontë, 258, 249, 257–58.

40. I want to stress that my reading of "The Yellow Wallpaper" emerged from my experience of and discomfort with the text and not from prior knowledge of Gilman's radical ideology. When I began to imagine political implications for the color "yellow" in the story, I thought the text might be reflecting unconscious anxieties, but I did not expect to find overt evidence of racism in Gilman's writings.

41. See, for example, Gilman's "My Ancestors," *Forerunner* 4 (March 1913): 73–75, in which the narrator represents all humans as one family; "Race Pride," *Forerunner* 4 (April 1913): 88–89; in which she explicitly criticizes Owen Wister's *The Virginian* for white supremacy; and *With Her in Ourland, Forerunner* 7 (1916): passim, in which America is chastised for its abuse of Negroes, Mexicans, and Indians.

42. *Concerning Children*, 4, cited in Gary Scharnhorst, *Charlotte Perkins Gilman* (Boston: Twayne, 1985), 66. Scharnhorst gives much more attention to Gilman's racism than does Mary Hill in *Charlotte Perkins Gilman: The Making of a Radical Feminist, 1860–1896* (Philadelphia: Temple University Press, 1980). This may be because Scharnhorst is dealing with the whole of Gilman's life and work, Hill with only the first half. But I do not want to rule out the possibility that Scharnhorst's gender and/or ethnic identity, or the five years' difference between his book and Hill's, made it easier for him to confront Gilman's racism.

43. Gilman, *Concerning Children,* 89 and 55; Gilman, in the *American Journal of Sociology* (July 1908), 78–85, both cited in Scharnhorst, 66, 127. See Gilman, "Why We Honestly Fear Socialism," *The Forerunner* 1 (December 1909): 9. This charge is also made of the Jews in Gilman's *The Man-Made World: or, Our Androcentric Culture* (New York: Charlton, 1911), 231. See Gilman, review of "The Woman Voter," *Forerunner* 3 (August 1912): 224; and see, for example, *Forerunner* 4 (February 1913): 47, and 3 (March 1912): 66. Gilman, *With Her in Ourland, Forerunner* 7 (October 1916): 266–67. See similar statements in "Growth and Combat," *Forerunner* 7 (April 1916): 108; and the following example from "Race Pride," *Forerunner* 4 (April 1913): 89: "Perhaps the most pro-

nounced instance of this absurdity [of race superiority] is in the historic pride of the Hebrews, firmly believing themselves to be the only people God cared about, and despising all the other races of the earth for thousands upon thousands of years, while all those other races unanimously return the compliment." In at least one earlier text, however, Gilman does note without blaming the victim that "the hideous injustice of Christianity to the Jew attracted no attention through many centuries." See *Women and Economics* (1898; rpt. New York: Harper & Row, 1966), 78.

44. Gilman, personal correspondence, cited in Scharnhorst, 127.

45. Gilman, "Immigration, Importation, and Our Fathers," *Forerunner* 5 (May 1914): 118; "Let Sleeping Forefathers Lie," *Forerunner* 6 (October 1915): 263 (emphasis mine).

46. Gilman, *Living of Charlotte Perkins Gilman*, 1.

47. Gilman, *Moving the Mountain*, in *Forerunner* 2 (March 1911): 80.

48. *Forerunner* 7 (June 1916): 154.

49. *With Her in Ourland*, in *Forerunner* 7 (June 1916): 155. It may not be accidental that Ellador changes the subject from race to sex.

50. Gilman, cited in Scharnhorst.

51. Gilman, "Let Sleeping Forefathers Lie," 261; Gilman, "Growth and Combat," *Forerunner* 7 (December 1916): 332.

52. Gilman, *Living of Charlotte Perkins Gilman*, 317; Gilman, *The Forum* 70 (October 1923): 1983–89; *Forerunner* 7 (October 1916): 277.

53. Gilman, "Immigration, Importation, and Our Fathers," 118; "Let Sleeping Forefathers Lie," 262; *With Her in Ourland*, in *Forerunner* 7 (June 1916): 153.

54. Gilman, "The City of Death," *Forerunner* 4 (April 1913): 104.

55. Gilman, "The Power of the Farm Wife," *Forerunner* 6 (December 1915): 316. See also "Growth and Combat," 332.

56. Gilman's autobiography echoes these sentiments when she names New York "that unnatural city where everyone is an exile, none more so than the American," and laments that New York has "but 7 per cent native-born" and that one-third of New Yorkers are Jews. When she travels one summer to coastal Maine, she "could

have hugged the gaunt New England farmers and fishermen—I had forgotten what my people looked like!" (*Living of Charlotte Perkins Gilman,* 316).

57. Gilman, *With Her in Ourland,* 151, 155. Ellador's racism (and Gilman's) is often tempered with "fairness." Here, for example, Ellador insists that "'I do not mean the immigrants solely. There are Bostonians of Beacon Hill who belong in London; there are New Yorkers of five generations who belong in Paris.'" But these seem to be exceptions, because only the immigrants belong elsewhere in "'vast multitudes.'"

58. Gilman, *The Man-Made World,* 27–28; 136, 249.

59. Gilman, "Personal Problems," *Forerunner* 1 (July 1910): 23–24.

60. Gilman, "Miss Tarbell's Third Paper," *Forerunner* 3 (April 1912): 95.

61. Gilman, "Personal Problems," 23–24.

62. See Gayatri Spivak, "Can the Subaltern Speak? Speculations on Widow-Sacrifice," *Wedge,* nos. 7/8 (1985).

63. Gilman, *The Man-Made World,* 136.

64. Alicia Partnoy, *The Little School: Tales of Disappearance and Survival in Argentina* (San Francisco: Cleis Press, 1986), 104.

65. Reading Gilman's remarks about polluting the melting pot, for example, helped me to see similarities between anxieties about immigration policy and anxieties about "letting too many groups into the literary canon."

66. Gilman, "Race Pride," *Forerunner* 4 (April 1913): 90.

67. See, for example, Gilman, "My Ancestors," 74.

68. See Gilman, "Why I Wrote 'The Yellow Wallpaper,'" *Forerunner* 4 (1913).

69. The strongest articulation of the pleasures of such reading is Sydney Janet Kaplan's "Varieties of Feminist Criticism," in *Making a Difference,* 37–58.

70. Ellen Messer-Davidow, "The Philosophical Bases of Feminist Literary Criticisms," *New Literary History* 19 (Autumn 1987): 79, 96.

71. Rich, "When We Dead Awaken," 35.

72. Adrienne Rich, "Heroines," in *A Wild Patience Has Taken Me This Far* (New York: Norton, 1981), 35–36.

☐ ELIZABETH AMMONS ■

Writing Silence:
"The Yellow Wallpaper"

> At best, woman was counted little more than man's toy
> among the upper classes, and his beast of burden
> among the lower social elements. In some countries even
> denied a soul, in none was she supposed to have any
> particular mental power, nor any need for its
> development.
> JOSEPHINE SILONE-YATES[1]

Frances Ellen Harper was thirty-five-years old when Charlotte Perkins was born. Their paths seem not to have crossed, and certainly their perspectives diverged. Harper, an avowed feminist, put race first. Gilman, an unreflecting racist, put gender first. She was exactly the type of white woman whom Harper, as far back as 1869 (when Gilman was nine years old), criticized because of her blindness to the paramount importance of the race issue.

Yet as authors, what Harper and Gilman shared across race and generation is powerful. They, perhaps more than any other two writers in my group, resolutely and constantly fused their political and their literary missions. Not claiming to be "artists"—though of course they were, and even had strong opinions about what art should do, their own included—they were immovably committed to the literary tradition that Helen Gray Cone identified in 1891 as women's "struggle between the art-instinct and the desire for reform, which is not likely

From *Conflicting Stories: American Women Writers at the Turn into the Twentieth Century* (New York and Oxford: Oxford University Press, 1991), 34–43, 207–208.

257

to cease entirely until the coming of the Golden Year."[2] Related to Harriet Beecher Stowe by self-declared affinity on the one hand (Harper) and by blood on the other (Gilman), the two, along with Pauline Hopkins, actively carried into the new era a tenacious nineteenth-century belief in the overt political—even evangelical—function of literature.

At the same time, placing Gilman and Harper side by side immediately calls into focus difference. Although *Iola Leroy* and "The Yellow Wallpaper" both deal with middle-class issues, and specifically with women's claim to physical self-definition and self-possession, crucial historical and contextual differences obviously separate the two texts. For middle-class white women, the issues of violence, sexual exploitation, and silencing were played out against a backdrop not of rape-lynch mythology but of domestic ideology; and the contrast clearly appears in the two works. Iola's story takes place in the world: Gilman's heroine is confined to one room of one house. Iola rejects the claim to her body of white men as a group; Gilman's narrator rejects the claim of one white man, her husband, to her body. Iola "speaks," despite the systematic effort to silence her (and all black people), by committing herself to a life of action and service in the world. Gilman's narrator "speaks," despite the effort to silence her, by writing her body on the walls of one room.

Gilman had to know that "The Yellow Wallpaper" would be shocking when it first came out. When she sent the story to William Dean Howells in the early 1890s in the hope of seeing it published in the *Atlantic Monthly,* she received in reply from the editor this terse rejection:

DEAR MADAM,
Mr. Howells has handed me this story.
I could not forgive myself if I made others as miserable as
I have made myself!
Sincerely yours,
H. E. Scudder[3]

After the story appeared in the *New England Magazine* in 1892, a reader complained to the Boston *Transcript:* "It certainly seems open to serious question if such literature should be permitted in print." This letter, titled by the newspaper "Perilous Stuff," concludes with the question (already emphatically answered in the negative): "Should such stories be allowed to pass without severest censure?"[4] Although some readers responded favorably, praising the story for its realism, its remarkable "delicacy of . . . touch and the correctness of portrayal,"[5] the shocked reactions of Horace Scudder and of the reader signed simply "M.D." in the Boston *Transcript* suggest how powerful the silence was that Gilman was breaking. Neither charged Gilman with lying. Rather her story was too true, the information in it too depressing. It should remain buried, untold.

"The Yellow Wallpaper" tells the story of a middle-class white woman's attempt to claim sexual and textual authority. Forcibly stripped of choice and voice, Gilman's narrator furiously affirms her right to self-determination—in the flesh, in the written word. She does so in the face of the fact that her right to write herself has been systematically denied her, the story maintains, by the violent process of feminization to which she, as a privileged white American woman, has been forced to submit.[6]

To expose as sadistic this standard white middle-class process by which a grown woman, under the supervision of a "benevolent" male expert, was required to turn herself into a helpless, docile, overgrown infant—that is, a feminine adult—Gilman evoked as context for "The Yellow Wallpaper" the late Victorian rest cure. Having been a patient once herself, she believed that it was in many ways simply an exaggeration of the "normal" process of feminization operating in the culture anyway. The intent of the cure, like the Victorian ideal of femininity it sought to instill, was to render a woman simultaneously and paradoxically all-body and yet (supposedly) asexual, a process that entailed strict prohibition of intellectual activity, fixation on physical reproductivity, and enforcement of childlike submission to masculine authority. Originally devised to treat soldiers incapacitated by the trauma of battle (the terror and profound lethargy that resulted were termed, rather benignly, "fatigue"), the rest cure responded to middle-class white women's trauma of unsuccessful role adjustment, which the medical establishment labeled "hysteria," by instituting a rigid and highly symbolic therapeutic regimen of enforced idleness and induced, infantile dependence.

In a typical scenario, the hysterical patient was admitted to the care of a learned physician and his attendants and then confined. Whether her disease manifested itself in symptoms of depression or of heightened excitability—she might be apathetic, morose, uncontrollably tearful, hypersensitive, delusional, or any combination of these—the patient found herself forcibly relieved of all physical and mental responsibility. Denied freedom of movement and intellectual stimulus (books, friends, writing, or drawing) in the first stage of treatment, she was transformed into nothing but body, a mass of pure passive, ostensibly desexualized flesh without self-control. As one historian explains in a discussion of the regimen created by S. Weir Mitchell, the most famous of the late nineteenth-century American rest-cure specialists and the physician whose treatment nearly drove Charlotte Perkins Gilman insane, he "made it clear to his patients that he was in total control and that their feelings, questions, and concerns must be disregarded."[7] With the physician properly installed as the sole authority, therapy then consisted of isolation, inactivity, and excessive feeding. In Mitchell's words:

> At first, and in some cases for four to five weeks, I do not permit the patient to sit up or to sew or write or read, or to use the hands in any active way except to clean the teeth. . . . I arrange to have the bowels and water passed while lying down, and the patient is lifted onto a lounge for an hour in the morning and again at bedtime, and then lifted back again into the newly-made bed.[8]

To summarize Mitchell's treatment: "The nurse spoonfeeds the patient, gives her a sponge bath, administers vaginal douches and rectal enemas, and may read to her for brief periods."[9] These reading periods, after a couple of weeks, could be extended to several hours, presumably, as a kind of reward.

The symbolism of this treatment is dramatic. Fattened, purified, and ceremoniously carried about like a sacred object, the re-covering Victorian patient of Mitchell's rest cure blows up to resemble a woman steadily and unchangingly six-months pregnant, or a pudgy baby that cannot yet walk. The two are the same, of course, in falling outside the conventional Victorian definition of what is sexual, a pregnant woman officially considered extrasexual, a baby supposedly presexual. Endlessly with child and at the same time *a* child, the successfully refeminized woman is at first forced and then later learns cheerfully to place her whole being in the hands of another, who, not accidentally, is a physician: the new priest, the new male authority, of the new scientific era.

Violence defines the physician's power in Gilman's story. When "The Yellow Wallpaper" opens, the heroine has been taken back in time by her physician-husband, forcibly carried away from modern, urban America to "ancestral halls," a "colonial mansion," a "hereditary estate."[10] There, in a "haunted house" "long untenanted" that perfectly symbolizes the repressive Victorian "separate sphere" to which she is being returned, the narrator is held prisoner in a room filled with images and symbols of coercion, torture, and death. Empty except for one piece of furniture, a bed, which is nailed to the floor and shows signs of having been gnawed by some previous inmate, the room has barred windows, a heavy gate at the top of the stairs, and rings in the walls. When the narrator asks to be released from this prison, she is told by her husband, in a joke worthy of Poe, that he would be happy to take her "down to the cellar, if I wished, and have it whitewashed into the bargain."

The relationship between this violent setting and the sexual exploitation and silencing of a privileged—in this case, literally a "kept"—woman emerges directly in "The Yellow Wallpaper." Under the supervision of modern medicine, the narrator has been moved back in time to be forcibly resocialized into conventional white middle-class femininity, a highly sexualized set of behaviors according to Gilman (despite its surface infantilism), and muteness. Against her will she is to learn in this "colonial" space, simultaneously imaged as a torture-chamber and a nursery, how to be a docile middle-class wife and mother and how to suppress her desire to write, the two in many ways being the same. Indeed, as this story about writing, about taking possession of language, proceeds, we realize that the desired transformation of the narrator has already *been* written on the domestic environment designed to contain her. The symbols of restraint—the nailed-down bed, the gate, the bars, the rings in the walls—announce the repression and self-denial, the excruciating idleness and physical inactivity, expected of her. The repellent flowery paper, with its repeating disembodied head that "lolls like a broken neck and two bulbous eyes [that] stare at you upside down," images the grotesque, idiotic cheerfulness endlessly required of her. The severe isolation and circumscription of the space (even the view is highly limited) declare the narrow slit of experience and vision permitted.

That this ugly, imprisoning environment is a bedroom emphasizes how sexualized Gilman believed the supposedly asexual Victorian ideal of femininity to be.[11] The aggressive sexual content of the classic rest cure, with its assault on almost every orifice of the passive adult female body, is obvious. To be sure, the narrator's torture-chamber is officially a nursery, a place where she is treated like a baby. Her erudite husband carries her to bed, reads to her, calls her "little girl," and smothers her in baby-talk, exclaiming, "Bless her little heart! . . . She shall be as sick as she pleases!" Cuddled and coddled, the narrator, in accord with the Victorian ideal of femininity into which she is being forcibly reinducted, is expected to be helpless and dependent. Still, all of this infantilization takes place, it is important to remember, in a room inhabited by an adult and one piece of furniture: a bed. Immovable, gnawed, only it has been left in the room. From the point of view of the physician, the male architect of the narrator's resocialization, the concept of the space in which she is confined is very simple. It is a jail; it allows an extremely limited view of the world; and it has at its center a bed. Site for a woman not only of birthing, dying, and sleeping but also, and probably most important for this story, of sexual intercourse and therefore a potent reminder in late nineteenth-century America of male sexual privilege and dominance, including violence, a bed, to the exclusion of all else, dominates the room in which the narrator has been confined and forbidden to write.

Yet she does write. Simultaneously denied her adult female body by the room (a "nursery") *and* defined as nothing *but* that body by the bed, the narrator, ostensibly shattered by the schizophrenic space/ideal, defiantly inscribes her body on and through the wall(paper). The political content of this act remains vivid almost a century later. As the late twentieth-century critic Hélène Cixous argues: "Woman must write her self: must write about women and bring women to writing, from which they have been driven away as violently as from their bodies—for the same reasons, by the same law, with the same fatal goal. Woman must put herself into the text—as into the world and into history—by her own movement."[12] Writing as a subversive act, as a dangerous move because it threatens the system of control constructed to contain women, is the subject of "The Yellow Wallpaper." To be written is to be passive. To write is to be active, to take action, to be the actor—to own and create one's self. And the action taken by Gilman's bound and silenced narrator, quintessential image of Victorian femininity, is radical. Venting her rage on the very domestic space that confines her, she permanently violates the silence imposed upon her by, as a theorist such as Cixous might put it, writing her body: both on the room, which physically bears her defiant inscription, and on the printed page before us. In doing so the narrator accomplishes a fundamental change in her relationship to the violence in the story. She moves from the position of victim to that of agent.

Initially, the wallpaper attacks the narrator. The paper displays "lame uncertain curves . . . [which] suddenly commit suicide—plunge off at outrageous angles, destroy themselves in unheard of contradictions." It thrusts at her "a recurrent spot where the pattern lolls like a broken neck and two bulbous eyes stare at you upside down." It "strangles." It shelters "a strange, provoking, formless sort of figure, that seems to skulk about." It turns backsomersaults and "slaps you in the face, knocks you down, and tramples upon you." By the end of the story, however, this exterior "surface" violence transforms into what it has been in part all along: the external manifestation of the narrator's internalized rage. The suicide, the dangling head, the suffocation and skulking and pummeling all reflect the narrator's feelings, the abuse she has absorbed and turned on herself. Now she releases those feelings outward. She gets "in" the paper, and its violence, formerly directed *at* her, becomes her articulated fury and agony. Paper as enemy gives way to paper as self as she and the strong woman "behind" the tortured wallcovering (the narrator's double, of course) work together to shake their bars. Liberating other women also trapped behind paper/violence, they rip and shred the hideous paper-for-decoration (fitting symbol of the creative limits of the domestic world to which the narrator has been consigned). They turn the room into, metaphorically, the liberated, torn text of a woman's body.

Inscribed on the flowery walls of the narrator's cell, then, is a parallel text to the one in our hands. The story anticipates Cixous's statement that "women must write through their bodies, they must invent the impregnable language that will wreck partitions, classes, and rhetorics, regulations and codes, they must submerge, cut through, get beyond the ultimate reserve-discourse, including the one that laughs at the very idea of pronouncing the word 'silence.'"[13] Gilman's narrator, like Harper's Iola, declares in her flesh one woman's triumph over the system of violence, sexual exploitation, and silencing instituted to control women. Supposed to be passive, she lashes out at her nursery/prison/boudoir. She bites the bed, rips the walls, and threatens to kill anyone who touches "her" paper (*YW*, pp. 34, 33). On one level an image of defeat—the narrator has finally gone mad—this concluding picture also represents victory. Violent, wild, physical, the narrator is the complete antithesis of the inhibited "lady" that Victorian America so carefully nurtured as a symbol of male power.

Read optimistically, "The Yellow Wallpaper" dramatizes the failure of the modern era's attempt to recycle Victorian ideology. The regime in the nursery does not work. All the right things are done: The narrator is secluded, sheltered from stress, waited upon by faithful servant, flattered and pampered by a loving husband, and given plenty of rest, fresh air, and modest exercise. To no avail. The trip back in time fails. Women such as the narrator will go mad before they will submit to the lives of infantile dependence prescribed as ideal by Victorian America.

But the story is also very dark and hopeless. By the end

the narrator has lost her mind. Moreover, the idea that women will band together in mutual support and accomplish as a group what cannot be won by any one individual remains just that, an idea. For the narrator, solidarity exists with the imaginary women in the paper. In real life, the other women in the story collude in the system's resocialization of the narrator. The principal executor of the system is another woman, paid for the purpose by the man in charge, and if there is any thought that the narrator's mother and sister might support her rebellion, it is quickly abandoned. Their visit on the Fourth of July leaves the narrator's situation unchanged: In real life and real terms, there is no Independence Day for the isolated woman in Gilman's tale. Viewed from this vantage point, the system has worked. The heroine has become the cripple her class has worked hard to create. Literally crawling, she offers a horrible picture of what the bourgeois white nineteenth-century ideal of femininity often really meant: bondage, masochism, madness.

The ways in which class and race limit Gilman's argument in "The Yellow Wallpaper" are very important. As Susan S. Lanser explains in an excellent essay, white feminist claims that the story is universal ignore its ethnic, class, and, perhaps most important, racial context. Focusing on the color of the paper itself, Lanser thinks about yellow in its turn-of-the-century context and theorizes that the paper is repulsive for Gilman precisely because it is yellow, the color that racist white Americans at the time, including Gilman herself, associated with Asians, Jews, Italians, and Eastern European immigrants. Unconsciously encoded in the wallpaper, in other words, is Gilman's own racism, and with it the limits of this story's "universality." Just as the class context of "The Yellow Wallpaper" establishes narrative boundaries, so the story's horror of yellowness articulates its racial boundaries and hidden racism.[14]

There is no question that Gilman's specific political agenda had to do solely with white women like herself. In her autobiography she recalls telling William Dean Howells, when he asked for permission to reprint "The Yellow Wallpaper" in *Great Modern American Stories* (1920): "I was more than willing, but assured him that it was no more 'literature' than my other stuff, being definitely written 'with a purpose.' In my judgment it is a pretty poor thing to write, to talk, without a purpose." Her purpose, she explained, "was to reach Dr. S. Weir Mitchell and convince him of the error of his ways."[15]

Whether or not Gilman influenced Mitchell,[16] her story contains a clear response not only to his rest cure but also to the larger cultural argument out of which his philosophy developed: the widespread, mounting scientific insistence at the turn of the century on fundamental difference between the sexes—and between races as well, even though Gilman was not perturbed by that part of the reactionary argument; indeed, she openly subscribed to and used it in some of her writings.[17]

As the historian Rosalind Rosenberg points out, for certain privileged, well-educated American women, by the turn of the century "the very basis of women's understanding of themselves was changing." Increased opportunities for higher education plus decades of political activism had produced a generation of professional women able to challenge traditional Victorian dogma about sexual differences. "Once the seed of doubt was planted," Rosenberg explains,

> it germinated in all directions. From questioning the extent of biological differences, women proceeded to challenge the universally accepted belief that men's and women's social roles were rooted in biology. Before they were through, they had challenged every tenet of the Victorian faith in sexual polarity—from the doctrine that women are by nature emotional and passive, to the dogma that men are by nature rational and assertive.[18]

This assertion of equality in the work of turn-of-the-century white female social scientists, which is equally obvious in fiction by women of the period, black and white, developed against a backdrop of intensifying scientific argument about white middle-class women's biological destiny. As historians explain, the increasing emancipation of middle-class white women at the turn of the century and the mounting reactionary power of medical science in the period are connected. It is not accidental that the most advanced men of medicine (Freud, for example) focused more and more brilliantly on defining women as a class as inferior and biologically determined at the same time that a growing number of women were representing more and more of a threat to the traditional Victorian order of society.[19] As organized religion gradually lost its power to dictate and enforce belief, science took over. The new dogma-maker, it pronounced the sexes innately and radically different.

One year before Gilman wrote "The Yellow Wallpaper," an article in *Forum* put the mainstream scientific conclusion for a general audience this way:

> All that is distinctly human is man—the field, the ship, the mind, the workshop; all that is truly woman is merely reproductive—the home, the nursery, the schoolroom. There are women, to be sure, who inherit much of male faculty, and some of these prefer to follow male avocations; but in so doing they for the most part unsex themselves; they fail to perform satisfactorily their maternal functions.[20]

Resexing the narrator, a middle-class white woman who is a new mother who rebelliously wants to use her brain and who therefore is failing in the performance of her maternal destiny, represents the scientific challenge—which Gilman presents as insane, of course—in "The Yellow Wallpaper."

Popularized by the turn of the century, the scientific insistence on difference, which owed a great deal to Darwin and Spencer,[21] was initially and most influentially developed for the general medical and scientific community by the American physician Edward H. Clarke. Offering biological "evidence" for inequality, Clarke maintained in *Sex and Education* in 1874 that the male and female brains were basically different. "The organs whose normal growth and evolution lead up to the brain are not the same in men and women," he argued; "consequently their brains, though alike in microscopic structure, have infused in them different though excellent qualities."[22] Among the different excellencies of women's brains, being smaller and lighter, was the fact, in Clarke's view, that they were not as capable of intellectual exertion as men's. The physician agreed with Spencer that women who pushed themselves mentally risked enfeebling themselves physically[23]—precisely the argument, of course, used by the narrator's physician-husband in "The Yellow Wallpaper."

Reasoning such as Clarke's generated a vigorous scientific and then popular literature about women's alleged intellectual inferiority to men, which was in turn used as evidence in arguments about the biological imperative of motherhood. The argument maintained that nature designed the sex to be breeders not thinkers. S. Weir Mitchell, for example, declared:

> Worst of all, to my mind, most destructive in every way, is the American view of female education. . . . To-day the American women is, to speak plainly, physically unfit for her duties as woman, and is, perhaps, of all civilized females, the least qualified to undertake those weightier tasks which tax so heavily the nervous system of man. She is not fairly up to what Nature asks from her as wife and mother.

Then, letting the political cat completely out of the bag, he asks: "How will she sustain herself under the pressure of those yet more exacting duties which nowadays she is eager to share with man?"[24] Ostensibly the argument holds that bourgeois women cannot even meet the demands of maternity, so how could they ever handle the more difficult challenges to which they aspire in the masculine realm of public accomplishment and action? Covertly, however, Mitchell is issuing a warning. If middle-class women are not contained in a separate sphere of maternal and domestic obligation, what is to prevent them from invading man's world wholesale and permanently?

That the argument was racist and class-ridden as well as sexist, though, again, Gilman was concerned only with the latter, becomes overwhelmingly clear in the many alarms about "race suicide" raised at the turn of the century. When Theodore Roosevelt wrote from the White House in 1902 to the authors of *The Woman Who Toils: Being the Experiences of Two Ladies as Factory Girls* (1903) that the "woman who deliberately avoids marriage, and has a heart so cold as to know no passion and a brain so shallow and selfish as to dislike having children, is in effect a criminal against the race, and should be an object of contemptuous abhorrence by all healthy people,"[25] the President of the United States was not worrying about women of color or immigrant women forsaking motherhood for work. Turn-of-the-century intellectuals and scientists asserting the biological imperative of motherhood wanted to control a specific group of women. As "The Yellow Wallpaper" demonstrates, what obsessed and frightened them was the possibility that middle class, American-born white women might actually believe in their own right to self-determination.

Blind to the antifeminism of her own racism, Charlotte Perkins Gilman was inspired by exactly the same idea.

Finally, the anger that drives "The Yellow Wallpaper" was in many ways intensely personal. Most obviously, Gilman's experience with Mitchell's rest cure, which was the consequence of her depression as a wife and mother, provided the impetus for the story. As a new mother the heroine of "The Yellow Wallpaper" epitomizes, according to the most advanced elite masculine scientific theory of the day, woman at her most "natural"—meaning, according to the experts Clarke, Mitchell, and the narrator's husband, woman speechless. The power struggle in which Gilman's narrator finds herself—like Wharton's Charity Royall in *Summer* sixteen years later, or Larsen's Helga Crane in *Quicksand* almost forty years later, *or* Gilman herself before "The Yellow Wallpaper" was written—is one of resisting the shifting but seemingly inescapable patriarchal definition (self-fulfilling, of course, in male-dominant culture) of motherhood as prison, flesh as destiny, and voice as silence. That Gilman never got paid for "The Yellow Wallpaper" because her male agent kept the money it earned seems almost unbelievably fitting.[26]

Less obviously, "The Yellow Wallpaper" probably had deep roots in Gilman's childhood. In her autobiography, the account she gives of her growing up focuses on the misery of her mother, a woman who adored her husband and loved having babies, only to have her husband leave and her babies grow up. Deserted, Gilman's mother—in the daughter's telling—grew bitter and fiercely repressed, deciding not to show any affection for her daughter in order to toughen the child. Life, as Gilman's mother had come to know it, brought women terrible disappointment and denial. Only in the dead of night would she allow herself to hug her daughter.

As a story about her mother, the early portions of Gilman's autobiography construct a family drama in which sexual desire in a woman leads to babies and death. (According to Gilman, her mother was warned that one more pregnancy would kill her, at which point the father left the family.)[27] On the other hand, denial of sexual desire, the celibate life that Mary Fitch Perkins knew when her husband left, resulted in furious repression and frustration. Either way, female sexual desire, motherhood, and masculine power were bitterly entangled for Gilman's mother, who even after years of separation and rejection remained her husband's prisoner, calling for him on her deathbed.[28] Looked at from the child's point of view, and Charlotte Perkins Gilman clearly both admired and hated her father, Frederick Beecher Perkins's power over his wife was so strong that she had to stamp out all that was free and physical and warm in herself, and try to do the same to her daughter. In a sense the woman on her knees at the end of "The Yellow Wallpaper," the prisoner of a charming man and an ugly empty domestic life that she cannot escape, is Gilman's mother as the child experienced her while growing up—humiliated, angry, crushed.

Even more salient, the alienation of women from each other and from their own bodies that Gilman learned in her childhood is deeply written on "The Yellow Wallpaper." It shows a powerful male figure designing the emotional misery of his "little girl" (in the story the wife, in Gilman's childhood the daughter), which is then carried out for him by an unbending, mature woman (in the story Jenny, in Gilman's life her mother). Indeed, the narrator's emotional torture probably reflects the pain that Gilman felt not only as an adult but also as a child. Certainly the secret nocturnal relief achieved in the story by the narrator's surreptitious writing and secret connection with the women creeping around behind the wallpaper echoes Gilman's desperate, secret strategies for escaping the emotional and physical amputation from her mother that she felt as a child during the daytime. Gilman describes how she waited in the dark to connect with her mother: "She would not let me caress her, and would not caress me, unless I was asleep. This I discovered at last, and then did my best to keep awake till she came to bed, even using pins to prevent dropping off, and sometimes succeeding. Then how carefully I pretended to be sound asleep, and how rapturously I enjoyed being gathered into her arms, held close and kissed."[29] Escaping only at night and in secret into the female arms that promised refuge from the emotional prison she knew during daylight hours, the plotting child clearly anticipates the fictitious grown woman's furtive nocturnal escapes into a female world of intimate bonds and wild physical abandon. The narrator waiting to get into the wallpaper's embrace and the child waiting to get into her mother's arms flee the same thing, a spiritually killing world created by a man who supposedly loves them—and run by a woman who acts as his enforcer. And they seek the same thing: a world where women rebel, unite, touch.

The importance of this echo is that it lays out in biographical terms what is also obvious in the story, the scope of Gilman's subject. The drama of patriarchal control in "The Yellow Wallpaper" is the same one that Charlotte Perkins Gilman felt as a child, saw in her mother's life, and then experienced again herself as a young wife and mother. The story is not limited to just one stage of her life as a woman, but applies potentially to all stages, from childhood to old age. It is not, moreover, simply a story about the desire for escape from male control. It is also a story about the desire to escape *to* a female world, a desire to unite with the mother, indeed with all women creeping and struggling in growing numbers, through the paper, behind the wall.

Above all, "The Yellow Wallpaper" is about using paper to connect women, a theme doubly insisted upon in Gilman's story—on the wall, on the page—and repeatedly voiced and demonstrated in the work of women writers at the turn of the century. The union and reunion pictured at the end of *Iola Leroy* and of "The Yellow Wallpaper"—homey and evangelical in the first instance, ghastly in the second—represent dreams of female connectedness and reconnectedness that recur throughout the period. The mother-loss that permeates both texts—Iola's literal search for and reunion with her mother, the narrator's rupture from her mother and subsequent bond with the women in the wall—foretells a major concern of women writers in America at the turn of the twentieth century as, collectively and individually, they faced the issue of leaving the old century.

☐ Notes ∎

1. Josephine Silone-Yates, "Parental Obligation," *Colored American Magazine* 12 (Apr. 1907), 285.

2. Helen Gray Cone, "Woman in Literature," in *Woman's Work in America,* ed. Annie Nathan Meyer (New York: Henry Holt & Co., 1891), p. 113.

3. Quoted in Charlotte Perkins Gilman, *The Living of Charlotte Perkins Gilman: An Autobiography* (New York: D. Appleton, 1935: rpt. 1975), p. 119.

4. Ibid., p. 120.

5. Ibid., pp. 120–21.

6. Some recent discussions of "The Yellow Wallpaper" are Susan Gubar, "*She* in *Herland,*" in *Coordinates: Placing Science Fiction and Fantasy,* ed. George Slusser (Carbondale: Southern Illinois University Press, 1983), pp. 139–49; Annette Kolodny, "A Map for Rereading: Or, Gender and the Interpretation of Literary Texts," *New Literary History* 11 (Spring 1980), 451–67; Elaine Hedges, Afterword, *The Yellow Wallpaper* (Old Westbury, NY: The Feminist Press, 1973), pp. 37–67; and Conrad Shumaker, "'Too Terribly Good to be Printed': Charlotte Gilman's 'The Yellow Wallpaper,'" *American Literature* 57 (Dec. 1985), 588–99. Also of interest is the idea that periods of cultural turmoil—and certainly the turn of the century was one—have a liberating effect on women's speech; see Patricia S. Yaeger, "'Because a Fire Was in My Head': Eudora Welty and the Dialogic Imagination," *PMLA* 99 (Oct. 1984), 955–73.

7. Ellen L. Bassuk, "The Rest Cure: Repetition or Resolution of Victorian Women's Conflicts?," in *The Female Body in Western Culture: Contemporary Perspectives,* ed. Susan Rubin Suleiman (Cambridge: Harvard University Press, 1986), p. 141.

8. Ibid.

9. Ibid.

10. Charlotte Perkins Gilman, *The Yellow Wallpaper* (Old Westbury, NY: The Feminist Press, 1973).

11. For extensive development of Gilman's belief that the Victorian feminine ideal was a completely eroticized version of woman, see *Women and Economics* (Boston: Small, Maynard, 1898; rpt. New York: Harper & Row, 1966). There she argues, for example, that even women's hands and feet have been made into secondary sex characteristics and a woman is expected to dress "in garments whose main purpose is unmistakably to announce her sex; with a tendency to ornament which marks exuberance of sex-energy, with a body so modified to sex as to be grievously deprived of its natural activities" (pp. 45, 53).

12. Hélène Cixous, "The Laugh of the Medusa," *New French Feminisms,* eds. Elaine Marks and Isabelle de Courtivron (New York: Schocken Books, 1981), p. 244.

13. Ibid., p. 256.

14. See Susan S. Lanser, "Feminist Criticism, 'The Yellow Wallpaper,' and the Politics of Color in America," *Feminist Studies* 15 (Fall 1989), 415–41.

15. Gilman, *The Living of Charlotte Perkins Gilman,* p. 121.

16. Gilman says: "I sent him a copy [of "The Yellow Wallpaper"] as soon as it came out, but got no response. However, many years later, I met some one who knew close friends of Dr. Mitchell's who said he had told them that he had changed his treatment of nervous prostration since reading 'The Yellow Wallpaper.' If that is a fact, I have not lived in vain" (ibid., p. 121). For an excellent discussion of Mitchell that focuses in particular on his own creative writing—the novels he published—see Eugenia Kaledin, "Dr. Manners: S. Weir Mitchell's Novelistic Prescription for an Upset Society," *Prospects* 11 (1986), 199–216.

17. One of the central arguments of *Women and Economics* is the implicitly racist one that women, and by this Gilman meant white, American-born women, should be liberated from Victorian restrictions, ranging from corsets to unemployment, in order to be stronger, healthier mothers of stronger, healthier (white) babies and thus future citizens.

18. Rosalind Rosenberg, *Beyond Separate Spheres: Intellectual Roots of Modern Feminism* (New Haven: Yale University Press, 1982), p. xiv.

19. See Ruth Bleier, *Science and Gender: A Critique of Biology and Its Theories on Women* (New York: Pergamon, 1984), p. 171. Also of interest here is Carroll Smith-Rosenberg's observation in a discussion of antiabortion debate at the turn of the century that the threatening figure changed dramatically depending on who was doing the analysis. When bourgeois women analyzed the abortion issue, for example, it was men, not middle-class ambitious women, who posed the threat: "In their pages, images of marital rape, of unwanted pregnancies, of marriage as legalized prostitution replaced male images of unnatural aborting mothers and willful urbane ladies. . . . For the women . . . the husband who forced unwanted pregnancies upon his wife, and not the willful and fashionable matron, constituted the dangerous and disorderly figure." *Disorderly Conduct: Visions of Gender in Victorian America* (New York: Oxford University Press, 1985), p. 243.

20. Grant Allen, "Woman's Place in Nature," *Forum* 7 (May 1889), 263; quoted in Louise Michele Newman, *Men's Ideas/Women's Realities: Popular Science, 1870–1915* (New York: Pergamon Press, 1985), p. 54. Allen, an Englishman who declared himself "an enthusiast on the Woman Question," declared in another essay in 1889:

> For what is the ideal that most of these modern women agitators set before them? Is it not clearly the ideal of an unsexed woman? Are they not always talking to us as though it were not the fact that most women must be wives and mothers? Do they not treat any reference to that fact as something ungenerous, ungentlemanly, and almost brutal? Do they not talk about our "casting their sex in their teeth?"—as though any man ever resented the imputation of manliness. . . . Women ought equally to glory in their femininity. A woman ought to be ashamed to say she had no desire to become a wife and mother. (Quoted in Newman, p. 127).

21. For analysis of Darwin from this point of view, see Ruth Hubbard, "Have Only Men Evolved?," in *Biological Woman: The Convenient Myth* (Cambridge, MA: Schenkman Books, 1982), pp. 17–45.

22. Quoted in Rosenberg, *Beyond Separate Spheres*, p. 7.

23. Ibid., pp. 8–9.

24. See Newman, *Men's Ideas/Women's Realities*, p. 85.

25. Theodore Roosevelt, "Prefatory Letter," in *The Woman*

Who Toils: Being the Experiences of Two Ladies as Factory Girls by Mrs. John Van Vorst and Marie Van Vorst (New York: Doubleday, Page & Co., 1903), p. viii. Although Roosevelt applied this statement to either the man or the woman who shunned parenthood, it is clear from the letter, as well as from the Van Vorst material which inspired it, that his concern was with women who shirked their biological duty.

26. Gilman, *The Living of Charlotte Perkins Gilman,* p. 119.
27. Ibid., p. 5.
28. Ibid., p. 9.
29. Ibid., pp. 10–11.

☐ Selected Bibliography ∎

Works by Charlotte Perkins Gilman

Herland: A Lost Feminist Utopian Novel. New York: Pantheon, 1979.

His Religion and Hers: A Study of the Faith of Our Fathers and the Work of Our Mothers. New York: Century, 1923. Reprint. Westport, Conn.: Hyperion Press, 1976.

The Home: Its Work and Influence. New York: McClure, Phillips, 1903. Reprint. New York: Source Book Press, 1970.

Human Work. New York: McClure, Phillips, 1904.

The Living of Charlotte Perkins Gilman: An Autobiography. New York: D. Appleton, 1935, Reprint. New York: Harper and Row, 1975.

Women and Economics. Boston: Small, Maynard, 1898. Reprint. Edited with an introduction by Carl N. Degler. New York, Harper and Row, 1966.

"The Yellow Wallpaper." *New England Magazine* 5 (January 1892): 647–656. Reprint. Afterword by Elaine Hedges. Old Westbury, New York: Feminist Press, 1973.

Suggested Further Reading

Berman, Jeffrey, "The Unrestful Cure: Charlotte Perkins Gilman and 'The Yellow Wallpaper.'" *The Talking Cure: Literary Representations of Psychoanalysis.* New York: New York University Press, 1985. 33–59.

DeLamotte, Eugenia C. "Male and Female Mysteries in 'The Yellow Wallpaper,'" *Legacy* 5, no. 1 (1988): 3–14.

Feldstein, Richard. "Reader, Text and Ambiguous Referentiality in 'The Yellow Wallpaper.'" *Feminism and Psychoanalysis,* eds. Richard Feldstein and Judith Roof, 269–279. Ithaca, N.Y.: Cornell University Press, 1989.

Ford, Karen. "'The Yellow Wallpaper' and Women's Discourse." *Tulsa Studies in Women's Literature* 4, no. 2 (1985): 309–314.

Golden, Catherine. "The Writing of 'The Yellow Wallpaper': A Double Palimpsest." *Studies in American Fiction* 17, no. 2 (1989): 193–201.

Hill, Mary A. "Charlotte Perkins Gilman: A Feminist's Struggle with Womanhood." *Massachusetts Review: A Quarterly of Literature, the Arts and Public Affairs* 21, no. 3 (1980): 503–526.

Jacobus, Mary. "An Unnecessary Maze of Sign-Reading." *Reading Women: Essays in Feminist Criticism.* New York: Columbia University Press, 1986, 229–248.

Karpinski, Joanne, ed. *Critical Essays on Charlotte Perkins Gilman.* Boston: G. K. Hall, 1992.

Kennard, Jean E. "Convention Coverage or How to Read Your Own Life." *New Literary History* 13, no. 1 (1981): 69–88.

King, J., and P. Morris. "On Not Reading between the Lines: Models of Reading in 'The Yellow Wallpaper.'" *Studies in Short Fiction* 26, no. 1 (1989): 23–32.

Lane, Ann J. *To Herland and Beyond: The Life and Work of Charlotte Perkins Gilman*. New York: Pantheon Books, 1990.

MacPike, Loralee. "Environment as Psychopathological Symbolism in 'The Yellow Wallpaper.'" *American Literary Realism 1870–1910* 8, no. 3 (1975): 286–288.

Masse, Michelle A. "Gothic Repetition: Husbands, Horrors, and Things That Go Bump in the Night." *Signs: Journal of Women in Culture and Society* 15, no. 4 (1990): 679–709.

Meyering, Sheryl L., ed. *Charlotte Perkins Gilman: The Woman and Her Work,* Ann Arbor, Mich.: University Microfilms International, 1989.

Pearce, Lynne, and Mills, Sarah. "The Marxist-Feminist Literature Collective: 'Women's writing.'" *Feminist Readings/Feminists Reading*. Edited by Sarah Mills, Lynne Pearce, Sue Spaull, and Elaine Millard. Charlottesville: University of Virginia Press, 1989.

Schopp-Schilling, Beate, "'The Yellow Wallpaper': A Rediscovered 'Realistic' Story," *American Literary Realism 1870–1910* 8, no. 3 (1975): 286–288.

Spacks, Patricia Meyer. *The Female Imagination*. New York: Alfred A. Knopf, 1975. 208–218.

Treichler, Paula. "Escaping the Sentence: Diagnosis and Discourse in 'The Yellow Wallpaper.'" *Tulsa Studies in Women's Literature* 3, nos. 1–2 (1984): 61–77.

Veeder, William. "Who is Jane? The Intricate Feminism of Charlotte Perkins Gilman," *Arizona Quarterly* 44, no. 3 (1988): 40–79.

Weinstein, Lee. "'The Yellow Wallpaper': A Supernatural Interpretation," *Studies in Weird Fiction* 4, no. 1 (1988): 23–25.

❏ Permissions ■

"The Hysterical Woman: Sex Roles and Role Conflict in Nineteenth-Century America," by Carroll Smith-Rosenberg, *Social Research* 39:4 (1972): 652–678. Reprinted by permission of the author and *Social Research*.

Excerpt from *The Madwoman in the Attic: The Woman Writer and the Nineteenth-Century Literary Imagination* by Sandra M. Gilbert and Susan Gubar (New Haven: Yale University Press, 1979). Copyright © 1979 by Yale University Press; reprinted by permission of the publisher.

"'Too Terribly Good to Be Printed': Charlotte Gilman's 'The Yellow Wallpaper,'" by Conrad Shumaker, *American Literature* 57:4 (1985): 588–599. Copyright © 1985 by Duke University Press, reprinted by permission of the publisher.

"The Gothic Prism: Charlotte Perkins Gilman's Gothic Stories and Her Autobiography," by Juliann E. Fleenor, in *The Female Gothic*, ed. Juliann E. Fleenor (Montreal: Eden Press, 1983), 227–241. Reprinted by permission of the author.

"A Map for Rereading: Or, Gender and the Interpretation of Literary Texts," by Annette Kolodny, *New Literary History* 11 (1980): 451–467. Reprinted by permission of the author and The Johns Hopkins University Press.

"Reading about Reading: 'The Yellow Wallpaper,'" by Judith Fetterley, in *Gender and Reading: Essays on Readers, Texts, and Contexts,* ed. Elizabeth A. Flynn and Patrocinio P. Schweickart (Baltimore: The Johns Hopkins University Press, 1986), 158–164. Reprinted by permission of the publisher.

"Monumental Feminism and Literature's Ancestral House: Another Look at 'The Yellow Wallpaper,'" by Janice Haney-Peritz, *Women's Studies* 12 (1986): 113–128. Copyright © 1986 by Gordon and Breach Science Publishers; reprinted by permission of the publisher.

"Gendered Doubleness and the 'Origins' of Modernist Form," by Marianne DeKoven, *Tulsa Studies in Women's Literature* 8:1 (Spring 1989): 19–21, 28–35. Copyright © 1989 by the University of Tulsa; reprinted by permission of the publisher.

"Feminist Criticism, 'The Yellow Wallpaper,' and the Politics of Color in America," by Susan S. Lanser, *Feminist Studies* 15:3 (Fall 1989): 415–441. Reprinted by permission of the publisher, Feminist Studies, Inc., c/o Women's Studies Program, University of Maryland, College Park, MD 20742.